THE BOOK WOMAN *of* TROUBLESOME CREEK

"Richardson's latest work is a hauntingly atmospheric love letter to the first mobile library in Kentucky and the fierce, brave Pack Horse librarians who wove their way from shack to shack dispensing literacy, hope, and—just as importantly—a compassionate human connection. Richardson's rendering of stark poverty against the ferocity of the human spirit is irresistible. Add to this the history of the unique and oppressed blue-skinned people of Kentucky, and you've got an unputdownable work that holds real cultural significance."

—Sara Gruen, #1 *New York Times* bestselling author of *Water for Elephants*

"Emotionally resonant and unforgettable, *The Book Woman of Troublesome Creek* is a lush love letter to the redemptive power of books. Cussy Mary is an indomitable and valiant heroine, and through her true-blue eyes, 1930s Kentucky comes to vivid and often harrowing life. Richardson's dialogue is note-perfect; Cussy Mary's voice is still ringing in my head, and the sometimes dark story she tells highlights such gorgeous, glowing grace notes that I was often moved to hopeful tears."

—Joshilyn Jackson, *New York Times* bestselling author of *The Almost Sisters*

"This is Richardson's finest, as beautiful and honest as it is fierce and heart-wrenching, *The Book Woman of Troublesome Creek* explores the fascinating and unique blue-skinned people of Kentucky and the brave Pack Horse librarians. A timeless and significant tale about poverty, intolerance, and how books can bring hope and light to even the darkest pocket of history."

—Karen Abbott, *New York Times* bestselling author of *Liar Temptress Soldier Spy*

"Kim Michele Richardson has written a fascinating novel about people almost forgotten by history: Kentucky's Pack Horse librarians and 'blue people.' The factual information alone would make this book a treasure, but with her impressive storytelling and empathy, Richardson gives us so much more."

—Ron Rash, *New York Times* bestselling author of *One Foot in Eden* and *Serena*

"A rare literary adventure that casts librarians as heroes, smart, tough women on horseback in rough terrain doing the brave and hard work of getting the right book into the right hands. Richardson has weaved an inspiring tale about the power of literature."

—Alexander Chee, author of *Edinburgh* and *Queen of the Night*

THE BOOK WOMAN

of

TROUBLESOME CREEK

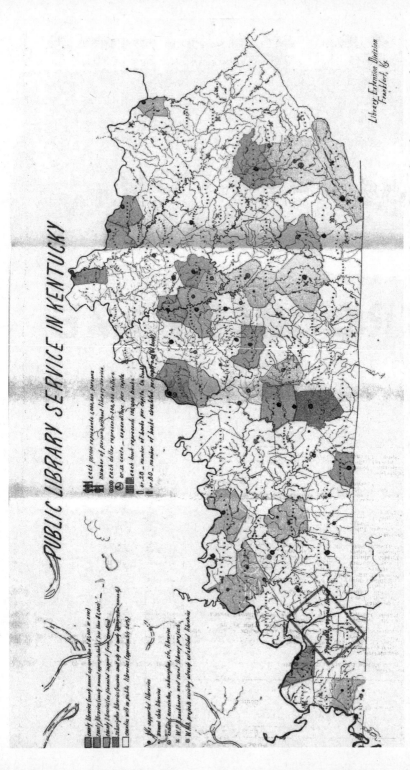

Courtesy of Archival Services Branch, Archives and Records Management Division, Kentucky Department for Libraries & Archives
1939 Map of Packhorse Librarian Project

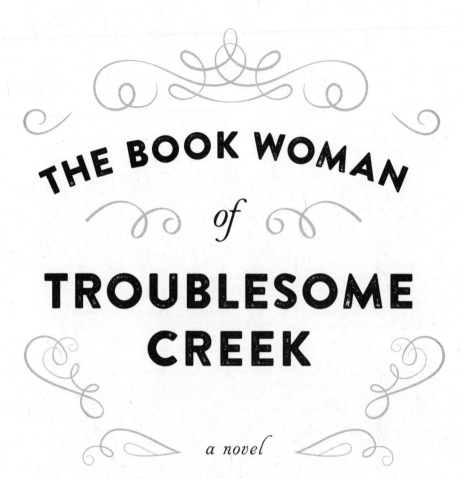

THE BOOK WOMAN

of

TROUBLESOME CREEK

a novel

KIM MICHELE RICHARDSON

Published by Sourcebooks Landmark, an imprint of Sourcebooks
P.O. Box 4410, Naperville, Illinois 60567-4410
(630) 961-3900
sourcebooks.com

Library of Congress Cataloging-in-Publication Data

Names: Richardson, Kim Michele, author.
Title: The book woman of Troublesome Creek / Kim Michele Richardson.
Description: Naperville, Illinois : Sourcebooks Landmark, [2019]
Identifiers: LCCN 2018033574 | (trade paperback : alk. paper)
Classification: LCC PS3618.I34474 B66 2019 | DDC 813/.6--
dc23 LC record available at https://lccn.loc.gov/2018033574

Printed and bound in the United States of America.
WOZ 25

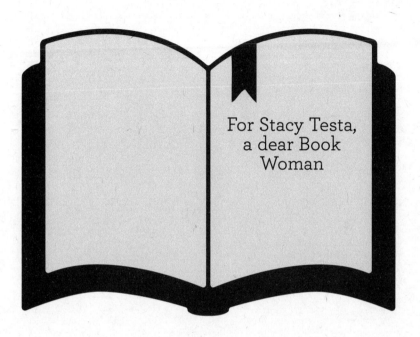

For Stacy Testa,
a dear Book
Woman

"The very existence of libraries affords the best evidence that we may yet have hope for the future of man."

—T. S. Eliot

Kentucky, 1936

The librarian and her mule spotted it at the same time. The creature's ears shot up, and it came to a stop so sudden its front hooves skidded out, the pannier slipping off, spilling out the librarian's books. An eddy of dirt and debris lifted, stinging the woman's eyes. The mule struggled to look upward, backward, anywhere other than at the thing in front of it.

The book woman couldn't keep her eyes off the spectacle as she shortened the reins and clamped her legs against the mule's sides. Again, she prodded her mount. Baring tall, sassing teeth, the beast lifted its muzzle into the balsam-sweetened air, the quavering brays blistering the sleepy mountain.

The woman stiffened, drawing the reins in tighter. In front of her, a body swayed back and forth below the fat branch from which it hung. A rope, collared tight around the neck, creaked from the strain of its weight. A kettle of turkey buzzards circled above, dipping their ugly, naked heads toward the lifeless form, their tail-chasing shadows riddling the dying grass.

From the scorched earth rose strange cries, and the librarian pulled her stunned gaze away from the corpse and toward the ground.

Beside a large toppled can, a baby lay in the dirt, the tiny face pinched, scalded with fury.

Mountain breezes dipped lazily, shifting, carrying the stench of death and its soiling. The weighted branch crackled, groaning under its burden. A bloodied sock inched down from a limp, cerulean-blue foot. The librarian gawked at the striking blue flesh and cupped a hand over her mouth. The stocking slipped off, landing beside the squalling baby's head.

The wind rose higher, then plunged, skittering across the sock as if trying to lift it, but it stayed stubbornly put, rooted to the earth—too heavy to be sent off by a mere summer breeze.

The book woman looked up, lifted one darkening hand in front of her own blue-colored face as if comparing her color to that of the hanging corpse. She examined her cobalt-blue flesh, then dared to peek back up at the dead body, bound, eternally rooted like the black oak to the hard, everlasting Kentucky land so many tried so hard to escape.

One

The new year was barely fifteen hours old in Troublesome Creek, Kentucky, when my pa adjusted the courting candle, setting it to burn for an alarming length of time.

Satisfied, Pa carried it out of our one-room log house and onto the hand-hewn porch. He was hopeful. Hoping 1936 was the year his only daughter, nineteen-year-old Cussy Mary Carter, would get herself hitched and quit her job with the Pack Horse Library Project. Hoping for her latest suitor's proposal.

"Cussy," he called over his shoulder, "before your mama passed, I promised her I'd see to it you got yourself respectability, but I've nearly gone busted buying candles to get you some. Let this stick hold the fire, Daughter." He hoisted the old wrought-iron candleholder higher by its iron-forged rattail and once more played with the wooden slide, moving the taper up and down inside the spiral coil.

"I've got a respectable life," I said quietly, following him out to the porch, taking a seat on the wooden chair, and huddling under the patchwork eiderdown I'd dragged along. The first day of January had brought a skift of snow to our home in the cove. Pa set the candle down and struck a match to light a lantern hanging from the porch.

Two winter moths chased the light, circling, landing nearby. A clean wetting mingled into woodsmoke and umbrella'd the tiny cabin. Shivering, I buried my nose into the coverlet as a cutting wind scraped down mountains, dragging soft whistles through piney boughs and across bare black branches.

In a minute, Pa picked back up the courting candle, raised a finger above the wick, and jutted his chin, the approval cinched in his brow.

"Pa, I have me a good job making us twenty-eight dollars a month delivering books to folks who's needing the book learning in these hills."

"I'm back to work now that the mine is running full time." Pa pinched the wick.

"They still need me—"

"I need you safe. You could catch your death in this cold, same as your mama. You're all I have, Cussy, all that's left of our kind. The very last one, Daughter."

"*Pa, please.*"

He reached down and brushed a lock of hair away from my eyes. "I won't see you riding that ol' mount up and down them dangerous passes and into dark hollers and cold creeks just because the government wants to push their foolish book airs into our hills here."

"It's safe."

"You could be struck ill. Just look what happened to that book woman and her mount. Foolhardy, and the poor steed was punished for her temerity."

Snow gusted, swirled, eddying across the leaf-quilted yard.

"It was along in years, Pa. My rented mount is spry and sure-footed enough. And I'm fine and fit as any." I glanced down at my darkening hands, a silent blue betrayal. Quickly, I slipped them under the folds of fabric, forcing myself to stay calm. "Sound. *Please.* It's decent money—"

"Where's *your* decency? Some of the womenfolk are complaining you're carrying dirty books up them rocks."

"Weren't true. It's called literature, and proper enough," I tried to explain like so many times before. "*Robinson Crusoe*, and Dickens, and the likes, and lots of *Popular Mechanics* and *Woman's*

Home Companion even. Pamphlets with tips on fixing things busted. Patterns for sewing. Cooking and cleaning. Making a dollar stretch. Important things, Pa. Respectable—"

"*Airish*. It ain't respectable for a female to be riding these rough hills, behaving like a man," he said, a harshness rumbling his voice.

"It helps educate folks and their young'uns." I pointed to a small sack in the corner filled with magazines I'd be delivering in the next days. "Remember the *National Geographic* article about Great-Grandpa's birthplace over in Cussy, France, the one I'm named for? You liked it—"

"Dammit, you have earned your name and driven me to nothing but cussing with your willful mind. I don't need a damn book to tell me about our kin's birthplace or your given name. Me and your mama know'd it just fine." He raised a brow, worrying some more with the flame on the courting candle, resting the height of the taper to where he wanted. And as always and depending on the man who came calling, how long he wanted the old timekeeper to stay lit.

Pa looked off toward the creek, then back at the candle, and set his sights once more over to the banks, studying. He fought between raising the timekeeping candle and lowering it, mumbling a curse, and setting it somewhere in the middle. A taper would be cranked up tall to burn for a lengthy visit, or tamped down short for any beau Elijah Carter didn't favor as a good suitor.

"Pa, people want the books. It's my job to tend to the folks who are hungry for the learning."

He lifted the courting candle. "A woman ought to be near the home fires tending that."

"But if I marry, the WPA will fire me. Please, I'm a librarian now. Why, even Eleanor Roosevelt approves—"

"The First Lady ain't doing a man's job—ain't my unwed daughter—and ain't riding an ornery ass up a crooked mountain."

"People are learning up there." Again, I glimpsed my hands and rubbed them under the quilt. "Books are the best way to do that—"

"The best thing they need is food on their tables. Folks here are hungry, Daughter. The babies are starving and sickly, the old folks are dying. We're gnawing on nothing but bone teeth here. Not two weeks ago, widow Caroline Barnes walked nine miles for naught to save her babies up there."

I had heard the poor woman staggered into town with the pellagra rash and died in the street. Many times I'd glimpsed the rash set in from starvation. And last month a woman up in a holler lost five of her twelve children from it, and farther up in the hills, a whole family had died the month before.

"But folks tell me the books eases their burdens, it's the best thing that could happen to them," I argued.

"They can't live off the chicken scratch in them books," Pa said, flicking the wick and hushing me. "And this"—he rapped the candleholder with a knuckle—"is what's best for you."

Jutted up high like that, the candle's nakedness seemed desperate, embarrassing. I caught the unsettling in Pa's gray eyes too.

It didn't matter that for a long time I'd shared Pa's fears about what might become of his only daughter, until the day I'd heard about Roosevelt creating his relief program called the New Deal to help folks around here during the Depression. We'd been depressed as long as I could remember, but now, all of the sudden, the government said we needed help and aimed to do just that. The president had added the Works Progress Administration last year to put females to work and bring literature and art into the Kaintuck man's life. For many mountainfolk, all of us around here, it was our first taste of what a library could give, a taste to be savored—one that left behind a craving for more.

I'd seen the flyers in town asking for womenfolk to apply for the job to tote books around these hills on a mount. I snuck an application and filled it out without Pa knowing, applying to be a Pack Horse librarian a month after Mama died.

"They gave *you* the job?" Pa had puzzled when I got it last summer.

I didn't tell him I'd bypassed the supervisors here by picking up my application at the post office. The job application said you could turn it in to the head librarian in your town or send it to the Pack Horse libraries' manager directly by mailing it to Frankfort. It didn't say anything about color, and certainly not mine. But I'd taken my chances with city folks I'd never meet instead of trusting it to the bosses here in Troublesome.

"Did no one else apply?" Pa had questioned me. "You can't work," he'd added just as quick.

"Pa, we need the money, and it's honorable work and—"

"A workin' woman will never knot."

"Who would marry a Blue? Who would want me?"

I was positive no one would wed one of the *Blue People of Kentucky*. Wouldn't hitch with a quiet woman whose lips and nails were blue-jay blue, with skin the color of the bluet patches growing around our woods.

I could barely meet someone's eyes for fear my color would betray my sensibilities. A mere blush, a burst of joy or anger, or sudden startle, would crawl across my skin, deepening, changing my softer appearance to a ripened blueberry hue, sending the other person scurrying. There didn't seem to be much marriage prospect for the last female of blue mountainfolk who had befuddled the rest of the Commonwealth—folks around the country and doctors even. *A fit girl who could turn as blue as the familiar bluet damselfly skimming Kentucky creek beds*, the old mountain doctor had once puzzled and then promptly nicknamed me Bluet. As soon as the word fell out of his mouth, it stuck to me.

Whenever we'd talk about it, Pa would say, "Cussy, you have a chance to marry someone that's not the same as you, someone who can get you out of here. That's why I dig coal. Why I work for scratch."

And the disgrace would linger in the dead air to gnaw at me. Folks thought our clan was inbreeds, nothing but. Weren't true.

My great-grandpa, a Blue from France, settled in these hills and wedded himself a full-blooded white Kentuckian. Despite that, they'd had several blue children among their regular white-looking ones. And a few of them married strangers, but the rest had to hitch with kin because they couldn't travel far, same as other mountain clans around all these parts.

Soon, we Blues pushed ourselves deeper into the hills to escape the ridicule. Into the blackest part of the land. Pa liked that just fine, saying it was best, safer for me, the last of our kind, *the last one*. But I'd read about those *kinds* in the magazines. The eastern elk, the passenger pigeon. *The extinctions*. Why, most of the critters had been hunted to *extinction*. The thought of being hunted, becoming extinct, being the last Blue, the very last of my kind on earth, left me so terror-struck and winded that I would race to the looking glass, claw at my throat, and knock my chest to steal the breath back.

A lot of people were leery of our looks. Though with Pa working the coal, his mostly pale-blue skin didn't bother folks much when all miners came out of the hole looking the same.

But I didn't have coal to disguise me in black or white Kentucky. Didn't have myself an escape until I'd gotten the precious book route. In those old dark-treed pockets, my young patrons would glimpse me riding my packhorse, toting a pannier full of books, and they'd light a smile and call out "Yonder comes Book Woman... Book Woman's here!" And I'd forget all about my peculiarity, and why I had it, and what it meant for me.

Just recently, Eula Foster, the head librarian of the Pack Horse project, remarked about my smarts, saying the book job had given me an education as fine as any school could.

I was delighted to hear her words. Proud, I'd turned practically purple, despite the fact that she had said it to the other Pack Horse librarians in an air of astonishment: "*If a Blue can get that much learning from our books, imagine what the program can do for our normal folk... A light in these dark times, for sure...*"

And I'd basked in the warm light that had left me feeling like a book-read woman.

But when Pa heard about Agnes's frightening journey, how her packhorse up and quit her in the snow last month, his resolve to get me hitched deepened. And soon after, he'd shone a blinding light back on my color and offered up a generous five-dollar dowry plus ten acres of our woodland. Men, both long in the tooth and schooling young, sought my courtship, ignoring I was one of *them Blue people* when the prospect of land ownership presented itself. A few would boldly ask about my baby-making as if discussing a farm animal—seeking a surety that their Kentucky sons and daughters wouldn't have the blueness too.

Why, for all Pa cared, it could be the beastly troll in "The Three Billy Goats Gruff" who wanted my hand. Lately, he'd been setting the timekeeping candle uncomfortably long for *whoever* was keen on calling.

But I couldn't risk it. The WPA regulations said females with an employable husband wouldn't be eligible for a job because the husband is the logical head of the family.

Logical. I liked my sensibility just fine. I liked my freedom a lot—loved the solitude these last seven months had given me—and I lived for the joy of bringing books and reading materials to the hillfolk who were desperate for my visits, the printed word that brought a hopeful world into their dreary lives and dark hollers. It was necessary.

And for the first time in my life, *I* felt necessary.

"Right there'll do it." Pa fussed one last time with the slide on the courting candle, then finally placed the timekeeper on the table in front of my rocker and the empty seat beside me. He grabbed his carbide-lamp helmet off a peg and looked out to the dark woods across the creek that passed through our property.

The snow picked up, dropping fat flakes. "Reckon he'll be showing up any minute, Daughter."

Sometimes the suitor didn't. I hoped this would be one of those times.

"I'll be off." He dropped a matchbook into the timekeeper's drip tray, eyeing the candle one final time.

Frantic, I grabbed his sleeve and whispered, "Please, Pa, I don't want to marry."

"What's wrong with you, Daughter? It ain't natural to defy the Lord's *natural* order."

I took his palm in mine and pressed the silent plea into it.

Pa looked at my coloring hand and pulled his away. "I gave up my sleep to ride over to his holler and arrange this."

I opened my mouth to protest, but he held up a shushing hand.

"This harsh land ain't for a woman to bear alone. It's cruel enough on a man." Pa reached for his hand-carved bear poker with the razor-sharp arrowhead tip. "I've been digging my grave since the first day I dug coal. I'll not dig two." He tapped the poker against the boards. "You will take a husband so you'll have someone to care for you when I no longer can."

He buttoned his coat and grabbed his tin lunch bucket off the porch boards, ambling off to his night shift down at the coal mine.

Hearing a horse's strangled whinny, I turned toward a rustling in the trees, straining to listen above the prattling song of creek waters. The courter would be here shortly.

I leaned over the wood railing and peered out. When I could no longer see the flicker of Pa's miner's lamp and was sure he'd disappeared into the woods, I reached over, adjusted the wooden slide on the timekeeping candle, and lowered the taper to where the wax would touch the old spiral holder's lip within a few minutes of being burnt—a signal to this latest suitor that a prompt and swift departure was in mind.

Raising my hands, I watched them quiet to a duck-egg blue.

Two

Barely another gray week had passed when Pa sent a new suitor to our porch. Gradually, the man got down off his mount and tied it to a tree. He was just one more hungry troll out there hunting, and one more I needed to run off.

Racing a thumb across my fingers, I ticked off the number of courters who had come calling. It had to be over a dozen, maybe higher, closer to two dozen if I counted the ones who'd never showed, who'd turned back at the mouth of our woods.

I watched the man lumber up the steps, eager for him to take his spot so I could burn the courting candle and be rid of him.

Fumbling, I picked up the box of matches and pulled one out. This particular chore of lighting the wick was always mine after Pa's hopeful intended arrived, and was done as soon as the suitor sat.

Hewitt Hartman plopped heavily into the rocker, nearly busting the planked seating as I lit the short taper. He hunched over a ripe belly, twiddling his hat, working his coated tongue around a big chaw before sputtering a greeting I couldn't understand. Looking down at his knees, he asked to see the land deed.

Silently, I went inside and brought it out, placing the paper beside the courting candle. I caught a whiff of shine from Mr. Hartman and moved over to the rail, laced my hands behind my back, watching the flame quiver, the wax melt ever so slow.

The man grunted several times while reading the deed. The

ten-acre dowry was more than generous. The land could be cleared for farming or timber, or even sold if a man wanted. Pa never wanted neighbors, never had those means, that mindset, or the money to do anything. But as his illness set in and his determination to see me wedded persisted, his thoughts had latched on to other ways.

Mr. Hartman leaned in toward the taper and studied the deed over the yellow light, a greed flickering in his dull eyes. Squinting, he snatched a glance at my face, then another back to the paper, and once more at me. Snapping the old document, he took a dirt-stained finger, running it down the page, his lips chewing over the fancy script. Again, he pinched off a flurry of peeks at me.

Finally, he cleared his throat, stood, and spit a wad of tobacco over the rail, the brown spittle painting his bottom lip and a few droplets speckling his chin.

Hartman picked up the courting candle, shoved it toward my face. Cringing, he dropped the deed and, in one weighty puff, blew out the flame.

"Not even for all of Kentucky." His old, rotted breath whisked through black smoke, taking mine.

Weren't a week later, Pa set back out my timekeeping candle, raising the taper to its longest burn. By the end of January and three courters later, he'd made sure he wouldn't have to again.

The man showed up in the early afternoon wearing a worn hat. He took his time reading the deed, then sat tight-lipped, raking his fingers through his thinning hair, snatching glances at the courting candle's flame. Several times he shifted, smacked his limp hat against stained britches, each move sparking a new plume of rancid odor. After two porch visits with the suitor, Pa gave his blessing the last week of January and signed over the deed, snuffing out my last courting candle. The old squire shot up from his seat and grabbed the document. Avoiding my face, he leered at my body, his eyes lingering on my breasts, taking stock of his new possession.

I clung to Pa on our porch. "I don't want to marry," I'd said, afraid. "I don't want to leave you." My eyes flitted to the old man waiting out in the yard beside his mule. He stared back, tapped his leg with the hat, each smack growing louder and more impatient.

"Daughter," Pa said, cupping my chin in his calloused hand, "you must take a man and live your life. Be safe." He turned away, took a ragged breath, and coughed several times. "*You must.* I have to make sure you won't be alone when I'm gone— keep my promise to your mama." His tired lungs wheezed and he coughed again, the coal mine thieving his time.

"I have my books!"

"It is a foolishness you have, Daughter." A sorrow clung to his stick-throated voice.

"I'll lose my route, my patrons. Please, I can't lose them." I gripped his sleeve and shook. "Please, not him."

"You'll have yourself a big family. The Fraziers are an old clan with kinfolk all over these hills."

"But he's kin to Pastor Vester Frazier." I pressed a palm to my galloping heart thinking about him, his hunt-hungry congregation, and their deadly baptismal waters down at the creek. "Pa, you know what the preacher does to folks like us, what he's done—"

Pa laid a hand on my shoulder and shook his head. "He doesn't associate with the likes of the preacher man, and he gave me his word that he'll protect you. It's growing late, Daughter. I must get ready. The Company has several cars they're expecting me to load today, or I'll lose my job. Get on now to your new family," he gently urged.

I'd looked at the man in the yard twisting the floppy cake-like hat in his hand, coiling our old Carter land deed, nervously shifting to one short muscly leg and then the other, small eyes darting between us and his bone-ribbed mule, anxious to leave. Gusts of wintry air tore across the brow of the woods, shaking branches and whipping his stringy gray-flecked hair.

"But, Pa, please, I'm…I'm frightened of him." I searched for my hankie, gave up, and wiped my runny nose on a coat sleeve.

"Mr. Frazier will give you his name and see that you have a roof over your head and food in your belly."

"I have a name, the *only* name I want! *Book Woman*."

Pa's eyes filled with turmoil. His face crumpled. I was sure he didn't want me to go, but he was more afraid not to let me. I was just as frightened to leave him, and more, for the likes of that out there in the yard.

"Please, Pa, you know'd how Mama loved the books and wanted them for me." *Mama*. Her absence ached in my heart, and I was desperate for her comforting arms.

"Your mama wanted you safe, Daughter."

Frazier moved closer to the mule, drawing in his shoulders, bracing against the bitter cold.

"He don't look safe, and he scares me something awful." The old cabin creaked, moaned like it were true, like it was trying to keep him away. "And he don't bathe… Why, his britches are strong enough to stand themselves up in a corner. I-I don't want to marry. Pa, please, I don't want to go anywhere alone with him, I—"

"Daughter, I would see you knotted right and give you a proper send-off if I could, but the Company ain't allowing nary a second off in a whole month for the likes of us miners—unless it comes with a gravedigger's notice or boss man's pink slip. In the morning, I'll rent Mr. Murphy's ol' horse, Bib, and bring your trunk on over to him. Make sure you're settled in. Go on, Daughter. He'll take you to the officiant, and you'll be Mrs. Charlie Frazier by tonight. Get on to your man. Go on, it's getting late." He flicked his hand. "Don't keep your man waiting."

His words landed like rocks on my chest.

Pa fished into his pants pocket and pulled out a clean handkerchief I'd just washed for him this morning, passing it to me.

I balled it up in a damp, trembling fist, unrolling, squeezing, rolling.

Pa's shoulders drooped as he turned to go inside. Gripping the latch, he paused at the threshold. "You belong to Charlie Frazier now."

"I belong here with my job! Don't take my books away like this. Please…Pa, no, don't let him take me away." I sank to my knees and raised begging hands. "Let me stay," I whispered hoarsely. "Please, Pa? *Pa?* Almighty Lord, please—"

The door shut tight, swallowing my prayer, taking my light with it. I wanted to run, to fold myself into the dark, rotted land, disappear under the cold Kentucky ground.

I raised the twisted handkerchief to my mouth and pressed, watching my hand grieve to a dark azure blue.

Radish red, he was.

What he did was worse than a rattler's bite, or what I imagined the snake's strike to be when my sixty-two-year-old husband, Charlie Frazier, first tried to plant his fiery seed inside me. Bucking, I knocked off the pillow he'd cloaked over my face.

"Be still," he hissed. "*Still, you blue devil.* Ain't gonna suffer the sight of your dead face." He pressed his other hand over my mouth and eyes, shielding himself, pumping inside me.

I wriggled free from his grip, bit and clawed at him, choking on my fear and fury, struggling for air.

He pummeled my stomach, pinched my breasts, and punched at my head until a blackness took hold.

The second time he poked me, a gray leeched into his dog-pecker-pink face.

When I came to, I was lying on a cold dirt floor. A voice floated above, and I tried to speak but nothing came out. Someone placed a cover over me, and I fell back into a shifting darkness until another voice roused me once more.

I struggled to lift my lids, but could only open one eye part-way, barely making out Pa's face.

"*Pa-ah*." The word broke in my throat. I stretched out a hand. A deep pain struck and I cried out, cradling my swollen arm.

"Daughter, don't try an' move." He lifted my head and brought a mug to my mouth. "Just sip this." Part of my lip had swelled to my nose, and the liquid dribbled out, down onto my chin. Pa dried my wet skin with his coat sleeve, tilted the cup, and tried again to give me a drink. I tasted the shine and spit and coughed, the liquid setting me on fire, burning my tender gums and split lips.

A different ache lit, hot and knifelike, and I sucked in a breath, pushed Pa away, clamping a hand to my ear, only to jerk it back and see the sticky blood that had leaked out the eardrum and covered my palm.

Pa dug out his handkerchief and pressed it against my ear. "You hold it there a minute." He placed my hand over the hankie and held up the mug. "Try and get all this down now." Pa raised the liquor back to my mouth, and I took a bigger gulp.

"That's it. Have just a little more, Cussy. It'll help some." When I finished, Pa set down the mug, folded me carefully in his arms, and stroked my hair.

"*Mama*," I whimpered and slipped my hand between his shoulder and my ear, pressing, trying to stop the stabbing pains. "*I want my mama*."

"Shh, I've got you, Daughter." He rocked. "Doc's here now, and we're gonna get you home and rested."

I squinted at the man standing beside the bedpost. "*Doc?*"

"You'll be fine, but his ticker done broke, Bluet," the mountain doc said over the sagging marriage bed, covering Frazier with a thin flannel sheet before tending to my broken bones.

Pa buried him out in the yard under a tall pine along with my courting candle.

Three

Somewhere between that first poke and the unfolding of spring, my bones mended, and I got three things: my old job with the Pack Horse librarians, an old mule I named Junia, and sign of Charlie Frazier's seed. Weren't but a few days later, I pulled up Frazier's devil-rooting with a tansy tea I'd brewed from the dried herbs Mama'd kept in the cellar.

The brisk morning nipped at my face, and I buried my chin deeper into Pa's oilskin coat and nudged the mule ahead to the home of our first library patron. We crossed over into the fog-soaked creek before sunrise, the dark waters biting at the beast's ankles, a willingness to hurry pricking Junia's long ears forward. Late April winds tangled into the sharp, leafy teeth of sourwoods, teasing, combing her short gray mane. Beyond the creek, hills unfolded, and tender green buds of heart-shaped beetleweed and running ivy pushed up from rotted forest graves and ancient knobby roots, climbed through the cider-brown patches of winter leaves, spilling forth from fertile earth.

Hearing a splash, Junia paused in the middle of the waters and gave a half-whinnying bray. "Ghee up, girl," I said, spotting the frog. "*Ghee.*" I rubbed the mule's crest. "Ghee up now."

The beast flicked her tail, still unsure, looking over into the trees toward the trail that led to Frazier's place. "Ghee, Junia. C'mon, we're on our book route." I pulled the reins to the left, tugging her head so she wouldn't look—wouldn't have to remember him too.

The mule was my inheritance, the only thing Frazier had owned, that and three dollars, some loose change, a tar-blackened spittoon, and his name. Before Frazier married me, I'd rented my mount for fifty cents a week from Mr. Murphy's stable, same as most other librarians. I had been satisfied riding his horse or small donkey for my book routes, but I just couldn't leave the poor animal tied to Frazier's tree to die.

The mule's coat had been blood-matted, and her open wounds oozed out of flesh that sagged toward the cold winter ground. But one look at the beast told me she had a will to live, could fight with a fierce kick and big bite. And I'd seen something in her big brown eyes that told me she thought we could do it all together.

Pa'd said, "It's trouble. Sell it! Ain't worth two hoots—a horse or donkey would serve you better, Daughter. You tell a horse and ask a donkey. Yessir, horses will gladly do your bidding, but a mule, well hell, that beast is just an argument, and with that one"—he shot a finger to Junia—"you're gonna find yourself wrestling a good deal of just that, negotiating with the obstinate creature." Then Pa'd turned away, grumbling, "That mule's only fit for a miner's sacrifice."

I'd balked loudly at that. If a mine was shut down overnight, a *miner's sacrifice* had to be made. Mules were sent in at daybreak before the shaft opened because of the fear of gas buildup over-night. The men would strap a lit candle or carbide lamp onto the beast and send it in alone. If they didn't hear an explosion, or see a smoking, flaming mule hightail it out of the shaft, only then did the miners know it was safe to go in and start the day's work.

Reluctantly, Pa let me bring her back home. I bought a bottle of horse liniment, a used saddle, and soft horse blankets for the old mule. It had taken a month for me to nurse the starved, beaten beast back to health. Another month to stop her from kicking and biting me. Not Pa, nor any man, dared stand beside her still, or else the ol' mule would sneak out a leg and sidekick them, stretch her jaw and take a hard nip of skin. But despite her temper with the men, I'd ridden her into town and marveled at how gentle and agreeable she was around the young'uns and womenfolk.

Junia lifted her muzzle, and once more I followed her stare, bent my good ear to the breeze, stroking my lobe. Doc said the other ear might never heal, and so far he'd been right. The muddle stayed put when I tried to test it by closing a palm over the good one.

Across the creek, a rafter of turkeys and their poults scratched for food. "He can't hurt us no more, ol' girl," I soothed the mule, patted her withers. "C'mon now, we're on official duty for the Pack Horse." Junia prodded the breeze with her nose. Quietly, I waited, letting her decide it was safe to journey on to our book route.

To my relief, she cast her eyes away from Frazier's path and moved toward the bank. Today would be busy. My Monday route was a long one. Some days I only had a few folks scheduled for drop-offs, but today I'd been given a new patron on top of the seven homes and mountain school I'd visit.

Climbing up the brush-tangled bank, we topped the hill, leaving behind the scuttles of squirrel and rabbit. The mule raised her muzzle and nickered, remembering we'd checked out the route last week to prepare for our first day back.

A train whistle lost itself over the rows of blue hills to the east, slipping rail song into the coves, hollows, and pockets of old Kaintuck. I let the sound fill me with its tune. Soon, my mind turned to the train passengers the big steel cars carried past the woodlands, through these old mountains cut with untold miles of rivers and creeks. What fine places the locomotive toted them to. I'd dreamt once of a train full of Blues journeying. Blues like me. Someone, somewhere who looked like me—

Junia snorted as if she'd heard my far-fetched thoughts. "It could happen," I told the mule. "There could be others out there like me."

In the distance, the Moffits' homestead peeked out of the morning light. Eager now, Junia pressed on, breaking into a fast trot when she saw the girl.

It was my first book drop since my January marriage, but seeing my library patron up here and waiting like that felt like I'd never left.

Spring had finally come, and I shed the dying winter, the death of my marital bed, and returned briefly to my ten-year-old child of yesteryear. I leaned into the raw spring wind feeling the spirit of books bursting in my saddlebags—the life climbing into my bones. Knocking my heels against the beast, I kissed my teeth in short bursts, urging her into a full gallop. Being able to return to the books was a sanctuary for my heart. And a joy bolted free, lessening my own grievances, forgiving spent youth and dying dreams lost to a hard life, the hard land, and to folks' hard thoughts and partialities.

Four

Sixteen-year-old Angeline Moffit stood barefoot in the mud-carpeted yard, hands on bossy hips, waiting, her tired orchid-pink dress billowing, whipping around long legs to Jesus, the tattered hem snapping a harsh whisper under a thin, holey housecoat, the bother set plain on her mouth.

"*Blu-eeet.*" She waved. "'Bout time, Bluet. It's April already! I missed ya. You got yourself a new mount. What's its name?"

"This is Junia."

"Oh, Junia's a fine name. Get over here, Junia. C'mere, you ol' apostle gal."

Angeline, one of my youngest library patrons, remembered me reading to her from Romans 16:7 about Junia, the only female apostle. The same Bible verse Mama'd read to me, and the reason I had given Junia the fitting name. I'd found out quick how clever the animal was, how you couldn't make her move along if she sensed danger ahead. At sixteen hands tall, a protector, a prophet, Junia'd already saved me from a bobcat attack, another time from a pack of mean dogs, and most recently from a slippery moss slope that was caving in.

The ol' girl had made us wait until I saw the bobcat and let it slink away, heard the dogs before any human could, and made me turn back to a spot where the wild dogs dared not enter. And she just refused to go up the mossy slope until I got off and saw the trouble with my own eyes, made a fool of myself testing it and tumbling down, landing hard on my tail. Junia wasn't skittish like my old horse or stick-legged like the donkey. She wouldn't dither over a problem none, but she'd defend and battle if it came down to it. Folks said a good trail mule was far better than a horse, that riding a mule was just as good as packing a shotgun across these dangerous hills. But Pa still weren't convinced of Junia's worth, nor trusted her cantankerous ways.

Junia nuzzled the girl's shoulder, took an instant liking, letting Angeline grab her reins and tie them to a tall, turkey-tail-covered stump. "*She's here.* The Book Woman's here with them books," Angeline yelled back to the cabin.

I eased myself off the mule and opened the saddlebag, digging. "Sorry it's been so long, but the winter was…and…" I let the unspoken words fizzle in the air, not wanting to talk about the marriage.

Angeline graciously brushed it off. "I heard. And it don't matter none. You're here now, and I sure have missed ya."

I wondered just how much she'd heard, and I felt the blue rise on my face as I pulled out *The Young Child's A B C, or First Book* and handed it to her. She clutched it to her chest and murmured a soft thank-you.

Digging some more, I found her a church pamphlet and a magazine. "Mr. Moffit's *Popular Mechanics*," I said.

"*Pop…Pop-a-lur Ma-mechanics*," she read and traced the title with a dirty nail, inspecting the photograph on the cover. "That's an airship, Bluet."

Fearfully, she looked up to the sky and whispered, "Hain't never seen it, but the mister swears he saw one floating over the hills. That aeroplane passed right over him, and he up and threw hisself to the ground."

I'd never seen one either, but I believed her.

"And"—Angeline shook a telling finger—"I know'd the president's wife climbed into one too, when she came to Kaintuck."

We both stared to the heavens, trying to imagine Eleanor

Roosevelt up there in the gray belly of a machine flying across our mountains.

"Hard to believe folks can reach our hills like that." Angeline barely breathed and cupped a hand over her eyes, searching the skies. "Pretty soon a fellar hain't gonna need his mount, or feet even. Them big machines jus' gonna pluck you up and do it for you."

She slipped her hand into mine, and I stiffened. No white ever touched a Blue friendly like that. No one but Angeline. And no matter how many times she'd reached for my hand, it still felt strange, and I'd quietly tuck it back to my side, feeling I'd somehow left a sin on her.

Still, I liked her soft touch, and it made me yearn for Mama and wish for a sister, maybe even a baby, a little. But there would never be a babe, nor another man for me. If word had reached way up here, I was certain the townsfolk had rumored that my color somehow killed Frazier—gossiped that a Blue devil had murdered a man in his marriage bed. It was a blessing, I reminded myself. No one would have me now, and I'd never be forced to marry again. My breathing slowed, and a small relief anchored that surety.

"Aeroplanes and trains," I said to Angeline, shaking a little inside from that thought and those darker ones I'd just tucked away.

"The world's a'gettin' so big, Bluet. Makes a fellar feel too small," Angeline barely whispered. "It's growing too fast. Right when you're looking smack at it, but you hain't really seeing it neither. Hain't natural." She tilted her head down toward the dirt, plugging her toes into the earth as if to root herself from being carried off.

"Sure is a'changin', Angeline." It gave me hope, though— hope that those big, loud machines might one day bring another of my kind. "I best be getting inside to Mr. Moffit."

"Oh, Bluet, he'll be happy to see ya. He's been in the bed. Done went and got his foot busted the other day." Her cheeks pinkened.

Eula Foster told me he'd been shot in the foot for stealing another man's chicken. "Maybe the new loan will ease his discomfort," I said.

She caught my hand again and led me up the stacked stone steps and onto her stick porch, grinning. This time I carried her warmth in my heart, savored a sisterhood I'd never had.

I ducked past an old hornets' nest hanging under the sagging eaves. Inside the one-room cabin, a house mouse darted under the black potbelly stove packed with a rotted smoldering stump. Daylight slipped through the curled paper coating the walls, dusting the shadows out of the home's corners.

A pan of wild ramps and turnips simmered atop the cast iron, filling the room with stinky steam. Yellowed newsprint lined moldy walls, with a smattering of Angeline's words dotted across the peeling pages.

"Let me get ya a seat," Angeline said and fetched an old, empty tin of Mother's Pure Lard from over by the stove's feet, dragging the big can loudly across buckled pine boards.

Splitting at the seams, a stained featherbed mattress that had been stuffed partly with straw butted up to a spider-cracked windowpane. Angeline's husband lay there by the sill dozing, the pain tracked across his face. With no money for a doctor, the wound wouldn't heal. The thirty-year-old looked scrawnier than the last time I'd seen him. His face had aged like craggy rock, and he had gray patches under his eyes.

A splintered ax handle poked out from under the bed where Angeline must've placed it, hoping there was truth in the old superstition that it would cut a person's pain.

Angeline put a hand on her husband's shoulder and gently shook him awake. "It's Monday and she's finally back, Willie. Right here she is."

He grimaced.

"I brought you a *Popular Mechanics*," I told him.

"Didn't expect you back, Widow Frazier." Mr. Moffit squinted up at me.

"Yes, sir, it's me, Book Woman, and I'm back now." I cringed at my new title, having realized as soon as Eula Foster had addressed me that it would stick. A week ago when I returned to the Center, Eula had crossed her unwelcoming arms and called out my new title, a mixture of disappointment and loathing sliding over her snipped greeting. The despair had knotted tight in my gut, leaving me to lower my eyes, afraid to witness the disgust in hers.

Mr. Moffit tilted his head to the bucket for me to sit as Angeline tucked a threadbare crimson counterpane up closer to his chin.

Angeline smoothed the covers, tucking him in a bit more. Satisfied, she slipped out the door.

I pulled the lard can closer to his bed, sat down, and opened the first page, holding the magazine high in front of my face. He turned his head toward the window.

We did this for our comforts. Mr. Moffit wouldn't have to stare at my face, and I wouldn't have to worry about making him uncomfortable. I didn't fault him, reckoning we both had disfigurements, some that didn't have a color.

Mr. Moffit knotted the covers closer to his chin, and I caught something I'd never seen before: odd-colored nails, not odd to me, being a Blue, but odd on a white folk.

His nails were a light blue, every single one of them.

I looked at my own, the blueness nearly the same. I snatched a peek at his face and ears, white like new milk teeth, and again glanced back at his nails, scanning the length of him.

At the foot of the bed a single toe stuck out from under the covers, his toe I'd never seen before. It weren't white neither. It was like the blue-eyed Mary in the hills, the two-colored bloom that nature painted lavender-blue on one side and white on the other. *Blue*, I puzzled.

Long ago, Mama'd said there had been some of us Blues who'd been born blue-eyed Marys like that. And others with the color who'd outgrown it in their youth. Those Blues who only showed their color on their nails easily escaped the affliction by keeping hands and feet hidden inside mitts and socks.

I wondered if Mr. Moffit had some other condition, or maybe it was because of the ailing from the bullet wound on his foot.

Mr. Moffit turned partway, his eyes closed. "Ready."

"Yessir. This'll be a fine article, Mr. Moffit."

He crooked his head back to the window.

"'Understanding Our Airships,'" I began. Mr. Moffit was never taught, and he liked me to read a few pages to him. "An aeroplane's engine is…"

I read five minutes more than what I intended, then peeked over the top of the page and saw him asleep. Quietly, I laid the magazine beside him. He'd pore over the pictures, then return it to me on my next visit to exchange for another.

Out in the yard, Angeline pointed to words she'd scratched into the dirt with a stick. "You learned me good. Look here. *Garden. Horse. Home. Angeline,*" she said proudly, and then gave me *The Little Red Hen* book she'd borrowed in December. "Sorry, Bluet. It got busted some when Willie had hisself a fit and threw it outside. I'm glad you're back 'cause he lit at me good for not being able to read him his own loan. Said a colored shouldn't be able to read better than me. Real sorry…" She latched on to my hand and laid the apology with a firm grip. I looked down at us bound together like that, tried to draw back, but Angeline squeezed tighter and whispered, "Hain't no harm. Our hands don't care they's different colors. Feels nice jus' the same, huh?"

It did. But Mr. Moffit didn't like folks who weren't his color. He used to demand that I stay put in the yard. But his longing for the printed word soon weakened his demands, and he eventually allowed Angeline to bring me inside to read at the small wooden table, so desperate was he for the books to help him escape his misery, misery at never having enough to fill his belly, not even enough spare coins to buy himself a couple of bullets to maybe shoot a rabbit, and now the misery at the poison inching its way deeper into him from his gunshot.

I'd seen it in his face, in his bony slumping shoulders, that he'd given up long ago, wishing every night that there wouldn't be a next. There weren't nothing sweet Angeline could ever do to help him that wouldn't bring on a bigger anger.

She caught the concern in my eyes and said, "Sometimes he gets so riled it scares me something bad. Has a meanness. Hain't no reason to always grumble like an ornery bear."

I loosened Angeline's hold and examined the spine on her old loan.

"Hope it don't rile Miss Harriett and Miss Eula too much, Bluet."

I stuffed her book into my bags. "Reckon it's nothing I can't get bound." I know'd Harriett Hardin, the bookbinder and assistant librarian supervisor, would preach a sinner's funeral, rile a'might indeed. And head librarian Eula Foster would pinch her mouth in dismay.

But it was too precious not to fix, what with the demand for books so high and the reading material so scarce.

The last time I brought in one of Angeline's busted loans, Harriett had wrinkled her nose and warned, "You tell Mrs. Moffit the government pays the Pack Horse librarians' salary. *And only that.* We don't have enough books nor the money to be replacing them. If she can't see fit to care for a library book in her possession, I will deduct the cost from *your* pay and suspend her from the route!"

The government men didn't supply books and printed materials to the Pack Horse service. They were donated by bigger libraries, in bigger towns and richer cities—from the women's clubs, and the Parent-Teacher Association, and Boy Scout troops even, their members spreading across Kentucky and Ohio.

Most books sent in were damaged, tattered, and castoffs. The government didn't give us a proper place to hold them neither. Troublesome Creek's post office offered its back room to the Pack Horse Library Project to use for housing, sorting, and repairing the materials.

"Hope it can be fixed," Angeline whispered worriedly.

"I'll take it home and bind it myself." I smiled.

"It won't happen again." Hesitant, Angeline held up the new book I'd brought her. "Read it to me 'fore you leave?"

We went over her new book, and she read the words without trouble. Angeline had a strong hankering to read and write. When she was done, she pulled a shriveled half carrot from her pocket and looked at me for permission. "For Junia."

Junia shot up her ears.

The country's despair had dug its roots into Kentucky and spread like ugly knotweed, choking spirits, strangling life. I didn't want to take from Angeline, what with the small scraps they lived off. But I also didn't want to offend her gracious offer.

In the side yard, toppled rows of dead cornstalks from the last season were scattered where the young girl tried her best to coax a decent crop from the tired clay and thin air. Beside it, a postage-stamped garden of spring carrots, beets, and turnips scratched for survival against weed, briar, and wild onions. Beyond, a mustard patch grew thick.

"Thank you, Angeline. Junia is much obliged." She fed it to her, knowing the twenty-year-old gray mule was smart and would eagerly keep toting me back to her. Greedy, Junia nosed inside the girl's pockets for another carrot.

Angeline pulled out something else, grabbed my palm, and pushed a tiny cloth package into it. "Can you get these to the doc for me? There's twelve of my granny's Bloody Butcher seed for him to come tend to Willie." She rolled my fingers over them.

I doubted the doc would come for corn. Wouldn't pay a visit for less than four dollars since he lived a good three-hour ride away from here by horse or mule.

"His foot's getting a bad sickness now, an' the nails a'turning blue. I don't want to bury him, not with a babe coming," she said.

"A baby?"

"In the summer."

"That soon?" I ran my eyes quickly over her scrawny body, tight cheekbones, and the bluish cast circling her pale eyes,

wondering how she could possibly bear the punishment of preg-
nancy. The greedy land had dulled her youthful looks.

She seemed soft and more suited for the fancy living in the
cities I'd read about, what with her delicate heart-shaped face
and long flaxen hair. Though I know'd Angeline worked harder
than two stout mountain women and was tough as a pine knot,
despite appearances. Still, I worried the young girl wouldn't be
strong enough for child birthing, that the old mountains would
steal more from her.

Angeline said, "July 18 it'll come. I've been counting."

"That's…uh…" The goodwill died on my tongue. "I'll get
these seeds to him."

Angeline picked up a stick. "I know'd its name I'm giving it.
Want to see?"

Surprised and curious she'd already given thought to the
baby's name, I sputtered out *yes*.

She crouched down with her stick and scrawled carefully in
the dirt, working each letter on her lips, scratching out two, and
then trying again. Satisfied, she stood and pointed. "*HONEY.*"
She poked her stick at the name. "I know'd it when I made
myself a tea and read the leaves, and they said it'd be a girl. I
want her to be real sweet like that." She rubbed her tiny belly.

"Honey. That's a fine name," I said, because it reminded me
of Angeline's sweet nature.

"Willie don't. He said it was a colored's name, and he won't have
it." Angeline swiped her hand down her dusty skirts and looked off
like she was counting the sunsets until she gave birth. Tiredness and
disappointment spread across her face. "Here Willie'd promised
to take me to the summer hootenanny to hear the men with the
fiddles. Don't reckon there'll be any dancing now."

I studied on the baby-care pamphlets back at the library that
the health department had dropped off and reminded myself to
bring one to her.

Angeline shook her skirts and placed a hand over her belly.
"Here I'm already sixteen, knocked up and about to get withered

from the seed, and hain't even danced myself a proper jig." She rubbed a bony fist over her eyes.

I lifted an arm. "I reckon you don't need a hootenanny to have dancing. Or a fancy fiddle even. It's free as rain and here for the taking."

Angeline brightened at that. "I know'd lots of songs, and I can dance some." She sang an old, lively ballad, twirled around once, twice, until she was laughing, her sweet musical voice filling the air.

"You have a fine voice," I said.

"I got lots more, Bluet." The girl sang another cheerful one and spun again. She glimpsed my feet tapping the ground, my hand bouncing off the side of my skirts. It was as if they had a mind of their own, and I stopped at once, fearing I'd made a spectacle of myself.

When Angeline finished her tune, she said, "Be sure an' tell Doc them seeds are from Minnie's lot. God rest her. An' her corn... Well, it's worth twice his fee if a man could pay in money. Three times, even."

She looked proud, like she had given something as big as the moon and worth all the heavens.

I dropped them into my pocket. "I'll be going to town in May, and I'll make sure he gets them."

"You can give 'em to Jackson."

I looked at her blankly.

"Jackson Lovett," she said. "Hain't seen him yet, but he's come home now. He settled in the ol' Gentry homestead an' Willie said he's always running to town for supplies. Hain't he on your route?"

"Mr. Lovett?" I touched the saddlebag, suddenly remembering there was a new stop today, though I hadn't heard who it was and only that it was a man Eula Foster had told me about, and that there would be *another* added to my already long route. "Yes, I think he is." I mounted Junia.

"He went and built a dam out west for the president, I heard." Angeline squinted up at me.

"Hoover Dam," I marveled, recalling the wonder I'd read about in magazines.

"*D-A-M*," Angeline spelled. "You ride her home safe, Junia." Angeline scratched the mule's ears, sneaking glimpses of me, and then said quietly, "I heard. Heard about that book woman, Agnes, losing her horse trying to cross Hell-fer-Sartin Creek. Heard the way it up and laid down in the snow and... Well, it passing on her like that was real bad."

I wondered how she'd found out about Agnes's accident, then realized I'd seen Mr. Moffit outside the Center in December. Or maybe the news came with the mail delivery that traveled the hills every two weeks. Though I never recalled seeing any mail in their home. Weren't no other visitors but me and the mail courier in these hills, except for Doc, when a fellar couldn't right himself with his own homemade tonic and could afford the physician's services.

"Willie used to have hisself kin planted up there in Hell-fer-Sartin. I did too," Angeline said. "Hain't never met any of 'em, though."

The small town of Hell-for-Certain—uttered and spelled as Hell-fer-Sartin, what an old preacher called it when asked about his visit there decades ago and what stuck to folks' tongues ever since—sat two counties over. Steep rocky inclines, twisty devil land, and one of the most difficult book routes a Pack Horse librarian could have.

Agnes's old rented horse, Johnny Moses, snapped a leg at the mouth of Hell-fer-Sartin Creek. Agnes pulled off Johnny Moses's fat pannier and packed all the reading supplies onto her back, leaving the dying animal in the snow. She stopped at the Baxter cabin and sent the man off to end the poor beast's suffering. Ol' Mr. Baxter was bound to make good use of every ounce of that rented meat and every inch of its hide until the owner came and fetched whatever was left.

Agnes had journeyed onward a good sixteen miles on foot, up and down ravines, coves, and passes, along the dangerous trails, missing not one patron on her book drop, somehow making it home with nary a scratch to show for her two long, troublesome days.

Angeline continued, "Never been to Hell-fer-Sartin neither. Most of my folk come from Cowcreek, where I was born. Where my Willie first met me." She shot me a soft smile. "But Mamaw always said some of our kin stayed put in them ol' hills of Hell."

We talked a few more minutes until Junia sounded a warning, shaking off my worrisome hand combing through her mane.

"See you Monday," Angeline said.

"Ghee up, ol' girl." I waved goodbye.

Angeline picked up her stick and dragged it through the muck, a lost lullaby spilling, calling up the long day. She paused. "Hear that?"

I strained my ears. Somewhere, a rain crow rolled out its gravelly whine. The bird sang again, and once more, this time longer, and I searched the skies for storm clouds. *Bright blue.*

"That's three times now," Angeline fretted.

Mountaineers thought the crow's calling came as a death warning. Angeline's eyes sought mine, and I saw the fear in them that the bird had sung it for her. Again the bird stuttered its mournful song.

Five

I rode to my next book drop, leaving the rain crow's warbles on the mud path, thinking about Mr. Moffit's wound and the baby coming.

It could've been me with child, and I shuddered to think how close I'd come to it, possibly birthing another Blue—and with Frazier's dirty seed at that, and during these hard times too.

I pulled in my shoulders, kneed Junia onward, and picked up a lively whistle to take leave of the dark thoughts, ignoring the dismay I'd pocketed at the Moffits'.

At the mouth of the woodlands, Junia rooted herself to a halt and perked her ears. After a bit of coaxing, I urged her on into the belly of the woods. Inside, dark earth, leaves, rotting logs, and crawling moss rose among the pine saplings, cottonwoods, and honey locusts and canopied the beaten path, pulling me deeper into my thoughts. Halfway through, a twig snapped and Junia stopped, swished her tail, and heaved, stirring me from my contemplations.

"Ghee on, girl, ghee." I rubbed Junia's briary mane and stroked her enormous floppy ears.

To our right, I caught a glimpse of what looked to be a haint, then blinked and saw the trick that had caused it.

Weren't no such spirit, just a man sly-eyeing me. He didn't fool me none with his pasty-white face. Darkly he was, filled to the brim with the blackness inside. And he weren't really hiding, more like in waiting, slumped against the bark, a boot propped up on a knobby root, not bothered by who saw him, I reckoned, and making sure I did, I know'd.

It was preacher man Vester Frazier, my dead husband's cousin. I'd seen him poking around the woods a week ago when I inspected my trails, and in town at the Center loitering near Junia. He'd been coming for me a good while, and more boldly since I'd been left widowed.

He'd done the same to others like me: Michael McKinney, the three-nippled midget who rode his goat cart bare-chested across the hills, a boy with pink eyes and skin and hair the color of a white lamb, the seven-year-old Melungeon girl who had fits that tonic and herbs couldn't quiet, and the Goodwin woman whose triplets Vester Frazier set his sights on, declaring *It ain't fitting for a Godly woman to birth more than one young'un, only beasts, and it is surely Satan's doings to plant multiple seeds in a female like that.* And there were the godless, those who'd never found a church, and a few ungodly others Vester Frazier and his followers thought the devil had given those peculiarities to. The odd markings with no names.

When Vester Frazier and his First Mountain Truth of Christ congregation tried to chase the devils out by baptizing those sinners down in the cold, fast waters of Troublesome Creek, the seven-year-old fell into a coma and perished, two of the triplet babies drowned, the paper-white boy was left a mute, and Michael McKinney suffered a broken limb and busted collarbone before escaping, never to be seen again.

Pa had done his best to keep me from Frazier's christening. When I was born, Pa said he'd chased the preacher off our land with a gun, picking the Bible right out of his hands with a single shot. When I turned six and once more when I struck twelve, Pa had to run him off again. Then Pa had Sheriff talk to him and thought he was rid of him for good.

That Frazier was on my route, way up here, terrified me. He had to be hunting me. I searched for his mount and saw that he'd hidden it and had lain in wait.

My breath came short and fast, and a pounding in my temples seized hold.

Alarmed, Junia backstepped. I jerked on the reins, kicking her flanks, urging her on past. But the mule wouldn't obey. Instead, she struck her ears forward, bawled loudly, and swung her head sideways, readying to battle Frazier.

I slid down off her, groping wildly for the straps, trying to latch on and lead her past the preacher man.

Frazier stepped out onto the path, and Junia blew her hot horsey breath in his face. He caught Junia's bit, yanking hard, cutting her mouth. She reared to get away, and he kicked her hind leg, sending her tumbling backward onto the dirt, a scream strangled in her chest.

"Junia!" I reached for her. "Please don't harm her."

The old mule tried to rise and shake him off, but Frazier had her locked down by his grip on the bit in her soft gums and a boot on her neck.

"You wouldn't be spreading the word of Satan on this fine day, now would you, Widow Frazier?" Preacher asked.

"Let her go. I'm on library duty, Pastor. Give us safe passage."

"On a sinner's path," he snarled. "God will surely cast you down unto the chains of darkness for your wickedness unless you seek salvation through baptism."

"It's for the WPA program. I'm on government business."

"Another sorry lot of devils. Let me give you Jesus, Widow Frazier. Help pull you through the fires so you can get forgiveness and bask in His salvation."

He bent over and slapped at his pant leg wet from Junia's slobber, keeping an eye locked my way.

The pastor half-bent like that reminded me of Charlie Frazier, and I shrank back. The same dirty hair, scraggly beard, and rotting-bark-brown teeth, him leering and looking like he wanted to give me a different salvation from Jesus's.

Junia's flesh quivered, and she fought to free herself from his grasp. Frazier jerked harder on her leathers, the mule's wild eyes swelling, pooling in a darkness from fear, maybe from a recognition of his horrid kin who'd hurt her before. Then she went still except for her heaving rib cage.

"You're hurting her. Stop!" I tried to pry off his hands. Junia's tongue hung limp out the side, her mouth slathered in froth, her bulging dark eyes ringed with a white terror.

"P-please, Pastor Frazier, let us go—"

His eyes flashed, and then he loosened his hold, swung out a lazy kick to Junia's soft gray muzzle, startling and sending her up and flying in a panicked scramble of twigs and dust.

"Junia, whoa, *whoa*," I yelled after her.

Frazier snatched my arm, jerked me back. "Anywhere you're tramping off to can't be good." His breath blew rancid in my face.

I turned my head. "I'm working, sir. I have to get to my next stop." I felt the color blazing across my skin, my hands needling a blackish blue. "Please...please let me pass, Pastor."

"Doing the devil's work by carrying sinful books to good and Godly folks. You're unclean, born of sin. In need of church."

"They...they's clean books, and my mama taught me the Lord's Word."

"You're a heathen!" He poked the words onto my chest.

"I know'd the Lord Jesus. Let me go now." I said this like a truth, although weakly with little might since we both know'd the Blues didn't have a church—I'd never been in one, or even been invited inside the smallest holler chapel. Home was church.

"She was soiled," he hissed, "godless, and is surely burning in hell for laying her sins, *you*, in Godly land."

"I ain't no such, Pastor! I ain't a sin." I tried to wiggle free from his bruising hold. "My folks said God's not just in your church. Mama know'd the Lord and read her Scripture daily. Weren't soiled—"

"She was the beast's slittail. And the only pure word is His written word from the church and what He directs me to give to you. You're a devil, girl, who's done her evil on Charlie, and sorely in need of that direction."

"Please, Pastor—"

"I can save you. God can cure you of that devil color." He gripped my arm harder. "It's my calling to bring home the lost, my duty to save my kin. Come with me now."

I looked around, seeing nothing but forest and nowhere to escape, the terror pummeling inside me.

There'd been stories from time to time. Whispers about women who'd been dropped right in their paths, taken viciously on the forest floor, ravaged by vile men. And I know'd Vester Frazier was a vile one.

When the Pack Horse program started, a librarian was accosted by a drunken bootlegger on her route, and her mount was stolen. Furious, the sheriff sent out a posse to find him. The lawman was fond of the library program and admired the services of the Pack Horse librarians. Pa said they'd found the drunk and brought him into town, publicly whipped him outside the Library Center, and then dragged his half-dead body back up into the hills by the very same packhorse he'd stolen. The offender had been left next to a pile of bear scat.

Sheriff said it was important to have the librarians in our area where there weren't any, and with only one school with old textbooks to read from at that. He declared whoever harmed a librarian, or dishonored or disgraced the Pack Horse women and their service, would meet harsh consequences. Then he nailed his warning inside the post office, and folks had cheered.

It made our jobs safer. And with Junia, I'd felt even more protected. I searched the trees for her, but she was nowhere in sight.

"Leave me be. Leave me, or the sheriff will bring down the law on you," I threatened.

"*Law.*" His lips flattened. "I don't give three shits about man's laws, or diddly-squat about that ol' stupid relation of mine."

Although the sheriff had married into the pastor's family, I'd heard he'd squabbled with Frazier over a track of land long ago, and there had been bad blood between them ever since.

"My pa'll"—my mouth grew hot and dusty—"my pa'll sic the law on you." The scratched words slipped through my teeth, weakening.

"You listen up, girl. There is only His law in this land." The preacher pulled me closer and rasped, "There's a stream just beyond the thicket. I can give you a baptism there, cleanse you good—and give you a salvation you never know'd the likes of and what poor ol' Charlie couldn't."

He would have his way with me, then drown me, I was certain.

He tightened his hold. "It was true that ol' boy could never hold on to his land or his whores. What is peculiar is that you'd be the last. You use your witching ways to do him in, maybe use some of that hot blue slittail of yours?" He rubbed himself against me and slid busy hands over my bottom and to my breasts, digging in his bony fingers to feel me.

I jerked hard, tried to break free, but he had a muscled grip. "Let go—"

"Come with me now." He held tight, moving his mouth to my ear. "I'll put a hot-white fire inside of you that'll burn out them blue demons for good."

Frazier wrapped his hands around my neck, yanked me to him, and soaked my lips with an ugly rough kiss.

With the back of my hand, I swiped my mouth, spit, and saw a trickle of blood where his teeth had scraped my flesh. He latched his lips onto mine again. I struggled against him, fighting a sickness rising from my belly, remembering the blood that had stickied my thighs when Charlie Frazier had rolled off me—the month I'd spent scrubbing between my legs, rawing, bloodying my flesh to rid myself of his stain.

Behind the pastor, I caught the long shadow of something, someone, then heard a loud thump and a startled braying.

Junia screamed and trampled toward us, kicking up a squall of black earth and rot.

"*Blue Witch.*" Frazier's voice burned. He shoved me to the ground and ran off into the woods with Junia thundering after him and chomping hard teeth, her maddening cries skinning the bark of pines.

Six

Junia returned from the woods alone. Shaken, I stood beside her and said a prayer. But as always, without a church, there was a falseness in my pleas, a disbelief in my folks' claim that God was everywhere, and soon a shamefulness took hold as I realized I was a sinner. No matter how much or how hard I prayed, I was still unchurched—left with a nothingness and belonging nowhere. And I know'd the Lord Jesus would surely see fit to stick me with more of nothing for the rest of my days.

The mule's shoulder quivered under my hands. It'd taken a good hour to calm her, and another to ease my nausea and try to rid my mind of Vester Frazier. The freedom and joy I'd felt this morning had been robbed. That he could steal it so easily left me both furious and scared. I looked at my timepiece, dusted off my skirts, and mounted.

We rode on and stopped at three more cabins. By the time we reached the Lovett place, my neck was crooked from watching my backside, my skin lit from the nerves.

Lovett's Ridge was a spectacle, and soon I relaxed a little and soaked it up. Layers of dark-blue mountains stacked in the distance, at every turn their cuts rolling, deepening, then lightening to shades of blue-greens from the day's passing clouds. The air blew fresh and breezy. Scents of apple blossoms lifted from a nearby tree, and honeysuckle clung to a crumbling split-rail fence as swallowtails and fat-legged bees flitted above the old timbers and dipped for nectar.

It was alive. You could feel the heartbeat of this mountain, unlike my home tucked in the dark, decaying hollow of old bark and moss, a place where it stayed dark during the day and grew darker at night. Lovett Mountain felt religious, churched, like it belonged.

"Ghee, girl," I said, still wary and circling Junia wide around my new library patron.

Tanned a golden brown like expensive old parchment, yet youthful in bone, Jackson Lovett knelt in the side yard, humming a gravelly ballad, his busy hands working the masonry around a busted well wall.

"Drop it on the porch," he said, barely glancing at me.

I pointed Junia to the steps and dismounted but held on to her reins. Inside my saddlebags I found a worn copy of *A Plea for Old Cap Collier*. I tried to get books I thought different patrons might like and always liked to fill their requests. But with such a shortage of reading material, and because I only got to the Center once a month, it was impossible to select a book for each patron. I lifted it from my leather pouch, and two other books tumbled out onto the grass beside Junia.

The mule toe-hopped and I tried to still her. "Easy, Junia. Easy." I bent down to gather the books beside her hooves, gripping the reins and tapping her knees to push her back.

Mr. Lovett came over to help. He reached for Junia's bridle. Before I could warn him of the mule's cantankerous ways, she pinned back her ears and bit him.

He snatched his hand away, shaking his wrist, cursing under his breath, and cradling the injury.

"I'm sorry, sir. *Sorry!* She's had a frightful day on the trail," I excused and promptly smacked Junia on the rump, lightly scolding her. "Real sorry. She doesn't like…uh…people much." I dug inside my bags, pulled out an old bandage roll, and offered it to Mr. Lovett.

"I've got it," he said, waving away my offer. He stepped onto his porch and grabbed a jar from the rail, opened it, and poured the clear liquid over his bite. "This alcohol will heal it faster."

I reached into my pocket for Angeline's seeds. "Mrs. Moffit asked that you pass these seeds to the doc for medical payment. Her husband needs tending to."

"It'll be a while before I get to town." He grimaced at his wound and then wrapped the hand in a strip of cloth while pinching glimpses of me.

"He's in a very bad way."

Our eyes latched, and I couldn't turn away. His were fine and spirited, yet there weren't nothing playful in them. There was something deeper, a touch of chance and danger, a conquering, but no harming in his gaze either, no fear I could rightly claim from it or could summon, or feel the need to tamp, to turn from. His eyes held a muddle of curiosity, loss, and other distant things I couldn't call up that had somehow taken root and fixed themselves to him in a strange way.

He broke our hold and examined his hand again.

"He's been shot, sir." Mindful of my boldness, I tucked my head to my chin, feeling my ears scalding blue, my face warming full of color to match my hands. "Hurt badly," I added, locking my hands behind me, wishing I'd worn the deerskin gloves Pa had made me.

"For stealing chickens," he said simply, inspecting his dressing some more.

I tucked the seeds back into my coat, worried my fingers over the tiny package. It was a lot to ask for a thief, and Mr. Lovett seemed far too busy to take hours off, what it would take to go to town and back. It didn't make sense. I would be in town in a few weeks and find Doc then.

Satisfied with his nursing, Mr. Lovett pulled a knife from his pocket.

I stepped back, tugged on Junia's reins, pulling her to me, fearful he'd hurt her.

"Junia, huh?" He stood in front of the mule and wagged his knife at her, studying her. "Is that your name, ol' girl?"

Junia flattened her ears, then struck out a front leg and kicked forward. Mr. Lovett sidestepped, missing her temper by a mere inch.

I yanked on her bit, scolding.

"Is that any way to treat a new friend?" Mr. Lovett said and grabbed an apple off the porch. He sliced off a piece of the fruit and held it out to her.

Junia turned her head, side-eyeing him and the fruit. Just when I thought she was going to ignore him, she knocked her head forward and snatched the whole apple from him.

"Junia!" I cried, now afraid he would surely beat her—or worse.

Instead, he laughed easily and slipped the knife back into his pocket. "Now, Junia, you've got yourself a fine mule skinner there. And I can see she takes real good care of you. You just keep bringing the book mistress back, and I promise to get you more."

Junia flopped her ears and chewed, studying him. The mule would never warm to him or any man after all the horrible things Charlie Frazier and his kin had done to her.

Mr. Lovett plucked his copy of *A Plea for Old Cap Collier* off the ground. "Have anything else? I like Cobb just fine, but I already read this when I was out west."

The old Kentucky author, Irvin S. Cobb, was popular reading for menfolk—a great humorist, and Pa used to enjoy reading his *Old Judge Priest* stories.

"No, sir, not today. These others are spoken for. And they're mostly what the courier dropped off at my outpost. I'll try and bring more next Monday. Anything particular?"

"I've been wanting to read John Steinbeck's latest."

"I go to the Library Center the second Tuesday of each month. I'll be sure and check for you." It was a treat to be able to pick out reading material for my patrons instead of just having what the courier left at my pickup station.

"Thanks. Do you read much?"

"Yessir, I started reading when I could hold a book, and I haven't stopped. Mama taught me with the family Bibles and old newsprints. We had pamphlets, an old church hymnal, some discarded oil cans and trash containers with advertising that she'd have Pa bring home to use for teaching."

"Mine did the very same." He looked out to the mountains like he was recalling gentle memories of it.

I wondered if his mama had been *book-read*. My mama didn't have the higher learning, but she'd read plenty enough to almost be. She got most of her smarts from her French grandfather and had herself the start of a small library with eight fine books Pa'd scraped and saved to buy for her. Mama'd insisted on me having the reading and writing same as her. And Pa'd agreed and built her a corner cubby to display the books even though he didn't particularly have the fondness anymore, just occasionally scanning an article in the newsprint or magazines, always saying, "A sneaky time thief is in them books. There's more important ways to spend a fellar's time."

I was pleased this patron liked books so much, surprised he could read or cared about reading. Most men around these parts wanted the mechanic magazines or catalogs.

A lot of hillfolk refused to read, while others had been forced to learn when their Kentucky sons went off to war, and letters arrived back home. But then I reckoned anyone smart enough to build a dam out west had to be clever.

"I have sorely missed the books," he said. "It'll be great to have new ones. I'd like several if you can spare them."

"I'll do my best, sir."

He called out to Junia, "That sure went quick. You don't like people much, huh? You liking me any better after that tasty apple, ol' girl?" Then he cocked his head toward me. "What about you?"

"Sir?" I asked, picking up the other fallen books.

"*You…* I know you like books. Do you like people?"

"I—I best get going. My other patrons are waiting for their Monday drops." I still had the school, Mr. Prine, the Smiths, and Loretta Adams ahead of me, and there was time to make up.

"Call me Jackson." He took a step toward me. "And you must be—"

Junia lit a ghostly shriek, bared her teeth, and pushed herself between us, blocking, gnawing at the air for another nip of him.

Again, I was grateful for the mule's orneriness.

Hiding behind Junia, I peeked over the saddle at him and murmured, "Cussy Mary, but some call me Bluet." I hurried and put the books back into the bag, then slipped my foot into Junia's stirrups and mounted.

"*Bluet.*" He chewed the name, chanced a glance to my hands and face. "And a right pretty damselfly at that. As pretty as those blue-eyed Marys." He nudged his chin toward an old tree bloused with a full skirt of the wildflowers, the colony of plants blooming in soft blues and whites.

"Ghee," I murmured to Junia, not knowing what to reply to this man's words, my face bursting with the color louder than any that could be scraped off my tongue. Then a bit firmer, and before my color could frighten him into taking it back, "*Ghee.*"

He gave the mule a pat on the rump. "Ride safe, Junia."

Junia swished her tail, pricked her ears.

I nudged her with my heels. She wouldn't budge. Mr. Lovett studied me. I dropped my weight into the saddle and dug my heels in again, but Junia weren't having none of it, determined to be mulish and ruin our graceful exit.

"Goodbye, Cussy Mary." He smiled, and this time his eyes did too.

I lifted my legs out wide and brought them down hard on Junia's side, making a crude flapping sound from the stirrup leathers, feeling a flush shoot up from my feet to my face. "*Ghee up!*"

Junia snorted and trotted away.

"Jackson Lovett," I whispered and stopped the mule on the trail minutes later and out of earshot from his cabin, turning his words. "What do you reckon he's about?"

Junia raised her upper lip and nibbled the breeze with tall, talking teeth.

Seven

We left our last patron, Loretta Adams, as shadow-draped mountains folded into a coal-dust sky. Eager for the safety of our cove, Junia led us there with nary a falter in her fast stride.

I pulled off her bridle and saddle, then the bags, and hung it all inside the tiny shed Pa'd reluctantly built for her.

Junia rolled on the grassy patch outside, enjoying her freedom. After a few minutes, I cleaned her hooves, then led her into the stall. Inspecting her coat, I found a few scratches and nursed the scrapes with salve. After latching her wooden half door, I tossed hay over her gate. The mule pushed her nose inside the small bin by the doorway and crooked her mouth, showing teeth.

"Long day, ol' girl," I said, tired. "Let me tend to me now." I tickled her floppy ears. Solemn, she eyed me and nudged my hand.

I fetched a bucket of water for the cabin and my book bag and then hurried to the porch.

Pausing, I leaned my forehead to the door, dreading the long night without Pa, the loneliness that came after he left for the mine. I never felt it so much out there carrying my books, but as soon as I stepped onto my porch, an emptiness loomed and struck when I thought about the fat, dark hours coming.

Creek waters rippled over stone, the murmurs swirling around the cove, as damp breaths of fog pressed down. Inhaling, I took a long pull of the night air to forget my troubles, to forget that Frazier was out there hunting. Sometimes on a clear night I would carry out a chair, sit in the yard with Junia, and watch the stars until my breathing slowed and I could muster enough courage to go back inside the cabin.

Pa must've heard I was home. Coughing, he called out for me.

"Evening, Pa," I said, stepping inside and trying to dip some cheer into my greeting. I set down the bucket and dropped my book bag.

Pa had just awakened. He yawned, scratched the stubble on his face, then pulled on his overalls over his long johns.

"You're late, Daughter."

"Sorry, Pa. It was a bothersome day," I admitted.

"Did you meet trouble out there?" Concern crawled across his coal-stained brows.

"I… No, sir," I fibbed and hid it behind a feeble smile. "It was a long ride my first day back. I caught folks up on their reading, and they wanted me to sit a spell."

I wouldn't tell him about Vester Frazier. It was one thing to find the intruder sneaking onto your land, a Kentucky law that protected all colors from the violation. But we Blues dared not mete out punishment if the harm was off our land.

Over the years, more than one mistreated Blue who'd tried to right a wrong, defend a kin's honor, or stand up to their persecutor had received a whipping or gone missing in these hills. Pa's uncle Colton, a hard-working miner, was one of them, dumped into an abandoned coal-mine shaft after he'd punched a man who'd accosted his wife. They didn't find Colton's bones for five years.

There'd been other talk—whispers from my folks when they thought I was asleep, or out of earshot—the tales of other Blues being hanged for something as simple as back-talking white folk.

"I got a new patron today," I said. "Mr. Lovett."

"Cause you any trouble?"

"No, sir. He's—" *What was he?* "He's a nice enough fellar. Went out west and built a dam for the president. He's bought the old Gentry homestead. Mr. Lovett hankered for the books, and I loaned him one of Irvin Cobb's."

Pa didn't say anything, just sat down on the bed and wrestled on his boots, then thrust his chin to the stove. "Went ahead and helped myself to the beans you made this morning."

Relieved he weren't in the mood to fuss about my job, I crossed to the stove, the old sloping floorboards protesting under my feet. I grabbed two slices of bread from a loaf I'd baked the day before, then scooped out some of the beans from the pot, straining the juices off. I mashed the beans, spread them onto the bread, packing the meaty sandwich into his lunch bucket, adding an apple and a stringy carrot from the cellar to top it off.

"Pa, let me fix you some tea," I said.

"No time. I'm running late myself."

"Another union meeting?"

"Yup."

"Mama said they were too dangerous."

"It's not a female's affair."

"But I'm afraid for you. Pa, if there's another strike, there'll surely be more deaths. Three miners died in the last one, and a few others were left beaten and crippled, spent for life. The Company's guards will take up arms again and shoot anyone who tries to strike. I'm frightened—"

"Daughter, take a look at the fright out there. They're mur- derers, gun thugs, them Company men are. Something must be done. Folks are worse off than before they arrived." Pa coughed. "We're working seventeen-hour days down on a rocky floor with bloody kneecaps in a black hole for scratch, and all the while fearing the next cave-in, the next blast that sends us to our fiery grave. Hell, we're worth less than that ornery beast of yours. Same as Daniel."

I was too young to remember, but when Pa's older brother, Daniel, worked the coal, the men tricked him into being a miner's sacrifice, saying they'd already sent the mule in because they'd just lost a Company beast two weeks before. Daniel went in first with a lantern, and there'd been an explosion. He cried out for help, but the Company couldn't dig him out without causing another collapse. For two days and nights, Pa stayed at the site, talking to his brother through a hairline crack in the debris and rock while Daniel lay in the cold, dark belly of the mine, tortured from blistering burns, begging for mercy. The third morning, when Daniel went silent, the Company sealed the entrance and called their chaplain to say a few words.

Pa's eyes filled with a sadness as he spoke. "Yesterday they suspended Jonah White after a pillar collapsed and came down on his working mule and broke the creature's back. Jonah had his arm crushed clean to the bone."

I rubbed my own arm Frazier had broken, horrified by the suffering of the miner and his mule.

Pa's voice cracked. "Boss Man told ol' Jonah he just bought himself a dead ass and then put a rock on the poor fellar's pay. A man best not let one of them Company mules get killed or harmed down there unless it's for checking leaks. They'll fire or suspend you like that." Pa snapped his fingers. "But let a miner lose his limb or die in that black hellhole and they don't blink, just replace him. They're stealing the very breath of the Kentucky man, the land." He knocked back a cough. "It's all disappearing, Daughter. The tracks of muck in and out of this town, up our brown-dying mountains. *Up*"—Pa's anger throbbed in his hardening jaw, and he hacked again—"up our dying ass! The devil Company won't release its tether on us until they are good an' sure they've fattened themselves on our black gold, spent us, and not a fast Kentucky second sooner."

"Let someone else go. Why do they always pick you? You haven't had a day off in over a month—"

"That's exactly why I have to, Daughter." He hooked the overall straps up over his shoulders, then shrugged on his coat. I handed him his lunch bucket and set his old carbide lamp helmet atop his head.

Pa's tired face folded into worry lines, and here his shift hadn't even started. He'd have to walk five miles to the mine. I wished he'd be willing to work with Junia so he could ride her, but he'd said, "I'd rather walk a hundred miles barefoot on briars than ride that cursed beast."

"You going to the Center this week?" He turned to ask at the door.

"No, sir, going the week after next." I glanced at the calendar nailed to the wall and saw my scribbles on the second Tuesday in May.

"I was able to clear part of the path for your ride."

"Thank you, Pa." I kissed his cheek. "Don't forget your bear stick," I reminded. You never know'd what four-legged beast, bear, pack of dogs, or mean two-legged ones would be out there lurking to do harm. I thought about Vester Frazier and tucked my mottling hands behind my back, away from Pa's eagle eyes.

"Get some rest, Daughter." And he was out the door, coughing his way to the airless job.

Rest sounded good. But there weren't none coming just yet. After a bowl of soup, I donned my apron to tidy the cabin, swept the big area rag rug I'd knotted last year, and mopped the dark wooden floors where Pa's coal-dusted boots had landed.

It was near impossible to keep a clean house when a man worked coal, and you couldn't get a second behind in your chores trying.

Even with my weekend off from the book route every week, it seemed like there was more to clean because of what more Pa kept bringing in.

I stripped Pa's mattress and boiled the soot-stained linens, wrung them in the yard, then hooked them over a rope tacked across the ceiling behind the woodstove, worrying about Pa's safety in the dark hole, worrying about leaking gas, explosions, and fallen rocks. It was enough to cause a right-headed folk to lose their mind, and it was all I could do to tuck back the thoughts.

I rubbed my chapped hands together, wishing I had Mama to worry with. She used to read the Bible, her novels, and sing French songs, her voice a soothing balm, distracting us both when Pa was at work. Humming one of her tunes, I made Pa's bed with fresh muslin sheets I'd sewn from the bolt of fabric he'd bought in town at the mine's Company store last year.

Finished with the bedding, I gathered a lantern and the pile of Pa's work clothes, washed them on the scrub board with a bar of lye out in the yard, soaped, rinsed, and washed again, wringing the fabric until my hands cramped, then emptying the black water four times until the clothes came clean of the coal dust. Last, I tackled my grubby long skirts, undergarments, and socks.

Back inside, I flexed my stiff hands, then remembered the bucket on the porch. I hauled in the old zinc tub, filled it, and dragged the bath over to the feet of the stove for warmth.

It took two more trips back to the springhouse to ready Pa's bath and still another to top it off. On the third, I cocked my ear, listened to the quiet, taking note of anything amiss. Junia called out to me softly, and I walked over and gave her a quiet greeting. The old girl's ears were relaxed, eyes sleepy, her stance loose. She would alert me of trouble.

Look to the beast, the bird, the wild dog, the critters, Pa'd taught me long ago. *God spent all their might on the ears so they would have protection. And that safeguard ensures ours.*

After one more good night to the mule, I lugged in the last bucket. In the morning, Pa'd come home spent, heavy in his bones and blackened. I'd have him strip to his waist, then kneel down over the bucket for me to scrub the sticking coal dust off his back, same as all the other miners who were fortunate to have family to help.

Up in the loft, I gathered a pile of my clothes for wash tomorrow, then took the pillow from my mattress and carried it all down.

With the clean wash hanging to dry, the cabin near spotless, and my chores done, I put on the teakettle and settled at our wooden table to cut fabric and paper into sheets and rolled glue across it all to bind Angeline's book.

From a nearby shelf, I pulled down the library scrapbook I had been compiling for my patrons, fattened with what I hoped were interesting things. I'd cut up a feed sack with a sunny floral print for the dust cover. In our spare time, us librarians made books filled with hill wisdom, recipes and sewing patterns, health remedies, and cleaning tips that folks passed on. Newspapers sent us their old issues, and we'd cut out poems, articles, essays, and other news from the world, and pack the mountain books. The scrapbooks had become a vital part of the library project and were passed from one little home to another.

I opened the book and pasted handwritten instructions for creating a broom from broom corn onto the opposite page from where I'd put a tatting pattern with a swatch of old lace some stranger had donated.

In between sips of tea, I thumbed through the pages. Two were filled with cartoons from the Sunday funnies the hillfolk favored. The mountain men liked *Dick Tracy* and *Li'l Abner*, while the women couldn't get enough of *Blondie*. And their young'uns clamored for *Little Orphan Annie* and *Buster Brown*. I'd made sure to take the time to hunt for comics, snip carefully from used newspapers and old magazines, and put them aside for more scrapbooks. I only had three scrapbooks and two were on loan, tattered and barely holding. If only I could get my hands on more reading material.

I reminded myself to look for Mr. Lovett's book and turned a few more leaves and stopped. Mountainfolk looked forward to this section filled with the latest home remedies from magazines and to the health pamphlets the government sent in. It made me happy that a lot of folks, especially the elders, insisted on sharing their own too.

Someone had written instructions for use of a lodestone, advised readers to wear the mineral around their necks to attract money, love, and luck. Beneath that was a note on cock stones from the old midwife Emma McCain, instructing women to find the small stone from the knee of an old cock and hold it during birthing to protect the babe. The midwife had dropped the note off at the library herself, insisted the cock stone worked, praised its worth, and begged me to paste the message into the book. Underneath the amulet's instructions, Emma had penned a special reminder written to husbands: *Wear a cock stone to excite and make your wife more agreeable.*

Wincing, I moved on to the following page. It advised to keep a mole's foot in my pocket to protect against toothaches. Pa didn't put much stock in that remedy, but he did carry a crystal rock, the old madstone he'd taken from the belly of a whitetail, same as most hillmen who were lucky to find one. The stone was said to protect against the mad dog and coon diseases. Once someone was bitten, it was necessary to stick the madstone onto the wound to draw out the poisonous rabies.

A few more sheets budded with soap recipes and cleaning tips; one touted a mix of water, vinegar, and lemon for sooty pine floors and winter-baked walls. A drawing with instructions showing how to make a stovetop took up a whole leaf. Construction of a two-seater outhouse filled another.

The poetry section I'd made filled several pages, and I paused to reread one of my favorites, "In a Restaurant" by Wilfrid Wilson Gibson. I loved how I could hear the music of the violin he'd written into it. Beside it, I'd pasted "Trees in a Garden" by D. H. Lawrence. The poem was a pretty one about trees, and I could almost smell the naked scents of woody barks, budding leaves, and fruits.

I closed the mountain scrapbook and admired the clean cabin while kneading my calves and thighs, tight from the day's long ride. Remembering my schedule, I went over to the wall and grabbed the Company store calendar.

The square on today's date was blank, and I made a note on Monday, April 24, marking it *1st Book Route, New Patron. J. Lovett,* and then looked over my schedule for the rest of the week.

On Monday I had nine stops, including the school. It'd been wonderful to see the children today, and I smiled to myself thinking about how excited they'd been to see me. Along the path, I'd spotted two older boys walking with buckets. The tallest one saw me, and his eyes rounded and he said to the other,

"Ain't going crawdad huntin' today, Thad. I gotta get to school. Yonder comes Book Woman!" Then he dashed off ahead of me.

In the schoolyard, a little boy climbed a tree and swung upside down from the back of his knees on a branch, crying out, "Yonder comes Book Woman. Book Woman's here!" The teacher had been so pleased to have the library service back, she didn't bother to scold the mischievous young'un.

I reminisced about visiting the other patrons my first day back. Martha Hannah dropped her clean laundry in the dirt when I rode into the yard. Mr. Prine actually stepped out onto his porch to quietly ogle me and share a small smile, an unheard of. And Miss Loretta had cried, though she'd never admit it, and instead insisted it was her old eyes ailing when I offered to get her a handkerchief. The memories warmed me, and I was suddenly struck by my tender affection for my precious patrons.

With the back of my hand, I dabbed at my damp lashes and blinked at the calendar. On Tuesday, I'd follow the creek bed and hand out reading materials to folks who would accept them. Wednesday, there would be the dangerous Hogtail Mountain to climb, the Evans home, and a visit to young Master Flynn. And on Thursday, I'd spend the day at my outpost, exchanging material for new books and whatever the courier had dropped off for me; sometimes, there were letters waiting to be handed out when the mail couldn't reach a home. There was Friday, my last route, where I would journey eighteen miles to get the material to Oren Taft's Tobacco Top community.

I made a few more notes and then, satisfied, set the calendar aside. Pulling my pillow atop the table, I rested my head and rubbed a hand across the embroidered blue hem, cuddling against the folds of the fabric Mama'd given me long ago.

She'd sewn us matching dresses with it when I was five. Soft blue ones with striking slashes of deeper blue that she'd some-how thought made our skin look whiter and a lot less colored. "A trick and it works," she'd said as she dressed us to go to town for a rare visit. "The color is like a bright-blue Kentucky sky that the angels dotted with bluebirds"—Mama'd winked—"and those sweet li'l birds are what catches the eye first."

She'd made Pa promise he'd bury her in it. I'd kept my dress and made the soft pillow slip out of the threadbare fabric after she passed, embroidering flying bluebirds onto the hem to remind me of her, us.

I glided my finger over the threads and stared out into the room, the sound of my breathing giving stingy life to the cabin's loneliness, my eyes glazing, fixed on the nothingness my home now held. My mind pulled to the Fraziers, and I turned to one of Mama's old French lullabies, imagining her hands stroking my hair, her airy fingertips tracing my face. Before long, my voice quieted, my lids grew heavy and closed.

I don't know how long I'd been dozing when I startled awake to Junia's brayings, and jumped up and scrambled across the room. Falling to my knees, I pulled Pa's shotgun out from under the bed and edged over to the window. Peeking through the curtain, I saw nothing but darkness. Junia called out again, and I moved to the door.

The shotgun wobbled in my grip as I fumbled with the lock. A curse slipped off my tongue, and I flung open the door and scampered down the steps. Lifting the gun to my shoulder, I scanned the yard for any wild creatures. *Nothing.* But I could feel something, someone out there in the darkness. I squinted at the tree line and then turned toward the creek. A noise struck to my left, and again I searched the woods. Weren't no small critter stirring through the leaves. It was a bigger movement, and I was sure someone was out there. *Maybe Frazier and his congregation, or some townsfolk bent on hunting Blues.* Once more the sound shifted, and I raised the shotgun higher and gripped the stock. I couldn't tell how many there were, or who it might be, but one thing I know'd: they were hunters.

Junia lifted a long, watery bray into the silence. I tilted my head, trying to hear, and picked up footfalls and more faint rustling. A fear pounded in my good ear, muddling my hearing.

The mule snorted, then quieted. I stood there a moment before the darkness enveloped, pulling a panic into my bones.

Inside, I slumped against the door. The long day back on the route latched hold of my nerves, doubled me over, leaving me gasping for air. The shotgun trembled in my hand. *Pa would take care of any creatures, but who would take of Frazier and the hunters?*

In a few moments, I straightened and carried the gun up to my loft.

Eight

The second Tuesday of every month, I worked at the library headquarters and May weren't any different. On those days, librarians were excused from their routes and would head to town.

At dawn, I traveled toward the Center through the hills. Spring winds knotted old winter grasses, and the scents of budding bloodroot, geranium, wild dogwoods, and creeping laurel sweetened the mountain air, but an uncomfortable crawl fouled my skin, and I was eager to be done with the monthly library chore and back to my book route.

I'd always feel like a thief sneaking into town, what with my big-brim bonnet and chin tucked tight to escape folks' wide-eyed stares and pointed fingers.

I tethered Junia to a place outside the post office and heard my name called. It was Doc. He nudged his mount toward us, and Junia blew at the horse, bossing the fine creature back.

"Bluet, it's good to see you about."

"Sir, I was coming to see you this afternoon."

"Are you okay, my dear?" he asked, concerned, straightening to get a better gape.

"I'm fit, sir. It's the Moffits. He's ill and—"

He held up his hand. "I'm off to tend to Mr. Franklin's gout."

"Yes, sir," I said, digging into my coat pocket for Angeline's seeds. "Mrs. Moffit asked me to give you this to tend to her husband's ailing foot."

I hurried over to him and held up the little packet. "They're from Minnie's lot," I remembered, hoping that meant something to him.

Doc opened it and shook his head. "It's a waste to tend to a chicken thief. I'd be healing his feet only to have him light off and rob decent folks again."

"He's getting worse—"

"He's a thief, Bluet."

I mumbled yes and no, then said, "Mrs. Moffit's with child, and she's real worried about her husband, sir. Weren't no med—" I stopped and tried to remember my grammar lessons. "There is...isn't any medicine in the home, sir," I said slowly.

He pushed up his spectacles and leaned down closer to me.

"Ain't none!" I blurted, then felt my skin washing in color. I looked around to see if anyone else had seen, and I spotted Mr. Lovett going into the Company store.

"Bluet, there's no place for thieves in Kentucky. And Moffit knows a chicken is more valuable than human life here. He got off lightly with just a busted foot. Most would say he should've been pocked full of holes and left as a sifter bottom." Doc leaned back in his saddle, satisfied with his homily.

I tucked my shadow-dark hands into the folds of my skirt, feeling Mr. Moffit's shame as if it were my own.

After a moment, he righted and said, "Tell you what, my dear. You tell Mrs. Moffit to come into town, and I'll give her a good examination for her and the babe. Free. You can come too, Bluet." He struck up a wiry brow. "It's been a while since I tended you. 'Bout three months since your marriage bed, I believe." He pointed a long finger toward my belly. "We'd want to check for that."

I shrank back, wanting to hide, to cover my face. For as long as I could remember, the doc had been curious about us Blues. He'd been coming to our cabin for years asking us about any ailments, begging to tend to us. The doc was friendly enough, a soft-spoken man, and seemed truly hungry for news of our well-being. But Pa insisted that it was only for the appetite of blood. Doc proved him right when he showed up shortly after Mama passed, begging for a sample of her skin and blood before burial. Pa'd cursed and ran him off.

"Well, I'm off to my patient. Come see me, Bluet." He turned his horse, dropping Angeline's precious payment in the dirt.

I scooped up the seeds and pocketed them. Dismayed, I hurried toward the back room of Troublesome Creek's post office. Someone had painted *Library Center* on a new sign above the door, even though folks rarely came into the Center. Our headquarters wasn't a library, and there weren't but a few in the whole of eastern Kaintuck, matter of fact. The small room was a place for the Pack Horse librarians to work and was only used to house and sort the reading material, bind books, and shelve them for the courier to pick up and deliver to our outposts.

I leaned over a table and opened the window inside the stuffy Center, welcoming the sun-soaked breezes. The cumbersome strikes of hooves echoed, and I paused to watch a wagon pull up to the side of the Company store. The old buckboard strained from the weight of stacked caskets, one of the stocks they always sold out first.

From behind, titters lifted and I turned partway. Across the room, the supervisors gossiped about the upcoming town dance in June, darting eyes around the Center in case someone slipped in. They sorted through stacks of magazines, pamphlets, and newspapers, their murmurs drumming the paper-soaked air, trailed by splinters of unkind laughter.

Silently, I unpacked a box of books, knowing their mirth came at another's expense.

The radio was switched on. Shortly, the tubes warmed up and batted about a newscaster's thinning words, rolling them out in bumpy conversation into the small room before the words became rich and steady. The Sears radio had been donated by a woman's club in Cincinnati, but the assistant supervisor, Harriett Hardin, only allowed the pretty cathedral-shaped radio to sit on her worktable, where it picked up the wobbly broadcast signal from the one station she ever permitted, WLOC, *The Mountain Table* program. A few other stations played jazz and big bands, but Harriett felt only heathens listened to jazz music, and the song and talk were too fast, too wicked.

Today, it was a female who talked on WLOC. I admired the way she pronounced her words so clear and beautiful, dropping the endings just perfect instead of losing them like folks around here did. I listened every chance I got and practiced the announcer's proper sentences.

Sometimes on my book route, I'd try them out on Junia. *Mrs. Abernathy and I shall meet you at Roderick's at eight. They prepare a scrumptious roast duck with a divine sherry sauce. There's not a better dish to be found in the city.* Occasionally I'd brave a few with Pa—until he'd raise a confused brow and warn me about putting on foolish airs. My tongue would tangle, and I'd be back to my old language of *Me and Mr.*, smacking the air with my *weren'ts* and *ain'ts*.

I leaned in to the newscaster's crisp voice and listened to her announce the Kentucky Derby winner named Bold Venture, mouthing her fine words to pocket them for later. When she mentioned a motion picture playing, I smiled, remembering how one of my younger patrons told me about taking the train to see *Mutiny on the Bounty* with his girl.

The woman on the radio said H. L. Davis's *Honey in the Horn* book had won the big Pulitzer Prize. Excited, I clapped out loud. I'd read the tale about the Oregon pioneers and loved it.

Harriett shot me a disapproving look, and I quickly turned back to my work.

A pile of old license plates that had been collected for the library waited under my table. I picked up a rusty plate and bent the end over the edge of the table to make bookends for the Library Center's table and shelves, making sure to set some bookends aside for my outpost.

The Pack Horse librarians didn't have time to come to town and do their daily routes. A special courier, usually a postal

volunteer helper, delivered the library books to the outpost stations closer to the hills for us carriers to pick up. My outpost was
a tiny, old boarded-up chapel that had seen too many hard rains
and floods from a nearby creek. Inside the church, there were a
few shelves built by volunteers and a donated table, which would
protect the supplies until I fetched them. But on the days we
Pack Horse librarians worked at the Center, we were allowed to
take home books to help lighten the load of the courier.

Outside, Junia nickered. I looked up to see Jackson Lovett
coming out of the Company store. He munched on an apple
while making his way over to the post office. Grinning, he
approached Junia and stood a few feet back from the hee-hawing
mule until he spied me in the window and held up the apple, a
question in his eyes.

Flustered, I nodded a silent yes, then lowered the brim on my
bonnet and sorted through more license plates.

Harriett sidled up beside me. "Jackson," she barely whispered to
herself, leaning her twenty-five-year-old plump body lazily toward
the sill. "Ain't he something of a man, going all the way out west
and building that big dam like that, making himself a rich living?
Smart. He invested his hard-earned money too. A right big land-
owner now, getting top dollar for his timber and minerals. Mmm-
hmm." Harriett smacked her lips. "Such a handsome, smart man
needs himself a smart, pretty girl." She pulled back her shoulders,
rapped the top pane for his attention, eager to be that girl. "Only
three weeks till Pie Bake. I wonder who the lucky girl will be?"

The first Friday in June, Troublesome always held its Pie Bake
Dance, a pie auction to hitch unmarried folks. Any single girl
could attend by baking a pie for the celebration. Pie Bake Dance
was a night of festivities on sawdust floors at the old feed store
that had since closed, pushed out by the Company like most
businesses. Grand fiddle playing, clogging, and flatfoot dancing
turned into a chance to get a marriage bed. Each pie would be
auctioned off to the men, and the highest bidder won the rest of
the evening's dances with that baker lady.

I'd never been, wasn't allowed to cross the threshold where a NO COLOREDS sign hung, but folks talked about it enough that it felt like I had. Eula and Harriett had slipped it into every conversation when I returned to the Center a few weeks ago. Talk of sewing new dresses, favorite recipes. Who was coming and who wasn't. I listened, snatched up bits of conservation, and fancied the dance for myself. On dance night, I would pretend it was my own in the silent hours inside my cabin.

Harriett mused, "I'd sure like to serve him a big slice of my peach pie." She sighed dreamily.

With a piece of steel wool, I knocked the rust off the corner of a license plate.

"Why in the world is Jackson fooling with that nasty beast of yours?" she asked and then turned to me, accidentally brushing against my sleeve.

Harriett screwed up her mouth, jerked her arm back, and jiggled it as if to shake off a bug.

She was afraid to touch me. The supervisor had reluctantly trained me for my route, but for only one day before abandoning me to go at it alone the very next. "I've been training and teaching the thick-headed Blue a full week," she'd fibbed to Eula Foster.

I snuck a glance back to Jackson and Junia, then mumbled a sideways apology to her for the contact, moved a step away, inspected another plate, and went to work on bending it.

"Why, look at you, Bluet!" Harriett cried.

I glanced up, Harriett's loud voice startling me.

Harriett's eyes flashed, a crawl of anger lit across, and then she spit out, "Your face is ripening into a blueberry. Why, it looks like an inkblot." She laughed. "Don't she look like an ugly ol' inkblot, Eula?"

Her scorn slashed at me, cutting. Sometimes I thought my embarrassment, my shame was exactly what Harriett wanted to see, trying hard to poke and make it happen. I pressed a hand to my cheek and watched her lace-colored face crinkle and harden.

Harriett plucked at her sleeves, flicked her fingers down her arms, and then stomped back to her worktable, each step feeling like a kick to my gut. Settling noisily into her seat, she turned up the radio.

Outside, Junia shrieked and just as quick quieted. Jackson stood in front of her at a safe distance now with the apple, and talked to her. Junia turned her head, sneaking a side-eye, then tossed her nose back and took the apple from his outstretched hand.

I couldn't help but laugh softly and then glimpsed over my shoulder at Harriett, busy with her mail. I turned back and gave Jackson Lovett a small appreciative smile.

Then he walked up to the window. "Cussy Mary, a friend lent me a new book, and I wondered if you'd heard of it?"

Curious, I leaned out.

"*Fer-de-Lance*?" He took it out from his coat pocket.

I turned and looked at Harriett thumbing through a magazine, loudly humming the tune playing on the radio before answering him. "Yes, sir." I kept a low voice. "That's the first in Rex Stout's Nero Wolfe series. A fine detective novel and mystery."

"You don't say? I do like myself a good mystery." His eyes were mischievous. "Thank you, Cussy Mary." He touched a finger to his head, struck off a friendly goodbye, a pat to Junia's rump, and strolled away.

Puzzled, I watched him until he rounded a corner.

When I'd finished with the bookends, I moved over to a stack of boxes filled with reading material that had just come in and pored through the new donations. This was the best part of my job, going through other big town libraries' castoffs, always surprised by the countless treasures those richer folks thought worthless, to be thrown away.

I pulled out two books, studied on which one to give Angeline, then set aside *The Tale of Mrs. Tittlemouse* for her. Then I eyed two baby-care pamphlets and saved those. A Doctor Dolittle book was at the bottom, and I dug it out, inspected, then tucked it away for a dear patron.

Digging deeper, I spotted an old English grammar textbook from a Chicago school. It was a perfect find, and the pages weren't torn or missing. I'd study the lesson book and then pass it on to Angeline. Maybe I'd have time to learn all the lessons so I could give her a few.

To my surprise, I came across a novel that looked new, one that Harriett had been dying to read: *The Stars Look Down.*

I weighed it in my hand, thinking about keeping it to read first. She loved the Scottish author and had been hankering to read his latest about an English mining town. If she found out I hadn't given it to her, there'd be hell to pay. Maybe the book would turn her sour mood into a more agreeable one. I walked over to her and held it up, hoping it would.

Suspicious, she looked at the book, then back to me like I'd set a rabbit's snare.

"I know'd how much you like Mr. Cronin's books," I said, placing it on her table, trying to brave a friendly smile for her.

She snatched it up, but not before I heard a gravelly "Thank you" and saw the pleasure in her eyes.

"Brand new. It sure looks like a grand one," I told her.

"Why, yes, yes. Oh, *Three Loves* of Lucy Moore was a grand one, you know? A masterpiece! When he drowned? The way she devoted herself to her son. All for naught. A tragedy…" Harriett flashed a sad smile that softened her.

I'd read the book too. The character, Lucy, was prideful, a determined pauper who could only have victory and worth through men.

"The monastery scene in Belgium," Harriett prattled, "when she—" The assistant supervisor stopped herself and stared up at me.

I loved the way Harriett loved her books. It changed her into something different, better, and for a minute I forgot who she was—who I wasn't.

"Oh, Bluet…*Bluet!*" She snapped her fingers in front of my face, scattering my thoughts. "Get to work," Harriett griped, though I could tell she was pleased to get the novel, even more to talk about it as if she were an expert on books.

I stiffened my silly grin. "Yes, ma'am."

I went back to my station and dug into another box for magazines and came up empty. Instead, I found a Vogue pattern for children's smocks and took it for the scrapbooks. There was some old sheet music that Winnie Parker, the schoolmarm, would love to have. I grabbed a few more health and hygiene pamphlets and put them in my growing pile.

Pleased, I stacked them neatly and moved on to the next carton, searching for a *Farmers' Almanac* for a patron who'd requested one. I dug deeper and broke off a piece of my nail looking for any Steinbeck books.

I found an old 1935 June magazine with a lady wearing a fairy-tale wedding dress on the glossy cover, and several books for Oren Taft who was on my Friday route. He was the holler dweller who lived over the mountain. I'd travel all day to get reading material to him for his small community. Despite the wearing day and unpredictable paths, it was always worth the journey to see his friendly face.

Under a pile of old textbooks and *Readers Digest*s, I spied a newspaper and grabbed it for the Smith household. The paper, dated May 5, 1936, was practically new, and not like the ones we usually got, often outdated by a month or more.

Feeling a rush circle my neck and flush upward, I rubbed my indigo-washed hands, thrilled at my find. Pressing the newsprint to my chest, I buried my nose in the still-fresh ink and inhaled.

It was the *Louisville Times*. I scanned the headlines about a gambling place that was raided in the city, read about Italy's invasion of a strange place called Ethiopia, then searched the pages and saw an even stranger advertisement for a ladies' swimming costume costing a whole $6.95, what would feed several hill families for a week. It was drab fabric, and not much of it either, but it showed a lot and drew the eye over every inch of the city woman's body.

Astonished, I couldn't take my eyes off the skin-tight dark union suit, the lady's shapely breasts, thighs, and legs slithering inside it. I came to my senses and guiltily flicked to a new page, fearing I'd witnessed something odd and knowing folks here would find it vulgar.

I stole a glance at the supervisor. She'd surely censor it, destroying the pages like she did Maugham's *The Painted Veil* that had been donated and any other reading materials she said would offend, taint, or tempt the morals of the deeply spiritual mountainfolk.

After turning more pages, my eyes rested on a flowered dress that cost $12.88. The slick city woman wore a draping flax-blue linen dress with a white scalloped border, matching felt hat, and clean-white gloves. A bolded advertisement above the picture read *Next Sunday Is Mother's Day*.

I ran a finger over the clothing, sifting through my thoughts of her. Mama'd had one good dress, and it was the same color. The very same one that matched mine.

For months and beyond, I would feel the swish of her cottony sky-blue skirts lingering on my skin as I picked up her duties, tended the daily chores in a home wrecked by aching loss, with Pa the stranger now, toppled in that grief. Occasionally, I'd stop to tilt my face into the ghosted airs of her fabric and fold a prayer into my sorrow.

How I ached for her, recalling her head bent to candlelight, her slender fingers dipping into beeswax to coat the thread to strengthen tired, old string, her swift, graceful hands working stitches into the fabric, her sharp teeth biting snips of thread, her nimble fingers knotting while I sat at her feet watching her rhythms birth a hymn sweeter than any birdsong.

"*Widow Frazier!*" the head librarian, Eula Foster, called out, walking up behind me and snapping the paper out of my hands. "I'll take that. And, Widow Frazier…oh *please* tether that bad-tempered beast of yours to the back of the building. Not on the side. She's causing a ruckus and scaring passersby."

At her worktable, Harriett whistled through her teeth over

the bookbinding and said, "I don't know how you put up with such an ornery creature, Bluet. Honestly, I'd done shot it for meat and skint it at the tree you took her from."

I nearly jumped out of my skin and bumped into Queenie Johnson, the thirty-two-year-old Negro Pack Horse librarian.

"That mule's a nuisance," Eula grumbled.

It weren't like Junia to fuss in this familiar place. "I'll take care of her." I whispered a pardon to Queenie. As I turned to go outside, I noticed Queenie was wounded. Alarmed, I asked, "What happened?"

"Just a nip." Queenie held up a scraped hand tracked with tiny specks of blood. "Only a scratch, honey. Old Junia got the devil inside her when the pastor happened by. He hit her with his stick, and she tramped around, tried for a piece of him, and done tore his coat sleeve almost off." Queenie choked back a giggle, pressing her knuckles to her mouth.

Harriett nailed Queenie with a stony glare and said, "Pastor Frazier baptized both my nieces. A fine God-fearing man that shouldn't be bothered by filthy *beasts*." She struck the last word and batted it to us.

Queenie ignored her, pursed her lips, and quieted. "The pastor whacked her three more times. So I figured I would help him out and calm her some, but Junia… Well, that old girl went for him again with those big, ugly, green-stained teeth. She missed once and plumb nabbed me instead."

"Oh, Queenie—" I said.

"She didn't mean it, though, and I could tell by her sorrowful eyes that she felt bad." Queenie grinned.

I looked past her. Through the screen door I spotted Vester Frazier across the street under the concrete lip of the Company store, dragging a stick along the sunbaked bricks, cutting a mean eye my way. A cold fear struck and had me reaching for the door to steady.

"*Bluet*, back to work," Harriett warned. I turned to reply *Yes, ma'am* and then I saw it, saw what I hadn't seen before. And I

suddenly know'd her fat hands had been under those cold baptizing creek waters with the preacher's and his followers when
they'd drowned the Goodwin babies and the others. Looking at
Harriett's open hatred set hot on her face, and then back outside
to Frazier, I felt ill. *Hunted*. The preacher shot me a hard grin,
sending me backward, stumbling into Queenie again.

Harriett grumbled to Eula, "I see Birdie's late again. I'm
gonna make that girl come in next week, and she ain't leaving
for her routes until she's inventoried all our holdings and given
us a full day in them stacks."

Queenie placed a hand on my shoulder. "You okay, honey?
Honey?"

"Yes…yes." I looked back out and saw he was gone. "I'm so
sorry she bit you. Does it hurt? Let me clean it for you." I glanced
back to the street once more. *Empty*. Relieved, I nudged my chin
to the tiny alcove, meaning to lead Queenie into the new ladies'
powder room and wash the wound, maybe freshen my face with
cold water, but Eula stepped in front of us. She jabbed a finger up
to the new NO COLOREDS sign above the ladies' door.

Queenie stared down at the tops of her shoes. Before she
became a Pack Horse librarian, Queenie had applied to the
program five times and had always been turned down. I'd seen
her applications, and they looked better than most. Each time,
Queenie'd write her name perfect and correct and give her age
and all the proper information. And each time, she was denied.

Last summer, Queenie had visited the Center and asked for
another application, but Harriett refused to give her one. The
next month Queenie came back. I was in the headquarters sorting when she barged in and dropped a letter onto Eula's desk
and announced, "Says I have a job. Says so right here from the
Women's Professional Project in Louisville, Kentucky."

Eula'd bent over and read out loud the WPA's order instructing her to give Queenie Johnson a Pack Horse librarian route,
her voice souring to the ending.

The supervisor's face paled to a wedding-dress white, and

she crumpled the letter, single-fisted, ordering Queenie to wait outside. Harriett turned as blue-faced as me, scattered her neatly stacked piles of church pamphlets, and threw two books across the room, one striking my arm.

In the end, Queenie was called back in and given a book to read out loud. It was the only requirement of the Pack Horse project for the job, and usually the read was a children's storybook at that. Queenie breezed through it, then pulled out a dictionary from her bag, and read two pages, and better than any of us.

Eula gave her a long and treacherous route, second to mine. And when Harriett refused to train her, Eula left it to me. Queenie was suspicious of me at first, but by midweek she'd warmed into her route and shyly offered me half of her fat biscuit. We'd stopped by the creek to break, and I shared my apple and she talked about her family.

We chatted on about books, went over the routes and patrons, and both marveled how lucky we were to be Pack Horse librarians, doing important pioneer library work, as the WPA administrator reminded us. I told Queenie how I'd done the same as her and bypassed Eula by sending the job application directly to the bosses in the city.

Queenie'd told me her husband, Franklin, had been killed in a mine explosion, same as her pa, leaving her to fend for her three small boys and her widowed, ailing grandma. Her mama died from the fever, and the tiny family was all she had now.

Again, Eula stabbed the air, pointing to the sign.

"Best go, Cussy," Queenie said. "I'll see you Wednesday as usual." She walked over to her table to gather her bags.

I stared up at the sign. It seemed a bad waste of paint and fine wood, of city running water and the fancy indoor latrine installed this winter when there were outhouses scattered around town. Weren't but a handful of "coloreds" around these parts anyway. Queenie, her kids, and her grandma Willow. There was Doc's housekeeper, Aletha, the woman who'd come from a place called Jamaica. Eight counting me and Pa.

Eula wagged her finger, but this time at me, her shaming eyes landing on mine. "You're only allowed in to *clean* it, Widow Frazier."

I looked down, knowing my place, knowing I was the one they were really afraid of, detested most.

It was difficult enough being colored, much less being my odd, ugly color and the last colored of my kind. Somehow, folks like Harriett and Eula made it worse, made sure their color, any color was better than mine. I was an affliction on their kind and mankind. And I was to stay put, and exactly where they wanted to keep me put. *Beneath them. Always and alone.*

"You know the rules. Blues and Coloreds outside," Eula said, shaking her head, darting her nervous eyes between Queenie and me. "We can't have you using the indoor facilities. We wouldn't want to chance passing on a... Well, we just can't have it!"

Harriett jumped out of her seat, sending her chair tumbling backward. "Good heavens," she screeched and pressed a fat finger to her warted jaw. "Why, they could pass a disease. Take yourselves outside to the well pump right now. And take that filthy beast home, Bluet, before I shoot it myself!"

Her eyes said she'd do just that, and would like to do the same to me. I scampered for my things and shot out the door past a bewildered Birdie, almost spinning the young Pack Horse librarian around.

Nine

The following Monday, I made it to Angeline's only to find her missing. I didn't want to disturb Mr. Moffit, so I dawdled out in the yard, wasting a good twenty minutes before reckoning she was out hunting food.

Junia slow-poked along on the paths. "Ghee," I pleaded when she stalled on the trail where we'd seen Frazier. I looked all around, rubbing the chills on my neck. After a few minutes, my nerves crawled, and I yelled, "We're late. *Ghee up!*" She wouldn't budge, and I became frantic and climbed down, searching the woods with a sharp eye, dragging her onto another longer path that cost us more time. When I mounted, she picked up speed, perking her ears to make sure he weren't coming after her. Bent, I scrunched down close to her head, keeping my eyes wide to make sure too.

We rode on to my next three cabins and left loans on the stoops of thimble-sized homes. I didn't have a book for Mr. Lovett, so I journeyed on past to my next patrons.

In the dust-bitten yard, a leaning chicken coop and tiny wooden goat pen nestled beside the tall one-room school, its chestnut harvested from the forest, the log gaps daubed with mud and grasses. Smoke percolated from the chimney, curling over black hand-split shingles and skittering up the side of a craggy, treed hill. The school door was shut, the yard empty of students. Junia called out a bossy neigh to the goat, and two chickens flew up from their perch and squawked back.

From inside the schoolhouse, small faces peeked out the narrow windows. I heard the scrambling of little feet and the sounds of smothered giggles before the door swung open.

Teacher Winnie Parker pushed through the doorway with a flared skirt of eight scruffy young'uns circling her. The thirty-six-year-old woman clapped her hands when she saw me.

I dismounted, and Winnie exclaimed, "Cussy Mary, you're here." She grabbed the reins and passed them to one of her older pupils. "Come with me, Miss Junia," the girl said and trotted the mule over to the hitching post.

"Book Woman's here!" the students sang.

"She's here sure enough," a littler one piped up.

"Miss Book Woman, I have you a big surprise!" A small girl missing her milk teeth pushed forward, waving a scrap of paper. "Mama said to give you her counterpane pattern for your scrapbooks."

I took the note and saw it was for a knitted cross-centered bedcover with a knotted fringe border. "That'll make a pretty counterpane, and a lot of folks'll appreciate knitting it. Thank your mama for me," I said, inspecting the pattern again before slipping it into my pocket. The girl blushed and gave a small curtsy before scrambling behind Winnie and the others.

A boy rushed up to me. "Miss Book Woman, I need a book about the war. 'Bout the World War. I'm going to grow up and go to fight!"

Another little boy said, "I want a book about China, like the one you brought us last year."

"It was *The Chinese Twins* the Perkins lady done wrote," a girl in tatty braids proudly announced. "Uh, Lucy...I reckon was her name."

"Lucy Fitch Perkins," I said, impressed.

"Yup! *The Chinese Twins*." The boy brightened. "And I'm gonna take the big locomotive and live there... Soon as I grow'd a little more, my ma says."

I loved that the books were growing their little minds. Pa was wrong. They needed books more than anything else this place had to offer. They were starved for the learning, the know-how on leaving this hard land for a better, softer one.

Winnie said, "Time to let her get her books."

"I brought you two new ones," I told Winnie.

Winnie's eyes popped. "Two? Heavens!"

Usually I couldn't get but one, but last Wednesday, Queenie had slipped it to me from her own bundle.

"*Farmer Boy* and *Mountain Path*," I announced. "Got something for you too, ma'am."

Winnie clapped her slender hands once more, shooing the class back into the schoolhouse. "Stay seated," she called to them before turning back to me. "Let's go have a look at the reading material."

I pulled out books from my bags, then dug around and found the rolled-up magazine and handed it to her.

"Oh!" Winnie peeked at it, the partly slick but tattered cover splatted with tape, its back replaced with stiff paperboard. She fanned through the dog-eared pages. "You remembered."

"It was finally returned, and I know'd how you wanted the loan. You keep it as long as you like, ma'am."

"Thank you. This'll keep me company until Albert gets home." She pressed the *Love Story* magazine to her face, breathing in the ink. "I'll take good care of it."

The magazine was one I'd kept in circulation for the women who secretly requested *excitement reads*, the one I'd snuck out of the Center last year before the supervisor could approve it, knowing she wouldn't allow it. The one I kept hidden from Pa.

Winnie had spent a long winter cooped up in her attic nest above the classroom, where she slept. Nobody else in the hills had the room or food to take in a teacher like that. Her man up and moved to Detroit to work in the big factory and hadn't come back for her yet. A lot of mountaineers sought work in the city, leaving behind their wives until they could care for them proper—get ahead with a few paychecks. I figured Winnie was lonesome, same as me. And any type of reading softened that.

"Weren't no trouble," I said, meaning it and feeling proud I'd gotten the magazine for her. I handed her the sheet music.

"Oh, new music too, my Lawd, thank you!" She examined the sheets. Then, "How's Elijah?"

"Good, thank you for asking. But he has himself some long hours of mining, and they's working him before his time."

"These hills birth the old. How are you this week, Cussy Mary?"

"I'm fit." Out of habit I tucked my hands into my pocket, hiding the coloring, though it weren't necessary here, and my skin was a comfortable gray-blue.

Winnie'd been the only one to come calling after Charlie Frazier died—the only one to bring a pie and sit with me one long Sunday, and then the very next, reading to me while I recovered from Frazier's beating. She never asked what happened or pried none, and I never offered, but I could see the understanding in her eyes. A mixture of concern and anger in there too.

Last summer, I'd been caught in a fierce summer storm, and Winnie had insisted on making me a pallet beside the school's woodstove for the night. It didn't feel right sleeping in a room below a patron, so when the rain quieted before midnight, I'd folded the quilts, stacked them, slipped out to my mount, and headed home, our lantern lighting our way like a bright firefly, the drizzling rain illuminated in swaying yellow shadows, combing the path ahead.

"Cussy Mary." Winnie held up a book. "Do you have a few minutes to read to them?"

I loved the way she said my name, always called me by my given one, never once by the doc's old nickname, or worse, the new title, Widow Frazier. She had kindly asked my partiality long ago when we'd met.

"Ten minutes maybe?" Winnie coaxed.

I didn't have myself even one, much less ten of them minutes. Junia had rode slow today, and waiting on Angeline had eaten up twenty of them. These hills stole a whole lot too, what with the lazy sun struggling to climb over the mountains and the nights dropping fat and fast. Time was something there weren't enough of in these parts.

My route was seventeen-and-a-half miles as the crow flies, but longer by mule. I was already late for my next stop. It'd be dark when I got home. I'd have to feed and groom Junia, and there was Pa's supper to fix before he went off to the mine, and I'd be left to finish my other chores.

But Winnie asked so sweetly. And if I hurried, and Junia didn't tarry or get difficult, I might not be too late.

"I reckon I have some time for the children," I said.

Inside the chalk-dusted schoolroom, Winnie led me over to the piano that butted up to the far wall. A wood ax and cross-stitch sampler of the Ten Commandments hung above the fine upright. An old regulator clock hung from the wall, its pendulum silent. Rough-hewn benches formed a neat line on slanted chestnut planks in front of the teacher's desk.

In the corner, a fire crackled, spitting sap and bark inside an old woodstove.

Winnie pulled out the piano stool for me. Two years ago, Doc had donated the pretty mahogany-and-spruce Story & Clark piano to the school after his wife passed, and he'd made sure to leave Winnie the beautiful red-fox-skin bench cover he'd bought from a trapper to fancy it.

She said it'd been the devil getting the horse-drawn wagon to tote the heavy furniture up the mountain. She worried it was too prideful and pretty. But folks came from miles around for the chance to see a real piano like that, to touch the gleaming wood and tap the ivory keys. It was a sight, and to this day, folks still happened by to beg a peek, or sneak a shy tapping.

Winnie smoothed down the slipping pelt and righted the fox's dangling head, tail, paws, and hind legs.

The young'uns gathered on the worn puncheon floor and sat in front of me in a semicircle. Henry, a frail ten-year-old, scooted close and snuck a rub of the fox's furry feet.

He tugged lightly on my skirts. "Book Woman, ma'am, I love the *Peter and Wendy* book. Please bring it again."

"I'll try, Henry." I smiled warmly.

The small boy looked sickly, and I know'd it came from hunger.

The mountain children were thinner than the young'uns in the picture books I brought them, and they'd noticed more than once and pointed it out, marveling about the fictional towns the characters lived in and all the food available there.

Still, I couldn't help notice again how the students waited for me, looked up at me, all quiet and not a single fidget or wiggle, as hungry for the stories in these books as they were for the food that always seemed sparse in this real land.

"Book Woman?" A small girl named Nessie raised her hand. "Can you git me a cookbook next time? Sister is going to Pie Bake Dance in two weeks, an' she needs herself a good recipe, ma'am."

"Pie Bake Dance, the Old Maid's Chance!" Several boys sang out, making kiss-smacking noises until Winnie clapped her hands.

"I'm happy to bring one for your sister," I said. We always had church cookbooks coming in from around the state. And there would be recipes in the newspapers and magazines.

I opened Laura Ingalls Wilder's book and read the first chapter of *Farmer Boy*.

Fifteen minutes later, I finished.

Henry raised his hand. "Ma'am, I'm gonna be a librarian like you when I get grow'd up."

A few boys snickered. "You ain't a'growin' up, and you ain't a girl, stupid."

"Am too," Henry said to the boys. "*Peter and Wendy* says all children grow'd up. An' I'm gonna be a librarian if I want."

"Ain't true," one snipped back. "It said *except one*! That's *you*, stupid."

Hurt, Henry shrank back.

Winnie glared her disapproval, quieting them.

Clementine, an older girl sitting back on her legs, popped up on her knees and said, "I want to join the Pack Horse, Book Woman!"

"'Cause you ain't never gonna get yourself hitched, bean-pole," said a tall, barefoot boy sitting next to her in baggy pants and a tattered shirt, who yanked her braid.

Clementine punched his arm.

He tried to pinch her back, nabbing her shoulder. "Here, I can help," he whispered as a tease. "You ain't blue enough."

Winnie gave a sharp, scolding clap. "*Quiet.*"

I softly cleared my throat and told the class, "The Pack Horse librarians ain't just for girls. We have a man who rides over in Woodford now. And, Master Norton," I said to the boy who'd pulled Clementine's braid, "we also have ourselves women in the project who are widowed with young'uns."

I heard of at least two other women whose husbands had left them to find work in the city factories. The librarians had fibbed to the WPA and said they'd been abandoned so they could feed their family until their men sent for them.

Norton dropped his head and murmured, "Sorry. Yes, ma'am."

Several students raised their hands, wriggling for permission to talk.

Winnie clapped her hands again for a hush. "Let's thank Book Woman for her visit, boys and girls."

Outside, I said goodbye to the teacher and mounted Junia.

"See you soon. Be safe, Cussy Mary," Winnie said, rubbing the mule's ear.

Henry ran out of the schoolhouse. "Book Woman! Miss Book Woman! *Wait!*"

He looked at his teacher, feet itching, a plea of permission in his weak eyes.

Winnie said, "Be quick, Henry. We've kept her long enough."

"Miss Book Woman, I've been saving this for you," he said, breathless, and then thrust out a grubby fist with a wadded-up piece of paper inside. "I got it for winning Mrs. Parker's spelling bee," he beamed.

Winnie placed a hand on his bony-ribbed back. "That's right," she said. "Henry spelled all his words with nary a hitch."

Henry passed it to Winnie who reached up and dropped the gift into my hand.

I peeled back a piece of the paper wrapper, and Henry cried, "Don't undo it, ma'am, don't…until you feel a'might hungry."

"Thank you. I'll save it then," I said, pocketing the curious little package.

"Has the new baby come, Henry?" I remembered he'd mentioned a new baby back in December.

"No, ma'am, but Ma thinks it'll be here soon. She's gotten too big to walk me partway to school now. She says I'm big 'nough to come all the way by myself."

Most of the schoolchildren did walk miles by themselves. A few had brothers and sisters to join them. Others would meet up with students along the way if they were lucky enough to live nearby.

"It'll be nice having yourself another brother or sister," I said.

"Yes, ma'am. I'm hoping this one'll live." He scrunched up his small face, worrying the thought. Shifting his body, he nudged the dirt with a bare toe. Henry's ribs jutted from a thin shirt that was too small, his collarbone cut sharp, an unnatural easel for his pallid face.

His mama had lost the last one. Or was it the last two? I couldn't remember. There were always new babies in the mountains if you didn't count the dying ones.

"A new little one," I said, trying to sound warm and positive and a tad excited.

"I like the new babies best." Henry grinned.

"Give her my best wishes."

"I can spell 'pineapple,' want to hear?" Henry boasted.

"That's a mighty big word," I said and waited. Winnie had spelling contests from the books I brought. It always pleased me to be a small part of it.

"*P-I-N-E-A-P-P-L-E*," Henry burst out. "And don't you open it none until you're good an' hungry." He scurried back to the schoolhouse.

"What could it be?" I wondered as I rode off.

Ten

As I left the schoolyard, low gray clouds rolled overhead. In the distance, a dog barked at the thunder, and the scent of passing rain sweetened the swirling billows of ghost fog.

I pulled out my great-grandpa's timepiece from under my coat, the silver watch dangling from a leather string hanging around my neck—a gift from my mama and one that'd been handed down to her from her grandpa in France.

Pressing down on its pumpkin crown, I released the latch, and the small, bubbled filigree pair case opened. I peeked inside the inner case and noted the black hands on the porcelain dial, then snapped it shut and stuffed it back down into my coat.

I left the school and rode into Bear Branch most of the way, walking Junia along the slippery tree-twisted route near the end, eager to drop off the *Time* weekly magazine at Mr. Prine's homestead and always keeping my eyes and ears sharpened for Frazier.

Though the newsmagazine weren't weekly by the time I got the copy, and was three months old or more, Mr. Prine, a widower who'd fought in the Great War, would accept only the *Time* for his loans.

I picked his old copy off the stoop and studied the newer one, the picture of someone with a mouthful of name—an older lady, Abby Greene Aldrich Rockefeller—on the cover. The magazine touted that she *has a nose for new talent*, and I reckoned she might in her fancy hat, stylish dark dress, and pearls.

I rolled up the January edition like Mr. Prine had asked me long ago and left the magazine stuck between his doorjamb and latch.

Close to three thirty, so I'd have to hurry now.

A few miles into my next drop, Junia stopped, and I realized we'd reached Saw Briar Trace. My old rented mounts used to do the same. Junia didn't mind and had took it easily the last three times, barreled through it even. But today she weren't too keen on taking the trail.

"Don't be scared none," I said, skittering down. Carefully, I led the mule along the brair'd path, smacking away branches with a high crooked elbow, my head tucked down to escape the thorny bushes.

I hated that Junia might get scratched some, but there weren't an easier way to reach our next drop. Tonight, I'd inspect her coat and put salve on any wounds. I needed to remember to ask Pa to clear the growth before it thickened in the summer. In the past, Pa'd insisted on renting Mr. Murphy's horse a few times to comb over my trails for any trouble, saying that if I was bound and determined to tote foolish books, he needed to make sure I'd do it safely.

Junia stepped lightly, zigzagging and dithering in her pace. I wetted my tongue with a ticking to hurry her on.

A smattering of orange pine needles and rabbit scat dotted the mud trail. Ahead, I spotted a deadfall with a cottontail's leg poking out. My belly rumbled. A family would have themselves a fine meal of rabbit meat, gravy, and biscuits tonight. I liked the tender part of the back the most, and for a minute I could almost taste the delicious meat.

I'd eaten the apple and bread I'd brought from home hours ago, sharing pinches with Junia.

Light-headed, I dug into my pocket for Henry's gift. "I'm a'might hungry," I said out loud, stopping.

Junia snuffled.

I unwrapped the paper and found a tiny Life Saver candy inside. Winnie had shared a nickel roll with me when she'd visited. She was fond of the sweet treats and would reward a good student with a piece.

I licked it. *Pineapple.*

The thought of Henry giving me his prize, this treasured bite, sat knotted in my throat. It was a grand thing. The little boy had lost one of his brothers to starvation last year, his pa had run off, and his mama was expecting. How long had the child held on to it for me, waiting to give it to me? How many times had the hunger pangs tempted him? Set his belly afire for the wanting? Yet, his love for words and books was stronger.

I covered the Life Saver with the paper and slipped it back into my pocket to save in my tin box where I kept my fine keepsakes: Mama's silver thimble and three brass buttons with the pretty scroll border, her tiny leather Bible, a letter written by my great-grandpa, and Pa's brown-bone-handled penknife he'd favored as a boy.

"Let's ghee, ol' girl." I climbed atop Junia and plucked a song from my mind, singing for the distraction, quieting my hunger.

At the Smith cabin, I rode Junia past the clothesline, a burst of soap and clean cottons swirling around us. The light of fading afternoon canted across grass folding into the darkening ground. I nudged Junia up to the window.

Martha Hannah and her young'uns crammed the warped frame, leaned their heads out, lit with a big cheer from seeing me.

The young mama stood peeling an onion. She swatted some of the children away, ordering them back to their chores.

"Sorry I'm late, ma'am," I said, feeling bad I'd interrupted her dinner chores. My mouth watered as I peeked past, smelling the skillet of chopped greens frying in grease. A girl poured corn kernels into a heavy pot of boiling water to make hominy, while her sister skinned a rabbit beside her.

"No bother a'tall, Book Woman. Have any of them newspapers in your bags today?" she asked, hoping.

"No, ma'am," I said, wishing I'd snuck out the one Eula grabbed. The city newspapers went fast and were rarely returned.

Most folks used the print to paper their cabin walls, keeping out drafts, holding in the warmth and fancying up drab rooms. The little ones made paper dolls out of them. "I'll be sure and try and save you one next time I'm at the Center," I said.

"Would you have any *Woman's Home Companion?*" She shifted, and I could see she was in the family way again.

The *Companion* was a popular request. Mountain women were snatching up new cures and remedies from the magazine, abandoning their old ways of healing.

"Sorry, ma'am, not today. I'll look for one at the Center first thing back," I said.

"Be obliged to git one. Nester Rylie's been reading it, and she told me in passing last year, she ain't rubbed groundhog brains on her babies' sore teeth or needed to use the hen innards on the gums of her teething ones since. And after she'd read about a good paste recipe that cured thrush, Nester said, none of her nine young'uns ain't ever had to drink water from a stranger's shoe again to get the healing."

From behind her I heard the rattle of a copper dipper in a water bucket. One of Martha Hannah's daughters passed it to her mama.

"For your ride, Book Woman," the girl said.

I handed her my worn leather-wrapped bottle Pa'd made, and she poured the sweet spring water into the container and passed it back.

We exchanged books, and Martha Hannah and the young'uns thanked me. The children snuck a touch to Junia's furry head, poked at the tufts of her spiky mane sticking up between her ears.

Junia edged closer to the sill, leaned into the frame, enjoying the curious hands, nosing around for any victuals. Startled, the smaller young'uns stepped back and screamed and laughed, while the two older ones squealed and boldly stroked her muzzle.

"Read us a story, Book Woman," one boy rang out.

"I wanna read *White Fang,*" another said.

"No, *The Call of the Wild,*" a bigger boy insisted.

"Shush, young'uns. Where's your manners?" Martha Hannah said. "Book Woman's had herself a long ride and even a longer one to go."

I wished I had time to chat and read, but Martha Hannah understood she was my second-to-last stop on Mondays, and I had little daylight left. We'd make up for it in the summer hours, I promised her.

Her husband, Devil John, a moonshiner, walked into the yard right past me, stone-faced, without a greeting.

Martha Hannah spotted him over my shoulder and snapped, "Git to your chores, young'uns. I need to git supper on the table quick. Finishing hulling them beans, Junior, and bring in the laundry, Lettie and Colleen." Her voice turned edgy and shrill. "*Carson!*" She leaned her head out the window and peered across the yard. "Lawsy, you still ain't hoed the garden? *Git to it!*"

Weren't two miles past the Smiths' place when I spied Vester Frazier. Not really him, but his sneaky shadows: a dirty boot and the hem of his long topcoat poking out from behind a thick Kentucky coffee tree. I heard a soft nickering from his nearby horse.

I sucked in a breath, feeling raw and exposed. That he'd been trailing me still left a sinking knot in my belly that rose in my throat like bile.

Junia must've seen Frazier too because she cried out and broke into a wild gallop. I held tight, letting her run off the path.

Ahead, I saw a woman and child collecting berries. Grateful to see hillfolk, I pulled Junia over and waited for them to pass. The boy stopped and pointed. "Look yonder, Mam." When they drew close, I lifted a friendly hand, hoping to tell them about the library services. But the small young'un dropped the berry basket he'd been toting and cried out, "Oh, Mam, look, it's *har*. It's Blue Ghost ya done tol' me about."

My greeting froze in midair.

She yanked the little one's arm so hard he stumbled and yelped. "Don't look at har, William," she warned, plucking up the basket and dragging him past me. The child's whimpers lifted into the natters of chasing swallows.

Junia shifted toward the lost berries, and I squeezed my legs against her sides and tugged the reins. "*Halt*," I ordered the mule.

The boy glanced back, and the woman tightened her hold and pulled him farther down the path, but not before I saw the wide-eyed fright in his eyes, the blame of childhood nightmares.

I lowered my head, grieved that I was his.

An hour later, I tethered the mule to a rotted porch rail and knocked on the door of my last patron. The seventy-five-year-old woman hollered, "Iffin' that's Bluet, get on in here, child."

Relieved, I looked once over my shoulder and stepped inside. Loretta Adams sat at her small table that had a worm-eaten wobbly leg. In front of her, two empty cups waited on the delicate walnut-stained doily she'd tried to center. Squares of fabric were piled neatly on the edge. A stack of sewing cloths lay on a tick-covered ottoman nearby.

Tallow candles cast warm light across the whitewashed walls and the homespun curtains, the scent of animal fats wafting from candle wax. Loretta held an Old Testament book in her aproned lap.

"Miss Loretta," I said softly, "it's me, Book Woman."

"I know'd who it is, child. Poor-sighted I am, not deaf."

"Yes, ma'am." I grinned and set down a book. Miss Loretta was nearly blind, a spinster who lived alone with only a nephew to check on her well-being. And then, only when he weren't out on a tear for a month or more.

Loretta still read some and had fine penmanship, but it wore on her eyes and she could only make out shadows at times, she claimed. Her hearing was good as most, her mind keen and full of sharp wit.

She boasted how she could still whip the tightest stitch of anyone in Kaintuck, sew the prettiest counterpane, or fanciest church dress—a fine seamstress in her day, and occasionally I'd pass on a letter to her from folks writing to ask her to sew a christening, wedding, mourning, or church dress for them.

Loretta's cabin was neat and tidy, though there weren't much to clean in the cramped area. The walls were darkened and baked from the woodstove, like all hill homes. But her bed was made, and she'd folded her quilt neatly across it, and I could tell she'd swept the floorboards and dusted some. A teakettle sat atop her lit wood stovetop, sweating from steam. A skillet of molasses bread rested beside it, sweetening the musty air, and another pot of water beside that.

Under the stove, two skinny cats, Myrtle and Milkweed, raised their furry white heads and yawned before returning to their nap.

Loretta swished a clumsy hand across the table and grasped for the china cups she'd put there. She found them and pushed them toward me.

"You're late today. Get the book, then get us some tea, child," she said.

I pulled out a wedge of pine snugged beneath the table leg, took my library book from the rickety table and propped it under the leg, steadying the rattling cups and placing the old table on solid standing.

I gathered the cups and walked over to the stove to pour our teas and then turned and took a hearty gulp from mine before giving Loretta hers, grateful she couldn't see my greedy thirst. I wiped my mouth with a sleeve, eyes locked on the bread.

"Help yourself to the bread an' bring the kettle over here and have yourself some more," she said. "There's plenty for seconds, child, thirds if you're hankering. We have us enough sassafras root and spring water in this ol' mountain to quench the whole country, an' plenty of sweet bread today."

Feeling my face warm, I muttered, "Yes, ma'am." Even though she couldn't see well, I felt Loretta could see other, bigger things that most eagle-eyed folks missed. Still, I wouldn't take her bread. It might be all she had to see her through the week.

I pulled out one of the old split-bottom chairs beside the table and sank into the woven seat Loretta had made with bark strip.

Loretta handed me her Bible, and I opened it to the Book of

Ruth where'd we left off and read until she tapped my leg with her walking stick some twenty minutes later. "Get on home, child. Darkness is near."

I rubbed my eyes. Mountain shadows had seeped into the cabin, marbling the walls in black splashes.

I stooped over, pulled the library book cautiously out from the leg, and replaced it with the pine wedge while my other hand gripped the table lip to keep the stuff from sliding off.

I held the library book a moment and then said, "Miss Loretta, this is a Doctor Dolittle book, and I think you might like it some—"

Loretta held up a shushing hand and shook her head.

"It's clean, Miss Loretta, and it's a good one about a nice doctor who talks to animals and—"

"Nonsense, child. And what I done told you before: I ain't letting you read me them government books."

"But—"

"Them's books about rubbish and devilish deeds. Foolishness. Take it on back."

"Yes, ma'am," I said, wishing she'd let me read her one from the library once in a while instead of her Bible.

Every time I brought one I thought she might take a liking to, she'd sour and rile on. "Them city books ain't fitting for my kind—ain't got a lick of sense in them pages for us hillfolk. Nothing but foolish babble an' prattle."

"No, ma'am. Yes, ma'am," I'd murmur agreeably.

Loretta said, "It was 1857 when my papa toted this fine Bible and four of his mama's teacups all the ways from Texas where he'd preached, settling in these ol' Kentucky hills a good four years 'fore me and Sister was born. These all that's left of the teacup set." She jabbed a finger at the two delicate white cups with a gold trim around the lips and on the fancy ribboned handles. "And this"—Loretta tapped the Bible—"was how he found his way. He had only one Book and wanted me to know it too."

"Yes'um, it's a good one," I said.

"Now, I know you have to bring 'em, child"—she puffed up and smacked her long, frumpled skirts—"but I still like mine best. And I ain't no cheat for it."

Someone had told Loretta I only made stops to deliver books, though I'd told her it weren't true. When she brought it up, I said there were folks on my route I'd only read to, just not from their own book. Still, Loretta got it in her mind if we used the library loan as a table leg prop, and she made me take it when I left, she didn't feel like she was stealing from the government.

"No, ma'am, you ain't a cheat," I said. "You're a fine hill-woman, Miss Loretta."

Loretta raised a proud head and bobbed it, her white bun unraveling, loosening a strand over her old, ailing eyes.

"You rest now, and I'll be back soon to read more," I told her.

Loretta pointed to the basket on the floor beside the door. "Get ya some root for you and your papa, child." She patted her hair in place and rose from the chair.

"Thank you, ma'am, much obliged."

I helped her hobble over to the narrow iron bed and took off her heavy shoes, tucked them under the bed frame beside her old Colt revolver. She fussed with her quilt and hung it over the bottom bed rail.

Loretta pointed to the bulging covers at the foot of her bed. "Oh, my bed pig needs filling," she said, standing back up.

"Let me get it for you, Miss Loretta."

"Bless you, child."

I pulled out the pig-shaped pottery from under the counterpane, took it outside and unscrewed the lid atop its fat back and emptied the cold water out in the yard.

In a minute, I'd filled the bed warmer with the hot water on the stove and tucked it back under Loretta's cover at the foot of the bed to give her heat that'd warm her for the night.

"My eyes are burning," Loretta said. "I'm a tad tired. Can you spare another minute to help me with my eye wash, child?"

"Yes, ma'am." I picked up a rag beside her basin on a tiny stand near the stove, dipped the cloth into the washbowl full of tincture, and wrung it. The tang of the old herb clung to my hand.

"Here, ma'am." I dropped the wet rag into her open palm, trying not to offend her with my touch.

Loretta moved clumsily, and the cloth fell to the floor, and our hands met.

A tiny gasp slipped past my teeth.

Before I could give the rag back, she groped for my hand, latched on, and said quietly in her old voice, "See all my fabric, child?"

"Sure is a lot."

"Well, them cloths are a lot like folks. Ain't much difference at all. Some of us is more spiffed up than others, some stiffer, and still, some softer. There's the colorful and dull, ugly and pretty, old, new 'uns. But in the end we's all fabric, cut from His cloth. *Fabric*, and just that."

"Yes, ma'am," I whispered.

"Now I know you're a Blue, but these old eyes don't care, nor feels the colors none. It feels the heart, child. And it's a fine one, and *you're* a fine hillwoman."

The hard day suddenly landed at my feet, leached out my skin, and swept up into weary eyes. A tremble took hold of my hand, though it should've been that of Loretta's old, weak one. But her touch was warm and firm, and she squeezed and pressed her other palm tightly on top, rubbing my flesh.

I tilted my head upward, shuttering my eyes, the hurt and loneliness pooling inside, swelling. I tried to pocket my feelings, but today more than ever, I missed Mama. Her love and mostly her gentle touch. As the days passed, I worried I'd forget her and know'd a certainty that because of my skin it would be unlikely I'd feel that kind of touch from another. I was a Blue Ghost, the spook in little boys' bad dreams.

My heart pained for Mama and for my ugly color and what Charlie Frazier had taken from me. There was the ugliness of the preacher, the hardness of this land, the shame weighing down my shoulders. It was always there inside. The disgrace had fixed itself to my soul like it had life, the rawness, black and heavy like a lump of Kentucky coal that would find its dirty way into our home.

A silence fattened and swelled as the candlelight herded shadows from nooks and crannies, tickling the cobwebbed ceilings.

Loretta gently untangled our hands and said, "Let me get my eye medicine, child."

I passed it to her, and she pressed the rag to her eyes, dabbing with the goldenseal wash she'd brewed to help cure them.

"Anything else I can get you, Miss Loretta?"

Loretta pulled two tiny eyestones from her dress pocket and pushed them into my hand. "Would you mind rinsing these, child?" I took the flat milky stones that she'd said had come from the innards of a hawk, and dropped them into the pan of goldenseal, swished, then dried them with a clean cloth the way she liked, and carried the rocks back over to her.

The old woman laid back on the bed and slipped a stone under each eyelid, shutting her bulging eyes, hopeful the hill remedy would be a cure.

"See you next Monday, Miss Loretta," I said. Beside the door, I squatted down to a basket stuffed full of ginseng, sassafras, and other herbs, picked out a small root and a big white willow bark, and slipped outside. I'd replace them this summer when the eyebright bloomed—bring her the old herb to nurse her eyes.

I hated taking from her, knowing she couldn't hunt the herbs anymore and relied on her nephew for it. But the willow cured pains, calmed swelling, and cooled the hottest fever. Maybe it would take care of Mr. Moffit.

An umbrella of coming dark and cold greeted me.

Junia gave a soft wind-down bray, and I mounted and pointed her toward home.

I looked back once to wave, even though Loretta wouldn't see. Her cabin was half-swallowed in shadow and rolling fog, haloed by fireflies chewing through the darkness.

Ahead, the dark forest beckoned. I stopped to search for him, feeling his sneaky eyes on me, his blackness smothering. He was out there hunting. And I know'd it weren't for supper. Junia shifted, lifted her muzzle, feeling it too. I kneed the old mule, urging her to hurry.

Eleven

Junia carried us home through the fog-drenched forest, not breaking until she saw the smoke curling from our chimney.

"You're running late again," Pa said as I came through the door.

"Sorry, Pa, folks are excited to have the library service back."

"You read to ol' Loretta?"

"Yes, sir, I read a good twenty minutes, then helped her to bed." I slipped out of my coat and hooked it on the peg beside the door.

"Good," he grunted as he bent over to roll up the socks under his pant legs. Pa know'd Loretta only allowed the Bible, and he had a soft heart for the old woman.

"I thought it was your night off. Where are you off to? Pa, you going out?"

"Yup. Last night, Lee Sturgil's woman took to the bed, and I promised to work his shift for him tonight so he wouldn't have a rock dropped on his pay."

"The sheriff's daughter is ailing?"

"Birthing bed," Pa mumbled, looking away.

Some of the coal miners had been calling on Pa a lot lately to work their shifts to avoid fines, keep them out of trouble with the Company bosses.

Remembering Loretta's tea, I dug out the root from my coat. "Miss Loretta gave us this. Let me brew you a cup of sassafras before you go."

"Another night, Daughter. I can't be late. Get yourself some supper and rest up. Doc came by and left one of his baskets." He crammed a foot into his work boot.

The old doc was the only one who did call beside the courters Pa had sent. More than once, the doctor had dropped off small gifts of apples, a jar of jam, or biscuits, all the while with whittling pleas to draw our blood, scrape our skin, or let him take us to the medical clinic in Lexington. Pa never answered the door and made him leave any gifts on the porch.

Appreciative, I plucked up an apple and lightly bounced it from one hand to the other. "Pa, I heard some stirring out there a while back." I pulled back the curtain and stared out the window into the fog, seeing nothing.

"I've seen a bobcat on the trail, and I thought I saw it over by the thorny locust when I came in this morning." He gestured to the door.

"Bobcat? I'm not sure it's creatures, Pa. I—"

"I need to get going so the sheriff's daughter can be taken care of. I'll have a look in the morning. Keep your eyes peeled."

"Yes, sir." I sighed that I had to, that there was one more thing out there hunting me. Maybe if I told Pa about the preacher, he'd stay home and we would both be safe.

I dropped the curtain and turned. "Pa, a few weeks back, the preach—"

But he was out the door before I could finish. I stepped onto the porch and watched his ghostly lamp slash into mists until I could no longer see him.

Frowning, I went back inside and rooted through Doc's basket. I found jam and bread and spread the preserves on several slices for my supper.

In the lantern light, I hurried and did my chores, stopping to build another fire in the stove with some birch bark and pine kindling from the porch. Carefully, I placed a tinder of curling birch on the stove's cast-iron floor, lit the nest, and stacked the pine splits atop the small flames. Fragrances of woods and resin filled the cabin.

Hours later, I fetched Henry's present from my coat and climbed the loft ladder. I dropped the Life Saver onto the table beside the cotton mattress Pa insisted on getting me when he brought me home from Charlie Frazier's. I'd always slept just fine on a pallet of quilts, but Pa believed the mattress advertisement that promised to *soothe hurt bones and give better rest* would help me heal faster. Pa had credit to spend at the Company store that he used for the purchase, saying he'd had a little extra that month.

But Pa didn't have as much as two nickels to rub together, and I know'd he worked eighteen-hour days for two weeks straight for that little extra. The Company didn't like for the Kentucky man to feel a dollar in his pocket, and they'd pay the miners mostly in Company scrip—credit that could only be used at the Company store—to make sure of just that. If a fellar balked at having to spend his pay there, he'd be dismissed right quick. The Company also let workers draw on their earnings before payday, happy to give out scrip as loans with interest to keep the families good 'n' indebted to them, insisting to any who might raise a brow, *It serves to smarten the miners, gives the coal man a vicissitude from improper business standards, and educates them on sound business practices, on acquiring sound credit.*

I changed into my nightgown, turned back the covers, and snuggled under the quilt. My thoughts pulled back to Henry's precious gift, the hunger he suffered.

Pa and I had seen our share of hunger. We only had the berries, morels, squirrels, rabbits, and other life we'd pinched from the forest. Sometimes Pa'd trade miners his kills for other foods we couldn't get, like eggs, corn, and fruit. Rarely could we afford the expensive staples at the Company store. The Company scrip and my paycheck helped us to stay afloat a little, despite Pa using most of it to buy up the store medicines rather than a doctor's stronger ones to fight his lung illness. Still, he stayed in debt purchasing newfangled medicines, the next sure-fix potion that the store would bring in. Like a small bandage, the store-bought medicine would hide his sickness for a little bit, so that he could go back down into the mine and make more money for newer cures the Company kept stocking and pushing on the miners.

Weren't but two of us to fend for. The three hundred or so scattered folks who populated our area lived in the woodlands and alongside creek beds, up slopes, and the few in town and out in the mine camp were mostly large families with many children.

That there was a medicine for Henry and all the Henrys out there, for the hunger and hungry, didn't seem right. Not much of the pox or influenza sickness in Kentucky as much as there was the hunger disease right now. That there were stores full of the cure for hunger kept me awake with that special kind of anger that comes from helplessness.

I picked up the Life Saver and pressed it to my lips, inhaling the tempting scent of the sugary hard candy. "And don't you open it none until you're good an' hungry," he'd warned.

I reached over, slipped Henry's gift into my tin box of keepsakes on the night table. "I'm not good an' hungry yet." I blew out the candle and said a prayer for Pa's safety, then Henry, and all the other Henrys in this land, though it wouldn't help any more than casting a wish on a shooting star.

Still, I stacked more prayers atop, begging the Lord to keep us and the young'uns safe, and cast a fevered one for a merciful Heavenly home for Caroline Barnes who'd walked the nine deadly miles to feed her starving babies—nine miles in the cold, harsh-driven Kaintuck hills. Nine miles of dying each lonely step in her own cold embrace.

I balled the anguish in my fist, and a gut-wrenching sound whisked passed my teeth. A whip-poor-will answered back, and I buried my face into the soft blue pillow and swallowed the sadness knocking against my throat, the horrors I felt coming.

Twelve

The May morning unfolded slowly in Kentucky's old hand, and soon a children's moon climbed into a bright new sky. For a young'un in the hills, the daytime moon was something to behold. The slow way of life and meager existence in these old, grandmother mountains meant that mamas put babes to bed long before dark, before the burning hunger set in.

I made my way toward a mountain in the distance, humming to pass the time, lifting my voice to the blue hills and pine warblers, content with the time we'd made so far. It had been two days since I'd seen Frazier up here, and I relaxed, hoping I'd seen the last of him.

Though there were only three stops on my Wednesday route, the first drop-off was my trickiest. It didn't help none that I had to walk it mostly, slowing guiding Junia some three thousand feet up Hogtail Mountain's twisty, narrow, mud-packed path. Sure-footed enough for the mule, but I couldn't chance it with me atop her. I'd nearly fainted from fright the first time she staggered the steep climb and turned a hairpin curve, her rump swaying just inches from the ledge, me only a split hair from the bottomless drop. One misstep and I'd be falling till summer, and they wouldn't find me until the land shed her thick canopy of green. I'd walked most of the climb ever since that scare. And today it was welcomed. I might see Queenie, and that gave me cheer. Most Wednesdays we would crisscross the paths on our routes and sit a spell.

I stopped halfway up the pass on a wide bend and told Junia, "Time to carry me, ol' girl." The mule took several switchbacks with ease until the path forked and she tried to take the spur trail and head back downward. I got off and walked again, leading her, hugging rock face and the scraggly treed banks the rest of the way up.

Rounding the last pass, we finally saw the fire tower.

Seventeen-year-old R.C. Cole peeked over his fire lookout, the wind lifting his copper-penny hair. Dressed in a holey T-shirt and frayed brown pants, R.C. lived sixty feet up in the Hogtail tower built by the Civilian Conservation Corps. I could see the eagerness in his waving arms, hear the urgency in his thundering feet on the steel platform.

He was waiting for my books that would take him even higher, he'd said. The boy wanted to study news clippings about the weather and forests, and he'd always beg me to bring him up a *Farmers' Almanac* or a *National Geographic*—anything that would help him work his way up to fire watch dispatcher, so he could get more pay for schooling to land a bigger job as a forest ranger.

The CCC had been his logical choice to start his career, he told me. They'd been building the fire towers with the home cabs atop the mountains of Kentucky ever since President Roosevelt formed the workforce. And the minute R.C. turned sixteen, he'd fibbed to the Forestry Service, telling them he was seventeen. He'd applied for the job to follow in his pa's—and now his mama's—footsteps.

His mama, Hallie Cole, was the first female fire watcher in Kentucky. When R.C.'s pa died from a lightning strike, Hallie'd taken over and manned the tower at Pearl Knob lookout some twenty miles east of here, and the Corps let her. The Pearl tower had been the Coles' home ever since it'd been built and long before the CCC took over.

R.C. had been living in the Hogtail steel cab over a year now, keeping a bird's eye on any fires in the mountains, weather watching for them too, alerting the Forestry with the special hand-crank radio at the first wispy tail of smoke or dark storm clouds.

I tied Junia to the steep metal staircase, dug out the loan for R.C., and pulled out the two letters the head librarian had given me to deliver.

R.C. bent over the steel wraparound deck above, a bigger itch of anticipation and excitement under him. "Miss Bluet," he hollered down, motioning for me. "Can you bring it up, please? I got myself a smoker, I think. And I have to keep watch!" He disappeared inside.

I walked up the eighty-four steps, winding around until I stopped at the trapdoor, gave the underside a sharp rap, and stepped aside. R.C. pulled back the wooden trap, and I climbed the four rungs up into his quarters.

R.C. said, "Book Woman! Hurry, come see."

He plopped down in a chair in front of his Osborne Firefinder, studied the circular topographical map, and then stood up to search out the four walled windows that wrapped his tiny cabin.

"What do you think, ma'am?" Lightly, he knocked on the Firefinder and pointed. "Right here. Think I got myself a smoker?" He peered out the window again and into the blue Kentucky sky, the vast woodlands and creeks and rivers, and glanced back down to the Osborne perched on the wood table.

R.C. offered me his chair. "Here, take a gander." He scooted a dirty shirt off the seat onto the floor and dusted it off for me with his forearm.

I handed him an old edition of *Forest & Stream* and letters from home and sat down, still catching my breath from the flight of stairs. R.C. fanned the pages of the magazine. I scooted the chair closer to the Osborne, but the leg caught on R.C.'s shirt, and when I tried to lift the chair up and move it, it stuck.

"Oh, sorry, ma'am." R.C. blushed. "Let me fix it. I can't have my insulators getting busted. They can save a man's life, you know."

Last summer there'd been a bad storm up here with lightning

clashing all around the tiny cab. He told me lightning scrawled writings across the sky, and there was an explosion like nothing he'd ever heard. Then something hit the big lightning rod on top, and a large, blinding fireball rolled off the roof, down the side of the tower, crashing to the ground, charring the earth.

After R.C. got over the fright, he walked out onto his deck. The railing and staircase were lit, glowing a hot orange, chasing him back inside.

He called the forestry office, and they sent two rangers up Hogtail Mountain that very next day. The men put glass insulators under the legs of his chair, instructing R.C. to sit and lift both feet off the wooden floor when a storm approached, even if it was miles away. Now one of those insulators, little glass boxes fastened to the bottom of each chair leg, had snagged a corner of his shirt.

R.C. righted the chair and stepped back. I took my seat. Peeking through the sighting hole of the Firefinder, I slowly moved the sights around until the crosshairs were aligned with the fire.

"That's over near Jewel Creek," I said, proud that he'd taught me how to use the Osborne, even more, trusted my word. "Could be fog rising, R.C., but I can't be sure." I stood.

"Could be." He studied some more and said, "I'll need to keep an eye on it and be ready to dispatch it to the Forestry." R.C. held up his magazine, frowning.

"Sorry, R.C., the *Farmers' Almanac* is still on loan. I thought this magazine might do till I get ahold of it."

"It's fine, ma'am. Much obliged." He hid his disappointment behind a sweet grin and studied on the *Forest & Stream*. "Looks interesting enough." He dropped it onto his narrow rope bed and opened one of his letters, scanning it with an appetite for news back home.

He was too polite to let me know I'd brought the magazine to him three times last year. I was hoping to get him a few lesson books in science and geography, a *Farmers' Almanac*, but so far there hadn't been any donated.

"Miss Bluet." He stuffed the letter into his back pocket and snatched two envelopes off his cold wood stovetop. "Can you post these two for me?"

"I'll drop them off tomorrow at my outpost for the courier, and he'll pick them up next week—"

"Any way to get it posted sooner? One's to Mama, and this one"—he tapped—"is to Mr. Beck. That's my girl Ruth's pa... But I need to get it to him quick as possible." His eyes pleaded. "It's an important letter, ma'am." He shifted his lanky frame onto one leg, then the other and back again, anxious for an answer.

Ruth Beck was his girlfriend. And every Saturday for the last year without fail, R.C. walked down the mountain and then hiked the four miles over to the train depot at Jasper Creek. He'd pay the dime to ride the train to the bigger town of Willsburg, where he'd meet fifteen-year-old Ruth. Then he'd buy the twenty-five-cent tickets at the new movie house and treat his girl to a fine date.

R.C.'s ears heated, and he blurted, "I, uh... Miss Bluet, I aim to ask Mr. Beck for her hand! If it ain't too much trouble, ma'am, to post—"

"Doesn't Mr. Beck work the mine?"

"Yes! Yes, ma'am, he surely does."

"I'll have my pa pass it to him tonight when I get home." I warmed, wanting to help the young lovers.

"Much obliged. I'd be most grateful, Miss Bluet."

R.C. chatted happily about his plans for a few minutes, hungry for company in his lonesome job.

A half hour later, I untied Junia and turned for my next stop.

"Don't forget my *Farmers' Almanac*, Miss Bluet. I aim to get my book-read education and become a forest ranger."

"I'll really try, R.C." I hated that he didn't have all the books he needed, that there weren't enough around to give him a better life.

"I mean to marry Ruth and bring her up here when her pa says yes." Leaning over the railing, he called out his vow again.

At the foot of the lookout's mountain, I followed a creek for an hour before stopping to let Junia drink. While I gave her a break, I sat down and pulled out the old grammar book from my skirts and read from where I'd left off, waiting to see if Queenie would pass by, stopping every now and then to make sure Preacher wasn't.

In a minute, I came upon an "essay" and called to Junia, "Junia! Come here and listen to this fine essay."

The mule looked up from her drink and clomped over, dribbling water onto my shoes.

I jumped up and faced her. "This perfect passage is from *The Wind in the Willows*."

Junia raised her mouth, working her jaw like she wanted to hear the words too.

I laughed and patted her neck. "Be still now, we have to study our lesson."

The creek chattered on, but the birds quieted, and I looked down at the page. "'Take the adventure, heed the call, now ere the irrev—'" I stumbled over the big word, then wished mightily for a dictionary. "'I-rev-o-cable moment passes!' Or is it 'ir-rev-oc-a-ble'?" I frowned, sure I'd said it wrong.

Junia nickered like I had.

"Well, Miss Smarty Apostle, I'd like to see you read it," I told Junia, feeling a warmth blooming on my face, though there weren't no folks around to poke at or make fun of me.

I cleared my throat. "Shall we continue, Junia?" I said with a fancy air and read on in my radio newscaster voice. "''Tis but a banging of the door behind you, a blithesome step forward, and you are out of the old life and into the new! Then someday, some day long hence, jog home here if you will, when the cup has been drained and the play has been played, and sit down by the quiet river—'"

As if bored, Junia did just that and meandered back over to the creek.

"'Take the adventure, heed the call, now ere the irrev—'" I repeated, and the troublesome word slid into a curse as I wished for a proper dictionary.

From behind me I heard soft neighs. Startled, I spun toward the noise.

It was Queenie on her old rented horse, Maude.

"Good day," she called out. Queenie had a kind grin on her face. "Couldn't help overhear your nice essie." She mispronounced essay. "Honey, are you holding lessons for Junia today? Maybe you should be reading her the Bible." She smirked.

I cringed at the mention.

Queenie didn't know that Frazier hunted me like a bobcat hunts a wounded bird. I'd seen the preacher pass her in town, and he'd never once looked her way, or saw fit to greet her. It was as if she was invisible to him, and I couldn't help but wish the same for me. The pastor had no quarrel with Queenie, with any fit black or white, only the odd and afflicted.

"No-no, that would be silly," I said and quickly looked around to search the trees, then checked on Junia, despite knowing the mule always scouted out trouble through her wide nose, her wheeling ears, and big eyes that could see all around her. But now she rested quietly on the bank, content. "Just silly," I whispered and smiled a little.

Queenie shifted in her saddle and nabbed a finger toward at me. "What's silly is hearing the smartest folks I know throwing away their own musical words to concrete them up with city airs."

I closed my book feeling doubly foolish, but a mite prideful for her generous praise.

"You have a right nice voice, an honest one without needing to fancy the words or fatten them with the untruths of cleverer words," she said and rode Maude over to a tree.

"I want to learn. Want to know'd...know all the words, Queenie." I raised my chin. "All 'em and proper-like too."

Queenie stared at me thoughtfully and dismounted. "Reckon some folks have the thirst for such. Needing to fill the brain till it busts wide open. My papa had the thirst and passed it on to me too."

She dug around in her bags and brought over some bread and

a book and then plopped down onto the grass and nodded for me to do the same. I sat down beside her.

Queenie opened up an old Webster's dictionary and turned the slick pages until she stopped, drew her finger to a word, and tapped. "Irrevocable," she rang out without so much as a stammer and in a sweet musical measure.

Again, she repeated the word and said, "It is irrevocable—final. You try it." She pressed the book into my hand.

I swallowed and looked down at the column of words and sang out the word with nary a hitch.

Queenie sang out a praise.

Proud, I licked the word a few more times before handing back the thick book.

Queenie laughed, and I know'd it was in praise of me.

She laid the dictionary beside my skirts. "You keep it till you're good an' learned."

"I can't—"

"Bring me new words when we meet again so I know the book and brain ain't gathering dust, till you is sure you're gonna bust from them. That's what my papa said when he loaned it to me." Then she was up, shaking her long skirts and righting her bonnet. "How's your papa?"

"All the time working. How's the boys and Willow?"

"Right good lately. Be better if we could leave. You ever think about leaving, Cussy?"

I shook my head. "Where would I go? Where would *you* go?"

"I'd go up to Pennsylvania and meet up with more of my kind. Don't you ever want to be around more of your kind?"

"Ain't no more of us, Pa says. I'd just be satisfied to be around kind folk is all."

"Heard they have some nice ones up near Philadelphia." Queenie nabbed me with a playful secret in her eyes.

"What else have you heard about Philadelphia, Queenie?" I raised a brow and met her gaze, hopeful of good news.

She lifted her voice in singsong. "Oh, I might've heard

something. Something about a librarian assistant job that's come open right inside the big city of Philadelphia."

"You apply, Queenie?"

"I did." Her eyes were bright. "Posted it a week ago."

"Philadelphia," I murmured, hardly able to grasp it in my mind.

"Miss Harriett gave me the posting herself. Insisted I apply. And I was just foolish enough to do it."

Next to me, Harriett would give anything to rid herself of Queenie.

"There's colored doctors for my sick granny and colored schools up there for my boys. I'll know soon," Queenie chirped. "Oh, mercy, it's a dandy of a place. I read there's a relief board that helps out families. With the president giving out relief, and his new programs going strong now and hiring more librarians, it's a blessing. It's a different world there, honey. Opportunity, the likes we've never seen, and ones that city folk won't try an' crush. Miss Eula offered to give me a reference. Oh, the chances we'll have now. Imagine."

I couldn't. Maybe there was opportunity and blessings for her color, but I'd never once seen one for mine. Yet, I wanted it for her so bad, it was all I could do to lock my hands behind my back to keep from giving her a hug. "The chances will sure be wonderful."

Queenie squeezed my arm. Just as quick, she broke away and wagged a finger at the dictionary. "Bring me new words—a brain full of them."

"Thank you, Queenie. I will. Good luck and ride safe."

"See you next Wednesday. Travelin' mercies, honey." She went over to Maude and mounted.

I watched Queenie till I could no longer see her. Thoughts about her opportunities, blessings, wishing then for mine crept in. I pictured myself in a big city like the bustling ones in my books—the friendly faces, getting a big librarian job, and Pa getting himself the finest doctor, the best medicines. Maybe in a big city I could find at least one more of my kind? A city like that might allow more than two colors, might let folks of more than two colors get on with their lives without trying to destroy them.

Absently, I swatted away a bee and then saw it, saw my sin in the darkening blue stain of my hands as I squeezed my fist tight, then even harder, and felt shamed by my useless envy.

Picking back up the dictionary, I lost myself in the B section longer than what I intended, until Junia blew for my attention. "'Benevolent,'" I said and let the word slip twice from my mouth. I pressed the page to my lips. "A benevolent lady. That's our Queenie Johnson, ol' girl," I told Junia and packed up.

The trail away from R.C.'s tower was easier than the one up. I dropped a church bulletin and letter off to the Evanses, an older couple who had no interest in chatting, rarely opened the door, and refused to look at me when they had to talk. They'd leave their loans on the porch railing, and then part the curtain and watch safely from inside. I'd quickly replace the books before hurrying on to my last patron.

Once in a while, Postmaster Bill would ask me to pass a letter to the Evanses from their son in Nebraska. Today was one of those. I'd always stare at the envelope and try to imagine what kind of place it was by searching the postmark and stamp for clues.

I wondered what folks looked like, what they did all day. I recalled reading in the *National Geographic* about a famous zoo there, and that the WPA had built some big cat and bear exhibits for it. I thought about the zoo and wondered why folks would do that, who would pay money to visit creatures like that. Free as rain here, and you could see all kinds of critters if you had a mind, a keen eye, and a quiet tongue. Nebraska folk sure had to be rich to fritter away money like that...

Junia trotted out of the Evanses' yard, and I heard the door creak open. Mrs. Evans called my name. "Book Woman, come here." I pulled Junia's reins and turned to her.

"Mrs. Evans, can I help you, ma'am?" She held the envelope in fidgety hands, then thrust it out toward me.

"Mr. Evans went over to Burl Top for the week. I need help reading Patrick's letter... I, well, I seem to have misplaced my spectacles again."

I'd never seen her with any, but know'd some proud hillfolk who couldn't read always claimed this to Postmaster Bill, some even going so far as to carry empty spectacle cases. Surprised, I slid off Junia. "Yes, ma'am, I'd be happy to read it for you." I took the letter and opened it. There were folded bills inside, and I passed the money to her. She shot me an embarrassed but grateful smile, and I gently cleared my throat and read her son's letter.

April 11, 1936

Dear Folks,

Abigail delivered a fit, healthy girl on the twelfth of March and we named our firstborn Sallie.

I purchased three more Herefords last month, and Maybelle birthed two fine bull calves a week ago. At fourteen, the old gal is my top breeder, and I plan to have her calve again in three months.

Abigail sends her love.

Your loving son,
Patrick

Mrs. Evans dabbed at her eyes with the hem of her apron and sniffed. "A granddaughter, and named after me. The *first* grand-babe, and here my son's already become a big cattleman. Thank you, Book Woman. Mr. Evans will be pleased."

I could tell she was, and a softness lifted her weary face, settled into her watery eyes as I handed back the letter. That I could bring a small joy to my patron, this happy news, lit my heart.

Mrs. Evans thanked me once more, then wrinkled her

brow. "Wait in the yard," she ordered and turned to go inside. Promptly she returned and held up something in a small cloth, then, hesitant, set it lightly on the porch rail for me. "I've done made up too much cracklin' bread again, and Mr. Evans ain't home, and it'll spoil. For your trouble, Book Woman."

"No, ma'am, weren't no trouble—" But she slipped back inside before I could politely refuse.

It didn't feel right taking the gift. The bread was likely the only thing she had to eat for the week. And food was the most valuable thing you could give someone—the most generous gift a Kaintuck folk could bestow on another.

Under the black willow tree at the mouth of Ironwood Creek, I waited for eleven-year-old Timmy Flynn.

Timmy lived just on the other side of the creek I could easily cross, but his mama refused the Pack Horse library service, refused to have me and the government books inside her home. But because Timmy didn't have a mountain school nearby, Mrs. Flynn had given her boy an old banged-up pot and lid and told him to place it under the big tree across the creek. I was to "leave the boy his reading there, as long as you and them government's books stayed good an' put there," she'd warned.

After a few minutes of waiting and calling for the boy, I took Timmy's old loan from the pot, placed the new one inside, and covered it with the metal lid.

Straightening my back, I felt something strike my arm and bounce off my shoe. A small stone had landed near my feet. Then I saw him peeking out from a fat spiceberry bush, full of mischief and merry.

"Book Woman." He grinned wide. "What'd you bring me?"

"Why, I brought you a smart book, Master Flynn. Come see." I cracked the lid teasingly. "It's about a nice boy named Danny."

"You're a nice blue woman." He ran to my side, scrunching

down to peek. Timmy's eyes lit when he saw his favorite loan, *Ask Mr. Bear.*

He snatched it up and then sat under the spreading crown of the willow, propped comfortably against the scaly gray trunk of the tree, and flicked through pages with small lightning-fast fingers.

The boy was skinny, the size of a child almost half his age. Before I could help myself, I placed the wrapped bread beside him. Surprised, Timmy dropped the book. "I already ate, ma'am," he said softly and stared down at the present.

Like most hillfolk, the boy had pride. I'd have to trick him into taking it. "I'm full and can't possibly eat it, and it'll go to waste if you don't help me," I told him, the hunger protesting in my belly. We had little money left, and even less game on our table lately due to Pa's sickness.

He hesitated.

"Sure would hate to feed those thieving ants," I coaxed.

The boy brightened. "No, ma'am. I'm happy to help ya, and I won't let it go to waste none." Timmy plucked up the bread. "I can eat anytime." He unwrapped the food and gobbled it all down in three mouthfuls, nearly strangling on it twice. Frightened for him, I raced over to his side, ready to pound his back. In a second he looked up, leaking tears from the choking. Crumbs clung to his face, and a bright gratitude lit his eyes. He brushed the scraps off his cheeks into his mouth and licked up every fallen speck on the cloth the bread had been wrapped in. In a minute he was back to his book.

I dropped his old loan into my saddlebag and pulled out a scrapbook. It was my grandest, full of recipes, pictures from newspapers, and smart tips that thoughtful mountainfolk had passed on to me. I wished Mrs. Flynn could see it. But I dared not walk it across the creek and hear her fuss.

I held it up to Timmy. "Hmm, look here. My satchel's plumb full, and I don't think I'll have room to tote my important mountain scrapbook back." I looked at the pot and then back to Timmy.

"Sure is a big'un, Book Woman."

"It is. I reckon I could leave it here," I told him slyly, "but the pot's not near big enough and it is surely not a good place for its safekeeping." I tapped my cheek, thinking.

Timmy squinted, scratched his head, thinking too.

"It's one of my finest, and I wouldn't want it to get ripped or wet. There's a tip on whittling that ol' Pell Gardner gave, and another that shows a fellar how to sharpen his pocketknife. And inside there's an illustration for making a good fishing pole."

At that, Timmy eyes widened, and he rose onto his knees. "Pa likes to whittle."

"I hate to be a bother, but do you think your mama would let you keep it at home…? Just this once, just till I can get back?"

Timmy bobbed his head, shot upward, and greedily grabbed it out of my hands. "No, ma'am, she won't be bothered none. Not a'tall! I'll keep it safe in the privy."

"Thank you, Master Flynn." I mounted Junia and added, "Tell your mama that Libby Brown has a real tasty sugar pie recipe inside."

"Pa and me loves sugar pie, and Auntie needs a good'un to take to the Pie Bake Dance next month!" Timmy ran off toward the creek, splashing across, crisscrossing carefully, the two books held high in the air.

Behind me, I heard leaves scatter. Junia swished her tail. I searched the trees, seeing nothing, but feeling something. Again, my eyes bore into the woodland, slowly scanning for him. Junia stared ahead, ears parked stiff, listening too.

Across the creek, Timmy let out an excited whoop and called to his mama.

Junia blinked and swung her head to the boy's cries.

Again, Timmy called out, "Look, Ma, Auntie, *look*, I have us pie!"

Junia's ears went limp.

I snapped the reins and chuckled. "Let's get home, ol' girl."

Junia brayed, then dropped her neigh into quavering nickers as if laughing too.

Thirteen

I'd been dreaming of making scrapbooks atop a fiery lookout when I awoke in the fat hours of slumber to Junia's furious screams. I lay there trying to rouse from my dream.

In the inky blackness, I blinked and rubbed my eyes, listening to the silence. I reached for the candle, struck a match, and peered at my timepiece in the light. Only a few minutes past four and still twenty minutes before I rose.

I plopped back onto the pillow, snuggling deeper under the covers. The May weather chilled, found its way into loose panes and log chink. Again, I heard the mule's high cries and then the loud blast of a shotgun.

I bolted upright and untangled my twisted covers.

Pulling on Mama's old housecoat, I rushed down the loft ladder, stumbled, missed the last rung, and fell hard on my knee. I rubbed off the hurt and went for the shotgun under Pa's bed, but it was gone.

Panicked, I lit a lantern and flung open the door.

The muffled light on Pa's old carbide lamp bounced around from his miner's helmet, flickered, then steadied and shone a brighter light over by the stall.

Pa crouched beside a body with Junia close by, pawing an angry hoof and loudly belling the night.

"Daughter, quick." Pa saw me and hollered, "Get the beast back. *Back!*" He took off his helmet, waved it behind him.

"Settle it down 'fore I use the shotgun again, and this time I won't miss. Hurry on, and round that damn beast up."

I saw Pa's gun in the dirt beside him and gasped.

"Junia!" I put the lantern down and ran to her with my hands raised. But Junia just shook her long head and tore at the earth with both hoofs, raring to fight. "Haw! Back now. Back. Whoa, whoa, girl." I sidestepped and tried to block her.

"Whoa, ol' girl. Easy there. *Easy.*" I slowly reached out and touched her side. Her flesh quivered, and I patted, rubbed, stroked her shoulder and gray muzzle while talking to her in low tones. Soon, she quieted and hung her exhausted head over my shoulder. I looked back and saw what had her troubled.

Him lying there like that, I was sure he'd come back from the grave, and it scared me so that I yelled out to Pa, "Is his ticker broke?"

"Get the mule in its stall," Pa ordered. "I said, get!" Pa lifted his helmet and raised the light over the body. "*Get now.*"

Junia startled and gave a shrill choking neigh. I grabbed a rope from her shed and hooked it over her neck, tugged, pulled her inside over muck and a splintered board. The wooden half door had fallen where she'd kicked it, the rope fastener sat on the ground broken away from its frame.

I pulled the gate up, righted it, and latched it with a piece of cord, then hurried over to Pa and knelt down beside him and Vester Frazier.

"Is he alive?" I whispered, torn between wishing he weren't and fearful he was. Frazier's head was matted with gore, and an ugly gash cratered the forehead. His jaw was split to his mouth, and his nose parked to the side, leaking blood.

"He has some life in him," Pa said, "and is going to be feeling a'might harder one if he comes to."

I noticed the ring of coal soot around Pa's nose, but his clothes were only lightly dusted, not filthy like usual. "Pa, why are you home so early?"

"Mine shut down. One of the sections collapsed, and the inspector sent us home."

"What happened here?" I eyed the gun beside his knees.

Then I saw it, a glint in the dirt, and my relief was washed away in a budding fury. Beside Vester Frazier's body lay a long hunting knife and another oil lantern snuffed out.

I plucked up my lantern and ran to the stall. Rubbing my hand over every part of the mule, I inspected her as best I could under the dim, flickering light. I raised the wick. It caught full and it burned brighter, and again I examined her.

"Just a scrape that's bloodied her rump, but no serious harm," I hollered to Pa and went back over to crouch beside him. "What will we do?"

"We help our fellow men, Daughter. We're God-fearing folk," he said simply, though I know'd he meant "careful folk" more, and worried about what could happen to us if a white person was found here, injured or worse. Like all Blues, I'd grown up to be "careful," learning when to bow down and when to cower.

"He's been hunting me." I barely breathed. "Sneaking around the hills for me, Pa." That he'd tried again, and so soon, sent a chill scuttling over my body.

Pa studied me, a coldness settling in his weak eyes. He swallowed what I thought was a curse, then knocked a fist against his leg.

I know'd he was remembering my marriage bed. Pa didn't say much then, but I saw it all in his eyes now.

"He didn't hurt me none." I placed my hand over his. "But Junia got scuffed some before she ran him off. She saved us."

Pa glanced over at Junia, surprise and admiration taking hold. "I've been meaning to tighten up that gate... Good thing I didn't get around to it. I reckon the beast got a sniff of his wickedness and busted out of its stall to stop him."

"Whatever we do, he's going to come after us, Pa. And keep coming until he has his day with me."

"Yes. But he's got to live now, or else we're in trouble. If this preacher dies, folks will pick up their ropes—"

"Wonder where his mount run off to, Pa." I cocked an ear, looking around, listening for it.

"I reckon the blast sent it hightailing back into the hills."

Frazier coughed, then moaned and stirred a little from his stupor, wincing. A stink of blood and fear rose from his body. When he opened his eyes fully and saw me and Pa hovering above him, he shielded his face with both arms.

"Let's get him inside," Pa said.

I stared at him and balked.

"Now." He cut me a warning look.

"Yes, sir." I gulped. We hitched the preacher under his arms and legs and carried him up to the cabin.

Inside, we laid Frazier on Pa's clean bed, the bed I'd made, and on sheets I'd scrubbed. Then Pa said, "The last thing we need is another dead Frazier. Best take the mule to town and get the doc."

Fourteen

"His body done broke," Doc said, pulling the coarse muslin over Frazier's gray face. He folded the stethoscope back into his medical satchel and glanced at me and Pa seated at the table and said, "That mule is dangerous."

Doc peeled the sheet back off Frazier and grimaced, studying him once more before draping the fabric back over the dead preacher's face.

I know'd Junia had spent her rage on Vester Frazier and busted his ribs and other innards, but the herb jar half-full of dead man's bells sitting by the kettle was new and something I'd noticed as soon as I arrived back home with the doc. An empty mug rested on a stool beside the bed. An uneasiness took hold as I wondered just how much of the foxglove Pa had given the preacher.

Pa told Doc, "The pastor had been hunting my daughter and meant to do harm."

Doc looked at Pa, then me, and back to Pa and nodded with the full knowing of that harm. Doc spied the jar and then picked up the empty cup.

"He came to and"—Pa's voice folded into a cough—"and I gave him some foxglove for the hemorrhaging until you got here. No more than I've given myself for a headache."

I wrung my hands in my lap, then tucked them under my bottom and felt the blue heat itching them.

"The beast busted him up good," Pa continued.

"You best shoot that striking mule before the town does it for you, Elijah," Doc said, slamming the mug back down onto the stool. "Shoot it right now!" He snapped his bag shut.

I flew up from my chair. "No! Junia was trying to protect me, and she stopped him."

Doc raised a hand and said, "Don't matter a spit. Now, Elijah, you know two Fraziers found dead—and both with Blue Carters—ain't gonna sit well, no matter what the excuse." Doc worried a hand over his whiskered cheek, rubbed his tired eyes, and slipped a hard glance at me. "Charlie, and now Vester."

I dropped my gaze downward, the ugly memory of Charlie Frazier's *broke ticker* loud in the cramped cabin.

Pa said, "He attacked us on *my* land."

"He's dead, Elijah. A dead white man in a colored's home. They'll burn your house for it. Hang you for sure," Doc said.

"Blue," Pa corrected.

"It's still a color to them, and one they're afraid of," Doc said.

"*Pa.*" I latched onto his arm. "We'll tell Sheriff how he came for me on my book route. The lawman pledged his protection to us librarians."

"He's Frazier kin." Pa worried a rough hand down his face. "Hell, half the town's related to a Frazier one way or another," he said, defeat wearing him down.

Doc mused, "Frazier clan runs thick, one of the biggest 'round these parts. Some of them are rotten, and some are decent-enough folk. The sheriff's a good lawman, of good cloth, and he takes his responsibility seriously enough"—Doc grimaced as if he was reminded of something unpleasant—"if not too serious sometimes. But this is two dead Fraziers." He shook his head.

"The preacher attacked me," I barely whispered. "I'll tell Sheriff how he tried to violate—"

Pa wrapped his hand over mine, pressed a hush into it. He squeezed once more, and harder again, a warning in his cold touch.

I swallowed my accusation and tucked down my chin. A woman violated would be damned—persecuted—and dismissed from her job like Postmistress Gracie Banks had been after she was raped last year and told. And there'd been more than a few other Gracie Banks who'd blabbered. Rarely was justice served and then only if the woman's kin took it upon themselves to mete out punishment in a quiet, lawless way. Disgraced, soiled like that, even womenfolk would silence, shun, and cast blame on the tainted female—make good 'n' sure she'd carry the sin of the man's stain for the rest of her days. Over the years, I'd seen that burden in a few women's hooded eyes around town. I remember Mama telling Pa when she thought I weren't listening that *the female's silence let those vile godless men walk free among their prey, boldly pass their sufferers on the streets of Troublesome with a sly tip to the hat, a smug pat to the crotch.*

"But he was hunting me," I said to Doc, my words weakening.

"On my land." Pa dropped my hand, stabbed a finger to the window. "*Carter land.*"

Doc drew a long, bothersome breath. "Folks'll surely think the worst. And fear of peculiarity, things that have no name, nor grasp"—his gaze fell on us—"will drive even a saintly man to do evil under this dark sky in this old, dark land."

Fear seized hold, and I looked at Pa's flushed cheeks.

Doc took a seat at the table, piano'd his long fingers across the scarred wood, and snatched more peeks at me. "We have us a problem, Elijah," Doc said, concern shrouding his voice. "A problem that needs fixing." Doc knocked the worry into the wood, softly cleared his throat. "Yessir, we do."

"Fetch us a drink, Daughter," Pa said, studying him. "The doc must be thirsty."

"Yes, Pa." Trembling, I pulled out an old whiskey bottle from the back of the cupboard, poured the men drinks, and placed the tin cups in front of them, meaning to take a seat too.

Pa grabbed my arm. "Check on the beast and make sure it's good and tucked in." He gently shoved me off. "Go on, Daughter," he said, a bit gruffer this time. "*Get.*"

I opened the door and glanced back over my shoulder.

The men had pushed aside their cups and tilted their heads together, ready for talk.

I stole one last glimpse of Frazier's sheeted body before going out. *A problem...that needs fixing*, Doc said, and I know'd somehow he'd meant fixing it with me.

Fifteen

I huddled on the porch in the darkness, my ear flattened against the door, trying to sip the words from inside. Behind me, Doc's horse nickered in the yard where he'd tied it to the post. Junia answered back in a worn, sleepy bray.

I pressed in closer. The conversation fell and rose, a clattering of broken sentences skating through the old cabin's chinks.

"Frazier did… He would've killed her," Pa said.

The doc muttered something I couldn't understand. Then Pa's angry voice stepped onto Doc's. "Dammit, man," Pa said. "When Frazier spent his last breath telling me God sent him a vision to plant his white seed inside her to rid the land of the Blue Devil, *I prayed he would die—*"

I covered my mouth to push back a gasp.

Pa mumbled something else. Then came Doc's softer tone.

More words crawled over and under, jumbling.

"Frazier was the devil hisself," Pa insisted.

"A man of the cloth," Doc said.

"A *charlatan.*" Pa coughed.

"He was an important man to some," Doc insisted.

"He had hisself the importance of a fool drunk," Pa bit back.

A hush grabbed the early-morning darkness. Then Doc's words sounded clear. "It's a lot to ask of a man."

Silence. I heard my name once, then again. They'd lowered their voices before the mountain doc added, "Hell, it's a mighty lot, Elijah, to ask a respectable fellar to look the other way and without…compensation—"

"*Pastor. Hide. They'll never know,*" one or both of them said, muffled.

More pinched talk uttered in fast, penniless words laddered atop confusion. *Blue, medical, Bluet, doctors, cure, tests* were mingled.

Then I heard Doc urge, "I'm a forthright man. Do me this small favor, and I'll ensure you and the girl's safety."

More puzzling talk.

Then from Doc, "I promise you'll live in peace for as long as I live."

I wrinkled my brow, tried to get the gist of it all, picked apart the word *favor*, sifting it over and over in my head.

"Give Bluet to me, Elijah, and I swear she'll see no harm," the doc pressed.

It felt as if I'd stepped right off the mountain and was clawing air to climb back atop. My heart knocked so hard, I feared it might be sounding against the door, and I slid a hand across my chest to quiet the noise.

I caught more rattled talk and further strings of hushed discussion that gave me no understanding, abruptly followed by a hard thump. Then chairs scraped against the floor.

Slinking back, I snuck off the porch and raced to Junia, a tangle of words muddling my head, my knees near buckling.

Inside the stall, I collapsed against the mule, buried my face and fright into her soft coat. She didn't move, didn't stir the slightest. And I know'd she must've felt something. Something coming at us fast.

Sixteen

"But I ain't ill, I'm just colored different," I cried to Pa two days later, knocking a dark, angry fist against my chest. "And I ain't any different than the white squirrel we've seen on Thousandstick Trace that scampers alongside the red and grays. They're all just squirrels, all the same—"

"Cussy," he urged, "I've had a trying shift in the mine, and I don't need more of it here. It's just a few trips to the city, and only once a month. It won't affect your route. Doc says he can carry you there on your day off and promises to see you home safely."

"Pa, please," I pleaded. "I don't want to go anywhere with him. I... Pa, it's Saturday, and I need to work on my scrapbooks on my day off." I crossed to the shelf of books. "Get my reading material stacked, clean this place, and—"

He caught my wrist. "You will go, Daughter. And you will let him and the Lexington medical facility do their tests. Help the doctor with his experiments."

I snatched my arm away, brushed off the coal-dusted prints he'd left behind.

"They might find a cure for our color, for you," Pa said with something that sounded a lot like hope. "Our burden would be gone." But the notion died on his tongue.

His words hit like a heavy slap. "I-I'm sorry. Sorry I couldn't be white... Sorry I'm not the daughter you wanted—that I was born your burden, Pa," I whispered, my voice swollen, pained.

His shoulders slumped, and his eyes welled up with sadness.

I'd never talked to him, Mama, or another soul like this, and seeing his grief and brokenness broke something in me. I looked away, balled up the loose fabric on my skirts, and squeezed, my anger dissolving, abandoned to heartbreaking misery.

Pa cleared his throat. "I want you safe, Daughter. It's the only way to keep us from the hangman's noose"—he jabbed a finger at the windowpane—"and keep him good and tucked in the ground out there. To keep the doc on our side and quiet."

I followed his finger. Two days ago, as morning slipped in and cast its rays over a sheeted Frazier, the doc slipped off for home, and Pa had sent me up to the loft, ordering me to stay inside. From my small windowpane, I saw Pa drag Vester Frazier's body across the yard and dig fast into the ground beyond Junia's stall, while the first light of day broke over him, burying the pastor in a stinking grave topped with manure and sticks.

"Pa, the doc knows he trespassed and tried to attack us."

"The doc only knows one thing: he found one more dead Frazier in the company of Blues. And that's exactly what he'll tell folks if you don't do as he asks."

My embarrassment reflected in his eyes.

"He attacked the mule, and she fought back. We didn't do anything," I said weakly.

"Blues don't have to do much, Cussy," Pa said quietly, the words needling, raising the hairs on my nape and arms. "Blues and many a colored have been hanged for less. Get on now. It's your day off and it's nearly six. He'll be calling for you in the hour."

For less. I stood there, my protest losing its starch.

"We have to save ourselves from the rope, Daughter," Pa said. Weary, he walked over to the chair and dropped heavily into it, bent over with elbows propped on his knees, hands rubbing his head.

At seven, Doc rode into our yard perched atop his horse. We took turns riding the steed to his cabin at the edge of town. In front of his home, he tethered his mount, instructing a young boy to tend it.

Doc's housekeeper, Aletha, stepped out the door and called a greeting to him, the lilt of music rising in her strange accent. "Gud mawnin, Docta. Mi ave a stew pon di stove—" Aletha stopped when she saw me. Folks said the old Negro woman from Jamaica had worked for Doc's kin in South Carolina. After Doc's wife, Lydia, passed, Aletha came here to help.

"No time to eat, Aletha," Doc said, taking the porch steps. "I'm here only to retrieve my bag and a journal. I have to get to Lexington."

"No nyam?" Aletha looked disappointed.

"If you'll just pack some fruit and cheese." Doc stepped around her. "And bring Mrs. Frazier in and offer her a cup of tea."

Aletha cast an eye my way. "But har a *Blue*, Docta."

Doc ignored her. "Bluet, come in. Aletha will see to it you get something to drink before our journey." He hurried on inside.

I climbed the steps, following after him. But Aletha moved in front of the door and put her hands on her wide hips. "No Blue inna Missus Lydia's yaad." She shook her kerchief-covered head, gestured over to the well. "Yuh jink from di well ova there," she said, her voice rising.

"Jink...well," I puzzled, following her finger.

"Yuh jink ongle from di well," she said again. "No Blue inna Missus's yaad."

"*Yaad?*" I said stupidly.

"Yaad, yaad!"

I flinched. Her words were musical, but weren't no song in there for me.

Aletha raised a finger above her head and poked it at Doc's home this time. "*Yaad.* No Blue inna di yaad, no Blue jink from Missus Lydia's fine china!" She stomped a foot and disappeared inside.

The door slammed, and I quickly retreated back down the steps to wait. In a few minutes, Doc came out with his things and rushed me around back to his motorcar.

My feet plugged the earth when I saw the big machine. The clunky black shoes I'd worn pressed harder against the ground while Doc tried to coax me into his big, steel motorcar, promising it was safe.

I'd seen motorcars and coal trucks around town, read about them in books and magazines, but I never imagined I'd come this close to one, let alone ride in one. I stared at the shiny steel-winged lady perched on the nose of it.

Doc must've seen my bewilderment because he grinned and said it weren't nothing more than a radiator ornament called "the flying lady."

Blushing, I pulled the brim of my bonnet down and stared at the ground, wondering why he'd put her there and naked like that.

Then he opened the heavy door. "Time is wasting, Bluet. It's just a horse with wheels," he insisted. "A 1932 Plymouth automobile, is all. Get in. You'll find it's a comfortable sedan."

I know'd what it was, but the leap from knowing to actually touching one seemed overwhelming. I looked at Doc and then back to the machine, and pulled out one of Pa's handkerchiefs from my pocket to dab my brow.

"Just a comfortable horse on wheels that'll take us to the city and see us back," he assured easily like it weren't nothing more.

"When will we be back?" I worried about leaving the chores I'd planned for today, and even more, about what Doc had planned.

"In the afternoon." He made a sweeping motion with his hand, pressing me to get in.

Carefully, I climbed onto a fancy broadcloth-covered seat, snatching glimpses of the big wheel atop a fat pole on the other side and the sticks and pedals on the floor.

With Pa's wadded handkerchief clenched in my fist, I squeezed the damp ball until my hand pained.

I stomped twice on the strange floor to be sure there was one underneath, testing the sturdiness, then inspected the walnut strip running behind the wheel with its strange metal buttons poking out.

Doc climbed in, and his hand moved feverishly, grabbing sticks, turning, pulling, and pushing knobs. A close roar said the engine had come to life. I pressed my back into the seat. In less than a minute, the heavy machine lurched forward, and we rode across bumpy country roads, bouncing.

I marveled at the speed, the loud engine and big tires biting at dirt and gravel, and know'd no sure-footed horse would ever ride like that, so smooth and fast and all at once.

Strangely, the sound of the motor and thrum of tires relaxed me. I passed time by looking out the window as the dirt road opened wider through rolling farmland bordered with stretches of stacked-rock fencing. After an hour, my eyes grew heavy, and the warmth of sunshine, the steady sounds and passing blurs lulled me into a sleep. Almost three hours later, the doc gently called my name, awakening me from my exhausted slumber. "We're in Lexington, Bluet."

I spotted motorcars rolling beside us, and beyond them, a curtain of tall buildings. It was surely a wonder that Lexington was only one hundred and fourteen miles from home, yet it might as well have been across oceans the way the city bustled with a different kind of life—respectably dressed people in heels, gloves, and fancy hats, the many high buildings, the dull roar of machines. On corners, men barked to passersby, waving newspapers, while folks clacked spiffy heels across paved streets, dodging motorcars.

I touched the collar of Pa's weathered oilcloth coat, brushed the folds of my homespun dress, and peered down at my unpolished laced shoes, tucking the heels quickly out of sight.

Doc stopped the motorcar to let people cross to the other side of the street. I watched several folks snatch up the newspapers on that corner, and I marveled that the newsprint could be had so easily and at their whim.

Once again, I pressed my face against the door's window, amazed at the hurried life, the folks rushing along the sidewalks, slipping into the many stores and shops, and dashing in and out of other unmarked doors.

It was a life I'd only read about in my books, and my hungry hands touched the glass, trying to touch the stories I'd read.

Doc said, "Go ahead, roll down the window. Just reach down on the door and turn the handle."

I fumbled with the crank, then finally opened the pane and breathed in smells of oil, gas, concrete, and other scents I couldn't name, tasted the peculiar spirit of the place, listened to the unusual buzz, the city's open hymnal.

The soot of the city, its oils and smoke and grit, filled my nose, burning, watering my eyes.

A motorcar hurried past us and honked, startling me. Another answered back, and still another and several more. Shouts, the pound of hammers, and music and loud greetings swirled from every direction. "There's so many noises. How do folks stand it?" I pressed my palms to my ears, swiveling my head to follow it all.

Doc laughed and sped on past until he turned onto a quiet tree-lined street that led to Saint Joseph Hospital. The wide, red-rose-brick, five-storied building climbed high into the noon sky.

Doc turned off the engine, jumped out, strolled around to my side, and pulled open the door. All I could do was gawk at the huge place, the porch with its generous sweep of concrete floor and tall pillars. Perched above was a long iron veranda. I'd only seen something this grand in magazines.

"Come on." Doc motioned to me, grabbed his medical bag from the back floorboard, and led me up the wide steps to the large wooden doors.

Inside, a woman in a dark dress and a strange white hat greeted us. Doc called her Sister and then leaned to my side and said, "Bluet, there's nothing to fret about. This is a Catholic hospital, the finest in Lexington, and she's a nun."

I was more interested in the grand foyer, the vast surroundings, and the massive furniture pieces scattered throughout the polished-tile entryway. It seemed like a concrete tree with branches of polished corridors in every direction.

I felt the nun's eyes on me and caught her inspecting me over her spectacles. I had half a mind to inspect her right back. Weren't no such person in Troublesome or in parts close around, but I'd read about her kind in the *Readers Digest* and *National Geographic*.

Doc said, "Good day, Sister, we'll see ourselves up," then took my arm and led me into the mouth of an empty white hallway that twisted and turned and branched into more hollow hallways lit up by electric bulbs. Several times I paused to gawk up at the lights, listen to the angry buzz of the bulbs, until Doc would latch onto my arm to pull me forward.

He paused to open a large metal door and led us up a staircase to another door, and again on a path that seemed to never end. Finally, Doc stopped at the large entry of an arched doorway. On the metal sign, two gray words had been painted at eye height so no one could miss them: COLORED WARD.

A Negro woman carried a fussy child past us, and a nun followed with another babe in her arms. A small boy peeked around the corner and disappeared just as quick.

"Here we are," Doc said, a little out of breath. To our right, I spied a door that read PHYSICIAN.

My heart thundered, and my throat cinched as if a rope collared it.

Doc pulled me into the room and shut the door. I backed up into a long metal table with rails. The smell of bleach and other unknown liquids was baked into the green walls. Medical instruments sat atop small silver trays crowded with sharp knives, bottles, cotton strips, balls, and little clumps of rags. A small basin was wedged into the corner. Beside it on the counter was a gauze-covered glass bowl filled with leeches. I recognized a lancet, one like those used in my hills. Sitting next to it was a bloodletting tool and glass cupping cups used to catch blood spilling out from a body.

Doc reached around me and grabbed a soft cotton wrap from a drawer under the sink and shook it open.

"Bluet, take off your clothes and your necessaries, and put this on for the examination."

I pressed a hand to my chest and shook my head, not willing to remove my coat, and certainly not my undergarments.

He frowned. "We're pressed for time. Let me get you a pill." Doc opened a metal cabinet with a glass door and pulled out a bottle, rattled out small pills. "Take this to calm your hysterics," he ordered, pushing it into my palm. "I'll get you water." Doc stepped over to the basin, and water ran freely out of a spout.

A knock to the door jarred me. A colored man in a white coat strolled in.

"Dr. Randall Mills," the mountain doc chirped. "I'm so glad you could visit today. Come in, come in. This is Cussy Frazier of the Blue Carters I told you about. She's called Bluet."

Dr. Mills moved in close, inches from my face, bobbing his head. "A real blue woman," Dr. Mills said and circled around me, his eyes grabbing up every inch of me. "Have you done a heart and lung exam, Thomas?"

"I'm ordering them today," Doc answered, sounding pleased.

"Astounding color," Dr. Mills said, touching my cheek.

I flinched and turned my head.

"Indeed," Doc murmured and tapped Dr. Mill's shoulder. "Randall, can I see you outside," and to me, "Bluet, be quick, take your pill, remove your clothing, and robe yourself."

The men stepped out of the room and shut the door quietly behind them.

I shook open the airy, threadbare robe and saw it had a long slit down the front—or was that the back? Shaking my head, I wadded it back up and placed it and the pill on the table.

Minutes later, Doc poked his head in.

"It's torn all the way open." I pointed to the gown.

He shook his head and pulled the door shut, leaving me alone once more.

A few more terrifying minutes passed before Doc swung open the door and stepped aside, letting in two broad-shouldered women wearing the nun robes.

The nuns gawked at me, then Doc snapped at them, "Sisters, strip her quickly and give her two Nembutal suppositories." He stormed out.

I pushed a protest past my fear-thickened throat and tried to go after him.

One of the nuns grabbed me by the coat, yanked it and my bonnet off. The other reached inside the medicine cabinet and pulled out a large bottle.

Together, they came at me, blocking me against the wall. I kicked and slapped at them, screamed and cursed until the larger one wrestled me to the floor, stuck her thick knobbed knee in my back. The other stripped off my skirt and then my undergarments.

I struggled to rise, but one had my head locked to the cold tile, her knee digging in deeper.

Then the other one knelt and lightly touched my behind, whispering, "Have you ever, Sister Doreen? Look, it's as blue as lake water on a bright day." She pressed her icy finger to my skin, poking before giving my bottom a stinging slap.

A killing rage grabbed hold inside me, and I let out a murderous scream as I tried to wriggle free, spit and bite at them, but caught nothing more than air. The large nun had me pinned down tight.

She laughed and smacked my bottom again. "Look at it now; it's plum purple."

"Get the Nembutal inside her," the one atop me ordered and dug her knee even harder into my back.

They pried me open, pulled back my skin, and inserted something hard and hurting inside my bottom. It went slippery, and warmed. Quickly they tossed the slitted robe over me. Then the nuns hauled me up onto the cold metal table, splayed my arms and legs high and wide, securing them tight with leather straps to the rails, leaving me open, exposed under the dangling, buzzing bulb above.

Weren't no time before my screams hollowed under a thickened tongue, and I could barely make out the doctors' faces hovering over me.

Drugged, I felt bare skin, their busy hands bumping, crawling over and down and inside me as their excited voices floated into a fading, gurgling string of words. "Take a swab... More blood here. More samples... More. We're going to make history. The best journals will fight for our articles, our analyses and photos."

I tried to move, but sleep sank its teeth deep, my lids grew heavy, and darkness came fast.

Seventeen

I stirred awake from a drugged slumber and realized I'd been shoveled into the back seat of Doc's motorcar. The confused memories of Saint Joseph and medical journals, samples, bolted my sore body upright. My crumpled bonnet had been placed under my head.

As I leaned my head against the window, I felt a sickness crawl into my belly and rise high in my throat, the hazy blur of trees and road rushing by, dizzying.

Moaning, I curled back down onto the seat, my breath short and fast. Soon, I escaped in sleep.

The motorcar bumped over something, growled its engine, and I awoke, raised a crooked arm over my face, the daylight harsh and hurting my tender eyes.

Instantly, I held out my hand. It was bandaged up the length of my arm.

I pressed on the dressing and felt the tenderness. Unraveling the cloth, I traced the tracks of blood on my veins, the skin bruised and swelling, the ugly strap welts, raw and deep. "Wh-what did you do?" I pulled myself slowly up and leaned over the seat, the fear tightening my voice. "What—"

Doc turned his head partway toward me. "Ah, you're awake. Good. Don't worry, it won't scar," he said quietly, and then more pert, "You'll be fine, dear." He snapped his attention back to the road. "Fine as one can be with chocolate-colored blood, I reckon."

Chocolate. I peered at my arm, picked up the cloth. Brown bloodstains riddled it.

"I'm sorry the nurses were rough with you, Bluet," he said, "but it was important—very—and we'll learn soon about your family's blood and how we can fix it—fix you, my dear."

I felt the spark of anger slip behind my eyes, prompting a headache. What I wanted most was to be okay as a Blue. I never understood why other people thought my color, any color, needed fixing.

"It'll be wonderful to fix you, won't it?"

Fix. Again, the chilling word caught in my throat, and I suddenly wished Mama *had* fixed my birth with some of her bitter herbs. Then I would've never had to suffer this horrid curse of the blueness. Still, Doc said it would be wonderful, and I couldn't help but wonder what my and Pa's life would be like if we were *fixed*. The confused thoughts made my head pound harder. I reached up and touched my neck, looked at my arms and leg, pressing for more tender spots. A cramp took hold low in my stomach and cut even lower.

"My innards. I'm...feeling cramps," I said, too tired to be embarrassed.

"You're fine. We took some blood and a sample of tissue from your cervix, a few skin scrapes from your scalp and the back of your shoulder, nothing that will harm or cause you permanent pain, and nothing that a good night's rest with laudanum won't fix." He rattled a bag and pulled out a pear. "Aletha packed this and some cheese here. Would you like to eat something?"

"I ain't hungry. It hurts, everything hurts." I doubled over. "I don't want to do this anymore."

"Only for a bit. I promise. Listen, Bluet, we may be able to cure you, make you white. Wouldn't you like that?" he asked gently and pulled the motorcar onto the side of the road.

Maybe there weren't anything a Blue should like better than becoming normal like that, but the pain and fear left me shaken and crowded out those possibilities.

"It would be safer, my dear. When you're white, you'll never have to worry about the likes of Fraziers, or others who might want to do you serious harm or worse because of your looks."

The words lay cold in my cramping belly. If I didn't let Doc have his way, there would be *worse* pains coming for me and Pa. *Many a colored have been hanged for less* looped in my brain and left a fear in the pit of my belly.

From the front seat, Doc rummaged inside his medical bag and pulled out a small bottle and a brown dropper and handed them to me. "Take one drop now and two drops of the laudanum before retiring to bed tonight."

It seemed like I had barely touched the dropper to my tongue, tasted, when my aches began easing. I inspected my arms more closely. The pokes and scratches weren't nothing more than a nuisance.

Curious, and then surprised that I was okay, I corked Doc's little brown bottle with the tiny plug and tucked it into my dress pocket while something bigger took hold in me.

"I need something to heal these scrapes," I hinted.

"Oh, yes, yes you do." He dug deeper into his satchel. "We wouldn't want you ill."

"No, sir," I agreed. "And we ain't had much food lately, and I get weak-kneed some—"

"Here, take this pear and cheese, and I'll bring more soon— see that you get some blocks of cheese and bread."

Blocks of cheese and bread! I almost clapped out a cheer.

"And here's a bottle of rubbing alcohol, dear." He handed me the bag and a larger bottle of the clear liquid. "And you can always use honey to dress the wound after you clean it with the alcohol," he added, reached in again and pulled out a full bottle of honey. "I want you to be comfortable, to have everything you need."

Any Kentucky woman know'd the worth of honey, that it was good for all sorts of ailments. It was just getting your hands on some that proved difficult.

Nearly forgetting the hospital and the harshness of the day, I clutched the prized bottles to my chest and managed to smile back before tossing it all into the soft belly of my bonnet. Soon, I grew drowsy and curled back down onto the seat.

Eighteen

We arrived back in Troublesome just before dark. The old mountain doc toted me back through the woods on his horse, seeing me safely to my cabin.

Before he left, I caught him staring at my crumpled clothes, unkempt hair, and fallen braids.

He dug into his coat. "I almost forget, Bluet. I picked these up for you in the commissary." He handed me two satin ribbons. "Uh, yes… Your hair ribbons were lost during the exam." He reddened.

Weren't no ribbons in my plaits, just twine. But I marveled at the lovely new white garlands, murmured a *thank you* that surprised me despite the intent in his wise eyes that the gifts were meant to bribe me into more testing. Generous, but it would all change if I refused.

My eyes searched the yard, landing over past Junia's stall where the preacher lay in his shallow grave. A shiver latched hold and rolled violently across my shoulders.

Alarmed, Doc said, "You're cold. Let me get a blanket from the pannier."

Instantly, I took a step back, wanting to take my leave. "I'm okay, sir."

The doc pushed up his slipping spectacles and leaned in closer to make sure of just that. "I can make you better than okay. Dr. Mills and I believe we can cure you. There's a good chance, Bluet."

It seemed far-fetched.

"Well, good evening. Rest well. I'll get a basket of food to you soon, and then I'll be back for you within the month, about the third week in June," he promised and mounted his horse, not waiting for my reply.

Pa was asleep inside. He fluttered his lids, and I whispered, "Go back to sleep. I'm just getting my reading material together for next week, then going to tend to Junia."

I set down my heavy bonnet beside the door, peeking inside at the gifts. Pa mumbled faintly and coughed, and I could see he'd gone to bed bone-tired, covered in the coal dust, though it looked like he'd at least given his face and arms a half-hearted swipe with a clean cloth.

"Shh, rest another hour," I said and covered him with his sheet.

Squinting, he groped for my arm. "You... Are you well, Daughter? He take care of you?"

"Yes, sir. Close your eyes now." I hurried to tuck the coarse muslin over him, not wanting to alarm or disturb him with the worries of the day, hoping he'd rest a little more—hoping he wouldn't see what they'd done to me in my eyes.

He hitched his thumb to the stool where he'd laid a coal-blackened envelope addressed to R.C. Cole. "Beck passed that to me for the fire-watcher boy," Pa said sleepily.

Outside, I picked up my book satchel and carefully packed Doc's bottles, the honey, and R.C.'s letter into it, then went to see Junia.

The mule bobbed her head, blowing, whinnying in loud brays, eager to see me. I unlatched the gate and led her out of the shed. She nuzzled my chin, stretched her neck for a scratch, then dropped beside me to roll in the grass.

Junia romped for a good while before I rounded her back into the stall to feed her. The gate wobbled and I fussed with it, sneaking glimpses to the grave. Pa'd tried to fix the door the day he'd buried the preacher, but the old stall guard needed a new post and stronger latch. After I'd finally secured it, I leaned back over to grab the soap, towel, and an old hand mirror of Mama's from the bin, then picked up my lantern and headed over to the creek to bathe, the warm spring day dropping behind the hills, a cooling curtain quivering on its tail.

Wary, I inspected my arms and searched all over. I'd read about medicine and what doctors do. But it was unsettling that it had been done to me. My parents and other folks in the hills cured themselves with nature—tonics, roots, barks, and herbs—unless some stubborn ailment didn't right itself from the homemade potions. They rarely called upon Doc.

I held the mirror up to my face. No matter how many times I'd looked, it always hurt like seeing something horrible for the first time. My skin was still darkened from the hard day, bruised a deep blue. How could the doctors ever change it? I was sure even the strongest potion couldn't do that.

Moving the angle of the looking glass to my backside, I checked my shoulders, calves, and bottom. Satisfied I wasn't permanently harmed and had scratches mostly on my pride, I dried myself with a towel.

When I got back to the cabin, Pa was rambling about, dressing for the mine.

"Pa, it's Saturday, do you have to go? Let me fix you some supper—"

"There's no time, Daughter. There's a special meeting tonight before work."

He meant *secret* and a union meeting at that. Those type of gatherings were as dangerous as cave-ins, explosions, and the miner's lung, and what the Company feared and fought fiercely against. The men clamoring for safer working conditions and more pay were the greatest danger to a mining company. And if the Company got word, they'd shut the meetings down with threats and violence, burn a miner's house or two, or make the leader of those talks disappear.

Pa plowed his socked feet into his boots by the door. "You do okay in the city, Cussy?" He glanced at me.

I wanted to fuss at him like Mama'd done when he had those meetings, beg him not to go, but I couldn't bring myself to argue with him or worry him none about my day. He had enough of that already.

Pulling the dirty sheets off his bed, I said, "Yes, sir. They took themselves blood and skin samples is all." Bent to the mattress, I balled up his linens and glimpsed over my shoulder. Seeing his alarm, I added, "Didn't hurt none. Just some scratches."

"Put some salve on it. And that reminds me. I mean to rent Murphy's horse this week and take the sickle and clean up some of your trails. Thin it all and cut back the briars for you."

"Much obliged." I appreciated he would do that for me and Junia. I picked up his lunch bucket and packed Doc's pear and cheese inside, adding a biscuit from the stove.

He grunted something I couldn't understand, grabbed his coat and bucket, then slipped out the door with a good night trailing over his shoulder, his hat lit and leading him onto a soft, wide path that disappeared into the fog, the tall silent pines soldiering him.

My belly rumbled, and starved, I gobbled down the rest of the cold, stale biscuits I'd baked this morning. Full, I put on fresh bedsheets, boiled Pa's dirty ones, hauled in his bath, and hurried through my chores. Last, I gathered strips of old fabric and scrubbed them with lye, boiled and rinsed and hung them to dry by the woodstove.

Soon, my mind returned to the hospital, and I went over to the mirror and stared and ran a light hand over myself, my face darkening as I tried to imagine what the doctors had done, how much of me they'd taken.

Exhausted in the bone but fully awake in my mind, I looked around for something, anything, to scrub, to wash away the soils of the day. Up in the loft, I shrugged off my clothing and necessaries, changed, and carried the clothes downstairs. When I had washed and rinsed the garments, scoured and scrubbed them again and then once again, until the fires sparked from my raw, bleeding hands and cleansed the day's muddle, my troubled thoughts, only then did I stop.

Satisfied, I rubbed my cramped hands with horse liniment, then sat down and pored through reading material, the newest loans and newsprint. The *Louisville Times* had an article about a fire in the Jefferson Memorial Forest that rangers had battled bravely. Excited for the find, I folded the newspaper to save for R.C.

I put aside a health pamphlet on baby care for Angeline, then went over and pulled one of Mama's novels from the bookshelf. It had been her favorite and mine too, and I clutched it to my chest, suddenly deciding just what I'd do with it. That it would be the boldest thing I'd ever done didn't matter after the hardness of today. Feeling giddy, I packed it with the others.

I remembered Winnie's student asking about the pie recipe and wrote out two different ones for her sister on a scrap of paper and tucked it in my bag.

Pleased, I settled back into the chair to read my other favorite, the *National Geographic*, slowly picking up every word, soaking up all the articles of peoples and faraway places, searching the smart magazine for others like me.

Hours later, I rolled up the dried strips of fabric, got my book satchel, and pulled out the medicine. My hands shook a little holding the precious bottles of laudanum, honey, and alcohol.

I moved over to the stove, reached above to the shelf for Loretta's willow bark. Filled with renewed strength and gratitude, I carefully wrapped it and Doc's gifts and tucked them into my bags.

Worth more than gold, more than chickens, it was exactly what Mr. Moffit needed to live, and what the Moffit family couldn't live without.

Nineteen

Under the quivering fog, Angeline labored in her garden, hilling a row of potatoes, a melody whisking from her lips, the May air tossing her loose hair. Beyond, gusts of spring winds brushed tips of a mustard patch and the waist-high stickweed beyond. Near the porch, a sagging clothesline hung limp between a tall post and a thick tree. Another breeze skittered past the dingy soaked sheets and raggedy clothing, dipping low and sweeping the laundry across the raw earth.

She stood and wiped stained hands on her skirts when she heard Junia's greeting.

"Bluet!" Angeline ran to us, nearly tripping over her long, muddied skirts, splashing barefoot through puddles and kicking up muck. "*Junia*," she cried and planted a kiss on the mule's velvet muzzle, pulled a small carrot from her pocket, and gave it to her.

I dropped to the ground and handed the straps to Angeline. She tethered Junia to the post.

"Is the doc comin'? We's been looking for him every day." Angeline asked with a rise in her voice on the *coming*, slipping her hand into her pockets and plucking out a homemade doll. "Look what I've made for baby Honey."

It was a tiny, faceless doll made from corn husks, its dress a scrap of orchid fabric Angeline had torn from her own skirts.

"It's mighty pretty." I pulled out her seeds I'd wrapped in cheesecloth. "Doc's really busy, Angeline. I'm sorry."

She took them and stared at the package for the longest time, a fright piling onto her pale sweaty face. "But Willie's got the bad fever now," she barely whispered, stuffing Honey's new doll back into her own pocket, her eyes shimmering. "I hain't been able to cool it none."

I fetched her *The Tale of Mrs. Tittlemouse* and the health pamphlet. "Angeline, I've got something else—"

"A *bad* fever," she said and walked away, shaking her head. At the bottom of the rickety porch, she dropped the seeds in the mud and disappeared inside the cabin.

"Angeline," I called after her, fishing inside my bags for the medicines. I hurried up the wobbly stones and high-stepped over the tall, scratchy weeds poking through the rotted planks. Pushing open the door, I peeked inside and softly said her name. Steam rose from a pot atop the stove. Scents of simmering wild grasses hung thick in the shanty.

Angeline knelt on the floor next to the bed, face buried in the covers atop Mr. Moffit, sobbing quietly, her tiny shoulders racked with grief and heartbreak. At the head of the bed, a homemade calendar that Angeline had fashioned from a worm-eaten board dangled against the bedpost. She'd carved out *HONEY* at the top. A scratch of berry-inked X's marked down the days until her baby's arrival.

"Angeline," I called quietly again, going over to her side. "Don't worry none. I brought medicine. Look."

Mr. Moffit groaned in his sleep, and the bedcovers slipped from his leg, showing his wound. The foot was angry red, pocked with yellowish-green pus, a festering sore that seemed to swallow most of his foot. The stink of infection wafted up, watering my eyes, roiling sickly in my belly.

Angeline stood and swept a hard hand across her damp cheekbones.

"I have willow bark for his fever"—I showed her—"and we can clean his foot with this alcohol wash." I pushed the bottles into her hand. "Then you can dress it twice a day with a layer of honey and bandage it with this roll. Here's some laudanum for his rest."

Angeline laid them gently at the foot of the bed, studying the treasures, gliding her dirty fingers over the bottles, while tears streamed from her eyes. She took a shaky breath, suddenly gasped, and clutched my hand to her belly.

"*Oh, oh.* Feel that? Honey's happy she'll have herself a pa," she exclaimed, her bright eyes widening.

I felt the baby's strong rolling kick and then released Angeline's hold. "Let's get that busted foot fixed," I said. Together we went to work, Angeline happily chattering about the baby, the future, and the town's Fourth of July picnic Mr. Moffit promised to take her to.

I boiled the willow and made a tea, then took a pan of water with a rag over to the bed to begin cleaning the wound. But when I lifted Mr. Moffit's leg, he roused awake and cursed me.

"Dammit, don't touch me," he bit, raising his head before collapsing back onto the bed.

"Willie, shush," Angeline said. "Bluet is going to make you better."

"No, no." He coughed. "Ain't having a colored touch me an' bring more infection."

"Willie!" Angeline said sharply. "Don't be ornery!"

I backed away and shifted my eyes to the floor.

"Bluet," Angeline said, "he don't mean it none. It's the fever—"

"Ain't having it." Mr. Moffit barked me back farther, and I stumbled over a boot.

I glanced at him and saw the fear on his face. His fear looked a lot like hatred, or something ugly that had rooted in him and his kin long before me. I turned my head. "Be well, Mr. Moffit."

"Oh, Bluet, he hain't hisself—" Angeline cried out with an outstretched hand.

"Don't forget to clean it with the alcohol before you put on the dressing," I whispered and quickly took my leave.

Twenty

Several hours later, I'd finished my drop-offs at the three cabins and rode into Jackson Lovett's yard, the smells of fresh rain, wild onion, and turned dirt rising into the breeze. Above, fat thunderclouds sailed off to the east, the sheets of rain curtaining layered grandfather ridges that rose beyond.

Jackson worked on a late-spring garden, taking a hoe to one of the many rows he'd cut.

Junia brayed and whinnied, a warning clinging to her last haw. Jackson pulled his shoulders up, laid down his hoe, and walked over to us.

"Easy, girl," I said as Junia snapped a leg frontward, cautioning him not to come any closer.

Jackson pulled a rag from his back pocket and wiped his neck. "Whoa, old girl. I plumb forgot it was Monday. But I'm happy to see you too."

I slid down the prancing mule, tapped her foreleg, pushed her back to try to right myself from a wriggling mess she was causing. Finally, I was able to stand and give a proper greeting, get Jackson's loan out of the saddlebag, and pass it to him.

He wrinkled his brow. "What's this?"

"It's your new loan. Well, not an official library loan. It's my mama's, and I'm loaning it out." It was a fairly decent copy of *Brave New World*.

Surprised, he inspected the dust jacket and thumbed through the pages.

It was a banned book here, but Pa'd saved up for six months and paid his foreman to fetch it from the city for him one Christmas years ago to surprise Mama with it. I searched Jackson's eyes, a worry gathering in mine.

"It's clean enough," I said with a challenge in my voice, but still buckling under a rising peacock-blue blush. I tucked my hands behind my back. The book *was* clean and less soiled than the real-life stories taking place in these dirty hills. In Aldous Huxley's fable of a future world where everyone was safe, no one suffered illness, starved, or did without, and there were no more wars. One of my favorite parts was when the law broke up an ugly riot. They didn't use guns, arrows, sticks, or fists. Instead, they sprayed a strange misty drug over the crowd that made everyone happy.

I imagined the law brewing gallons of Skullcap and using the old nerve tonic and mad-dog herb to do the same when needed around here.

Brushing a lock from my face, I tucked it back under my bonnet, then unclasped my feral hands, now worried I'd been too bold in front of this patron. *What if he went to the Center and told?* I could lose my job for passing a banned book. They would banish me from the books forever. Maybe even think up a worse punishment. At that, my hands itched to snatch the book back and flee.

Jackson said, "Your mother has good taste."

"*Had*, she done passed."

"I'm sorry for your loss," he said with sincerity, and looked again at the book. "Hmm, clean you say? I've been sorely wanting to read this one but never could get my hands on it. Thank you, Cussy Mary."

I was pleased. More than pleased. Thrilled.

"Let me get your library loan," he said and strolled across the yard and into his cabin, returning a minute later with an apple and the Cobb book I'd left with him the last time, along with a different book atop it.

He handed me his loan and a copy of *Sons* by Pearl S. Buck. "Have you read it yet?"

"No, but I've heard good things about it, and I've read *The Good Earth*. It won the Pulitzer." I tried to hand the book back.

He raised a palm. "It would be my pleasure if you'd read it. And, yes, *Earth* deserved the prize, but I lost that one out west. An excellent book."

"I liked O-Lan best," I said, thinking how O-Lan know'd she was too ugly to be loved.

Jackson stared at me a moment, then said, "She was the real hero, you know?"

"O-Lan was sure enough brave." I admired him saying so. "And I liked how she didn't have to say much neither."

"What's unsaid can be just as important," Jackson commented.

I nodded, excited to be able to talk about books with him.

"I especially liked Farmer Lung's love of the land," Jackson said and looked admiringly out at his own. "The power of land held a connection I could reckon with... For me, the earth gives life, and without it, we have none, not the smallest breath."

"Pa says if we hurt it, it won't feed us. That's what the Company's doing."

"He's right. And the Company is careless. I haven't see a lot of bees up here like when I was young. You hurt ol' Mother Earth, and she's going to paddle your hindside. The same as she did to Farmer Lung."

I clutched the book to my chest. "I'll start on it tonight."

"If you like it, I have her other in the set, *A House Divided*. You're welcome to read them both."

"Much obliged. I didn't think I'd ever get to read her others. Miss Eula and Miss Harriett scolded that her books weren't proper for Kentuckians and could lead to tempting the good morals of our people, and offend deeply religious minds."

"Miss Eula and—?"

"The librarian supervisors at the Center."

"I imagine they might make a small mind bigger." Jackson grinned playfully, tossing the apple from hand to hand.

"Reckon that wouldn't be such a bad thing," I said, taking in his easy smile and friendly chatter. "Much obliged, I best get back to my route."

"And I need to get the soil worked before I can cut the timber and daylight's gone an' bedded." He was strong like a tree, the cut of his face like the mountains surrounding us.

"You sure have yourself plenty of room to build up here," I said, not wanting to leave but knowing I should.

"Eventually I will. It'll take a lot of work. And I'm not a rich man, just a fool one with a strong back." He straightened, loosening the creaks and cramps of overworked bones.

I clasped my hands. "I don't mean to pry."

"I don't mind. I'm selling the lumber. I've got more orders for it than I can handle by myself. Enough woods and work to last two lifetimes."

I hated to think of it all bare, hurting the earth like that, but there was big business in timber and bigger money if a man wanted to work hard. "Sure is pretty."

"I'll take only enough trees to have myself a proper barn, to thin these woods some and bring new growth."

I nodded. And then because I had said too much, stayed too long already, "Let's get to our books, Junia. Thank you for the loan. Good day."

"It's a fine read. I can't wait to hear what you think of this one." He followed me over to Junia.

I stopped. That he would care astonished me, and I could only bleat out another thank-you.

"How's the ol' girl doing today?" he asked the mule and held up the apple.

Junia pricked her ears forward, wiggled her back muscles as I mounted her.

Jackson took out his knife, cut a big slice, and held it up to the mule.

I shifted in the saddle, an uncomfortable rumble vibrating my belly. It had been ages since breakfast, and dinner was still two drops away.

Junia snatched it up quickly, her big choppers savoring, enjoying.

Jackson took a bite, swallowed, then said, "Would you like some?" He cut another slice and lifted up a fat piece to me.

It was a kind present. This and the one in my bags would save me till supper. Before I could think twice, I leaned over Junia's side to take the slice at the same time Jackson stepped over to me. I grasped the fruit, our hands touching.

Junia screamed, swung her head sideways, braying loudly at him. The apple slipped from our hands and fell to the ground.

I jerked on the mule's reins. Jackson nearly tumbled backward.

Junia stomped on the fruit, then barreled out of the yard with me holding on tight, her indignant cries cobbled across Jackson's amused laughter.

Twenty-One

A short time later, the clouds parted as I rode into the schoolyard, scattering a brood of chickens and a cluster of loud, chasing boys.

Winnie rushed out of the schoolhouse, shooing the hens and students out of her way.

"I didn't think you'd make it this Monday, Cussy Mary," she said. "So glad you did."

I stayed atop Junia. "Sorry, I'm running behind today. I'll fetch your books," I said, feeling guilty because I'd tarried too long at the Moffits and Jackson Lovett's.

Winnie sent Clementine back inside for the loans.

The children, all hankering for a peek at the new material, circled around their teacher. I called over Nessie and handed her the recipes for her sister to bake for the big dance, and she spun around and curtsied, then waved the paper. "I'll have to learn her, 'cause she can't read. Thank you, Book Woman." The other girls gathered around her as she read the recipes to them.

I scanned the student's faces searching for Henry. He stood in the back of the group, a weakness in his eyes.

In a minute, Clementine flew back out of the building, stumbled, and dropped the books, kicking up a kaleidoscope of swallowtails.

Henry dashed over to her and scowled, picked up the books and dusted the jackets off on his pant legs and sleeves, scolding her as he ran up to me.

"Here you are, ma'am," he said, and blew on the books, again swiping the covers with his arms.

Henry's face was more hollowed, his bones again poked out of ragged clothes that had been passed down too many times and were tight and ill-fitting.

"Thank you, Henry." I bent over and caught the red, glossy necklace circling his neck, the thick scaly rash on his palms. He had the pellagra and was starving to death. And right before my eyes.

With a steady hand, I took the books from him and slipped them into my bags, stretched around to my other satchel, pulling out my saved dinner. I held up the apple.

"Everyone inside." Winnie clapped loudly, hurrying over to me, and gave a sharp startling clap once more, sending Henry and her pupils skittering back into their classroom and Junia toe-hopping nervously. "Inside. To your desks. Now," she warned, and clapped once more. Dampness blotted under the armpits of her dress, spreading to her chest.

When they were all inside, Winnie said firmly, "You can't feed one, Cussy Mary, without feeding them all. They *all* have the hunger, just some of their bodies are able to hide the sickness better than the others."

She was right, and it wouldn't be fair. Ashamed, I lowered the fruit to my side.

Winnie clasped her hands. "If only we could get more outreach programs up here. If only they could send a block of cheese with every book, a loaf of bread." She tilted her head to the sky as if telling it all to God.

I wished it too. Their hunger for books could teach them of a better life free of the hunger, but without food they'd never live long enough or have the strength to find it.

"Just one damn block of cheese," Winnie scratched out in a whisper.

I thought about the cheese Doc promised. If I could bargain with him for more food, I could give it to the schoolchildren.

Winnie sighed, stroked Junia's neck, then gently took the

apple from my hand, slipped it into her dress pocket. "Henry's new baby didn't make it," she said quietly.

Saddened, I turned to the schoolhouse and saw a blush of boys peeking out the window. One was Henry.

"I'll make sure I give this to him." Winnie patted her pocket. "Ride safe and give my best to Martha Hannah and the children." She turned, her long skirts bristling as she hurried back to her charges.

From inside, Henry pressed his head to the pane, watching me. I tossed him a smile and vowed silently to get him food. The boy broke into a sluggish grin, struggled to raise the window— once, then again—but was too weak. He coughed, pressed his rash-reddened hand to the glass, and mouthed, *Goodbye, Book Woman.* Then he was gone, his handprint a milk-ghosted blur disappearing into glass, a shiver left needling my spine.

Twenty-Two

After we left the schoolyard, I stopped on the path and double-checked my bags. I didn't have a newsmagazine for Mr. Prine so I headed straight to Martha Hannah's, looking forward to having an extra moment to chat with her and the young'uns.

I sang lightly as Junia rode us around a covey of oaks, trampled over squawroot and showy jewelweed, until she stopped and sounded an alarm.

I'd been thinking about the medical tests, the food. How much I could get from the doc in exchange for giving him more blood. I wondered just how much blood a person could lose, then remembered the article I'd read about Marie Antoinette's bloodletting she'd gotten while giving birth. How it didn't hurt her none to lose the blood.

Then I turned my mind to the book Jackson Lovett loaned me and became so riddled in thoughts of him that I hadn't kept a keen eye on the paths. I'd been speculating about his life, his kin. Jackson Lovett had burrowed into me like a tune I couldn't turn off, like the popular Benny Goodman song "Blue Moon" that played on Harriett's radio from time to time. I scolded myself and vowed not to pry into my patron's affairs, to keep a quiet tongue around the man next time. I'd been too bold and risked my job as well.

Junia blew hard as if shaming me, and I snapped my head up and pressed a hand to my galloping heart, half expecting to see Frazier lurking in the woods, still stalking me.

I cupped my eyes against the sun, relieved to see Martha Hannah's husband, Devil John, and not another Frazier. But his stance offered no relief, but something more, something disquieting and unbending, and I feared troublesome for me.

"Book Woman," he called out, standing there in his thin britches and faded shirt, a long rifle strapped over his shoulder. Devil John Smith was a moonshiner and, folks whispered, one of the best. He wore a black floppy hat with a raccoon dick fastened above the brim, what the bootleggers placed in a still's copper worm to direct the flow into the catch jug so there wouldn't be any loss of shine, and a handy way to alert a thirsty fellar he was in the business.

"Mr. Smith." I chanced a wobbly smile, stiffened atop the saddle.

"Ma'am." He tipped his hat. "I've come to tell you there's a problem with them books," he said soberly.

I felt my smile slip downward.

Junia blew a hot breath, and I wrapped the reins tighter around my sweating hands.

Devil John went on. "The young'uns won't do their chores, and yesterday, Martha Hannah was nearly an hour late with my supper. An hour! Them books are doing that—surely making them lazy. The girls are letting the laundry an' sewing pile up around their ears, and the boys are reading at the creek when they ought to be fishing and working the garden. Plumb can't get 'em to work 'cause they's so busy sitting and reading them foolish books you're bent on bringing. And I can't have it. Won't have it."

"I'm sorry, Mr. Smith," I said, secretly touched they loved the books so dearly. Without the loans, his young'uns couldn't learn because the moonshiner refused to send them to school. No man, no Kentucky law, could make a hillman do that. Most folks hadn't even heard it was law. The land had its own decrees, held tight its hard ways of handling harder things. Folks would pack their little ones off to school only if it suited them, and not because of something written somewhere far away by city folks they'd never seen, or would ever see.

"They've wasted the kerosene and burnt all the candles and damn near broke me," Devil John complained.

I reached into my satchel and held up a tape-covered magazine and a scrapbook. "Maybe these will help, sir."

Devil John grimaced, shaking his head. "Ain't got no use for any more of them highfalutin books that fritters away time. It's costing me good oil and wick and food, Book Woman! My farming's gone to seed from laziness. *Wasteful*."

"This is *Boys' Life*. And look, sir, here's a good mountain book full of housecleaning tips and sewing."

He balled up his fists, crossed his arms.

"Mr. Smith, the Boy Scouts just sent this latest magazine in. It's about hunting and fishing, and there's Bible stories inside."

He took a minute mulling it over.

"Sir, *Boys' Life* teaches a young'un how to knot rope, make a good fishing cane, and trap rabbit. Good hunting tips inside there, sir." I dismounted and walked the magazine and scrapbook over to him. Though it was said he never partook, only bootlegged to provide for his family, Devil John still smelled of sweet mash from working his still—the angels' share and what folks called the escaping spirits inside barrels. He loomed over me in his cow shoes, the large wooden blocks carved into cow hoofs that he'd attached to his boot soles to leave hoofprints and trick the revenuers.

"Mr. Smith, there's also an interesting article on tanning and some nice prayers they can learn. There's some old church bulletins and a pastor's sermons inside the scrapbook."

"*Sermons!*" he boomed, locking eyes with mine. "I don't need a charlatan's fire-wagging finger up my ass. The likes of that ol' devil Frazier pastor's falsehoods in my home."

Junia blew hard and stomped a hoof. I gasped and tore my eyes away, shaking inside, but not before I heard something more in how he'd said it. My mind pulled to Frazier's attack.

I'd seen a shadow and heard a noise that day. Had Devil John found Junia and sent her back to me? Had he seen Frazier accost me? Seen where Frazier lay?

Devil John saw a lot in these woods, know'd every stick and stink of it. Finally I caught my breath and squeaked out, "No, sir. Yes, sir."

He frowned and scanned the woods, thinking. "It's been a while since I've seen the false parson man, and if I never hear from him again, it'll be none too soon."

I swallowed my agreement.

He quieted a bit. "My Martha Hannah sees to their Bible studies—reads to 'em at first light and every night," he clipped, darting his eyes to the *Boys' Life* and then to me, and once more back to the magazine, before snatching it from my hand and quickly fanning the pages.

"Yes, sir, I'm sure Martha Hannah does a fine job. And there's a lot of other fine things in the scrapbook for her, some tasty recipes for her to make." The book shook a little in my hand. "There's a pattern for britches and instructions for making a good hickory basket and a couple of canning recipes. Lot of fine chores in there, Mr. Smith." I opened the scrapbook and showed him a recipe for sweet bread and another for a meat-and-onion pie. "That's Mrs. Hamilton's prized pie." I tapped the page and handed to him, hoping he'd let his wife have it.

"My garden ain't even hoed 'cause they's been reading too much." Still, he took it and pondered whether to trust what I'd said. Not knowing how to read, Devil John weighed it in his hands and snuck glimpses at me and the recipes. He opened the *Boys' Life* again, tapped a title beside a fish. "What's this say, Book Woman?"

"A boy's guide to fishing," I slowly read, underlining the words with my finger.

"A boy's guide to fishing," he mouthed and trailed the print. "This word here," he pointed, "says 'boy.'"

"Yes, sir. Boy, *b-o-y*."

He worked his tongue over the spelling. "This one's 'fishin','" then?"

"Fish-ing," I slowly pronounced, pausing my finger at the syllables. "*F-i-s-h-i-n-g.*"

"Fish-n'." He followed earnestly, mouthing the letters again, and then stole another glance at the scrapbook I held.

Junia nudged my back, rested her head on my shoulder, and kept her big eyes nailed on him.

"Uh, Mr. Smith, did I mention that Mrs. Hamilton's husband also has a dandy tip on picking the best witch sticks in there?"

Devil John tucked the *Boys' Life* under his arm and flipped through the scrapbook.

"Real good diviner tips, sir." Mountainfolk and bootleggers always looked for good water and places for new wells. Diviner Mr. Hamilton was a reputable water witch, and he'd used his forked peach switches to find water for decades, staking the spot when the twig pulled to it. It was true nary a soul ever dug a dry hole when Mr. Hamilton witched for a well. Hamilton's finds were so accurate that folks said he could tell a fellar how many feet down the water was by the number of times his switch nodded over a spot.

"Well, I reckon these can't hurt none. Might get 'em working," Devil John said lazily, tugging his beard. Another long moment passed, then, "But only bring the canning and recipe books after planting and after harvest. *Only that. Only then.* They'll not have the others till winter, and only after I see to it they've finished their chores. And not a minute sooner." He clutched the books in the crook of his arm and lifted a finger. "Not *one* Kentucky second sooner, Book Woman."

"Yes, sir." I swallowed hard. "Please give Martha Hannah and the young'uns my regards." I watched him slip catlike into the trees despite his big, clunky cow shoes. A dangerous man and also a strong, providing one, but someone you dared not cross. I wiped a damp brow and hurried Junia onward toward Miss Loretta's. We wouldn't rest until safely through the forest.

Twenty-Three

When R.C. Cole spotted me late Wednesday morning, he raised his arm, let out a whoop atop the tower railing, and flew down the steps barefoot like a bald hornet had lit after him, the steel stairs trumpeting an echo across Hogtail Mountain that clanged against rock face.

At the bottom, he absently shoved me his loan, practically dancing for the envelope while tucking the newspaper I handed him under a sweaty arm without even a glance.

"I found an article about a forest fire," I said, and gave him the letter from Mr. Beck and went over to mount Junia, leaving him to his privacy.

He ripped open the envelope. I heard a hiss, turned, and saw his paling face, the tears blurring and reddening his eyes.

"He done said no," R.C. murmured, swiping the back of his hand across his lids. "*No.* Said I wasn't good enough for Ruth, and my work ain't honorable, an' I ain't got myself a proper home for his daughter." R.C. rattled the letter. "He aims to have her take a coal miner for a husband." He thrust a fisted letter into the air. "A *coal miner.*"

I whisked out a sorry for him.

"I get good pay, and I'll get more when I'm a ranger. I'll build her a fine home, finer than any coal miner could." He slapped the letter against his leg. "I will!"

"I know'd you can do it, R.C. Just keep reading, and I'll keep bringing the books."

"Look." He lifted the paper and tapped the page. "He says he won't give her hand to anyone in the *We Poke Along* program. Calls it lazy work."

I winced. That's what some folks called the WPA program. A lot of men around these parts would rather starve than participate. They thought it was charity, dishonorable, and downright sinful to take the 75 cents a day the government offered to erect simple outdoor privies for folks who had none, build access roads into the hills and around, or lay split-timber bridges across creeks. *Lazy work*, the prouder hillmen claimed.

R.C. stretched his neck up to the watchtower, misery rippling across his freckled brow. *"But I love her..."*

He slowly folded the letter and rolled it into the newspaper, tucking it all into his loose waistband. "I ain't letting her go. Ain't letting a dirt digger have my girl."

I cringed thinking about Pa and the other miners, but know'd the young boy was hurting and didn't mean it.

"I've got to get to the train depot. Get my bride," he said and clenched his jaw and took off down the mountain, his feet pounding the declaration into the red-dirt path.

I didn't know a lick about matters of the heart other than what I'd read in books, but my hand curled into a tight fist and lifted up his declaration for a victory.

Twenty-Four

For the rest of May leading up to the Pie Bake Dance, there was talk about Vester Frazier's disappearance, and a few suspicions on his whereabouts, everything from him running off with a floozy to him falling prey to a hungry bear or pack of mean dogs. Folks around here had heard about my short union with Charlie Frazier, but they didn't know spit about his kin accosting me.

The talk didn't bother me much. Folks know'd the Blues were unchurched and didn't associate with the preacher. But I couldn't help fearing he'd be discovered, worry on what Devil John might've seen, worrying more that Doc would let something slip, or someone's hunting dog would come along and dig him up. Lately, I'd been peeking behind Junia's stall, scattering leaves atop the preacher's grave, piling on more sticks, rock, then dragging logs from the woodpile onto it. Made sure he stayed good 'n' put, couldn't push his devil-rotted, fire-wagging fingers up from the black earth and grab himself another sinner.

Pa'd fussed at me and ordered me to stop, saying I was making it worse by stacking a big marker like that. But I couldn't stop fretting over Frazier's grave, stop piling on more debris. The last week of May rolled in, and Pa made sure I wouldn't fuss the matter again. I awoke and found the site cleared, the hole empty, and Pa's conversation just as vacant.

Folks' talk drifted from the missing preacher to the union fighting for more pay and better working conditions for the miners and the young boys picking slate down in the hole and making pleas for better living quarters in the mine camp on the other side of town. The Company came back with a vengeance against the union; there was more violence, threats of shutting down the mines, and coal miners' strange disappearances.

Beginning with Pa's.

Two days earlier, I had come home from my route and found him gone, thinking he was off to one of his meetings. But the next morning, when he still hadn't returned, I was beside myself. I'd paced the cabin spitting out prayers, wearing the old floorboards until the rhythm of the creaks and groans skint my nerves and drove me outside. I ran over to Junia's stall and cried out, "We've got to go find him."

We trailed Pa's route to work, searching for any clues of an animal attack, anything that might lead me to him, until we saw the mine in the distance, and I pulled the reins and brought Junia to a halt. I was frantic for news, but I didn't dare go closer and I couldn't ask openly in town. Hoping to get word of Pa's whereabouts, I'd penned a letter yesterday when he still hadn't returned. I addressed it to Mr. Moore, a coal miner I'd heard Pa speak kindly of, and then boldly rode over to Queenie's house and asked her grandma Willow to give it to her. It'd taken half the morning, and I spent the rest of the day riding the mule hard to make up the lost time taken from my book route.

Pa'd been gone three days now, and I hadn't three seconds of peace worrying it all.

And when the couriers had left notes at the librarians' outpost requesting we come into the Center a week early to help with the large delivery the railroad had left, I was more than eager, hoping Queenie would bring news of Pa, or I'd see him in town.

Inside the Center, I sorted the mail and reading material at my table, keeping an eye on the Company store across the street and on the lookout for Pa. If I heard noises outside, I'd rush over to the window to see if it was Queenie, hoping Willow remembered to give her my letter.

Several times I dropped things, the nerves whittling me down. When Harriett slammed a stack of catalog cards onto my table, I jumped, knocking books onto the floor.

"What's wrong with you?" she snapped, looking at me suspiciously, slapping down more cards. "You sick or something?" She took a step away from me. "You've been clumsy all morning."

"No, ma'am. Sorry," I mumbled, and picked up the books and began sorting the cards into the makeshift filing cabinets we'd made from cheese boxes the Company store had set out for trash, while Eula and Harriett gossiped about the upcoming dance this Friday.

Out of the corner of my eye, I spotted Doc outside, and he raised a friendly hand in passing. He still hadn't dropped off the promised basket of food, and I wished I could ask him about it. Doc had mentioned the last time we drove from Lexington that he'd pick me up the third Saturday in June, so I reckoned I'd have to wait till then to talk to him.

I looked over at Eula and Harriett talking about the Pie Bake Dance, tempted to slip out and speak with him, but I quickly lost my courage when he disappeared into the Company store. I'd make sure to ask him for the food on the way to the city. It was a relief knowing Winnie would have it for her schoolchildren, and for a few minutes I let myself imagine the students stuffed and happy, looking like the fattened children in my storybooks.

Eula changed the conversation and chatted about the Penny Fund that Lena Nofcier was starting, and I perked at the mention. Miss Nofcier was the chairman of the librarian service for the Kentucky PTA and pushed each member to donate a penny to purchase new books.

It sure would be something to have a room full of new books—satchels brimming with 'em—and to see the looks on the hillfolks' faces. It would be thrilling to hand out stacks of the latest newspapers, and brightly colored magazines, and books with their perfect new covers, fresh ink, and crisp pages.

I kept an eye on the street and filed the catalog cards, picking up pieces of Eula and Harriett's other tattles, one about a partial cave-in at the mine, the Company shutting down coal production and pulling out, somebody's lost hunting dog, and the recent births of several babies.

I'd heard about the cave-in weeks ago when Pa told me about the two small boys who had to be dug out.

Both of the women dropped their voices to a near whisper, looked around in all directions, and right past me. They didn't care if I heard. My presence was of no more matter than a spent moth on a sill. Still, I'd kept an ear bent, listening for the hard and hurtful things others might say about me and mine. Seems I had learned to hear a lot of talk that other folks didn't think I could.

Harriett prattled while binding a book. "Mrs. Vance had her babe seven months after she wed, though she's claiming a sudden fever brought it early."

"It had fingernails on it like an old woman's," Eula said. "Nine months of nail growing if I've ever seen one."

"Nine months after he first came a'courtin'," Harriett snorted.

"Oh, did you see Mable Moss's new baby?" Eula's eyes rounded. "It was born with an ugly red stain across its long tongue that ran out onto its lip that ain't lifted."

"Uh-huh. And Mable's done insisted the baby got it by falling off the birthing bed," Harriett said. "I pity poor Mr. Moss having wed the homely girl only for her to give him a long-tongued liar."

"It is surely the mark of a liar," Eula agreed gravely.

I moved up by the women to stack books onto the old loft ladders we'd hung across the walls for the books. Stepping behind their tables, I kept an eye on them and an ear cocked to their words, hoping for any news of the missing miners, of Pa.

They whispered about other folks' latest ailings, Harriett's newest, and the Lysol douche she was using to cure it. I stretched my ear to listen to Harriett's shocking illness.

"It's—" Harriett stood and leaned over her table toward Eula, grabbing the edge. In an elaborately hushed voice, she said, "Well, I'd had this horrible itch." Harriett pointed to Eula's privates, then jerked her flushed face up when Eula's gaze fell below Harriett's belly. "I couldn't go to the physician. It wouldn't be proper." She paused, snatched glances all around again for anyone who might've slipped into the Center, her face coloring ripe red.

Eula bobbed her head in sympathy, though there weren't none in her rounding eyes.

"Well..." Harriett dipped her voice lower and caused me to strain. "Then I spied an advertisement in *Movie Mirror*. Mind you, I was only checking it for any filthiness that might offend our God-fearing patrons when I saw a picture of the brown bottle of Lysol, touting the inner rinse that would clean and kill germs."

I had also seen the feminine hygiene advertisements in magazines and newspapers. The pictures of the weeping lady with a dainty hankie to her eyes showed she'd been a *good mother, good housekeeper, good hostess, good cook*, all those things, until 6:00 p.m.

The feminine wash advertisement scolded the sad lady, insisted the perfect homemaker did one disgraceful thing her husband couldn't forgive by forgetting her smelly lady parts. It warned womenfolk about the dangers of neglecting intimate personal hygiene and reminded them to use the *feminine wash to keep from wrecking a marriage*. A *powerful germicide*, the product promised, and one that removes all kinds of powerful things and even stranger things I'd never heard of like "organic matter"... *It will keep your man happy and is a surety for a happy marriage.*

I squeezed another book onto the shelf and glanced outside, gave a prayer for Pa's safety.

Harriett continued, "I had my cousin over in Virginny send me the Lysol right away. But when Postmaster Bill handed me my package, it was busted open. That simpleton gave me the bottle right in front of God and everyone." Harriett pressed a hand to her chest.

"Oh my!" Eula knocked a fist against her own.

"The postmaster blubbered something about 'spring cleaning,' and I snatched it from his hands and took it home, and fast. *Lawd*, that Lysol fixed me good and proper," Harriett said, proud of her new cure. "Just in time. Oh, Cory Lincoln's coming to the dance on Friday," she added and this time louder.

Cory Lincoln was Harriett's cousin she was sweet on. He got hired on at the coal mine after being released from the penitentiary last month. And by *just in time* she meant it was the upcoming annual dance and pie auction time.

"I finished my dress," Harriett told Eula and raised a sly brow.

"Oh," Eula exclaimed. "Did you use the lace on the hem or—?"

"You'll see," Harriett singsonged, her eyes mischievous, holding a secret.

They talked excitedly about which man might win their company for the dance night, speculated on who they hoped would, and side-talked about the other girls, handpicking dull suitors for them, bursts of cackling punctuating each insult.

I pushed books into the ladder rung and moved to the next section, then heard Junia fuss outside and went over to the window. She pawed and strained from her tethered post.

Jackson Lovett stood in front of her, dressed in high-waisted stylish pants held up by suspenders like I'd seen in the magazines. He had a bouquet of blue flowers tied together with a ribbon. It looked like he was trying to get past her, maybe come inside the Center, or more likely pick something up in the post office. But the old mule blocked him.

I watched, knowing who'd win the argument. I wanted to raise the window and caution him, but the thought of doing so in front of the supervisors stopped me.

Junia blew at him, her loud snorts filling the quiet, sunny morning.

Peeking over my shoulder to the supervisors and back to Jackson, I lifted the window, careful not to disturb the already frayed rope cords that held the lead weights. I was determined to warn him again about the old mule's temper.

I glanced back once more to Eula and Harriett, tucked tight as fatted ticks in their gossip.

I stuck my head out just as Junia pricked her ears forward, hovered over the flowers and sweetly raised her nose over the bouquet, then snatched them, gnashing them in her teeth, chewing them like they were her special gift from him, gobbling them in one bite. She flopped her ears at him, pleased.

Jackson struck a mild curse and pulled the ribbon loose from her jaw. A flower fell along with it, both fluttering to the ground.

Junia showed her teeth as if thanking him, brushing his hand with her soft mouth.

"You like flowers too, old girl?" Jackson softly chuckled, scratched Junia's ear, and patted her neck—and she let him, the first man I'd ever seen her allow that privilege.

I pressed my hand to my mouth and choked back a giggle, surprised at the quickly eaten flowers, at my astonishment for how the two got along, at my wishing.

"Those were for a pretty lady," he said to Junia, not giving any hint that he'd seen me gawking out the window.

I wondered who Jackson might be courting, what old woman he was visiting.

Jackson looked up and around and then directly at me. He called out, "I imagine Junia's like all the ladies, liking herself some pretty flowers now and then."

I took a small step back from the window and bumped into Harriett, who'd snuck up behind me. She screeched and knocked me aside with her hip.

Harriett's eyes pulled to Jackson, then back to me and once more at Jackson.

"See you soon, Cussy Mary," Jackson said.

Smiling the whole time, he picked up a single bloom from the dirt, tucked it into his shirt pocket, tipped his hat, and strolled away.

"You've been staring out there daydreaming all day. Get back to work." Harriett slammed the window shut, rattling the heavy glass and snapping the old window pulley rope on one side, the weight clattering down inside the frame. "Keep it shut! It reeks enough in here without letting in your filthy mule's stinky droppings too."

Harriett raised her chin, pinched her nose, thudded back over to her table, and plopped heavily into her seat, scattering papers. "Stinkin' inbred," she huffed.

Eula pretended to read her mail.

Harriett clucked to Eula, "Jackson's a fine one to greet our Blueberry. A charitable man to pity her, waste greetings on her kind."

I turned away, kept my eyes on Junia outside, a tear weighting my cheek. I know'd Harriett's mama had married kin, that *her* kind had relations with close relatives. It just didn't show up in her pasty-white flesh, only in the small eyes hugging her sky-saluting nose. Her clan was the same as most kinfolk in these parts. Courting was hard, and a horse and mule could only travel so far, making it difficult to meet and marry outside these hills. Still, my great-grandpa'd done just that, all the way from France. And here Harriett was the one who pined after her cousin.

I turned partway to Harriett. She had her head bent over a box of catalog cards. *Stinkin'*, she'd called me. Tilting my head, I rolled my shoulder into it and sniffed under my arm. I smelled the same as everyone else, better than some.

"I said, get back to work," Harriett squawked.

I snuck one more glance out the window for Pa, worrying where he could be, before slinking quietly over to the shelf.

Another librarian walked out of the post office into our room, and a hush fell over the room. Eighteen-year-old Birdie, the youngest Pack Horse librarian, walked past me. Her route was along the rocky creek beds and across the river into the neighboring community of Silver Shale. Birdie would tie her horse to a tree on the banks, take a small boat to haul her books across, then hike her route the rest of the way.

She was a thin, tall girl who Harriett poked fun at and called

Bird Nest, always taunting her by asking if she was hiding one way up there, each time with a cackle at her own sorry, worn poke.

"Howdy, Bluet." Birdie shot me a bright smile. "I had a devil of a time rounding up Ol' Paul. That lazy horse didn't want to get moving and wouldn't come out of his stall. Me neither." She winked. I smiled back. Birdie grabbed a box of outdated textbooks and pulled the carton atop an empty table, yawning. "And the baby fussed most of the night."

Birdie's husband had moved out of Troublesome for factory work in the city, leaving her alone with the babe till he could fetch her.

"Morn'—" I whispered.

"Morning, Bird Nest," Harriett snipped into my return greeting.

Birdie said, "And a good morning to you too," and mumbled an added "Miss Bird Brain" behind Harriett's back.

Constance Poole walked into the Center, bigger than two singing Sundays in her pretty dress, snappy and stylish, as she breezed right past me. "I've got some new sewing patterns for your help," she told Eula, the last word dripping airish. Constance was the head of the sewing bee club, and she would donate quilt and dress patterns to the Center from time to time for the mountain scrapbooks. She always enjoyed stopping by to tell stories about her monthly sewing club: the young talented ladies who always had so much fun trading fabric, threads, and cheerful conversations.

Eula and Harriett huddled around her and bent heads to the matters of the Pie Bake Dance, sharing giggles and fast whispers.

After a few minutes, Constance told the supervisors she was off to shop for thread and pie ingredients. "Just three days to the big dance, ladies, and I still haven't decided on my pie," she told the supervisors. Constance stepped far around me, snipping off a short greeting of "Widow Frazier" as she swept past.

Queenie came in through the back door and dropped her pannier onto a table, then rummaged in her sack.

Harriett switched on the radio.

I fixed my eyes on Queenie, trying to see if they held a secret for me, that she'd gotten my note, word from Pa, but Queenie was flitting about.

"Morning, Queenie," me and Birdie called out, while Eula and Harriett swallowed any regards as if she weren't there.

Queenie murmured hello and busied herself, rooted inside her bags.

"Start on the crates the railroad left," Harriett ordered Queenie.

"Not today," Queenie snipped back.

Every six weeks or so, crates of books came in from library centers around Kentucky. We'd exchange books and send them back, packing the wooden boxes with about fifty books each, to be hauled over to the railroad depot. The L&N Railroad donated the shipping costs, carrying the books to other Kentucky libraries and dropping new ones off to us, free of charge.

Unpacking the new books, loading the crates back up, and then setting them out to be picked up could be backbreaking work. Harriett always put it off on Queenie first, saying it would silence her sassing mouth, and if she wasn't around, she'd push it on me.

Queenie pulled out an envelope and wagged it at Harriett. "I got the job. *Assistant librarian* for the big Free Library of Philadelphia. I'm here to shelve my books and then off to the post office to send my acceptance. Pack them yourself." Queenie walked over and slapped the envelope onto Harriett's desk.

Harriett leaned back, and her hands flew up. She wouldn't touch the envelope. Eula rushed over to her assistant's desk and opened the letter.

Eula glanced at the note and then back to Queenie. She finally folded the letter and stuffed it back into the envelope. "Post a job opening, Harriett," Eula said, wiping her hands with a hankie. "Let everyone know."

"Gladly," Harriett chirped and snapped up a long sheet of paper and began to write the advertisement.

"Spread the word, librarians," Eula said to me and Birdie. "We can't lose this route."

It would be hard to get someone to apply for the tough route, and the patrons would suffer, dearly miss their books. I ticked through all my patrons, my daily routes, and stopped at one of my male patrons.

"Yes, ma'am. Congratulations, Queenie," Birdie sang out, interrupting my thoughts.

Queenie beamed.

"Congratulations," I said, but worriedly searched her shining eyes, looking for any hint of news of my pa.

"That sure is a wonderful promotion," Birdie said.

"Sure is, Miss Birdie, thank you," Queenie said. "And $4.85 of extra wonderful a month."

Harriett made a hissing sound. "That's a crime to pay a darkie more. Why, we only get 95 cents more a month, Eula. *Eula?*"

"Indeed," Eula barely breathed, her hard eyes pounding on Queenie's backside.

"Eula, you need to write a letter immediately and ask for more," Harriett griped. "I'm going to send in a complaint to the Philadelphia library and tell them it is shameful to waste top dollar on the likes of *them*." Harriett nailed a scowl onto Queenie and cut a bigger one at me.

I know'd my job was about to get harder with Queenie leaving, and with me being the only colored, I'd suffer twice as much. But even Harriett couldn't steal my grin. I was so proud of Queenie. Admired her courage and envied it at the same time. Philadelphia. Assistant librarian.

I joined her side. Queenie held out her hands, and I took them eagerly and squeezed.

"What grand news," I said, meaning it. "It'll be a fine place for you and your family." I held onto her a bit longer, search-ing her face for news. "*Pa.*" I dropped the word in a whisper. But Queenie's eyes were jeweled with tears, and she didn't see anything but her future out of here. She said, "Oh, honey, they have a great collection of Charles Dickens letters and, oh, the manuscripts and—"

"You'll get to see it all, touch them," I said, knowing how fond she was of the old author.

"They're training Negro librarians now at the Hampton Institute." She wiped her wet cheek with the back of her hand.

"You'd sure make a good one." I pulled out my clean hankie, handed it to her, letting my hand linger on hers. I leaned in closer and barely whispered again, "Did you get—"

"Back to work!" Harriett ordered. And to Eula, "*Lawd*, these lazy coloreds'll use any excuse not to work."

Queenie sassed her with her eyes.

A few minutes later, Queenie sidled up alongside me, shelved a book over my shoulder, and gently bumped me.

She pushed a note into my hand and whispered, "From your papa. I'll come by before I leave." She slipped back over to her worktable to get the rest of her books.

My heart pounded so hard I feared it would rip the buttons off my dress and knock itself out. Quickly, I stuffed the letter into my pocket and hurried to shelve the last books in my pile, dropping nearly half of them onto the floor along the way. Harriett mumbled something rude, and I rushed to finish. Done, I grabbed my bag and one newspaper out of a handmade broom-handle rack beside Harriett's table and was out the door, the screen clapping into the supervisors' fury.

"Widow Frazier—" Eula cried out.

"*Bluet!* Bluet, you need my permission for newsprint," Harriett yelled. "Get back here, or I'll see you down on them bloody-blue knees scrubbing my ladies' latrine and polishing the floors. Eula, make her—"

For once, I didn't care what Harriett thought or what punishment she'd dish out to me. I had myself a newspaper for my patron, Queenie was going to be the assistant librarian in a big city, and, the very best, Pa was safe.

Twenty-Five

I waited until I was a far piece from town before I rested. A relief washed over me that Pa was alive. Nothing was more important than my only family left, and I forgot about everything but him. Then, fear of what Queenie'd done hit me cold. If the Company had found her with the letter, passing notes from union men, they would have beaten her, then burned her out of her home, maybe murdered her, gone after her family. That I'd put Queenie in danger by using her and her patron to get word to Pa left me shamed, terrified for her.

It was just last year when the Company had gone to Gordon Brown's home at the miners' camp after they'd found his wife passed letters from her husband to gather miners for a strike. When they didn't find Mr. Brown, they ransacked the house, destroyed every stick inside, then lay in wait all night to shoot her husband. The next day, when Brown still hadn't come home, the Company bosses evicted the wife and their seven children. Not a week later, a sympathetic barrister in the next county went to meet with Company bosses on behalf of the Brown family and other wronged miners. Two days later, the young lawyer was killed when his motorcar was bombed.

My hands picked up a tremble and I touched my pocket, pressed my palm against the letter. Queenie was safe. Pa was safe. That's all that mattered, I told myself. Slowly, I scanned the trees, looking behind me and all around. Twice, and then a third time to make sure I was alone.

Junia led us along a wooded path as I tore open the envelope and read as best as I could, again pausing to look over my shoulder in case Company bosses were afoot.

Pa's letter said he was near the Tennessee line in *family talks* and was in good health and would be home in two nights. *Family talks* was code for *mine meetings*.

Another two nights…

Here he'd never been out of these hollers more than two minutes. I worried about these talks and the trouble he could be getting himself into—the unrest with the miners, the dangers they were stirring up.

Mama'd fretted it and loudly when she was alive. But every time I'd try to talk to Pa about it, he'd rail a bit, then walk away grumbling.

Junia halted, and that's when I saw it in our path. The mule pawed and stomped a warning, but the rattlesnake stilled, slowly coiled itself into a tight S, rose partway up, forked its tongue, and wagged its rattler, refusing to slither away.

I pulled Junia's reins, nudging her to circle around. But the ol' girl weren't having none of it. Flicking her tail, she stared off to the left and bared chomping teeth.

I snapped the reins.

The snake shook its rattler harder, raising it.

"Back, ol' girl. Ghee around now," I cautioned.

The mule snorted, backstepped, and teetered, raring to stomp. I tugged again, ordering her to pull back and around, like we'd done before, and to give the creature time to cross.

"Back, Junia, whoa, *whoa*," I commanded, dug harder into her sides. "*Easy!*"

Then I was falling, hitting the earth, tumbling toward the snake. My hands went to my face, and I curled myself into a ball to ward off its deadly strike.

Hooves pounded the earth, and then a strangled cry shivered

the pines. For a second I couldn't make out if it was mine, Junia's, or another's.

I let out a few hard breaths and dared to open my eyes. To my horror, Pa's letter rested next to the snake. Wriggling, I rolled over onto my belly, crawled, inched toward it, and slowly stretched out my arm, my eyes locked to the serpent, my fingers almost on the paper.

An explosion rang out, and Junia bawled into the thundering blast of gunshot. I recoiled and cradled my head, a terror striking like no other that the Company had found me out.

Dropping my face into the dirt, I wrapped my arms over my head, the weight of my crime pummeling my chest, shoveling me into a shallow grave, my flesh exposed, bait for the snake's poison, for the Company men's bullets. Seconds later, footfalls sounded, then quieted, and I risked raising my head slightly to peek.

Angeline stood on the leaf-scattered trail with her arm clasped over a small pouting belly, an old rope looped loosely around her swollen waist and knotted with a dead rabbit dangling against her skirts, a floppy brown hat atop her blond head, the sulk dragging her mouth, a polkstalk gripped hard in her white-knuckled hand.

"Junia, you ol' ill-tempered Apostle. *Scat!*" Angeline lightly knocked the mule's knees with the butt of her gun, tapping her away from the dead snake. "Back. That's my supper, and you hain't gonna smush it 'fore I can get it in the skillet."

"Ang...Angeline," I barely breathed, and pulled myself onto my knees. I pressed my hands to my pounding chest, took another quaking breath, and slowly rose.

Angeline latched onto my arm and helped steady me upright.

"The mule—she wouldn't go off the trail," I said.

Junia nickered loudly. She had her nose aimed to the side, ears flicking, looking at nothing but a smatter of rock in tall grass.

"Dammit," Angeline said, and dropped my arm.

She broke down her single-shot, pulled out the spent shell, retrieved a new one from her skirts, and reloaded. I scrambled for Junia's reins. Aiming the barrel over to the base of the rock, she fired, sending up dirt, grass, and a knot of baby snakes.

Burnt gunpowder filled the air.

Angeline rushed over to rocks. "Got 'em. It's the nest, sure 'nough," she said. "That's why Junia wouldn't go around, scared she'd step on it." Angeline poked it with her gun. "That ol' rattler was gonna make sure she didn't either." Angeline turned back to me. "Oh, Bluet, you hain't hurt none, are you?"

I let out a breath. "Fine. Thanks, Angeline." I slapped the dirt off my sleeves, flexing my hands, and inspecting for any injuries. "I didn't expect you out here."

Angeline plucked a torn leaf from my hair, rubbed off a smudge of dirt from my cheek. "I'm getting food now that we's got some bullets from the tinker man passing through. Willie traded him some ginseng root."

She looked a little wild standing there, fierce, her tanned feet comfortable atop ancient knobby tree roots like the earth was her Cinderella slipper. The loose plait in her light hair glistened in a blade of sunlight.

For a minute I envied her, wanted to send Junia home, unlace my heavy, tight shoes, and run free with her to escape Frazier, the doc and his medical tests, and everything damning me—to hunt and fish in the woods like I'd done as a child. To be wilded. Have a wilded heart in this black-treed land full of wilded creatures. There were notches in these hills where a stranger wouldn't tread, dared not venture—the needle-eyed coves and skinny blinds behind rocks, the strangling parts of the blackened-green hills— but Angeline and hillfolk here were wilded and not afraid. And I longed to lift bare feet onto ancient paths and be wilded once again.

Angeline said, "Willie'll be out here fetching victuals soon. He's getting well now. Been hobbling out to the garden and back every day. Them bottles you gave us sure are curing him."

"I'm glad to hear it."

Angeline lifted my hand to her mouth and kissed it. "Thank you for saving him, Bluet."

I snatched it back.

"You ought not do that, Angeline. Someone might see you touching me. A Blue. And they could cause you trouble. It might anger Willie—"

"Hmph. Willie totes his pride in a beggar's cup. He wouldn't be here if not for you. And hain't caring a snit 'bout those that don't care none for me and mine." She gave a bright smile. "Here it's already June, and Honey'll be here next month and have herself a pa now 'cause of you." Angeline bent over and grabbed the snake, tying it to her rope. "And I got us fine meat, more'n one supper's worth."

Supper. I licked my lips, tasting. There'd been so little of it lately. Tonight I'd hunt for nettles to have soup.

Twenty-Six

I cooked a pot of nettles on Friday, hoping for Pa's return. The bright-green broth simmered atop the stove as the June breeze slipped into the warm cabin, stirring the earthy scents, the long day beckoning the dusk.

I tried to read Jackson's book, but I jumped up at every creaking board and rattling pane, and soon the uneasiness drove me out to the yard. Restless for Pa's arrival, I searched the trees, startled at every falling leaf and acorn. Darkness was near, and I watched as the last bird hurried to its nest.

Unable to stand it any longer, I grabbed a lantern and rode Junia toward Troublesome.

In town, we circled around the Company store several times, the night sky cloaking us. I checked in back of the courthouse for Pa or any miners, and over at the post office, hoping I'd see him, then moseyed over to the old feed store.

Music and merriment spilled out. Surprised, I halted Junia, dismounted, and tethered her to a post. I'd forgotten about the Pie Bake Dance, that it was the first Friday in June. Slipping up to a side window, I peeked in.

The menfolk had slicked-backed hairdos and clean-shaven faces. Most dressed in city jackets and tall-waisted britches, huddled in small groups, eyeing each other and the women. It was a fancy to-do and only something I could touch in my books.

I marveled at the ladies' tight-fitting dresses of bold prints with their big, puffy sleeves, pretty buttons, and smart-looking belts. I glimpsed a few Bette Davis–style hairdos like the big movie star wore in the magazines. Sitting in straight-back chairs, the ladies waited for the pie auction, tapped snappy heels on weathered boards, chatting nervously with each other and sneaking peeks to the men and pie auction table.

A long table brimmed with pies. Behind it, three men played the fiddles while another cupped a harmonica, their saucy tunes whisking lively around the smoky hall, escaping through cracks to the quiet streets of Troublesome. A few bold fellars picked partners, and the couples danced gaily on sawdust floors through wisps of tobacco smoke.

I spotted Constance Poole. Her sewing ladies crowded behind her, watching out of the corner of their eyes as she talked to the men. Tonight she wore a stylish pear-green dress, a silk sash drawn tightly around her slim waist, her perfectly coiffed hair swept back with a fancy matching ribbon. Constance chatted with two woodsmen, and I watched them lean in and dote on every word.

I glanced at the table of pies and wondered which one she had baked—how many would pitch for it. I thought of my own recipe with its hints of sweet, dark sorghum and buttery crust that I would sometimes make for Pa. For a moment I let myself fancy a man bidding on it, and then giggled at the thought and clamped a hand over my mouth. I hadn't heard my foolery since Mama passed. To hear what had been silenced for so long felt like I'd stolen it from another. I tested it again, louder this time.

Junia snorted, collaring my vanity and falseness, and I cut a shushing eye at her and turned back to the window.

Harriett stood over in a corner hanging on her cousin's arm, her new dress hemline boldly short, nearly naked leg to her knees.

A man struck out a verse from "Liza Jane," and the fiddlers picked up the lively tune while everyone moved to the middle and formed two lines, the ladies on one side and the men on the opposite. The two at the far end stepped forward, greeted each other with a curtsy and bow, and hooked arms and began circling around each other, clasping palms, kicking up their heels down between the lines. Another took their spot and did the same to the claps and toe-tapping of others.

It was all dreamy, like a slick city magazine advertisement. Resting my chin on the sill, I pressed in closer.

The fiddlers slowed their tune to a soft, sweet melody, the notes bending into the raw warbles of the harp player as couples broke off from the line to dance in corners.

I felt the music in my hips, the light air sweeping into my singing hands. I wanted to twirl, dance again like Pa and Mama'd done on our porch when my uncle would stop by with his fiddle. At the end, Uncle Colton would slow down his tune, and Mama would sing an old French lullaby, "Au Clair de la Lune." Her voice would lift softly into the damp night air, lose itself in the droplets of darkness. I'd join in to sing the beautiful French words, while Pa's gravelly voice would pick up a chorus in English. Mama always had a tear in her eye when he'd finished.

> "By the light of the moon,
> My friend Pierrot,
> Lend me your quill
> To write a word.
> My candle is dead,
> I have no light left."

Swept up in the wonderment, the gussied-up folks, the music, and the exciting might of it left me awestruck. In my nineteen years I had never witnessed such, couldn't imagine the splendor of the Pie Bake dance that Eula and Harriett spoke of, much less it happening in Troublesome.

Glued, I didn't see him slip up behind me until it was too late. His whiskey breath was hot on my neck, and his big arms circled around, grabbing my breasts. My scream rippled across Junia's.

The man pushed himself into my back and slurred drunkenly

into my ear, "Now, why's a sweet thing like yourself outside here all by your lonesome, sugar?"

"Leave me be!" I tried to move, but he tightened his hold. The terror rose in my throat, thick and bile-tasting.

"That ain't no way to treat a friendly fellar wanting some pie."

"Let me go. *Please!*" I tried to push away from the brick and escape. But he had me pinned hard against the building.

Out of the corner of my eye, I watched Junia strain and buck, trying to break free of her post, her cries climbing into the music. She'd kill him if her tether broke.

Again, I screamed out and struggled against him. He shoved my forehead into the brick, cutting my head, his clamped hand over my mouth, snaking his other one downward. "Give ol' Allen some of that tasty pie, sugar."

A loud thump sounded, and the man went limp and fell to the ground. I spun around and saw him wriggle in the dirt, cradle his head.

Sheriff Davies Kimbo stood over him, holding his gun.

I backed up into the shadowy wall.

"Allen Thompson," the sheriff called, "you got one minute to get your sorry drunk ass back over to Cut Shin. I catch you 'round here again, you'll be spending time in my jail." He kicked the man hard in the side and smacked the butt of the gun against his palm. "*Git.*"

Junia's cries carried into the night air, low and quavering.

Turtle-like, the man rose, unsteady, holding a hand to the back of his head, the other to his gut. He wobbled and tumbled into me. Then his mouth flew open when he got a look, and his red-mapped eyes rounded big and ugly. "*You!*" The drunken man stabbed a finger. "Gotdammit, you's a circus freak!" He spit at me, and the dribble landed on my chest. I raised my arms over my face, backed into the wall, trying to escape.

Cursing, the sheriff grabbed the man by the shoulders and threw him into the street. The drunk scrambled away.

Sheriff turned to me and I tucked my head, moved deeper into the shadowed lip of the building.

"Who's there?" Sheriff took a step. "Bluet"—he squinted—"that you, girl?"

I mewed out a weak "Yes."

"Why are you in town?" Sheriff holstered his gun.

"I, uh—"

"Does Elijah know you're here?"

I cast my eyes down.

"You on book business? What are you doing here, girl?"

I tried to think up a lie. Before I could, he pointed to the feed store door. "The Pie Bake. You trying to go to the dance? Is that it?"

"No! I... Oh, no, sir. I just wanted to see what it was like."

He shook his head and frowned. "Now, Bluet, I got myself a daughter 'bout your age who used to go to the dance before she wedded, but rules are rules. I can't have you breaking the law, offending these folks on their big to-do night." He poked his heavily whiskered chin to the NO COLOREDS sign. "I got a bunch of rowdy imbibers in there who I'm responsible for. And I can't do that if I'm tending to your kind. Get on home to Elijah, girl."

"Yes—no, sir. I'll be on my way. Sorry for the trouble, Sheriff. It won't happen again."

I turned toward Junia and took two steps before Sheriff called out, "By the way, Bluet, you seen my relation anywhere up there on your book routes? Ol' Vester near your part of the woods? That ol' boy's been lying low."

I paused, the question nearly toppling me. *Lying six feet low.* My mind rattled and looped around the horror.

Sheriff went on, "Preacher man's nowhere to be found, and as much as I don't miss that, I'm hoping the ol' boy didn't get himself into trouble."

"Preacher Frazier?" I asked casually, keeping my eyes parked on Junia, forcing myself to keep walking toward the mule and not look back at the lawman. When I reached Junia, my hands pressed into her fur, stroking, petting, drawing a strength. "No, sir, Sheriff, I never see a living soul on my book route—nary a one but my patrons."

Oh, but I'd seen the dead ones, and I know'd if Sheriff could see my eyes in the dark night, he'd see them in there too.

Twenty-Seven

I rode the mule hard back to the cove, vowing not to breathe a word to Pa about going to town, and praying the sheriff wouldn't either. I didn't need Pa going off and trying to defend my honor, to place us in bigger danger.

Restless, I did chores while I waited for his return. When I finished sweeping the floors, I paused at the mirror to smooth back my hair, studying my reflection, thinking about the ladies at the dance, their fancy dresses and stylish dos. I leaned into the looking glass and twisted a lock around my finger, and then remembering something I'd seen, emptied my satchel and thumbed through the old magazines until I found it again. Using penciled sketches, the article explained how to curl hair with hairpins. Below that illustration, a lady showed how to craft strips of fabric to make pretty locks. I scanned the room. Weren't no such hair fasteners in my home, but I had plenty of rags.

Up in the loft, I rummaged through Mama's old trunk and found a leftover piece of old material she'd saved. I carried it down the ladder and cut it up into narrow strips, then dampened the rags using a small pail of water.

In front of the mirror, I pulled out a section of my hair, carefully wrapping the ends around the strip of fabric a couple of times, rolling it all to my scalp before tying the rags into tight knots.

When I finished I stared at myself. An old ballad spilled from my lips, and I stretched out an arm and pretended to accept a dance with a fine man who'd won my pie. I twirled around the room once, twice, and again and again until I stubbed my toe on Pa's bedpost and yelped. I winced and limped back over to the looking glass. Feeling foolish and looking it, I yanked out all the rag curls and turned my darkening face away from the mirror, untangling my damp hair, scratching at my head.

After a fitful night, Pa waltzed in at dawn, spent and grumpy. A bruise bloomed on his eye, and a cut climbed across his cheek. He slapped a bulging knapsack onto the table. "Got you some rabbits. Done got the damn bobcat too." He pointed to the porch. "I'll make you a warm muff for next winter. And 'fore I forget, I ran into Doc out there. He reminded that he'll pick you up two weeks from Saturday."

I knocked the bag onto the floor, sending the limp critters flying across the old wooden floor. "Pa, you have to stop going! These *talks* are dangerous—"

"Hold your tongue! The men picked me, and I have to speak for my fellow miners to get better pay and safer work conditions! It's thievery down in the shafts, the lung sickness waiting to snatch your last breath. The miserable long hours. And the Company bosses who'd murder anyone who wants better than that—they scalp our land, leave behind the dirt an' ash, their broken coal trucks and ghost camps. They've left their filthy, fancy boot prints everywhere on everything, the poor 'tucky man's back. Why, even the fish are dying from the poisons running into our streams."

"Why you? Can't someone else do it?" A clamminess slid into my hands, and I couldn't help but wonder if the other miners chose him because of his color—because they believed his life was of less value, like the mules they sent in to check for leaking gases.

"Pa, is it because you're a Blue?"

He wouldn't answer, but I could see it there in his eyes, the truth he hid, and I wished more than anything that he was white, and that the burden of his dangerous work wouldn't be doubled by our ugly color.

If only I could keep him safe. I felt a catch in my throat and realized more than anything now, I wanted the whiteness for him. A peace that he'd never had. And for a moment, I allowed myself to think how life could be easier, safer, for both of us if we weren't colored. I sent up a silent prayer that Doc would find a cure, and quick-like.

"Pa?" I touched his sleeve. "Is it because you're blue—"

"It's because I'm a Kentucky *miner*, and a damn good one!" he barked hoarsely.

"Oh, Pa, forgive me. I didn't—" My words broke apart. Swathed in my own misery, I wrapped my arms around him, tightened, and soon felt his forgiveness in the steady pats to my back.

Doc arrived at 7:00 a.m. for our Lexington trip on the third Saturday in June, just as the morning fog crawled up cedar bark, snaking its way out of our cove.

Inside his motorcar, Doc passed me the latest issue of the *Lexington Herald-Leader* newspaper. Despite his kind gift, I was glum. I wanted to ask about food, but it felt too needy. I thought to ask him about the tests coming, but I was too afraid to hear his answers. We rode mostly in silence to the hospital except when he pointed out landmarks and offered the names of big horse farms.

"Magnificent beasts, aren't they?" he said. "Those buildings are stalls."

"They live in those?" I said, astonished.

Doc slowed, and I gawked at the stately buildings that housed the kings of horse racing, the princes of Kentucky, stared at the magnificent beasts grazing on land as green as emeralds, lush as velvet, content and fattened in their riches.

"They do indeed." Doc nodded.

"Ain't never seen anything so fancy. Such big mansions. And built just for beasts at that. Reckon their masters live in castles?"

"Castles indeed," he said, smiling. And I searched the countryside, trying to glimpse one.

When we pulled into the hospital lot, I found my courage and turned to Doc and said, "I'll do your tests, but not with them nuns." As bad as I wanted the whiteness for me and Pa right now, and the food for the young'uns, I'd seen a scarier color in the nuns' mean hearts and was terrified they would kill me.

Doc raised a brow.

"I mean it," I mustered, shaking a little inside from my daring, and peeled back my coat to show him Pa's hunting knife sheathed in cracked red leather. "They's—" I caught myself. "They're not going to touch me again. And I'll not take off my necessaries!"

I saw the beginning of a protest in Doc's face, but then he said, "We'll make sure they're not a bother to you, my dear... and I'll protect your modesty."

Emboldened, I held his gaze and waited for his promise.

"I give you my word."

I dropped my flap. "And I need food, a lot of food," I said, thinking about the schoolchildren. "We've been hungry. *Starved.*"

"There's a carton in the back. You'll find it full."

I turned around and saw it brimming with cheeses and bread. Relieved, I pressed my face to the window, stared out at the vast grounds, my own heart full of gratitude, near bursting.

Mistaking my gratefulness for worry, Doc reached over and patted my shoulder. "We'll find a cure, Bluet. We will."

To have food for the young'uns and now his declaration would be a fancy like none in my books.

Inside the hospital, we passed the nuns, and I cut them the meanest eye I could give, a rumbling hiss in my throat threatening to slip off my tongue and scratch. Doc hurried me along to the Colored Ward, not stopping when one of the nuns greeted him.

Inside the ward, a little girl stuck her head out of a room. When the young'un saw me, she let out a shriek and started crying.

A nun came running and scooped up the hysterical girl, shielding the child's face from mine.

Doc grabbed my arm and dragged me past. Inside the quiet examining room, Dr. Mills and the mountain doc asked lots of questions and made notes with each of my answers.

"Do you drink? Does your family partake of alcohol? Run a still, maybe mix it with something other than grain?" Dr. Mills asked.

I tightened my mouth, glared back my noes.

"Bluet and her father are hard workers, of good character and moral cloth, Randall," Doc said softly, but a little miffed.

No one had ever said such about Blues, and I looked at Doc, appreciative, and saw he meant it.

"Any illnesses, ailings?" Dr. Mills looked at me closely.

I raised my hand to my bad ear, lightly touched it, and shook my head, not wanting to tell him about Frazier and the ailings he'd left me with. The busted arm still pained me sometimes, and the ear was just about spent.

A smart-dressed lady wandered into the room, sat down quietly in the corner chair with a pen and pad, and took notes too.

I eyed her warily, making sure she wasn't a nun in disguise.

The doctors examined more charts, X-rays. "The heart and lungs are normal," Dr. Mills said. "What about the father, Thomas?" He turned to Doc.

Doc glanced at me and then said low, "He's an ailing coal miner. We'll discuss Mr. Carter later, shall we?"

They took my temperature, asked me curious questions about kin. "Do you know about your kins' backgrounds?" Dr. Mills asked. "Their names? Who they married?"

"Yes, sir. Would you like me to write them down for you?"

"You write?" he asked.

Doc placed a hand on my arm and said, "Our Bluet is a librarian for the Pack Horse project. A smart book woman for our little town." His voice was proud, like a papa bragging on his child.

"Librarian? In Troublesome?" Dr. Mills said, wrinkling his dark forehead, exchanging glances with the Doc.

"Yes, a librarian, and in Troublesome." Doc smiled at me.

"Get her a pen and paper, Miss Palmer," Dr. Mills said to the woman.

"Yes, sir." The lady handed me a pen and clean sheet of paper, and I bent over the table and scribbled down names while the doctors hovered over me peeking at my script.

Deliberately, I slowed, fancied it up some like Mama'd taught me, looping my letters fat and just right, giving them the perfect slant.

I paused and raised the tip of the pen to my lips, tapped, and thought some more.

Weren't many of my kin I couldn't name, but there were a few I'd missed, couldn't recollect. There'd been cousins and great-aunts and great-uncles, a few I'd never met, those who'd been shamed, suffered embarrassment, and were driven deeper into the hills and hidden coves, and still others who'd been hanged, ones who had fled the old Kaintuck mountains and were lost and had eventually died out, Pa'd said.

"I'm the last of me, Pa says, and I am not sure I have them all. Pa would know best."

Doc said, "That's fine, my dear. I'll have Elijah help fill in the rest."

It seemed Dr. Mills weren't convinced of my smarts, and he tacked a chart onto the back of the door with lines of letters and asked me to read them from the top.

"I already showed you I know'd my letters." Offended, I crossed my arms and refused. Doc quickly explained about the special eye chart that would check my vision. "If your vision isn't strong, Bluet, we could correct it and fit you for spectacles."

When I passed the test, they asked about food, what we ate and didn't eat.

"Rabbit, squirrel, berries, and lots of poke sallet...same as most when we can find it," I ticked off. "Pa sometimes trades his game, and hunts roots and herbs to exchange for eggs, corn, and tomatoes. Sometimes we have turkey or wild boar." I didn't tell him that lately there hadn't been much of anything with Pa's sickness, other than the rare sack of rabbits he'd surprised me with.

The men asked the ages of every single kin I could remember, and how long they'd lived.

I perked. "Except for Mama being struck with the influenza, and Pa having the miner's sickness, all my kin are healthy and lived good long lives, near their eighties and some past ninety, my folks always claimed. Except Daniel and the ones who'd been killed because of the color... At least a few I know'd of, more that Pa hasn't talked about. We have the notes in our Bible back home."

"Remarkable longevity, don't you think, Thomas?" Dr. Mills piped up.

"We're strong enough when left alone," I said.

Doc's face reddened like the hospital's rose brick. The colored doctor's gaze fell away. Then Doc cleared his throat, picked up a paper, and studied it. The lady taking notes stopped and gave me a gentle smile, like she was proud, maybe pitying too.

Dr. Mills coughed lightly. "Well now, let's see." He studied me in silence for an uncomfortable time, then turned to the old mountain doctor. "I'm stumped, old boy."

Doc grew excited. "Have you read Scott's report about the hereditary blood disorder he discovered among the Alaskan Eskimos and Indians?"

"Why, yes." The other doctor's eyes lit. "I recall he speculated it was caused by an absence of a certain enzyme. Could it be the same?"

Doc answered, "I'm not sure. It might be something to consider."

"I'd like to admit her. Keep her for a few days, maybe a week," Dr. Mills said. "Miss Palmer, go get the papers."

The woman nodded and slipped out the door.

Alarmed, I stuck my hand inside my coat, gripped the knife handle. "I ain't staying," I said icily, backing up toward the door.

"No need for that, Randall," Doc said, his old eyes watching me. "Bluet has her job and her father to tend to. We wouldn't want to keep her from her ailing pa and her important government job."

Dr. Mills shook his head and folded his arms, leaned back against the cabinet. "I don't need consent, Thomas. I could quarantine her. It would be, say, in the public's best health interest," he said slyly. "My duty to the people—"

"The hell you will!" Doc thundered. "I will not allow you keep this healthy young woman locked up here for *your* interest! You of all people should know what persecution feels like. You've worn those scarring leathers your entire life."

Dr. Mills flinched, touched the small of his back, like he had indeed.

"Step out into the hall, Dr. Mills," Doc said. To me, "Bluet, stay put."

The doctors left and shut the door.

Outside I heard their voices rise, jumbling over one another. It got quiet for a bit, then I heard cussing. And more cussing, and even more hard-flying words. Then someone or something thumped against the door. I scurried over to the far wall and reached for my knife just as they walked back in.

Dr. Mills tugged at his crumpled white topcoat that had slipped partway off a shoulder.

"Now," Doc said, smoothing down his own coat and running fingers through his winter-white hair. "Bluet, I think I'd like to take more blood samples to conduct this new testing to see if the Blues lack the same enzyme as the Indians and Eskimos. Would that be okay? You'd just need to roll up a sleeve, nothing more."

I looked over at the jar of leeches and bloodletting tools, and Doc's eyes followed.

"We'll take it from an arm with a syringe, and only a small amount. Won't hurt a bit, Bluet," he assured me. "Then we'll take our leave because we've already used enough of Dr. Mills's time." He cut an eye to the doctor. "Isn't that right, Randall?" Dr. Mills brushed a hand down his topcoat and reluctantly nodded.

I lifted my arm up a little.

"Very good." Doc said. "It could make you a little faint, maybe even a little nauseated." He reached for the needle. "But it'll pass quickly."

Alarmed, I tucked my arm back to the side, looked at the doctors. I'd passed out when the nuns gave me the medicine. They'd done all kinds of horrible things to me while I slept.

"Don't worry, it's only a tiny pinch. Then I'll see you back to Elijah safe and sound," Doc pushed. "If we're to find a cure, it's the only way, Bluet. The only way."

Pa's words rushed back in. *It's the only way to keep us from the hangman's noose.*

"It's absolutely necessary to find a cure," Doc pressed. "I want to see you cured. Help your pa. Don't you?" His eyes softened.

To think I could rid myself of not just my color but Pa's too, and the attacks and all the pains that came with it, would be worth the dangers now. Worth the frightening tests. Thinking about home, the folks in Troublesome, my job and Pa's, there weren't nothing I'd like better right now, and I rolled up a sleeve. The doctors gaped at the blue arm darkening from my excitement.

"Bluet?" old doc asked again.

"Yes!" I blurted, raring to take my leave, to get out, to not waste any more time.

I shoved my arm toward him.

Twenty-Eight

There'd been two blocks of cheese, three loaves of bread, one jar of jam, four pieces of fruit, and a dozen small squares of molasses taffy in the food carton from Doc. I'd counted it three times and each time touching it all with shaky hands. In the distance, a church bell lifted from the valley, calling up Sunday service. *Sunday, and what better day than the Lord's Day to help the children.* Most would arrive to class tomorrow with empty bellies. So I stole away with Junia in the morning darkness with the damp June air on my face.

My lantern cast ribbons of light across the empty schoolyard, and I snuffed out the flame, slid off Junia, quickly untied the heavy pannier she carried. In the dimness, chickens rolled out soft clucks. Junia hawed back, shushing them.

Tiptoeing up to the porch, I went to the corner post and tied the food sack to a beam, high and out of reach from any critters.

I stepped out into the yard and inspected my work. Standing there as the sun rose over the mountains, lighting the old shadow-sleeping land in oranges and dusty yellows, felt like a prayer, like I was standing in Sunday church. And I couldn't help bowing my head to pray to Him, giving thanks for this blessing. To think that the young'uns would have their bellies full in the morning was worth doing Doc's tests.

"Let's get home, ol' girl," I said to Junia and mounted, my heart full, near bursting.

On Wednesday, I was frightened by a loud banging on the cabin door that clattered the panes, threatening the old glass.

That night I'd been sitting, reading about Wang Lung's youngest boy in *Sons*. Startled, I jumped up, flipping the chair backward. My bare feet slapped across the wood floors, and I scrambled for the shotgun.

"*Bluet*," the familiar voice boomed from outside the door, "it's me."

I pushed the gun back under the bed, ran over, and opened the door with a pounding heart. "Doc, what are you doing out... Oh, you nearly knocked the color off my skin." I pressed my hand to my chest, then laughed nervously.

Doc grinned and raised his medicine bag. "I aim to do just that. Let's get inside, and quick. I have something to show you." He plopped down his satchel on the table. "It was tricky, but I've learned of your illness."

Puzzled, I quieted.

"Well, my dear, you and your kin have methemoglobinemia."

"Met...globe, what?"

"Sit down. Let me explain it."

I took a seat, and he picked up the fallen chair next to me, righted it, and joined me at the table.

"It's a blood disorder, Bluet." His eyes twinkled. "The new blood tests revealed that you're missing the same enzyme as the Indians and Eskimos. You have what's called methemoglobinemia," he said again.

That there was finally a name to my peculiarity astonished me; that it could be as big as that word scared me.

Doc must've seen my relief and fear because he reached over and patted my hand. "You're fine. Will be just fine. It's a rare heredity disorder that causes the blueness. Your parents carried the same recessive gene. A very rare gene."

"*Rare gene.*" Stunned, I still didn't understand.

"The Carters all have this in their blood, from way back to your great-grandparents and beyond. You and your kin's blood simply isn't oxygenated. And that makes it harder to reach the body tissues. Your skin." He lightly pinched the fat between his thumb and finger.

"Met...heme." I struggled with the big word again.

Doc raised a finger and said it real slow. "Met-he-mo-a-glo-bi-ne-mia."

I tasted the word on my tongue. Then braved it again and a little more correctly. "Met-he-mo-a-glo-bi-ne-mia."

Doc nodded his approval.

I said it once more to claim it.

He reached into his bag, pulled out a stethoscope, and listened to my heart. "Very good," Doc said. Then he took out a glass bottle and a needle. "Now, the very best part. This is a drug called methylene blue, my dear. It came to my attention that it might be the perfect antidote."

Confused, I peered closer at the big needle.

"I'd like to give you a shot. If it works, you won't have to go back to Lexington anymore. I can study...um, tend to you here in Troublesome."

At that, I quickly rolled up my sleeve.

"We'll start with a hundred milligrams." He filled the needle. "The drug will give your blood more oxygen and reverse your color. They started using this a few years ago for an antidote to carbon monoxide and cyanide poisoning."

Cyanide. I'd read about it in my books.

"You let me know if anything bothers you, if your ticker acts up, gets to hurting."

Hurting. I pressed a hand over my heart and held my breath. Some medicinal herbs could right a person just fine, or stop a ticker dead.

Before I could change my mind, he shot the injection into my vein. I flexed my elbow, rubbed the tiny prick. Moments later, I watched in awe as my hands turned to a normal white.

Doc clasped his palm over mine. "A miracle," he exclaimed, "nothing short of. Bluet, you're as white as flour! Come see." He pulled me over to the mirror hanging beside the pine washstand in the corner. "Astonishing," he whispered. "How do you feel? Any discomfort?" He listened to my heart again and murmured, "Good."

"I feel same as before, Doc." But I turned back to the mirror and know'd I wasn't, nor would never be. I brushed my hand slowly over my face, poked my lips that had colored a pretty pink, my cheeks a soft rose. *Normal.* I peered again at the stranger looking back at me, then looked at Doc, questioning.

"Modern medicine," he exclaimed.

"I'm a stranger." I stared at my reflection.

"A right pretty stranger at that," Doc commented. I gazed back to the glass and inspected closer.

Pretty. Could it be? My neck looked white, like linen that matched my hands. I raised a palm and lightly braced it against the base of my neck. A tear rolled off my cheek, then another and several more, splashing onto my white hand. I was white, and that pretty white stranger was me. *Me.*

Doc squeezed my shoulder.

Except for his rope of veins, his hands and forearm nearly matched mine. I lifted my dress to my ankles and peered down at my feet. "They're even white," I said unbelievably.

"Flour white," Doc said again, and proud.

"*White.*" I pinched my cheeks, smacked my lips together twice, astonished they didn't turn blue. Then I parted my mouth to utter my surprise when, suddenly, a pain seized my scalp and my head pounded. In seconds, my belly lurched. Covering my mouth, I flew to the door, raced out into the darkness. In the middle of the yard, I bent over and emptied my stomach, once, and then again.

From behind, Doc called, "Bluet, my dear—"

I swung a hand out, motioning him away.

Doc touched my shoulder. "The nausea usually disappears. A brief thing, just a nuisance, don't worry."

"My head hurts," I said.

"Let's get you back inside and check your heart, get you some rest. It's just temporary," he said again and took my arm.

Temporary it was.

The flour white, that is.

By the time I woke Thursday morning, I could see the miracle drug leaving my skin, emptying itself into my piss jar. I carried the chamber pot down the ladder and tossed the blue urine outside.

Doc came by shortly after Pa got home.

My skin had nearly returned to blue. Still, I had the whiteness, and Pa could see for himself the medicine worked.

"Elijah," Doc coaxed, "at least have a tablet if you won't take the injection. I've brought enough for both of you to take for a week, and I'll bring more. Just one a day'll do it." He set the pill bottle on the table.

"Take it," I begged. "It'll make things better—"

"Try one, Elijah," Doc urged.

Pa said, "Look at me, man." He held out his coal-stained hands, pointed to his dust-blackened face, then thumped his chest, smacking out a flurry of coal dust. Again, Pa hit his chest and coughed. "The only thing that I'm needing fixed is this black sickness inside of me. Have you any tonic to cure that, Doctor?"

Doc grimaced and squeezed Pa's shoulder. Most of his patients suffered from the lung disease.

Dismayed at Pa's refusal, I scooped a dipper into a bucket of water, took a big gulp, and swallowed a tablet, hoping he'd change his mind. "Pa, please, just one. *One.*"

Pa waved a hand, dismissing the offer.

Doc asked Pa questions, the names of our relatives. Absently, Pa told him. The doctor took out a pad and wrote them down, then pried some more, needling him for information on our kin.

Shortly, my heart banged and seized hold of my head, all of it churning, turning my belly. I lifted my hands to see that I'd turned back to white.

Baffled, Pa coughed violently. "White as a lily. Lily," he barked out.

For a moment I felt like his perfect little girl. I smiled and fetched him some water.

"A white daughter." Pa hushed the words and took a sip. Shocked, he sank down on the chair and studied me. Doc talked to him more about the tests and the medical journal piece he planned to write.

"Pa, you can go to the mine as a white man. Take one."

But Pa weren't listening to me or the doc, and a few minutes later, I flew out the door to relieve my stomach same as last night.

Finished, I crept back inside. Pa gawked at me, alarmed. "Daughter, are you hurt?"

Doc shook his head. "No. It's temporary, Elijah. Like the drug."

"Temporary? Then it's a vanity, not a cure," Pa snapped.

I winced.

"She should feel better directly. It's just a little discomfort that'll right itself, Bluet," the doc said with sympathy in his voice.

"Prideful," Pa grumbled. "Dangerous."

"It's a safe cure," Doc insisted. "And Bluet's strong."

Pa scowled. "Belladonna cures ails too, and it'll turn mean an' slay the strongest."

"You can quit the medicine any time, dear, if the reaction is too much," Doc said to me.

I could only murmur "yessir," but the thought of giving up my new color and going back to my ugly one sickened me more.

Again, I urged Pa to take one too, but he just gave me a stony stare.

Excited, Doc told Pa everything he'd discovered about the Blues, our ancestors, the rare gene, and our missing oxygen, while Pa kept a sharp eye glued to me the whole time, watching me, watching my skin.

But I barely noticed him. My eyes kept going to my hands and bare white skin, and I couldn't stop touching myself to see if the new flesh felt any different.

I peeked into the looking glass and saw Pa's reflection. He cut a disapproving look, and I stepped back. But in a minute, I returned to the mirror to stare at myself, delighted, spellbound by my normal, pretty white skin. Soon, I was practicing smiles and whispering at my reflection in my very best radio-newscaster voice.

Twenty-Nine

After Doc left, Junia's long, quavering bray sounded and I peeked out the window, surprised to see Queenie.

She nudged her mount closer to the porch. "I'm going to pick up my last pay," she said and slipped down off her horse, then stopped, pressed a hand to her chest. "Lord love Betsy, what has happened to you, honey? You lost your color. Plumb lost your blueberry now."

It was said without meanness, but her words still made me flush. I rolled up my sleeves; the late June weather was sticky and hot.

"Mmm-hmm." She glanced at my arms.

"Doc gave me some pills to try. Reckon they's working."

"Well, they sure 'nough work. *Lord.*" She grabbed my hand and inspected. "As if you wasn't pretty enough before, you're a'might prettier now. All of you!"

I blushed even harder at her compliment.

"Come on. You must come to town with me and show those bossy ladies your pretty self. They'll have themselves a passel of kittens and scratch each other up just as sharp when they get a look-see. Especially that ol' stinky polecat pussy, Miss Harriett." She tugged at my hand, laughing. "Come on, it's Thursday, and you only have to go to your outpost today."

"I was going to pick up my pay later, but I reckon going early won't harm none. Let me get your dictionary."

She held up her palm. "You keep it, honey, 'cause where I'm going, they'll have rooms full."

"But it was your pa's."

"My dear papa would be mighty pleased if you were the keeper of the words. I would too, and besides, you'll keep giving me your words. Only difference is you'll be posting them in letters."

"*Letters.* Liaison, litany, lithe, luminary, luxuriant," I said my latest new words, smiling as they flew musically out into the air.

"Don't you have yourself one fine, fine lexicon," Queenie said, just as proud. "You've made it up to your *Ls* and so quick. Keep it, honey. We can't have you stuck in the *Ls* like that."

"Much obliged. I'll take good care of it and write you."

"Maybe you can visit me one day. Be real nice to see the city together."

"Sure would be something," though I'd never have the money for such an extravagance.

"You try and come visit, honey." She patted my arm. "It'd be real good to see different folk other than hillfolk."

We rode to town. When the nausea returned, I had to stop once and dismount to empty my stomach by the path, heaving, my breaths coming hard.

"Lord," Queenie called out and rushed up behind me. "You okay, honey? Here, let me get you something for your sour belly. Did you have yourself a proper morning meal?" She fussed over me, swept the hair back from my face.

"It'll pass once the medicine takes good root. I'm fine," I said between shallow breaths.

In a minute, she pressed a jam-packed biscuit into my hand and ordered me to eat.

I pushed it away. "I'll not take your food." I wouldn't dare. It would be thieving, and all because of my vanity. The thought knotted my belly, and I pressed a fist into it.

Queenie laid a soft hand on my shoulder. "You will because I know plenty, know'd you'd give me yours. Eat, honey."

I sat on the ground and ate while she made sure I gobbled every bite. When I wiped away the last crumb, I felt stronger and was ready to journey on.

Queenie ordered me to rest a few more minutes, and by the time we mounted, a half hour had passed and I felt pert, excited, and scared about how folks would look at me, what they'd say.

Queenie chatted about her new job. "To think I'll be there in time to celebrate Independence Day. *My independence.*" She smiled. "I reckon that city'll have itself a grand parade." She shot me a look. "You should go to Troublesome's this year."

"I've never been but once." I ticked off the eleven days until the Fourth.

"I reckon they couldn't stop you now that you lost the color."

I chewed on the notion.

Queenie pulled back to her job. "I aim to get myself a librarian degree."

"A degree," I said in awe.

"I've dreamed of opportunity forever," she said. "To think how important it is for one to have chances over everything. They give the body life."

I plucked up her words and turned them over in my mind.

She went on, "My sons and their sons will have it, and they won't be tethered to their color, choked by the leashes of those who would cinch the tightest with the longest of ropes."

Before today, I couldn't imagine there would be such opportunities in my blue world. Now, my mind slipped over her bubbly talk, and it stole away to new thoughts of what might be, what I might become, dipped into fanciful worlds away from here.

Safe in my mind, I had enough courage to take those opportunities I got from books and magpie them away as my own.

We arrived in town, tied our mounts in the back of the post office, and walked into the Library Center together. Queenie chattered cheerfully and made me excited for her, for the both of us.

As I stepped inside, I smoothed my skirts and began to roll down my sleeves when Harriett spotted my face and arms. She let out a gasp, then jumped up and screamed, "Out, out, *out!*" Harriett stabbed a finger to the door. "I knew you had the disease in you. You was just waiting to pass it to us Godly folks. Both of you. *Out!* Eula...Eula, make them leave!"

Postmaster Bill poked his head around the post office's doorway and said, "Widow Frazier? Widow Frazier's *sick*." He crooked his head back and told someone in the post office. "Sir, ya may want to see her."

At that, Doc came up behind the postmaster, holding his mail. He pushed Bill aside. "What is it, Bill?"

Postmaster Bill pointed to me.

"What in tarnation... What's going on?" Doc demanded, confused.

"Oh, Doc, it's one of the coloreds. The Blue one," Harriett screeched. "Look! She's turned white from her disease and is going to infect us all."

Eula, taking big gulps behind a hankie pressed over her nose, had rushed to Harriett's side.

I wanted to turn and run for home, but Queenie latched tight onto my arm.

"I said *get out*," Harriett ordered. "Get your filthy sickness away from us. You're fired. Eula, dismiss her—"

I felt the air leave me. Queenie patted my shoulder, whispered something soft into my ear.

Doc stepped forward. "She is not sick. Mrs. Frazier is my patient, in my care, and I have declared her fit and of sound mind as any two strong men in this land."

"But she's white. *White*," Harriett said.

"And a fine, pretty white if I've ever seen one. And I've seen myself many, Miss Hardin," Doc snapped, glaring at her over his spectacles.

Harriett's eyes filled with rage. She raked them over the length of me. Then her chin lifted, and I glimpsed the tilt was unspoken jealousy.

"But look at her, all of her." Harriett pointed to my face, neck, body. "Her whole figure, her—"

"Silence, madam!" Doc barked and nailed his finger to

Harriett's face, then slowly lowered it to her belly, poking. "You, my dear, would do well health-wise to attend to your own figure, and if you cannot watch *that*"—he jabbed his finger again—"be forewarned, nor will any man."

The old doc had a fury and might I'd never seen, a glint in his old eyes that rent a youthful, strong spirit.

Queenie tightened a giggle, tapped a finger to her lips.

Harriett bared her teeth and hissed.

I realized I was holding my breath and slowly released it before I fainted, or worse.

Doc thrust a hard jaw toward the assistant supervisor.

Clutching her chest, Harriett opened, then snapped her mouth shut. Her lips quivered, and a harder anger spiked in her eyes, spilling hot tears. Again, she worked her mouth, clenched a fist. Afraid, I cast my eyes downward, stepped back. She picked up her skirts and ran into the ladies' room, slammed the door, rattling wood and windows.

Eula plopped into the nearest chair, eyes downcast, wringing her handkerchief.

"Bluet," the doc boomed, and loud enough that I know'd Harriett heard, all of Troublesome even. "May I say you're looking quite lovely today."

Queenie murmured in agreement, and my face burned with pride and embarrassment. Never in my life had folks talked about me being pretty. My tongue tried to scrape off a proper thank-you, but the words stayed locked, bubbling inside like a drowning frog.

"Yes," Doc said. "I'd wager the fairest lady in all Kentucky... Mrs. Johnson, Miss Foster." He tipped his head to us. "Good day, ladies." Doc slipped out the door.

I let out a ragged breath.

Eula still had her hands in her lap, folding and unfolding the hankie, as if waiting for someone to tell her what she should do next, or maybe even do it for her.

Gracious, Queenie did just that, stepped over to her and said, "Miss Foster, I'm here for my final pay, ma'am."

"Yes, yes of course," Eula managed hoarsely, dabbing her mouth with the handkerchief. She stood, picked up an envelope off her desk, and set it on the edge. Queenie took it.

Eula swallowed twice and said, "The—" She sniffed and took a small breath. "The Pack Horse librarians thank you for your service. Godspeed, Widow Johnson."

Queenie gave her a tight smile, then reached over and touched my arm. "I'll write to you, honey, as soon as I'm settled. You write me back."

"Sure will," I promised. And Queenie was out the door. The screen clacked twice, cheering her on.

I stared after her, thinking of the places she'd see, the people she'd meet, the opportunities she'd have. Finally, she'd be living the books she'd read about.

Eula called my name. "Widow Frazier."

"Ma'am."

She slid my pay envelope over to the edge. "Your pay."

"Thank you, ma'am." I slipped it into my pocket and headed toward the door.

Birdie strolled in with her baby hitched on a hip and stopped and turned to me, her young eyes dulled from restless nights. "Bluet, you're—"

"White," I said happily.

"*White*. Oh! You're white."

I nodded. "Doc gave me a cure."

"Oh my," she said. "So pretty, and the prettiest li'l daisy I've ever seen. Isn't that right, Samuel?" She jiggled him up and down on her hip. The baby squealed with delight, poked a finger into his drooling mouth, and grinned at me. "Yessir, our Bluet's a looker, and one the boys are gonna want to hook," she told him teasingly. "And look at you, Samuel, already a'flirtin'."

Harriett walked out of the ladies' room.

"Uh-huh. One pretty lady," Birdie said.

Harriett's heel landed beside me. She leaned her head

dangerously close to mine. "A pig in lipstick is *still* a stinkin' pig," she spat, her wet hiss spinning in the air as she swept past to her desk.

I turned. Her red eyes bored into mine. And I held them, locked, and lifted my chin two-man tall, snatching back some of the humankind that had been stolen.

Thirty

It had been a perfect June morning, and I rode away from town pleased I had money to give Pa, pleased with my new color.

I found a spot along the creek to let Junia drink from and dallied a little longer, thinking of clever talk I could have with Mr. Lovett next Monday, eager to show him my new color.

I mounted and headed to my outpost, anxious to see what the courier had dropped off. Soon, the hardness of my morning spent at the Center, Queenie's leaving, Harriett and Eula's fussing caught up with me, and in a few moments a headache reached my temples and tightened a band around my head.

I pressed a hankie to my forehead, fanned my neck. On Knob Trail, I passed a few folks headed into town, a man with a cart full of wares, and a woman and small child carrying baskets. A few minutes later, I heard the high whinny of someone else's mount.

I pulled Junia's reins to the right, stepping slightly off the path to let the rider pass.

The mule stopped and pricked her ears when she saw him.

Jackson Lovett rode toward us on a strong chestnut horse. Junia blew twice to let them know to step aside. He galloped onward, stopping beside us. "Cussy Mary, I'm taking my new horse into town to meet some men about timber. And here you are, and just in time to say hello."

His smile disappeared. Leaning forward, his eyes fixed on

me, brows knitted in concern, a worriment peaking in his eyes. Again he searched my face.

My skin grew hot, and my mouth became dusty as I called out a greeting. Then everything blurred and I was falling. Falling. *Falling.*

I came to on the ground, Jackson's head bent over mine, his hands cradling, rubbing mine.

I'd fainted or died, maybe both, I couldn't be sure. But I felt a dreamy grin on my lips, a warmth in his touch of a kind I had never known.

He squeezed my hand and called to me once, twice. "*Cussy Mary.*" He tapped lightly on my shoulder, rubbed my hand. I bolted upright, sat up, and scanned my surroundings, sure I was dreaming it all.

"Cussy, are you ill?" He gripped my arm, and I blinked and pulled to his voice and saw his wide eyes darken. "Talk to me. Are you hurt? Are—"

"I'm...I'm fine. It's only the medicine." I pressed my hands to my warm cheeks, shook away the grogginess.

"Medicine?"

I pulled myself to my knees and drew breaths. Jackson lifted me to my feet.

Junia gave a weak bray, kept a big eye pinned to us.

"I, uh... Doc found a cure for my color." I patted my hair and dusted my skirts, feeling horribly embarrassed.

"And it makes you faint?"

"No, it upsets my belly and gives me fierce headaches. This is the first time I've had this...this type of spell. It usually rights itself as the day wears on and the medicine gets out of my body—I turn back to blue." I shook my skirts again.

"Turn back? It's temporary?"

I hesitated, wanting it to be forever—for him to see me like this always. "Yes," I said, feeling a sadness rise, as I searched his eyes for disappointment. "It's...uh...temporary."

Jackson shook his head. "You could've broke your neck just

now." He waited, thinking, then, "Lots of cures are worse than what they aim to cure. Are you stuck with it, or can you toss it?"

"Ah," I stammered. "Doc said I could stop any time if I couldn't take the reactions."

I felt a flush color my ears and crawl over my face. It was vanity that made me use Doc's medicine and keep using it. And one of the deadly sins of the Lord Almighty. Now Jackson thought I was foolish and vain.

"There's nothing wrong with your color, being you," he said firmly. "Nothing wrong with what the good Lord gives us in His world, Cussy Mary."

He didn't know, couldn't know, the load I'd carried as a Blue, the scorn and hatred and gruesome marriage. How dare Pa call me vain and now Jackson. *How dare he too?*

"Nothing wrong—" Jackson repeated.

I stepped back and shot out a shaky hand. "No, Jackson Lovett, you're wrong. There is nothing wrong with *your* color in *your* world, a world that wants only whiteness."

He flinched, and his eyes filled with a mixture of hurt, sadness, maybe pity, I couldn't be sure, but I wouldn't wait to find out.

I spun on my heels and grabbed Junia's straps. Hoisting myself up, I snapped the reins, and we broke into a fast run.

"Dear Lord," I said when we were far away, pressing my face, the shame, into Junia's fur. "God, what has happened to me? Who have I become, and how small have I become? Mama would be so ashamed."

And thinking about her, and the burdens my folks carried, and the grace they'd carried them with made me feel smaller.

Thirty-One

The second hot day of July wore on me, and I rested more times than I dared on my route up Hogtail Mountain, each time feeling sicker and weaker. It'd been nine days since I'd started taking Doc's medicine, and I still felt bad, still thirsted for water, especially in the mornings. It seemed like with each passing day, the medicine was making me feel worse. So much that I took to leaving all loans on the porches, avoiding my patrons. Today, I tried to get food down, but it came right back up.

Junia's big eyes worried over my shoulder, and she nuzzled my back the second time I emptied my aching belly onto the road.

My skin felt feverish, and my throat was raw from retching.

With a pounding head, I finally reached R.C.'s fire tower.

R.C. poked his face over the rail, waved, then disappeared back inside.

I tied Junia and looked up the steep staircase. Digging into the book satchel, I pulled out R.C.'s magazine and the Fourth celebration flyer the Company store left at the Center to be passed out. I hoped R.C. didn't have himself a fire somewhere, prayed I wouldn't have to climb to the top today, of all days. Still, I always wanted to please the patron and leave the loan where they wanted it.

I waited a long time, but didn't hear his footfalls on the metal stairs, or his voice calling down to me. I'd have to brave the climb. I cursed the blue drug and then my vanity as I trudged up the steps to the first landing. Overhead, I heard R.C. open the door and clomp down the stairs.

I blew a shaky breath, grabbed the railing, and waited.

When R.C. came into view above me, I covered my mouth to silence a cry.

But R.C. beat me to it. He ran toward me, leaving behind a girl who'd been trailing him. "*Book Woman*. Miss Bluet, what happened?" he hollered, jumping the last three steps onto the landing beside me and dropping his old loan. The steel rattled, crawled up into my feet, and echoed into my aching head, leaving me to sway a little.

He'd been in an accident, maybe worse. His face was bruised blue as the color that stained my chamber pot each morning since I'd been taking the methylene.

"Here, have a seat." He pointed to a step. "You're white as the fog up here after a heavy rain."

How many times had I envied those words, *white as*? How desperately I'd wanted those words for my own, a prideful thing. I could stop this madness now, toss the medicine, but I craved the color more. "I am a little under the weather, R.C."

Over his shoulder, a girl stood behind him. She was reed thin with big doe-brown eyes. There was a cut on her mouth, and one eye was swollen and bruised purple.

The boy looked worse. His nose sat crooked, and an arm hung limp and twisted to the side. A front tooth was missing, and a good part of his left ear had been clipped.

"R.C., what happened? Does it hurt—?" I asked. "You must be in a lot of pain. Here, you sit." I scooted over.

R.C. waved away my concerns. "Hold on, ma'am. Stay seated, and I'll get you something to help."

"I'm fine. Please don't trouble yourself," I pleaded, worried he'd hurt himself more fussing after me, but he was off, racing up the steps, thundering his way back to the cabin.

The young girl stared at me, rocking on the balls of her feet.

She glanced up the stairs and said quietly, "My man's a good one. Smart. He's gonna learn me the books too."

Feeling ill, I could only bob my head.

"My daddy said we could live with him, but that tin room up in the sky there"—she raised her chin—"is bigger than Daddy's whole cabin," Ruth chattered on. "R.C. turned him down. Said he's looking to grow our babies up here, just like his folks done with him. He's gonna work hisself up to forestry dispatcher and then get the schoolin' to be a forest ranger. Be the lawman of the whole forest. He's real smart like that," she said again, proud.

"He is. I'm sure you'll be happy here." I wished it.

"I sure is happy to be with my man. My brothers were real ornery, and my daddy and them whipped me a lot, but R.C. sweared he won't whoop on me."

R.C. came tromping down the stairs. He handed me a mug of water and shoved a generous piece of yellowroot into my hand.

I murmured thanks in between tiny sips and gnawed on the root while R.C. and Ruth watched. In a minute, the herb eased my ails. Standing, I gave my thanks again, set the cup on the rail, and pocketed the yellowroot. We swapped out his old newspaper loan for a fairly decent copy of an *American Forests* magazine and the flyer.

"This just came in from Lexington," I said, pleased to give it to him.

"Oh, Miss Bluet, this magazine is surely a great one," R.C. exclaimed. "It's gonna be the best! Look, Ruth." He handed her the advertisement for the Fourth celebration. "Here's the celebration I told you about." R.C. showed her the flyer and pulled her up beside him. "Shoot, ma'am, I plumb forgot my manners. This is Ruth. Ruth Cole, my bride. Ruth, this is Book Woman, but you can call her Bluet, though she don't look much like a damselfly today." He grinned.

"Hello, Ruth." I mustered a smile.

Ruth looked down at her bare feet. "We's met, R.C." She dropped into a half curtsy for me. "Howdy again, ma'am."

R.C. beamed. "Do you think you can bring her some of them female magazines and scrapbooks, ma'am? I'm gonna learn her to read."

"I sure will."

"Ruth, you best go back up and watch the Osborne, hot one comin' up today. I'll see Book Woman down."

She gave a shy wave and said, "Hope to see you at the Independence celebration tomorrow, ma'am. R.C. done told me all about it. And the Forestry is giving my man two paid days off starting tomorrow."

R.C. led me down the steps.

At the bottom, he said, "I never did thank you proper for bringing me the letter the last time, ma'am. Mr. Beck didn't want to let Ruth go, and he whipped her." He tilted his head up to the sky, squinting. "I had to fight him for her."

I'd heard some unfavored courters did that. Had to fight for a bride. A test to join another clan.

"I'm sorry, R.C.," I said, letting him talk it out.

"Him and his sons tore into me, busted me some." He wrinkled his broken nose and winced, then rubbed a shoulder. "Didn't matter none when this was already busted." R.C. thumped his chest. "I took their whippings, and they was mean ones all right... But I got my licks in, mind you," he added. "After, they said I'd earned her, and we drank to it."

His smile was childlike, but a manliness settled into his face after what he'd done. "We had us a preacher over in Crooked Branch officiate it, and afterward, her family put on a right good feast."

"Congratulations on your marriage. Be well." I dared to lightly touch his arm.

He didn't pull away, just scratched his head and beamed. "I'd take a dozen whuppings for that girl."

I stared at him, awed by what lengths folks go to for love.

"Yessir, two dozen, even," R.C. said proudly.

I couldn't imagine finding any man that would take one for me, and for a moment I tried.

"Feel better, ma'am. And you be sure an' nibble on that root and get yourself well. You're mighty important to us and all. Can't have you sick, or worse."

Worse. The word slid over me, leaving its biting mark. That the drug could cause such fierce reactions made me suddenly wonder if it could get worse.

Thirty-Two

Heat trembled atop skinny pine forests and licked at mountain rock that rose above Troublesome. The hand on my pocket watch hadn't struck eight, and the July morning was already boiling, the blanket of air clammy, pleated with buzzes of excitement over the town and its tiny Independence Day celebration.

I snapped the pair case shut, slipped the timepiece back into my skirts, and watched from atop Junia behind a thicket of brush and tall briar on a knoll as folks set up tables below, went about fancying the town for their big two-day celebration.

Several times I glanced at my pale hands, each time feeling relieved, my excitement growing as I dared to go down and join the white folk.

Women carried cakes, pies, and tasty eats and arranged them on red-checkered cloth tables. Menfolk sliced watermelon and made a dandy spread of deer sausage and other game they'd trapped for the festivities. Folks gathered at the Company store to chatter. Families claimed patches of grass in shady spots and spread out quilts and baskets groaning with prized recipes.

I ran my hand down over my thick saddlebag. It held a Scripture cake, one of the first recipes Mama'd taught me so I'd learn my Bible verses while baking. I had cut the cake with cinnamon, figs, and a dollop of expensive sorghum I'd saved up for and had Pa tote home from the Company store after Queenie had suggested I attend the celebration. Pa usually balked at spending money like that, frittering away hard-working pay, but he weakened when I told him it was Mama's recipe. I'd made a smaller cake for him, and he'd ate it heartily, grunting compliments in between mouthfuls.

Surely it was good enough for today.

Impatient, Junia nickered for us to go. I fought again to get my gumption up, wavered between turning for home or joining the townsfolk. I stared down at the crowd, lifted an arm, and admired my new color. I didn't have to watch this celebration from a window, and I took a deep breath and snapped the reins. "*Ghee.*" The mule agreed and hurried down the slope.

I led her over to the post office, dismounted, and watched the coming and going of happy folks, curious wide-eyed children, men gussied up in their Sunday duds and smart hats, and women in new-sewn dresses. Young'uns played tag and kick the can in the dusty street. A group of small girls held up new apple dollies their mamas had peeled and carved out from fat Granny Smiths, showing off the funny-face whittled fruits. Three boys sat on a stoop at the post office with a pile of forest sticks and made whimmydiddles, digging out notches on the wood toy with their pocketknives, carefully selecting more sturdy twigs to make the wooden spinners to top them. "Ghee-haw," one of them shouted, raised his new toy, and furiously rubbed the notched whimmydiddle with a thick stick to make the top spin.

A few folks had set up display tables to sell deerskins, coon caps, rabbit foot charms, and other pelts they'd fashioned from their hunts. Junia lifted her nose toward a large cast-iron pot hanging over a small fire. The aroma of turtle soup filled the air with garlic and onion and other spices.

The Company store had set up a stand under a banner, and red, white, and blue streamers with Old Glory were mounted beside it. A man in a yellow bow tie stood in front of the wooden booth barking at passersby. "Get your tickets for a chance to win the celebration quilt from Troublesome's finest sewing club. Tomorrow at dusk one lucky winner takes home this year's quilt. Right here, step up 'n' get your ticket," he barked.

The booth was stocked with hand-held flags, spangle sparkler lights, rockets and firecrackers, candy treats, and other notions they would give to the townsfolk. The Fourth was the only time out of the year the Company shut down the mine for a two-day holiday and donated goods to Troublesome. Families would come down from their hollers, across creeks, and out of coves to enjoy the free festivities, stuffing themselves and having an excited social with their neighbors.

My folks had taken me once when I was little. We'd gone with Uncle Colton. A fight had broken out when a drunk put his hands on Colton's wife. Words and slurs had hit the Blues like punches, and Pa had grabbed Uncle Colton, his wife, Mama, and me, and rushed us back to the holler. That was the last time I saw my uncle—the last Independence Day celebration we'd attended.

"But I'm white now, and a respectable librarian," I told Pa last night when he insisted I stay home.

"Daughter, no good will come of you going to mingle with them folks," he'd warned.

"I'm the same as them now, Pa. Look at me, look at my color."

"I don't like it," he grumbled. "Those that can't see past a folk's skin color have a hard difference in them. There's a fire in that difference. And when they see you, they'll still see a Blue. No city drug's gonna change small minds, what they think about peculiarity. For them like-minded folks, there is no redemption for our kind. Stay put where you belong, Cussy."

Two young'uns raced past me, brushing my skirts. I recognized one of them as Winnie's student. He stopped and turned back to me, waving a handful of sparklers. "Book Woman, looka here." The boy raised the fireworks higher. "It's July 3, and these are for me! I'm eight today, and Pa says all these fireworks are for my birthday! An' we're gonna celebrate it Thursday *and* Friday." He grinned and was off to catch up with his friend, not even noticing or caring about my color. Again, I checked my hands.

The celebration crowd was growing larger, and laughter

floated down the street. I tied Junia to her spot at the post office, straightened my skirts, and carried the cake toward one of the gathering tables the townsmen had built, suddenly aware that the excited folks weren't really paying attention to me at all, that Pa was wrong. I belonged, same as everyone else.

With a lightness in my step, I found myself smiling. I spied Jackson ride in on his horse and watched him secure it next to the Company store. Harriett, in a new flower-blossomed dress, rushed up to greet him, full of the once-a-year fever that came with the town's special day.

She jabbered happily at him, trying to keep up with his long strides until Jackson said something to her, tipped his brim, and moved on to a small group of men. One of them, Mr. Dalton, Troublesome's banker, greeted him with a friendly slap on the back, and the other men shook his hand heartily.

He didn't see me when I bustled past toward the sewing circle. Likely, he wouldn't want to neither after the fuss I'd made on the trail. It was just as well. He was a patron, and only that. I'd been foolish to think our friendship meant more, or could ever be.

I approached the table with seven women around it. Constance Poole and her sewing bee chattered gaily over the folds of fabric, putting the finishing touches on the celebration quilt. From a few feet back, I admired their workmanship, studied the red, white, and blue blocked star design, and listened to their excited talk.

I reached up and touched my collar, then inspected my capped sleeves, my own needlework. I'd searched through magazine advertisements for dresses and hairstyles, then through our trunks and found some old lace and a few seed pearls of Mama's, and sewed them around the neck and onto the sleeves of my old soft, brown dress to make it more fashionable and less drab. For the past week, I'd practiced rag-curling my hair into soft wavy curls. This morning, I awoke hours before dawn and carefully worked damp ringlets around the strips of fabric. When my hair dried, I pulled it all back loosely with Doc's new white ribbons.

I could see Constance Poole and the others sharing amusing stories as their busy fingers lit across the quilt, expertly stitching and knotting. One lady urged Constance to go over and say hello to someone, *exchange a proper festive greeting*, she poked, *sure would be a fine one to court*. The others chimed in agreeing, whispering, and then I heard his name. Constance glanced over her shoulder, right at Jackson. Her cheeks rosied as the girls' voices chorused into giggles and gossip about Troublesome's latest eligible man.

Their lively talk covered a few other men, tales of courtship, but twice I caught Constance sneaking glimpses back at Jackson. I could tell she was sweet on him. They would make a handsome couple, her with the lovely ivory face and him with the strong, handsome one. They could be one of the dashing couples I'd seen in the magazines. *A Cinderella and the Prince.*

My old color crept into mind, doubt pricked, and I looked away, feeling dimmed by her beauty, knowing my new looks were just temporary—that I could turn back into a pumpkin just as quick. Checking my hands, I was relieved to see they didn't betray my jealousy.

A group of young'uns chased each other past the table, their screams jarring my thoughts. Clutching the cake, I smoothed down my skirts with my free hand and patted my ruffled collar, anxious fingers traveling upward, worrying my new hairdo.

The cake suddenly felt heavy in my other hand, the heat just as heavy and pressing. A dull headache throbbed at the base of my head, crawled up behind the ears, and I blinked and slightly rolled my shoulders to dismiss it. Silently, I counted the steps that would take me safely back to Junia, each number niggling, telling me to turn back to her now. The table of ladies exploded with laughter at something that I didn't hear. I searched their pink faces, glanced at my arms. *I'm white, white*, I pounded the declaration into my brain, chasing off misgivings. Taking a breath, then another, I stepped up to Constance.

"Miss Poole, ladies, happy Fourth." I held out the cake and shot them my best smile. "Uh, ma'am, I made a Scripture cake and thought the sewing ladies might enjoy a slice. It was my mama's favorite…an old family recipe passed down from her grandma."

Constance's eyes bugged, and a gasping hush locked the other women's wagging tongues.

"Why, Widow Frazier, you've turned white. Are you unwell?" She snatched a hankie from the folds of her skirts, patted a shiny forehead and pinched mouth. The other women scooted together, clattering their chairs against each other's legs, their six faces pinned to mine and snaking over the length of me.

"Fine, ma'am. I added an extra dollop of long sweetnin' to the recipe." I thrust the cake out, tried to give it to her. But she flinched, fell back against her chair.

"I just… Well, I wanted to stop by and see if I could join you, maybe lend a hand on the quilt. I've got a tight running stitch, and my mama always said it's one of the best she'd seen and—" I slipped a finger under my dampening collar, tugged lightly, and searched their faces. And then because it might be friendlier, safer, I added, "Sure don't remember a Fourth as hot as this one."

Uneasy silence batted around the group, shivering the hot, steamy air. Nearby a firecracker went off, making us all jump and leaving the ladies bleating nervously.

Constance balled her hand over a working patch on the quilt.

"I've got a decent chain stitch too, and my blind stitch is…" I hesitated, desperation sneaking into my wavering voice.

The woman looked to her companions, a silent question passing over each one. A fretful answer in their narrow eyes. I darted a shy smile around the group, hoping. Constance cleared her throat. "Widow Frazier, we have seven in our sewing bee, and we'd like to keep it at a comfortable *seven*."

She turned her head back to the women's approving glances, tossed a grim, satisfied smile to her group, picked up a needle, and dipped in and out of the quilt, picking up speed. A heavy moment passed, hard whispery voices buzzed, before the ladies lifted their prattle back to sewing and the affairs of the celebration, dismissing me.

"*Have you ever*. A heathen making a Bible cake," one spat out low.

"Disgraceful. Spectacle," an older woman hissed while her seatmate snuck a pitying glance my way. A younger girl with dimples and cold, blue eyes looked at me like I had the nuisance of a small bother. Another shot a look of triumph, and still another's eyes burned with anger.

Disgraceful. Spectacle. Heathen. I tucked my head. The hurtled words battered me like stones. The air felt like I was wearing it and had caught fire, trapping me.

Another firecracker went off and broke my prison, sending me scurrying back to Junia with the cake clasped in my hands. I chanced a peek back to the table of tittering ladies, then pinched my wrist and watched the white skin pucker and sink back into the flesh, into my shame and sadness. Again I pinched harder, dug in, the punishment not near enough for my grave transgression.

I'd been foolish. Reached the *worse*. The drug had not redeemed me. I didn't belong at this bright, happy gathering with these lively folks and bubbly chatter. I belonged in darker places where darker thoughts kept me put, where sunlight, a cheerful voice, or a warm touch never reached me. Weren't no pill ever going to change that.

I threw the cake into a bush and mounted Junia, glancing once more at the crowd. Across the street, Jackson talked to a group of smiling men and women. He lifted his head my way, raised a hand, and called out, "Cussy Mary..."

I couldn't bear for him to see my disgrace, see me for who I really was—who I'd become in their eyes. "*Ghee!*" I kneed the mule hard, and she raced off toward our dead, dark holler.

Thirty-Three

Even though the Pack Horse librarians had two days off for the Fourth, I left the celebration and rode to my outpost to be alone, stopping twice to empty my belly, the medicine and nerves wearing me. Determined, I climbed back into the saddle and continued on.

While I was there, I'd pick up the courier's new parcels for my Friday route. I couldn't let down the small community that would be waiting for the new loans tomorrow, and I needed to be in the chapel with my dark thoughts. Soon, those hard feelings dissolved and my belly righted as I delved into the reading materials and escaped to my books.

On Friday, it took all day to reach my patron through the darkly passes. Toting my heaviest book bags, weighing close to fifty pounds, wore on Junia.

The mule plowed heavily along rugged passes thick with vines, branches, and briars, crossed trickling creek waters, and twisted around thickets of scrub pine and beyond until we came to a pinhole passage that kept us from going any farther.

The skies opened, and down came steady rain, pushing up scents of new earth and aging rot. I didn't mind. It helped numb my thoughts of the sewing bee, of Jackson Lovett, what had been said, and what was best left unsaid, and now what would never come to be. I lifted my face and let the rain wash it, pelt at me.

I could see the patron ahead. Weather never stopped him, and despite feeling poorly, I wiped my face and waved.

Soft light he was, and just as welcoming, bathed in his own sunny color, forty-year-old Oren Taft stood grinning in tattered, wet clothes, a bright-green cap atop his long brown hair as he waited beside the small headstones rising from the weeds.

I returned his smile, feeling the warmth of it on this cloudy day.

Not far from the tiny graveyard stood his grandparents' abandoned home propped on leaning sticks, the gray walls sunken, the rotted weather boards gaping, weakened from years of rains and damp woods and the patching of thickening wisteria under a roof buckling to rainy skies. Wild roses climbed up crumbling chimney rock, creeping over a pile of broken stone, their soft, pink blooms tangled with the wild purple wisteria, lifting a slight fragrance into the rain, rising up on the dismal day.

"Good afternoon, Book Lady, I didn't much expect you today, it being the Fourth. Thought I would chance it, and I'm mighty glad I did," he said cheerfully, standing guard over two tow sacks.

"Afternoon, Mr. Taft. Happy Fourth, sir."

The mule stretched out her neck and blew at him.

Mr. Taft stepped out of Junia's path over to his grandparents' home, wisely distancing himself from her temper until I tethered her.

I tied Junia to a tree next to a broken gravestone and unloaded the books onto a board under a thick arch made from grapevine Mr. Taft had woven into a cover for the books.

Mr. Taft's tiny community of eleven families lived over the mountain from where we were standing in a place called Tobacco Top. An impossible pass for even the smallest of beasts. They were holler dwellers, the poorest, and what most mountainfolk looked down on. Without fail, every Friday, he'd meet me at his old family homestead after hiking the eight miles to get the reading, drop off his loans, and tote his new ones back to the isolated families waiting.

Mr. Taft snuck glances at my face, puzzled by my new color.

"Are you well today?" he called as he walked toward me. "I hope they ain't working you too hard."

I stacked the reading materials neatly under the arch. "Fit, sir, just spent from the rains." I pulled my floppy hat down over my white forehead, let the rain trickle off the wide brim and onto my shoes.

The drug still made me sick every time. And at least once a day, Pa needled me to stop taking the tablets and threatened to throw them out.

Mr. Taft pulled out a small cloth bag. "This'll cure any ails. My woman said to give you these and to thank you for the books."

I opened the bulging bag, and the scent of strong onion tickled my nose. Inside were fat ramps.

"There's a note she tucked in for you," he said.

I pulled out the paper and held it under my brim of my hat and out of the rain.

"It's mighty good and some of the finest biscuits in these parts," Mr. Taft assured.

"It sure looks it." It was a recipe for ramp biscuits with hog jowl.

"You just crisp up that jowl, then put 'em and these ramps into your dough." He patted his slim belly. "Better than my granny's."

"Pa'll love it, and folks will surely use this fine recipe. Much obliged to your missus. Thank you both."

I handed him back the bag, reluctant to take the ramps, and especially after I'd thrown away the cake at the celebration when so many hungered.

He shook his head. "Oh no, ma'am. My woman will skin my hide if I don't give 'em all to you."

It would fatten a lot of meager meals. Meals I feared I'd be taking from others. Meals I didn't deserve. I glanced at his rail-thin arms, busted shoes.

Mr. Taft pushed, "Real good in the eggs, and if you get yourself a fat turkey, well, my woman stuffs it full with 'em." Again, he rubbed his belly. "Good eats."

"She must be a fine cook."

"Yes, ma'am, ain't none better in these mountains. Best biscuits I've ever had on this good earth." He beamed.

"Thank you, Mr. Taft. It's a fine gift. I should get your loans into my satchel and your new ones into your bags before it kicks up a real storm."

We finished our exchange, and again Mr. Taft thanked me mightily while tying up his bags.

I mounted Junia and watched him while he secured his books. Like me, he'd never missed a day, nary a one in sleet, snow, or rain. He was a big extension of my borrowing branch, a librarian in his own right. So much so that I called out to him, "Mr. Taft?"

"Ma'am?"

"There's a new posting down at the Center for a Pack Horse librarian. And I thought of you, sir." I stopped, worried I'd gone too far, been too bold for this humble man. Would he see it as charity, scold me? I glanced again at his shoes, the leathers pocked full of holes and peeling away, then back at him, hoping I hadn't offended him. Just when I was about to work up an apology, he raised a brow.

"Librarian?" His face opened up with pleasure and surprise.

The job was still posted. It'd been hard to find someone to take on Queenie's route. But if anyone could, it would be him. "Yes, sir, we have us a few men in service now, and you'd make a fine one. The pay's decent."

"Pay?" His eyes widened. "Been a long time since I've seen that."

The supervisors would hire him, if for nothing else than to have a man around to preen in front of, help with the crates and bulky packages, the heavier jobs.

I looked over at his family's old home. With some patching, it would make a good outpost for the carrier to drop off the loans for him.

"At the Center?" he said.

"Yes, sir. You can pick up an application at the post office too."

"Thank you kindly, Book Lady. It'd be an honor, and a good fortune for me and mine. God bless you." He hoisted his book bags higher on his back. "A librarian. Ain't that something now. Won't my woman be surprised." He shook his head, still trying to grasp the notion. Then: "*Where's my manners?* I hope you get to feeling pert soon, ma'am. I miss seeing my bonny Picasso." He grinned.

I stared at him blankly, and he added, "Picasso's painting of the pretty blue lady, the *Woman with a Helmet of Hair* that I'd seen in one of the magazines you brought us? You remind me of her. Your fine color. My woman always said God saved that best color for His home." He pointed a finger up to a patch of blue sky parting the gray clouds. "Guess He must've had Himself a little left over."

Astonished, I could feel my face warm. No one, not a soul, ever said my old color was fine. *The best.*

Then he was off.

The mule kept her eyes on the man till she was sure his distance was safe. "Time to go, ol' girl." I watched him a moment and then flapped my legs against Junia's side.

Mr. Taft hauled the books onto his back like the storybook Santa Claus, whistling into the rainy air, then meandered down the path and disappeared into the foggy, needle-eyed opening at the end.

Thirty-Four

The weekend found me fainting again as I stepped off the bottom rung of the loft ladder and spilled into Pa's arms. When I came to, Pa scolded my vanity and my new color and damned our Blue affliction. "Dammit, Cussy." He gripped my shoulders. "You'll not have the pills and your route too. It's prideful, dangerous, and I forbid it!"

I escaped his hold and crumpled to the floor. Pa knelt down beside me, his bones stiff, creaky, and took me into his arms and cradled me, rocking. "My daughter, I'm sorry. I'm so sorry for giving you this damn curse. Dear God, how I wish I hadn't. Dear God, forgive me." A tear sprung from his eyes, splashed onto my arm. Frightened for us, ashamed of my foolish airs, unable to witness the hurt, his sadness, I could only press my face into his chest and sob.

It was the last morning I took the methylene blue, the last time I missed what I could never have and what was so foolish to miss. My pride, the hardships I placed on Pa and me, came at a bigger cost than I could bear. I couldn't lose anymore, and I wouldn't lose my route. The pills had already worn down my spirits, whittled my nerves. I had to get my books to folks, to hell with the color of my skin.

Jackson's words back on the path held a hard truth too. There'd been Oren Taft's words yesterday, and the more I thought about his Picasso Blue Lady, her *fine color*, the *best color*, the more I reckoned God wanted me to have it. If it was good enough for Him and the famous artist, it had to be enough for me.

Blue had to be enough for me, I vowed. The next morning, I looked into the mirror a little afraid. The white had quickly faded and the blue rose on my flesh, deepening, bruising, as I narrowed my eyes and whispered to my reflection, "This must be enough. I *am* enough."

Pa slipped up behind me, silently placed his gnarled blue hands on my shoulders and squeezed lightly.

Doc didn't seem to mind. "That's fine, my dear. We wouldn't want to add more discomfort to your burdens." And I caught that by *burdens* he meant my lot in life—my color.

"Should you change your mind, Bluet, call on me and I'll get you more," Doc had reminded when he'd dropped off a small basket of bread and fruits. He'd been busy minding his own— writing for the medical journals, drafting new letters, he'd said— before doing a quick check of Pa's lungs and heart and mine too.

But his visits became short, and far and few between until we rarely saw him at all, and then only in passing when he'd wave and give a cheery greeting.

Late afternoon, I rode into the empty schoolyard. A hot breeze teased the long July day as I plucked lightly at my damp collar and fluffed my sticky skirts. The goat and chickens ignored Junia's worn call. New diddles poked their feathered heads up from the bottom of the coop, curious of our arrival. A hen flew down from her perch, protective of the baby chicks.

The school was unusually quiet for a Monday, and I thought they might be having a test. Mountain schools didn't have much of a schedule, keeping more or less to nature's calendar. Fewer school days in the harsh winter meant more and longer when it turned mild. On the hottest days, the students would take their lessons outside under a shade tree.

Winnie appeared in the doorway holding her loans. I nudged Junia over to her. The second I slipped off the mule, she rooted herself, refusing to let me tether her. "Ghee." I pulled on her reins once, and then again. She wouldn't budge. I dropped the lead, knowing Junia wasn't going anywhere and I didn't have to win every argument.

"Cussy Mary," Winnie said, stepping down off the wooden stairs into the dirt yard. "The children will be sorry they missed you again."

"Sorry, ma'am." Last week, when I was ill, I'd snuck in and left the loans on the stoop, not wanting them to see my new color, or the illness caused by it. "You've discharged them early?" We exchanged books.

"The school's closed for the day. The superintendent came by for his annual meeting and to look over the children's studies. I suppose it was about time since he's missed the last two years."

Together we tucked the old loans inside my saddlebags. "Yes, ma'am," I said and mounted.

"The superintendent said the WPA is building a new stone school."

"A stone school," I said, astonished. It was something Winnie had dreamed of. Everybody had.

"I won't see it." Winnie fidgeted with her apron and patted the tight knot of hair on the back of her head. "Albert sent word to the superintendent for me. He says I am to join him in Detroit. He'll pick me up at the train depot on August 8."

"He'll be happy to see you, ma'am. Will a new teacher be sent?" I asked, sorry she would go.

"It may be a while. I wish I could delay my move till we can find a teacher. I asked, but..." Winnie looked down at her hands, rubbed reddened fingertips over her short nails. "Well, he's anxious for my arrival."

"I'm sorry you can't stay."

"Me too, but you know how that is. It could be six months to a year before they find my replacement."

Winnie had taught the longest of any before her, for nearly three years. It was impossible to get a teacher into these hills, and for chicken scratch at that. Most weren't cut out for it, and they'd pack their bags midyear.

"I'd like to wait around, just a little longer." She sighed. "But the superintendent said he wouldn't give me permission to stay unless my husband granted it."

It must be hard on Winnie to leave her students. Still, there was nothing she could do without her husband's consent.

Winnie wiped her brow, patted her flushed neck. "Cussy Mary, I need a favor."

"Happy to oblige."

"Some kind soul had been dropping off a few food sacks, but they only stretched so far, and"—she rubbed watery eyes—"well, it's Henry. He won't be back. The boy's too weak now. His mama has requested a drop-off and read."

Gloom seized. "Yes, ma'am. I'll make sure to add him to my route."

"I've written out the request for the Center. Godspeed," Winnie said, passing me the note with a squeeze to my hand, and hurried back into the empty schoolhouse.

Ɔo

The teacher's request was waiting for me at the Center on Tuesday. The next day, I skipped my fire-tower route and journeyed toward Henry's with a heavy heart, riding miles until I found the tiny cabin stitched into a mountain, tarred with black pine and stingy sunlight.

In the yard, two crows drank from mud puddles. Overhead, more cawed before dropping down to scar the yard. Two sick chickens peeked around the corner of the cabin, their combs and wattles festered with the fowl pox. A rawboned dog dozed on the crumbling porch. Junia snorted, and the pup raised its mangy body and flattened its flea-bitten ears before slinking off.

This old land had more dead stirring than sleeping, and Henry's mama, a pale, gaunt spirit, bore witness as she opened the door.

"Ye is here. I prayed for ye to come, Book Woman," she said weakly, planting a hand on her chest. "I'm Henra's mama, Comfort Marshall."

Weren't no solace to be found in a pretty name that the fates had cruelly robbed and left marked.

"Ain't long now," she said. "I thank ye for coming, Book Woman. The Good Lord'll take away Henra's pain by the 'morrow an' carry ma sweet boy to His home."

"Victuals, ma'am." I handed the woman my food sack. Her dead eyes filled with limp surprise. Doc had dropped off a carton yesterday, and I'd stuffed everything into the sack to bring to the family.

"Thank ye, thank ye. Come in... Ah, let me give ye—" Henry's mama looked over her shoulder, desperately searching for something, anything to give in return. She dug in her apron pockets, patted her sides, and then thumped her hollow chest. "*This.*" Reaching under her baggy dress, she pulled up a leather cord that held a metal-blackened crucifix of Jesus on it. "It was my mam's," she said, slipping it off her neck and holding it up like it was a sack of gold. "Ye take it now an' Jesus'll protect ye."

"No, ma'am," I said gently. "Jesus needs to stay with you." I crossed the threshold. If ever there was a place He was sorely needed, it was here.

"God bless ye, good Book Woman." She kissed the prayer onto dead Jesus's feet and dropped the cord back over her neck, rubbing the medal with gnarled fingers.

Inside the quiet shanty, a faint smell of corn lifted. A heap of young'uns piled under coverlets on an old corn-shuck-filled mattress. They poked their heads out as I entered, the stiff stalks crackling beneath their weight, candlelight shivering across their faces.

The family's opened cupboard was bare except for a bag of black walnuts that'd spilled out of its mouse-nibbled sack. An iron skillet of morel mushrooms with mustard weed sat atop the stove, the dryland fish and grasses, the family's only food. Beside it, another pan filled with a soup of wild thistle wafted into the air as it simmered.

A small boy knelt in the corner relieving himself through a knothole in the boards; a naked baby cuddled next to the potbelly stove and chewed on a stick.

Henry's mama pointed across the room. "Henra," she called faintly and hobbled her hard time across the floor, leading me to where he lay curled on a stingy pallet next to the wall.

"Book Woman—" Henry tried to smile and reach up for me, but his throat seized and a cough rattled the greeting.

"Henry," I whispered achingly, "I brought you this." I showed him the book.

He was too weak to take it.

"*Peter and Wendy*," he mewed, focusing his eyes on the cover.

"That's right. I've brought you Mr. Barrie's wonderful tale."

"It…it's surely the best, ma'am." Henry tried to push himself up on his elbows, but fell back shivering, his bones knocking taut flesh.

I knelt beside the boy and pulled a coverlet over him, tucked the dirty flour sack someone had tried to fashion into a blanket over his small frame. His shoulder blades and hips poked through the rough material. Henry's lips were faint blue, his cheeks hollowed with dark patches.

Light leaked through the gaping holes beneath the floor. Under it, chickens huddled in the dirt, clucking, the stink of soil and disease rising through splintered boards.

I opened the worn book, flipped to the beginning, and pulled out a small horse-shaped badge I'd patched together from pieces of fabric and pressed it into Henry's palm.

"Here's your librarian badge, Henry."

He squinted his feverish eyes.

"Raise your hand, sir."

Henry held it up, and I grasped it. "Henry, I do hereby make you an honorary Pack Horse librarian. Do you promise to take care of your patrons, bring them books, and read to them?"

Henry's watery eyes bloomed, and he swallowed the knotted promises, gulping them all down. Proud, he pressed the home-made badge to his heart.

Behind me, I heard a low, painful sob. Henry's mama clung to the doorframe, apron to her mouth, dabbing at soaking eyes, her bony frame toppled with grief.

The children in the bed chorused soft murmurs, popped up, the toothless surprises pasted on their sickly, pallid faces, their scaly necks and cheeks roped with the pellagra rash.

I motioned to his shy brothers and sisters. "Come on, little ones. Don't be afraid none. Gather 'round while our newest Book Man reads to us."

Henry's face swelled with pride. Again, he tried to rise but collapsed, his mournful cry whisking past tight-tucked teeth. I fitted the cover back over him and rubbed his frail shoulder.

Henry's mama nudged quietly. "Git on, childrun. Lissen to Book Woman."

One by one they slipped out of bed, crowding in silently beside me and Henry on the floor. The smallest girl curled up beside Henry, laying her head heavy on his arm. With pained effort, he cast a wincing smile at the little one, struggling to lift the blanket to share it with her.

I shrugged off my bonnet, folded and placed the soft fabric gently under Henry's head for a cushion. Leaning in close, I opened the book and held it up to Henry's face.

"Book Man, will you read us *Peter and Wendy*?"

Henry nodded solemnly, then raised a finger to the page, under-lining each word with a flesh-bitten nail, graveling out the first sentence. "All chil—" He looked up at me and swallowed loudly. "All children, except one…" Henry paused toward the end of the sentence to cough, his eyes ablaze with happiness, the fever licking his light. He coughed once more, and lifted his "grow up."

Thirty-Five

Devil John stepped onto the path as I made my way home from Henry's. I'd been huddling inside my grief and didn't see him until Junia warned me.

"Book Woman," he said, taking off his hat, twisting it in his hands, and pulling on his long beard. "I wanted to let you know the young'uns been working now. My garden is in, an' the chores is getting done. Martha Hannah has the girls caught up on their sewing, and supper's been on the table an' on time."

"That's real good, sir," I said.

All I could think of was Henry, wishing I could cradle him. But I had no right to take a mother's important last rite away. I'd left the dying boy in his mama's arms and quietly slipped out to give dignity to the family. Henry would be gone by morning, and probably all of the Marshall family within three months.

Devil John said, "Carson, that's my oldest, asked if you could bring him some more Boy Scout reads. That boy likes his reading more than anything," he added more with pride than bother. "Lights through the pages and helps Martha Hannah read to the babies now. Takes a hankering to read to me, and"—he paused to clear his throat—"well, he sees fit to sharpen up my spelling a bit. I have me a list of words I'm working on for the pestering boy." He reddened, but I could see he wasn't annoyed, just pleased with himself.

"That's real nice of Carson, sir."

"Well, he killed himself a fat boar and brought home a pail of trout. I reckon you bringing the Boy Scout read won't bother none."

"I'll try to bring it next Monday," I said, eager to pass and be on my way.

"And a better Bible for Martha Hannah too. Her fingers done licked the words off most of the pages."

"Yes, sir, we get lots of Bibles." It was true. We handed them out to every patron, and many were donated from Lexington, Louisville, and Cincinnati, so many we never asked for those loans back. It was like folks in the city had thrown away their religion, given up on Jesus.

In this moment of emptiness, of mourning, I wondered if I should too.

I could feel Devil John's eyes on me. He could see mine, red and swollen. I tried to light a smile his way. "Good day, sir. I'll fetch the material to you next week."

"A Bible and the Boy Scouts, and only them," Devil John said, and studied me some more before pulling out a pint of moonshine from his backside and setting it on the path. "I imagine it's a bit wearing for a book woman to tote all them books to the folks around here. And I reckon all that hard work wears on a soul."

He put on his hat and was off.

I slid down off Junia, took the shine, and placed it in my bag.

Two hours later, I made my last stop, handing Timmy Flynn a new read from atop my mule and stashing his other loan inside my bags.

Timmy plopped down by the tree and pushed his nose into the new loan.

I turned to leave and heard someone call for me. "Book Woman, Book Woman, *wait*."

It was Mrs. Flynn.

"Hol' up!" she ordered.

I winced and hoped she wouldn't fuss today. It'd been bold to leave the scrapbook, but I'd thought she would find something useful in it and dearly wanted to gain Timmy's whole family as patrons.

Mrs. Flynn splashed across the creek, holding up the scrapbook, her frayed calico hems darkened from the waters, feet teetering carefully across slick rock. Her bonnet slipped off and hung loose down her back.

Breathless, she stopped beside Junia and held up the book. "Book Woman, this! Bring me another one like *this*." She shoved it into my hand, then lit off back across the creek toward home.

I stared after her. My tense shoulders slumped some, and a full breath whisked out. After all this time, she'd requested her first loan and would become my patron. The family would be reading together. And despite the hardness of this sad day, a small joy lit my heart.

Timmy glanced up from his book and grinned. "Pa said that was the best sugar pie recipe Ma'd ever made. Auntie too. She made it for the dance and said she done caught herself a big, strapping man."

On the path away from the Flynns', I followed the creek toward home. Minutes later, Junia pulled toward the water and I climbed down and sat on the grass to let her rest, drawing my knees under my chin. A bee panther flew down beside me, landed atop a grasshopper, feasting on its midday meal.

I scooted away from the ugly robber fly. Soon, Junia moseyed back over to me. I pulled out my leather-sheathed bottle from the bags and saw that it was empty. My throat was parched, but I dared not drink from the creek. You never know'd who'd built an outhouse upstream, or what had spilled out from the mines.

I stared at Devil John's hooch and tried to decide if that would quench my thirst. "*Hard work*," Devil John had said. Feeling it, I grabbed the moonshine, took it over to another grassy spot by the bank. Creek waters slid over slick, gray rock, and I rubbed a thumb over the old glass as I inhaled the scent of rushing creek waters.

Far away, someone played a fiddle, tickling the mournful notes, the soft music laddering into tall boughs, carrying across the long day.

A wood thrush whistled overhead and folded its flute song into the strings.

I pulled the stopper out of the bottle, lifted the moonshine, and swallowed a mouthful, coughing back up some of the burn, spitting, wiping the dribble off with my shoulder.

I chanced another swallow, coughed some more. Once more. And then again. The liquor—smooth now—warmed my belly and tamped the trouble inside me.

When it hit my head, I had myself a talk with the Lord, with Henry's Jesus, railed to the dear Almighty God, shocked and afraid of how angry I was at Him for what he'd done to Henry and his brothers and sisters.

"Lord," I whispered, "what did little Henry ever do to You to make him suffer Your wrath? What could the boy have done?"

Junia edged closer to me and blew out a powdery neigh.

I thumped the earth with a fist and yelled, "Why, oh why didn't You love him like I did?" I swigged more corn liquor, then wiped the droplets of panther's breath off my chin.

"Why couldn't you let him grow up?" I curled myself into a tight ball on the blood-soaked Kentucky soil, wailing for Henry and all the Henrys in these dark hollows who'd never be a *common grown-up*. Stuck forever as Peter Pans.

Thirty-Six

I almost missed it at the outpost when I'd stuffed the courier's pamphlets and flyers inside my bags. And I'd stared at it in disbelief, rubbing my fingers over the elegant script used to write my name, marveling over the mere sixteen days the letter had taken to reach me.

I held on to the envelope all day, vowing not to open it until I returned home from the outpost. Several times along the path, I stopped, pulled out the envelope, stared at the Philadelphia postmark.

In the evening, I sat cross-legged on my bed and pressed my very first friendship letter to my bruising-blue lips, smelling the small envelope, turning it over, holding it up to the candlelight, doing it again and in a trance of wonderment.

I traced a dark finger over Queenie's city address, the smart fancy script, the blue ink. Leaning into the light, I took Pa's knife and slowly and oh so carefully opened it.

July 9, 1936

Dearest Cussy,

We made it to Philadelphia safely. I rented an apartment fourteen blocks from the library. It is crowded with five of us in this tiny two-room flat with no porch or hills to escape to.

Philadelphia is gray from its bootstrap to the top of its tall concrete buildings. The city nights are without stars, and I miss that most. It is hot, noisy, and never beds itself. How odd that Troublesome rises late out of its smoky-blue shadows and struggles for the light when the city won't shut off its blinding one!

There are beggars on the streets everywhere you look. One thief stole my bag, and another knocked down my young Aaron and snatched his hat. Hunger abounds. Men, women, and children stand in long food lines for their meals.

It's hectic here, and folk are always busy flittering about like bees. Oh, I wish you could see this big city and the people skittering to and fro! The white folk in this big place don't even look at me like they do in Troublesome.

The library is big, bigger than the whole town of Troublesome. I haven't seen all of it, but my boss, Mr. Patchett, promises to take a day off soon and show me around. Mr. Patchett is from England, and calls me a quick study. He says I'm a capable female and smart-enough Negro. He has urged me to apply to the Hampton Institute Library School, and insists on giving me a letter.

Write to me soon, honey.

God bless you and your papa,
Queenie Johnson

I read the letter many times, until the candle lost its fire and would no longer hold—till the morning light and fanciful and frightful dreams of city life had lulled me into a restless sleep.

Thirty-Seven

I rode the mule toward the Moffits' homestead as the fog parted and the sun broke through another morning, the last week of July bearing down, just as miserably baked as the fiery Fourth had been.

We saw it at the same time. Alarmed, Junia cantered, then teetered at the edge of the Moffits' yard. The mule's rear legs slid beneath her belly until she was nearly sitting. Thin, white foam gathered at the corners of Junia's mouth, and her eyes were ringed white as she fought to sidestep away, anywhere other than facing the thing in front of her.

I couldn't take my eyes off it as I struggled to control Junia and kicked her flanks. She rose stick-legged, straining her neck, ready to bolt. Keeping my eyes locked ahead, I seated myself firmly in the saddle, speaking gently to the trembling animal. Again, I kicked. When the beast high-stepped backward and sideways— every way but forward—I lifted my heels and brought them down hard. Junia burst into an awkward gallop, careering into the yard before skidding to another halt. I drew the reins in tighter. In front of me, a body swayed from the fat branch of a tree.

Angry cries sparked from the earth, and I dropped my gaze to the ground.

A baby lay in the dirt beside the large toppled can of Angeline's Mother's Lard. Swaddled in her mama's housecoat, the child's tiny arms quaked, fisted upward to the corpse, its eyes dead, body limp, rocking in a tight half-spin from a warm gust of wind.

The branch creaked, moaned under its heavy burden. A bloody sock slipped from a dangling methylene-blue foot and landed beside the wailing baby.

I dared another peek and looked up, then raised my hand in front of my blue-coloring face, comparing my darkened flesh to that of the hanging corpse.

Junia pawed the ground, turned her head, and blew hard.

I slid down and ran to the infant, picked the newborn up, and rushed toward the cabin. "Angeline, Angeline," I called to her.

Inside, Angeline lay on the bed atop soiled sheets. On the floor, blood had spilled and a slime of afterbirth spread, seeped through the boards' cracks. The air was raw, wrapped in iron, festering in the hot cabin.

Something had gone horribly ugly and wrong in the child-birth. A blood-specked hunting knife lay nearby on the floor, the baby's shriveled life cord draped over it.

"Bluet—" Angeline said faintly, stretching a bloodstained hand to me.

"Oh, Angeline," I cried, surprised she was alive.

"My babe...my ba-by," she choked and sputtered.

"Right here." I rushed and knelt down beside the bed, the scent of blood, old straw, and moldy sheets hitting my face.

"Give her to me. My Honey girl. She needs to feed—"

I placed the baby in the crook of her arm next to her breast. The child's breathy cries quieted as she rooted for the nipple.

Angeline winced.

There was so much blood. Far too much. Blood that would stain—birthmark the pine floors forever red.

"When did you have her?" I asked.

"I've been birthing her since yesterday morn'. She jus' came maybe an hour or so ago," Angeline said, pinching her words. "But Willie got mad, Bluet, and took her. Took Honey from me." She kissed the baby's head, and her sob clung wet to Honey's forehead. "Feared he was gonna hurt her...real bad. Said she smelled."

"What? Why would her pa do that?" I looked out the dirty pane, wondering how I would tell her about Willie out there like that and the bad that would be stinking on him.

"Willie wouldn't have her. Wouldn't have our Honey." Tears filled Angeline's eyes. "He said he'd married hisself a white, not a colored. And folks would know'd he didn't."

"Colored... But that's not true—"

"He didn't want her. *Me.* Said he'd rather die than be scarred with us."

Angeline pulled back the baby's wrap, and I saw it. Saw what Willie wouldn't have and wanted to hide. The baby weren't entirely blue, but she wasn't white neither. Honey's skin was smattered with the sticky blood of her mama's life, but you could see the soft blue running over her, faint like a coming-twilight blue, and the bruising-blue fingernails.

The baby kicked, and I saw the tiny toenails were the same.

"Willie has the Blue in him—it showed itself when he got sick," Angeline said breathlessly. "*I married myself a colored an' didn't know'd it.*"

Doc's words rushed back to me. *Your parents carried the same recessive gene.* Then Angeline's long ago words. *Willie used to have hisself kin planted up there in Hell-fer-Sartin. I did too...*

Could it be?

She coughed. "Don't matter none, and I tried to tell him so."

I thought about Willie's nails, the glimpses I'd seen. "I need to fetch Doc."

Moaning, Angeline shook her head. "It's hurting so bad. Hain't time. I can feel it leaving me an' the cold a'comin'."

A red stain spread across the thin sheet below her legs, deepening in the thighs and bottom.

"I have to get the doc," I said.

"Don't leave me. Hain't got time..." She grimaced and

moaned. The baby jerked and gave a sharp cry, then stilled to nurse. "Bluet, you"—Angeline weakened—"you take Honey."

I leaned away from her. "Take her?"

"There's no one else. He'll never come back for her. Weren't no one but me and Willie. My kin's dead, and Willie never had hisself a pa, and his ma left him with strangers when he was a babe."

"Angeline, please let me get you help. You need a doc." I looked around the tiny cabin for anything—herbs, something to help her. The home was empty except for the newspaper-coated walls that were fat with printed talk and Angeline's writings. I pressed fingers to my knotted forehead and tried to think.

"Hain't time now," she wheezed as she raised herself up on a shaky elbow, clinging to the babe with her other arm. "Seen this with my ma when she birthed her last one. Keep her, Bluet," she begged and then slumped back down.

I whipped out my hand to protect the baby's head. "But I can't—"

"She's a Blue, and hain't no one gonna love her. No one but you." Angeline's knowing eyes reminded me, hollow in the slanted light.

I touched the baby's hand, my own eyes filling, my mind grappling with losses, the unbearable pain of loneliness. Nary a townsfolk, not one God-fearing soul, had welcomed me or mine into town, their churches, or homes in all my nineteen years on this earth. Instead, every hard Kentucky second they'd filled us with an emptiness from their hate and scorn. It was as if Blues weren't allowed to breathe the very same air their loving God had given them, not worthy of the tiniest spoonful He'd given to the smallest forest critter. I was nothing in their world. A nothingness to them. And I looked into Angeline's dying eyes and saw my truths, and the truths that would be her daughter's. Know'd that without love, in the end, her babe would have no one, nothing, and would be fated to die alone in her own aching embrace. *Nothing.* The truths collapsed in my chest, crushing.

"*Please*, you're all she has," Angeline implored.

The baby twisted, and a weak cry slipped from her breath. I picked up her little hand, stroked the cupped blue fingers.

This child would suffer it all, and alone. Every hard hate. Every minute of damning solitude. Honey deserved love and more than the stingy spoonful that the white world would see fit to give her.

"Please, Bluet. Please promise you'll be her ma."

Ma? Her ma.

"Please help my baby." Angeline rolled her head, sweat popping on her forehead. "Dear Jesus, help… Take this Blue for yours."

"Shh, shh, don't worry none," I comforted. The child would bear the horrific load of being the last Blue now, the one hunted and harmed if I didn't protect her. "I'll take her, Angeline, and I will love Honey as much as you do. I promise." The words spilled out from deep inside me, from that place deeper than thoughts, from the deepest pocket of my guarded heart and wounded soul. And I silently vowed to God to love this babe, keep her safe from the harm and hate me and my family, and their families, had suffered.

It stops with Honey. I closed my eyes and lifted a fierce declaration to God, to mankind.

Angeline pulled my hand to her mouth, kissed and pressed it to her pale, wet cheek.

I took her hand and kissed it back and placed a light palm on Honey. "*Promise*," I said to her again.

Angeline's breaths came harsh as she pointed a finger toward the magazine. "It—it…it got busted some when Willie had hisself a fit," she said shakily, but still with that soft, shy smile.

I picked up her loan, the old copy of a *Good Housekeeping* magazine. The cover with a little brown-haired girl reading a book had been ripped off and left on the floor smeared with a bloody footprint. *Willie's.* Beside it lay the corn-husk doll Angeline'd crafted, now torn and scattered in shreds.

"Reckon it's nothing I can't get bound," I said, struggling to smile back.

"Read it for me?"

"Yes."

"Read the page about the pretty mama and happy baby to Honey an' me. Read that, Bluet."

I opened it to where Angeline'd marked her page with scrap paper and saw the beautiful, stylish mother in a pretty spring dress and white heels. She sat in a finely crafted rocker and read to a plump, smiling baby garbed in a beautiful ruffled gown. The babe held an expensive dolly in matching clothes—a baby that would never know this harsh land, go hungry, perish from starvation, or lose a mother.

I read the title. "'Having the Happy Baby.'"

Angeline murmured to Honey. "I want you to read everything when you grow'd some, know your letters same as me—same as your new mama taught me." She looked up at me sweetly, kissed the baby again, and closed her eyes.

I ran the back of my hand lightly down her cheek and across her jawline, wanting to remember her for Honey. Angeline sighed softly, and I read aloud for five minutes, peeking over the top of the page to see her pale face lighted with pain, nestled beside Honey's peaceful one, droplets of breast milk coating the sleeping babe's mouth.

Though she was a Blue, Honey didn't look any different than any other sleeping baby in her mama's arms, but she would grow up and feel the world's different eye on her color.

For another five minutes I read the article, my words faltering, choking with tears, scratching out strings of rushing sentences as I glimpsed the frail sixteen-year-old mama fading.

I paused when Angeline coughed again and said drowsily, "Me and Honey, we loves you to read to us."

"I love reading to you," I whispered. "I love you, Angeline."

"Sure is pretty words, jus' like Heaven." She fumbled for my hand, wrapped hers over mine, and pressed both to her mouth, tucking our double fists closely under her chin. "I want you to read lots of books," she murmured to the sleeping babe. "Books'll learn you, Honey."

I kept reading until her grasp went limp, and a few minutes beyond until my tongue couldn't scrape off another word, and my soaking eyes dared to see her dead ones.

The magazine slid to the floor. A prayer hummed softly on my lips. Another, and another. The pleas to a God I'd abandoned now begged for Angeline's revival, chewed across the newspaper-lined walls for her parting.

"*God.*" I struck a fist into an empty spot on the mattress, scattering straw. The bed swallowed my fury, rocking the mother and child. The baby startled, whisked out a cry, then settled.

I climbed into bed beside Angeline and the sleeping babe. Curling up next to their bodies, I cradled my arm across them both, and wept, howled—a dry howl, an empty riverbed droughted from heartache, hurts, and hardships—till the sobs rent the hollows, the deep rock caverns of my soul, and brought forth rivers of agony.

Thirty-Eight

For a long time, I laid on the Moffits' bed and stared out the window, busted in grief, then folded myself into the hymn Pa'd sung to Mama on her sick bed.

> *I've wandered far away from God,*
> *Now I'm coming home;*
> *The paths of sin too long I've trod,*
> *Lord, I'm coming home.*
> *Coming home, coming home,*
> *Nevermore to roam;*
> *Open now Thine arms of love,*
> *Lord, I'm coming home.*

I softly brushed a lock from Angeline's cheek as I finished the chorus.

Something buzzed past and pulled me out of my misery.

The first blowfly landed on the sill, its skinny black feet twitching, eager to feed from Angeline's flesh. Outraged, I cried out and flicked it away.

Another one quickly replaced it, its ugly eyes parked on Angeline.

I swatted.

The baby kicked, and I jumped up, hurrying to cradle her in my arms. What would I do with a baby? A Blue one at that?

I draped Angeline with her eiderdown counterpane, walked out to the porch with the newborn, and sat down on the stoop. I stared up at the tree, rocked the babe in time with her dead swinging pa. On a branch above Mr. Moffit, a cardinal trilled sweetly into a distant train song, the hymns washing the old mountains.

I forced myself to turn away. Old-timers believed when a cardinal called close by, it was the dead kissing you, and for the first time I thought it might be true.

I pressed Honey to my bosom, cupped her face, shielding her. I kissed her head, stroked her pale-blue cheek. She was the very last of me. And I cradled her closer, feverishly wishing I could take the title back from the helpless infant.

Junia was at the end of the porch with her backside to me and the tree, like she couldn't bear to see it either. The mule's head hung cheerless, her flesh quivering. She wouldn't come to greet me.

I tried to right my mind. If I called on Pa to help, folks might cast blame on us for the deaths. Worse, they might hurt Honey. Would anyone miss this baby? Care? I worried if Angeline and Willie'd been receiving mail, and if the old postman would've seen Angeline's pregnant belly. She'd been so tiny beneath all her skirts. In all my time spent with the Moffits, I'd never seen letters for them. Surely, they would've had me read the letters if there'd been some. I know'd her relatives had died, and not much else about him, except he came from parts deeper in the hills. But it was like the world never know'd those two had rooted here and scratched out a life, fought every day to stay alive. Had I been the only one to bear witness? Would anyone else notice they were gone? Still, I had to see to it that Honey's folks got a proper burial.

The infant stretched in my arms, fluttered her lids. I set her down beside me, stood and cupped my hand against the sun's watering rays and turned to the west, thinking.

In a minute, I walked over to Junia. "We have to take this baby to a safe place," I told the mule. "And we have to do it very carefully." Junia nuzzled my neck, and I stroked her mane. "Let's get our Honey home for our sweet Angeline." Junia pricked her ears as if she understood, gazed big-eyed and solemn to the porch, hoping the girl with the carrots would appear. I pressed my cheek to Junia's soft muzzle and kissed it. "From Angeline."

Pulling the reading materials out of one of the saddlebags, I stuffed them into my other. I dared not trust my trembling body to carry the child in my arms. The empty satchel was roomy enough to tote the tiny baby who was no bigger than the cloth doll my mama'd sewn me long ago. Satisfied, I took my bonnet and made a cushion before placing Honey inside, careful to make sure she was cradled safely, bending back the leather flap for air.

I mounted Junia and turned her toward Jackson Lovett's place, the closest on my route, with a prayer he'd be near and willing to help with two burials.

"Easy, girl," I said, and looked over my side and down at a sleeping Honey before snatching one last glimpse back at the Moffit cabin.

In a moment, I found one of Angeline's cradle songs tucked in my heart. Junia whisked a gentle whinny into the honeyed melody. I lifted the lullaby higher and sang for the baby. Though she weren't sad none or scared like me.

Thirty-Nine

I rode up Lovett Mountain with misgivings. Several times I turned around only to double back, the growing unease sticking to my dampening collar.

When I didn't see Jackson in the yard, I dismounted and took Honey from her bag. I stood at Jackson's door for a long moment, flexing a fist before braving a knock. I hadn't seen him in weeks, not since the Fourth of July. Every time I tried to drop off the books, he was nowhere to be found.

Maybe he didn't want to be found, didn't want to be around me and the books anymore.

Dismayed, I turned to take my leave when he opened the door wearing nothing but his work britches, a pencil tucked behind his ear. Books and papers lay scattered on his table inside.

"Cussy Mary, come in." He barely glanced at me, turned back, and grabbed clothes off a chair, tossed them across the room, stacking papers and books on the table to clear a spot for me. "Excuse this mess. I wasn't expecting company."

"How are you?" Jackson called over his shoulder. "Listen, I'm sorry about keeping the book so long." He rubbed his head while scanning his quarters. "Ah, here it is. I've been going back and forth to Georgia lately to help out a friend with his turpentine camp." He turned back to the door, opened it wider, and held up Mama's book. "It's good to see you—"

The baby squirmed in my arms. Jackson stared at her,

confused, and then laughed. "Where'd you get that?" He raised
a brow at Honey. "You delivering for the stork now?"

He glanced at my face, took note of my shabby appearance,
Angeline's smeared blood on my skirts, and I saw the alarm in
his eyes. "What... Are you okay? What happened, Cussy Mary?
Please...please come on in." He stepped aside.

"The Moffits," I rushed, "it's the Moffits—they's dead. *Dead.*"

"Slow down." Jackson motioned me inside again, flicking his
hand. "What are you saying?" he asked and darted his eyes to
the baby.

"She's the Moffits'. Was the Moffits'," I babbled and stepped
over the threshold. "The mama done gave her to my care before
she passed from birthing."

"Where's the papa?"

"Hanged himself."

"What—?"

I peeled back the baby's covering. "Mr. Moffit told his wife
he wouldn't have her—colored and all." I felt the child's loss
splinter in my heart. "He went and took his life out in the yard."

"Damn. Is the baby okay?"

"Honey. That's the name Angeline gave her. She's not fussing
none." I peeked down and saw she was sucking on a knuckle,
content to soak up her surroundings.

"I need help, Mr. Lovett—"

"Jackson. Call me Jackson."

"Jackson, I need milk. And I need to get them buried up there
before the critters take 'em. Can you help?"

"Where's their kin?"

"Weren't none. That's why she gave me the baby. I have
money to pay you—"

Jackson waved his hand, hushing me. "You mean to bury a
chicken thief? Take in the orphan?"

I drew Honey closer as if the ugly word would reach out and
lash her. "I-I..." Hot tears struck, and I took a step backward.
"I'm her mama!" I punched the words and claimed it for the

truth. "*Her mama.* And I aim to bury the Moffits, and proper-like, Jackson Lovett. Do it myself." I was out the door, my angry skirts swishing a curse across the threshold.

"Hold up," he said, following me down the steps.

Junia blew, swung her head back and forth, tried to break free of her tether.

I yelled at him. "Stay back...back till I can get my babe out of here!" To Junia I raised a hand. "*Whoa.* Easy, easy."

Jackson retreated back to the porch as if annoyed by Junia's protection.

With Honey tucked securely in the crook of my arm, I untied Junia with my free hand, gripped the mule's reins, and led her out of the yard.

Jackson called out, "Cussy Mary, I'll see they get a proper burial."

I stopped and turned to face him.

"As proper as one can get in this graceless land." His eyes were sad and troubling. "I'll have them buried 'fore sundown. You have my word."

All I could do was nod and breathe out a raspy *obliged* before continuing onto the path.

Forty

I held Honey by the stove while the pap I'd made for her cooled. In a few minutes I dipped a cloth into the breadcrumb broth and dribbled the mixture into her tiny open mouth. Pa stood nearby, allowing a stretch of silence to smother our quarrel.

"Daughter, it ain't right," he finally said.

"Pa, I mean to keep her." I set down the feeding rag and rocked the babe. "She's mine—"

"*Silence.* What would folks say? An unwed mother with a babe? *Think.* This ain't a critter you can just up and take a fancy to."

"A *Blue.* I'll take a week off, then let folks think she's from Charlie Frazier."

Nobody'd be the wiser. Just Jackson. Doc might from examining me, but he never saw Angeline and was too busy with his medical journals and patients. I didn't think either man would tell, and ghosts couldn't.

I added, "The timing would be right, and a lot of womenfolk hide their budding bellies behind the thick skirts. Pa, look. Look at her, she must be our kin. She's a Blue!"

"Nonsense, she's sickly. You're the last Blue."

"She's strong sure enough, and it's not true. Doc says all Blues are related somehow. Kin to ourselves. Mr. Moffit had the Blue in him. I seen it with my eyes. Same as Honey here. And her mama must've had it in her genes too." I held up the sleeping baby. "They were *Blues,* Pa. Just like us."

Pa looked closer and muttered a low curse. "It was rumored my uncle Eldon had a bastard out there. Could it be he'd found another Blue that weren't known?" Pa rubbed his whiskers.

"It happened to Great-Grandpa. It has to be. We can't leave our kin orphaned."

"They said Eldon's woman ran away to Ohio, never to be heard of again." Pa studied Honey and scratched some more at the thought.

"Pa, Eldon's woman gave her baby away. Gave Willie away. *Please*. I have to take Honey as mine. Give her a home, a mama. Ain't no one—not a single soul on this black-and-white earth— gonna do it if we don't. Please, I promised the mama."

He touched the baby's blue fingernail and traced her cheek. Something softened in Pa.

"My patron, Henry, passed," I whispered. "The boy died of the pellagra, Pa. The Kentucky sickness took him, and it'll surely take her too. Without us, it'll happen to her. Our last kin."

The baby's eyes fluttered open, and she squinted up at Pa. A tiny smile pulled at the corners of her lips as she twisted to suckle his finger. Pa ran a pinkie over her mouth, turning it all in his mind. Honey rooted, latched hold of his little finger, sucking.

Pa's eyes grew round as he watched her a second. "What kinda ma are you?" he grumbled, snatching back his hand. "Make her a pallet over by the stove, then get that ornery critter of yours to town and fetch this hungry babe real milk!"

I stared at him, dumbfounded and grateful.

"Go on now 'fore she gets to fussing and disturbs me," he said and turned away.

"Yessir." I stepped out the door, grinning as I raced to Junia.

Forty-One

After I saddled Junia, I looked in on Pa and the babe and saw that Honey was sleeping. Pa had settled into a chair near her pallet and fallen asleep too, holding one of my children's storybooks in his lap.

I headed toward the Moffits' homestead, eager to make the stop before I went for the baby's milk. I needed to make sure Honey's folks got themselves the burial Jackson'd promised.

As we got close to the broken-down cabin, every few steps, Junia would switch her stride and walk sideways, her nose arrowed toward the Moffits' home, a soft bray blistering her lips like she was calling for her friend Angeline.

The air smelled of mud. Turkey buzzards circled above, pressing blackened smudges against the hard Kentucky sun.

I found Jackson around back with his horse tied to a stick post. He stood over the potter's ground where he'd dug up two fresh mounds under a half-broke tree, the only shade back there. Jackson rested an arm on the shovel with his back to me, head bowed in what looked like thought or prayer. A damp circle bull-eyed his shirt as the July sun hammered its waves of heat onto everything.

I slid off Junia and fumbled with the reins before dropping them. Instead of staying put, the mule trotted toward Jackson, blew over his shoulder, then—to my surprise—nuzzled his arm.

"No flowers today," he told her solemnly and rubbed her neck.

I stepped up beside him and reached into my pocket. "Thank you, Jackson. I have your pay." I pulled out money.

He dropped the shovel and raised a palm in protest. "For the baby. How's she doing?"

"I got her settled in. Pa's tending to her. She seems right fit."

Jackson pointed to one of the graves, cleared his throat, and said, "Takes a mighty special woman to take in a mother's baby like that, Cussy Mary. To raise Mrs. Moffit's babe."

I studied Angeline's grave. The mound of loose dirt. Even it was sparse. "She's a right special baby," I said more to the heavens, hoping the words would reach dear Angeline.

"And a lucky one." He dug into his pocket, pulled out hair that had been braided into a small ring, and gave it to me. "I thought Honey might want her parents' locks. Snipped them off for her keepsake." A sorrow clung to his words.

He'd done that for Honey—thought to cut off small locks of her folks' hair like that. Jackson'd woven each of their strands, then carefully weaved those two together into a third, the one that represented Honey.

As if reading my thoughts, Jackson said, "My mama died of smallpox when I was twelve, and I lost my twin baby brothers a week later." He grimaced. "I can still see my papa saying it was important to honor the dead by keeping a part of them living. He'd tucked their locks into our Bible. I did the same to his, two years later after he drank himself to death."

"I'm sorry." Without thinking, I told him, "After Mama died, Pa went on a tear, ran off into the woods somewhere. He soaked his boots in the shine, had himself a mighty battle with devils and angels, I reckon. He didn't come out of the hills for three nights and not a second sooner and until the miners found him and dragged him home. I thought I'd lost them both."

I'd never shared anything about Pa's tear before, not to anyone. That Jackson could draw this story out of me so easily frightened me, and I searched his face to see if my words did something to him too.

Jackson nodded with the kinship of knowing something no one else did. "I ended up leaving these hard parts when I was fourteen and swore I'd never come back. Wandered around the country till I settled out west. Worked a lot trying to forget it all. But, hell, anyone knows a Kentucky man ain't gonna let the wandering legs plant themselves anyplace other than here—can have hisself one foot on foreign soil, but the other is always pointed home."

His words were measured with regret and relief, a flash of old hurts sweeping across his eyes.

I gave Jackson a sympathetic smile and said, "My great-grandpa came from a small village in France, but my folks always claimed he came here to collect his 'tucky heart. They say I favored him, and they named me after the town he was born in."

"*Cussy*, France?" Jackson looked at me like he saw something new. Then, "Well, I didn't think it was because of your mouth."

I smiled at that. "It's a right pretty place from what I've seen in the *National Geographic*." I peered at the ring he'd made. "Much obliged, Jackson. This is a special gift, and I'll keep it in the Bible for Honey." I held up the keepsake, peered at the tiny woven ring of Willie's dark hair and Angeline's blond. A precious piece of their life, for Honey's new life that she could hold forever. I pressed it to my mouth with a silent prayer and slipped it into my pocket, grateful for what Jackson had seen fit to do.

"This old land." Jackson stared off. "It sure makes a man yearn for it and want to flee it altogether."

"Ain't never had the chance to leave," I said and wondered if he would again, wondered if I'd ever. At that thought, a peculiar new ache seized me.

Jackson darted his eyes to mine and held them.

"Queenie Johnson wants me to visit her. She says there's opportunities in Philadelphia. That it's a fine place to raise colored young'uns." For the first time I thought hard about Honey, what kind of life we could have there, reckoning anyplace might be softer, better than here.

"Cussy Mary, I've been wanting to apologize for my words back on the trail that day. I had no right telling you how you should feel. No right claiming knowledge on things I could and will never feel. I've never known harm or exile because of my skin. Nor felt the lash of leather whips or angry tongues because of it."

I shifted uncomfortably.

Jackson stepped toward me. "Forgive me. I was damn foolish, blind, because I only saw a smart librarian, a fine lady. I see more now...see your burden and grief, and I am sorry for it."

A silence fell as I searched his anguished eyes, grasping the words.

He was about to say something more, then stopped and pointed to the hill behind the graves. "I'm not finished here."

My eyes followed his.

"There should be some sort of markings." Jackson climbed up the rocked slope and picked up two hand-sized stones, weighed them and scampered down. He placed one at the head of each grave and stepped back to inspect them. "I'll take them home and see if I can chisel proper headstones for them. Bring 'em back tomorrow at first light."

"I'm much obliged."

Jackson scooped up a handful of dirt beside the covered plots, letting it sift over the graves. He bowed his head.

I followed his lead, grabbed a fistful, and sprinkled it over the hungry earth.

"Go in peace, you've earned your sleep. God rest," Jackson said, picking up their stone markers. He walked them over to his horse, stuffed them into bags. Then he was off, galloping away.

For a while I stood over the graves, babbling to Angeline, praying, promising her that I'd take care of Honey till she was good an' grown—till the day I died. I looped my prayers and declarations until the ground seemed to shift, and Junia brayed a warning. I squeezed my eyes, and then opened them and saw the buzzards had tightened their circular pattern. Their afternoon shadows hungered, had grown bigger.

Forty-Two

Honey was a week old when I traveled the mile and a half to Loretta Adams's door and knocked.

"Iffin' that's Bluet, get on in here, child."

"It's me, Book Woman, ma'am."

"And poor-sighted I am, not deaf," she answered back, as always.

Candles flickered and cast extra light in the cabin. Loretta sat at her table, her head bent to fabric, sewing.

"I'm making a new apron. This one's so tatty." She plucked the yoke of her old one she wore.

"Sure is looking pretty, Miss Loretta."

Loretta whipped a few more stitches into the new cobbler's apron, inspected its cotton lace trim. "You haven't been by," she chided. "I don't have the tea made." She stuck her needle into a pincushion and pushed away the long apron panels.

"No, ma'am. I'm not here to read today."

I walked over to her chair and bent down. "I'm here to show you Honey." I lifted back the baby's light covering and moved her closer to Loretta's face.

Honey made soft noises.

"Honey? A baby?"

"Yes, ma'am, my baby. She's mine."

She didn't respond, and I know'd her manners wouldn't allow her to pry.

Loretta peered closer at Honey, and the babe cooed, struck up her tiny fists, and yawned. "Let's put her on my bed," Loretta said.

Myrtle and Milkweed crawled out from under the woodstove, and Loretta scatted them out the door. The old woman hobbled over to the bed faster than I'd ever seen her move.

"Let me hold her, child. Could you open the curtains wider?" She sat down on the mattress, and I placed Honey in her arms.

I pulled back the homespun curtains, and the light spilled across Loretta's adoring smile.

"Miss Loretta—"

"Have a seat. *Sit*," Loretta urged and patted the spot beside her, intent on studying Honey.

"Thank you, ma'am."

"She's precious." Loretta lifted Honey's small blue hand, gently stroked her tiny fingers.

"Yes, ma'am, she's a good babe sure enough."

"Perfect. I haven't held myself one of these in ages," Loretta said in a strange choked voice. "Thank you for bringing her by."

"Miss Loretta, I need to ask if you would be willing to keep her while I'm on my route, if you'd feel up to it, that is. I'd pay you square, and the babe don't need much—"

"Up to it? You don't need eyes to know what Honey needs, child. I raised my li'l sister, fed, cleaned, clothed, and rocked her, and she was a fussy babe too. And she grew into a fit child and a fine young woman. Raised her boy after she passed too. I can sure 'nough take care of our sweet Honey."

I sighed, relieved. "Yes, ma'am, I thought you'd do a fine job is why I brought her to you. And I'll pay on time."

"I won't accept money," Loretta said firmly. "Can't accept pay for being in the company of this angel." She shot Honey a big, toothless grin, dipped her wagging head to the babe. "An angel, the prettiest petunia," she told Honey. "A right purty blue-eyed Mary beauty…"

"I insist, ma'am. It wouldn't be right."

"Ain't having it." The woman blinked and rubbed her tired eyes, and I could see they were paining her.

I figured Loretta would be too proud to accept payment. I thought a moment and said, "Only if I can pay Doc to drop by and treat your eyes with his fine city medicine."

"Doc's a smart man," she said. "Know'd him a long time."

"He is, and he'll care nicely for you, Miss Loretta. He could fit you for spectacles."

"*Spectacles*." Loretta peered out the window and then squinted down at Honey.

"They'll help your weak eyes see—and they'll fix 'em up good as new."

"Oh, to see again." She pondered, rubbing them. "That would be a fine thing. Fine thing as any." She picked up my hand, squeezed it. "Thank you, child, thank you for bringing me Honey. She shan't want for naught. I'll tend to her right good."

My heart told me Miss Loretta would do just that. "I'll make sure I fetch you milk and bring clean diaper cloths."

But she didn't hear, for she was under Honey's sweet spell. Loretta bent over and brushed her lips across the baby's soft head, picked up her tiny hand, spread the fingers, and kissed each nub. When Loretta raised her eyes, I could see they were bright and shiny, youthful and strong.

"Me an' Honey's gonna get along jus' fine, child," she said, handing her to me. "Where's my broom?" Miss Loretta jumped up like a spry young'un and began bustling about. "I have to get this place cleaned. Oh, land sakes! I must shake out the rugs. Clean my stove. This place ain't fit for a new babe. Not for my Honey girl."

Forty-Three

The babe was barely two weeks old on August 7, 1936, when Pa lit a new courting candle, pouring the hot wax onto a glass drip tray he'd fashioned from a saucer and cementing the naked taper in the puddle to burn later for an alarming length of time. A straight thread of smoke rose toward the wooden beams, then shivered from a breeze that blew through the open window.

"This'll do just fine," he said. "Have to do, since I don't have money for a new one. I can't be digging up your old courting one and disturbing the dead like that," Pa fussed.

I circled around him with the baby in my arms, alarm pricking my flesh. "Pa, don't do this."

"*Daughter*," he hushed, letting me know the discussion was wearing him.

Pa leaned over and blew out the candle. Satisfied, he carried it onto the porch. He was determined. Determined to get his unwed, baby-ridden daughter hitched, and his grandbaby a pa.

I placed Honey in the crib he'd built her and followed him.

"Pa, please, I won't marry again."

"Cussy." He raised the candle. "I'm gonna see you get your respectability just like I promised your mama. And make sure Honey'll have herself a papa. This stick *will* hold the fire, Daughter."

"I *have* my respectability—"

"Honey needs herself a father, and you need yourself a man. A good one who'll properly care for you."

"Please. We're fine. I have myself good pay with the Pack Horse, and Loretta watches Honey while I work."

"Loretta's old...and...blind," he rasped, swallowing several coughs.

"She can use the money I give to the doc for her each month. And she did a right fine job with Honey so far this week. Remember Lila Dawson? She's blind, widowed, and has raised herself four babes—"

"I won't have it!" He smacked the railing, choking. "The mine's shutting down in a week, and I need to make sure you'll be taken care of!"

"You can get work with the WPA, Pa. There's so many easy jobs now for men needing 'em—"

Pa cut me a hard, scowling eye. "Beg for scraps, take the government's relief? If a man can't make do, he does without."

"They have lots of respectable jobs for men—"

"You mean for me to take their Paupers' Oath?" he said, deeply offended. A coal-stained hand flew to his chest.

I winced. It was true. Anybody who wanted a job with the WPA had to swear to poverty, take the oath, and leave their pantries and cupboards opened in case a government man might happen by and snoop around to make sure you were remaining good 'n' poor. I'd been lucky. The officials hadn't ventured into our cove yet. And not from lack of trying, but because we were tucked so deep, no matter how many times I'd given the proper directions to the supervisor who'd passed them on to the government men, they'd given up and turned back.

"Pa, let me take care of us. I don't want another courter— another husband." I wrung my hands, cracked and darkened from boiling Honey's diapers and Pa's clothing and sheets. "We'll be fine, you'll be fine."

"Let me tell you, Cussy, a miner's life is a short one."

"*Oh, Pa.*" I fanned his words away.

"Daughter, they buried eight of 'em last January after the collapse. Sealed that pit with them eight poor souls trapped inside it."

I had heard the horror of it all. How the men and young boys were trapped so far down in the midnight dust and crumbling rock, no one could reach them. Then a leak of poisonous gas put them to sleep. There weren't anything left to do, no way to rescue them except to cover the tomb and have a preacher hold a burial service at the face of the mine.

"Now, I ain't departing this earth and leaving my two girls to the likes of what the greedy man's leaving in our hills." Pa jutted out his chin.

I warmed at him including Honey as his, and was touched at how easily the babe had grown on him and tamped his moodiness the last two weeks. She'd brought a light into our dreary home and heavy hearts. And the warmth of it all had given me a peace like no other. Still, my belly knotted when he talked stubborn and scary like that.

"Pa, it ain't right you working yourself up so. We could go to the city, to Philadelphia. They have fine doctors who care for coloreds."

"*Enough.* I promised your mother." He coughed for a bit more, the anger attacking his lungs.

I plopped down into the chair. "Pa." I turned the conversation. "Who would want to marry a Blue? A Blue with a Blue baby?" I clasped my cold, fearful hands, folding them into my skirts. "It can't be anybody any good."

Pa cringed, and his gray eyes rested over on the creek.

"I don't want to leave my home. Leave you," I said.

"Cussy." He sighed and dropped into the chair. "It is I who must leave you. The doc says I'm not in good health."

"We'll go to Lexington and get better medicine. To a real city hospital. Please, Pa, let me stay and care for you—"

"This place ain't fit for you and Honey."

"I can provide for my own babe, and I don't need a husband to do that. I have my books."

His voice thickened. "You and the child deserve better. Deserve what I couldn't give you and your mama."

"Who could give us better? Who would want to? Even the homeliest white woman is prettier than me. To them, I'm a blemish, Pa, an outcast… Pa, please look at me."

He wouldn't. But I saw his reddening eyes, the color peaking under his coal-stained grimace.

"There's only a handful of eligible men left in town," I said quietly. "Most of them already turned me down. The others are too scared."

His shoulders dipped a little. "I have to see that you and the babe are cared for."

I pressed him again, "Who would marry a Blue? *Who?*"

In the distance, someone whistled lightly, toppling a horse's whinny. The tune trickled softly through the pines, down the singing waters, and across smooth rock.

"That one," Pa said, and raised his pointy chin toward the creek. He picked up his hat and lunch bucket, whisked out a good night, and was down the steps and off to the mine.

Over in her stall, Junia brayed and blew warnings, hawing long bellows.

I leaned over, listening to the courter's faint melody growing stronger, pressing my angry hands on the railing, and then over my ears.

I grabbed the courting candle off the table and tossed it out into the yard. The saucer danced violently in the air, then shattered on rock, sending the candle loose and tumbling—my signal that I was not available. I'd tell Pa the courter lit off when he got a closer look at me.

I sat back down and hummed a tune of my own, studying my hands, watching as they faded into a soft, misty blue.

Forty-Four

Like the warmth of winter candlelight cast across a beloved, worn book, he was. What he did was blazing with boldness when Jackson Lovett plucked my courting candle out of the dirt, carried it up the porch, and stuffed it into his pocket that night.

"Cussy Mary," he'd said. "I'll be needing this for my daughter when she gets her first courter."

I stood. "*You?*"

From behind his back, he pulled out a fisted posy of pretty blue-eyed Marys.

"If you and Honey'll have me?"

There was a promise in his voice, hope in his eyes, and a lick of stubbornness in his face.

"Me and my babe have ourselves everything we need right here, Jackson Lovett."

With his other hand, Jackson reached out and took mine. I pulled it free and turned away, afraid, crossing my ugly blue hands under my arms. Afraid of the feelings running through me.

From her stall, Junia nickered into the coming night. Out in the yard, Jackson's steed blew back. Frogs and other night critters trilled and beckoned the cooling darkness, rolling into my discomfort.

Jackson set the wildflowers on the wood railing, circled to face me, gently clasping my hands.

"I ain't accepting charity, Jackson." I untangled our hands

again and turned to go inside. "I don't need it. I have myself a respectable position, a proper life with my books. And I will make it a good one for me and Honey." I grabbed the door latch.

"Cussy Mary." He stepped closer, put a finger under my chin, seeking my eyes, trying to lock us together. "The WPA makes exceptions for married women now, and I'll see to it you get permission to tote books. You and those books are a shining light for our people. For *me.*"

I'd heard, but still I pushed him away with mistrustful eyes.

"I read the paperwork," Jackson said. "Despite those ladies down at the Library Center who were none too helpful when I told them why I wanted to—for you."

I could see Harriett's and Eula's pinched, confused faces, their reddening cheeks and tight-fisted envy.

"Cussy, I went to your papa and sought his permission to give you a proper courting, to ask for your hand."

Wide-eyed, I spun to face him. "You...*you* went to Pa?" I asked, surprised Pa hadn't gone to *him* to wheedle a courtship.

"Sure enough. The first time, after you brought those books to my hill, the second was after I saw you at the Library Center. There was a third after a certain mule ate your flowers." He cleared his throat. "A fourth and fifth. Your pa turned me down six times in all. *Six times.*" He held up six fingers, wiggling them, and shook his head.

"Six?"

"And there wasn't going to be a seventh, and I had to explain just that to Elijah Carter," he said firmly. "Same as I did with those fussy library ladies at the Center when they tried to keep the paperwork from me."

"Why would you marry a Blue?"

"I told your papa I love you, and I'm telling you now, and I'll damn sure nail that surety to every Kentucky crag, post it on every town door. I love you, Cussy Mary. And I will love our children, blue or white, it matters none."

Forever I'd let the darkness and brokenness live inside—let

others keep it there. His words were as fine as any prayer, and I wanted so bad to fall into his arms and get the salvation, but after accepting for so long what other folks thought of me, it was easier, safer not to.

"I promised your papa I would love and protect you and the babe. I promise you this now."

To think that the baby could be safe, protected, was what every Kaintuck mama longed for in this wild, unforgiving land. Still, I had my route, my books, and I felt a safeguard, a necessity in those treasures, and found my own strength like no other.

"I give you my word—my absolute love," he said. "Cussy—"

I placed a steadying hand on the splintered board of the old cabin where I'd been born, raised by my folks, the one who was no longer here and the ill one who barely remained.

"No, Jackson, I can't. I won't leave my pa sickly and alone."

"There's room on the mountain for Elijah—all of us."

Ever so gentle, he ran a thumb over my cheek.

The pain of poverty, years of shame, scorn, and loneliness paled, and I tried to break free and grasp the hope, embrace this wonderful, odd sentiment called love.

"I love you. *You.* And I mean to be the good man you deserve and promise to become the better man that you'll make me. I want to sit by the hearth every night, read to our young'uns, and grow old together. Please"—he held out his palm, waiting, his words wrapped in a strangeness I'd never heard—"Cussy Mary, be my bride and leave this dark hollow. Come up to the mountain with me."

In that moment, I looked into his eyes and know'd he meant the tender words, every one of them. And I know'd I wanted to be on that mountain with him forever.

He pulled me to him, pressed the promises onto my lips, setting them afire in roaring reds and oranges.

"For my beautiful book mistress," he whispered, plucking up the flowers and pressing the sky-blue and white velvet blossoms into my hands.

Weren't a single soul who'd ever breathed words like that to me, ever uttered or saw me as anything other than a color, an ugly color—and said so too—or ever made me hear it as a truth. But Jackson Lovett did. And for the first time in my life, the ugliness vanished, and I felt a light dance in me and rise out of the darkness.

"Marry me?" he asked.

I heard a pureness in his proposal, the prayer from his heart, and a certainty that he'd been saving it a lifetime and just for me.

"Marry me, Cussy Mary, and I promise to spend every waking breath trying to be worthy of you."

My voice became strangled with tears. I could only nod a feverish yes.

Forty-Five

Hours after Jackson left, I couldn't rest, had to keep moving, couldn't help marveling at the new feeling of love, its energy.

I checked on the baby many times, fed her and changed her cloths. Honey must've felt it all too because she wouldn't go back to sleep. She wasn't crying or fussing neither. I picked up *Milly-Molly-Mandy* and began to read to her. "Once upon a time." I flipped open the storybook and stopped. "See the girl, Honey?" I pointed to the picture of the young'un dressed in a frock. Honey blinked and stared at it. "Her name is Milly-Molly-Mandy." I lightly scratched Honey's chubby tummy, and she squirmed and cooed. "Look at your pretty, smart self." I smiled. "You're eager to learn all the words." When I finished the first chapter, she closed her eyes and quieted.

Out on the porch, I folded diapers and hummed a ditty, the tingle of Jackson's kiss still fresh on my lips. In a bit, I picked up a book on the table and flicked through it. The lantern cast a soft light across my busy fingers, my mind near bursting, picturing the three of us reading together. I'd show Honey my route one day and introduce her to my patrons. I thought of the opportunities the young'un would have. How the Pack Horse library, its books, had opened my eyes to places and folks beyond these hills, breathed a new life now with Jackson. Honey'd have it all. *Books'll learn you* were Angeline's last words to Honey, and I vowed to give the babe all the books. Give her what dear

Angeline wanted, and the dreams I was desperate for her to have. Lighthearted, I shut the book and returned to my task.

The tittering neighs of someone's mount brought me back. I looked up from my laundry and saw the ghostly lit lanterns, two mules approaching, and what trailed behind them scraping the ground.

The cloth fell to the boards, and I slowly rose, swallowing my cheerful thoughts, the fear weighing my legs, stitched tight in my belly. One of the beasts was harnessed with a stretcher.

I squinted at the men's dark, drawn faces and flew down the steps feeling the gallop of my heart reach my ears.

"Pa? No, Pa...Pa—" I ran into the yard and collapsed by the stretcher, shook his shoulders. "Pa? Oh, Pa, wake up." I kneeled over him screaming, then shook him, my voice an ugly crackle, strained from pleas to wake his lifeless form, my hands desperate to bring the dead back to life. "*Please.*" I clutched his coal-stained shirt, shook harder, clawed at the coarse fabric, the remnants of the mine breathing its last deadly breaths of coal dust into the air. "Don't leave me. Wake up and let me tell you about the courter. Pa! I'm getting married." I grasped his cold lifeless hand and cradled his coal-stained head with my other one. "Pa, oh, Pa, the stick held the fire." I leaned into his face. "*Took hold fine.* And he's a fine one you picked. Pa, don't leave us," I begged. "Please don't leave." I laid my wet, burning cheek against his hard, cold one.

The beast's nervous brays, nickering mingled with my rasping cries, spirited into gusts of grieving winds that plucked at the house boards, old chinks, and window cracks, carrying bursts of the night madness through pines.

"Ma'am," a man's soft voice called above. I peered up as the coal miner dismounted and approached with a lantern. "Ma'am. Uh, Miss Cussy, I'm Howard Moore. Mighty sorry to be bringing him home like this." He grimaced and shook his head, squeezed his red eyes shut. "We was pulling pillars tonight."

It was one of the most dangerous jobs of a coal miner, one

that most shirked from: the Company's last job where the men took out the pillars of coal that held up the roof of the tunnel to keep the top of the mountain from collapsing.

"Elijah got trapped. Mighty sorry." Mr. Moore set down the lantern, played with the carbide helmet a second. He brushed off the coal dust on Pa's lamp, then held it out. "Your pap was one of the best, ma'am. Volunteered to pull pillars with me when no one else would. A good, hardworking man who took care of us all. He made me get out first. Insisted. Then I couldn't find him at the mouth… By the time I got back to him, he weren't long for this world—" The miner choked and rubbed a tight fist across his coal-stained mouth. "I held Elijah's hand, and we prayed and talked a few minutes 'fore the Lord took him. He will be sorely missed and will cast a long shadow over these ol' Kaintuck mountains."

Soft murmurs of the other men echoed the miner's.

He wiped Pa's hat on his sleeve, handed it to me, and I clutched it to my cheek, pressed the sooty helmet to my trembling lips.

The miners trudged up the hill to our small family cemetery and dug hard into the night. Later, when I heard them talking softly on the porch, I peeked out and saw them passing drink. A coal miners' tradition. One or more would stay with the body, keep watch over their fellow miner, never leave the dead man to face his last earthly moments alone until he was tucked good 'n' safe into the ground.

Around 5:00 a.m., I heard a horse's high whinny and opened the door.

Someone rode into the yard on a horse-drawn cart. I walked out to the porch, raised my lantern, and saw the coffin it carried. Then I saw the man who had ridden it.

Jackson.

I raced down the porch steps. Jackson jumped down from the wagon and opened his arms, taking me in with his strong clasp. "I stopped in town to have a late meeting with Amos Dalton about timber when I heard about the mine accident. I'm sorry, Cussy Mary. I saw the miners leaving for your place. I wanted to help. They chipped in and made sure Elijah would have a fine coffin, and I borrowed the cart from Amos to get it here. We'll see Elijah has a proper burial. Preacher will be out at first light."

To have lost Henry and Angeline in such a short time, and now my only parent. The grief spilled forth, swallowing me. Jackson drew me closer and I buried my face in his chest, and huge sobs racked my body while he held on to me, his arms steady and healing.

At dawn, I found Mr. Moore sitting on the grass beside Pa's covered stretcher while the others were half-asleep on the porch. The men roused and told me Jackson had gone off to ride in with the preacher.

The sky turned into a gray beast. The winds whipped off hats, plucked at our overcoats, and whistled prayers through the treetops as we laid Pa to rest on the knoll up in our old, small Carter cemetery beside Mama and the other Blues.

Forty-Six

Pa always believed a marriage in the fall would bring a union of rebirth that'd bud slow, grow steady and strong from the dying season, while a marriage made in the hot summer would be short-lived and quick to wither. We set our wedding date for October. Honey would be three months old, fit and ready to make her first visit to town.

I'd bought dress fabric from the dry goods store that had opened after the Company store and mine closed down, and used the simple Butterick pattern I'd found in a box of library donations at my outpost.

The dress hem rested comfortably at my shins. It was a pretty print of golds and chocolates, with a matching sash, a modest scooped neckline, and long, soft sleeves. Perfect. Not too severe, not too prissy, my marriage dress fit the fine fall weather we'd been having.

"Ain't that a good-lookin' dress, child. And these stitches are some of the best I've seen," Loretta'd declared on her porch, peering through her new spectacles when I'd showed it off to her. "Why the fabric's a sure match for the ol' 'tucky mountains and your special day."

The hills had trotted out the boldest colors this autumn, blushed in scarlets, pumpkins, and golds. The dying leaves shimmered in lifting breezes, somehow breathing life into the dying season.

On the morning of October 20, I stood over Pa's grave and thought about him and the days since his passing, his long shadow alive across the slumbering mountains. "Pa, I miss you and Mama. It's my wedding day, and I wish you could see it— see how the books brought us together. I am filled with love. Jackson's a good man, the finest. Honey is fit an' growing. We're going to be just fine. *Fine.* You rest in peace now." I laid a hand on my parents' headstone.

An hour later, Jackson rode us into Troublesome and parked the little horse-drawn wagon at the post office. Before he helped us down, he held up a finger. "I've got your wedding present." He pulled out a brown package from inside his jacket.

"But I didn't get you one," I protested as he took Honey and handed me the gift.

"Open it," Jackson pushed.

Carefully, I unwrapped a book of collected poems by Yeats. "Thank you. It's beautiful." I rubbed my fingers over the gray buckram and beveled edges, traced the title on the leather label.

"It'll be the perfect start for a library, Cussy Mary."

"*Library,*" I whispered, awed by his love of books.

"Our library." He opened the collection to the title page, looked at me, and read the inscription he'd written along with a verse from one of Yeats's poems underneath. "For my dear bride and book woman, Cussy Mary Lovett, October 20, 1936:

> "'*And shy as a rabbit,*
> *Helpful and shy.*
> *To an isle in the water*
> *With her I would fly.*'"

I traced his script with a fingertip to magpie the precious words away to my heart. With him, I would fly wherever the winds might take us. Jackson placed his hand over mine and the book and squeezed.

He lifted us down from the buckboard wagon, tethered the

horse to a post, then carried Honey in one arm and looped his other around mine.

Harriett and Eula stepped outside the Center, their faces flushed, eyes straining.

I'd never told them my business, and they'd never cared to ask. Still grieving Pa, I hadn't come to the Center in September and stuck to my book route. And when October rolled around, I'd missed the Center again after Honey fell ill with a fever. Mindful, I'd followed the WPA's regulations and made up those two missed days with weekend book deliveries.

Jackson turned his head to the library ladies, grinned wide, pausing to tip his dandy new felt hat. "Ladies. It's a fine morning."

I looked up at his joyful eyes.

"Yes, ma'am, a mighty fine day to marry Troublesome's finest gal," Jackson practically crowed.

Harriett and Eula had their hands planted to their chests, mouths agape, inviting flies.

Honey pulled off her new bonnet, and I tied it back onto her head, swept a kiss across her chubby sweet cheek.

Eula's face softened a little at that. She took out a handkerchief from a pocket and dabbed it over her eyes and pressed it to her nose.

Harriett elbowed her sharply and whispered something. Flustered, Eula leaned away and shook her head. Then Harriett hollered, "*Bluet!*" She raised her arm, waved. "Bluet, you missed two days at the Center." She stepped off the stoop. "You be here Monday, and on time! You'll be crating books all day and the next for Oren."

I was delighted to hear they'd hired Mr. Taft, and it didn't bother me none to do the heavy lifting. I'd do their work all day, every day, as long as I had the books and spent my nights with Jackson. I glanced up at him and warmed in anticipation of our first night.

Jackson felt it too. I caught the yearning in his bright eyes and saw his love would be tender and beautiful.

"Bluet, seven sharp, not a minute later," Harriett snipped, her order bouncing down the street.

Jackson turned and in a smooth voice said, "I'll make sure my bride's not late." Then he winked in a shameless manner at the library ladies before pulling me into a fiery public kiss.

Honey squealed, and Jackson pecked her cheek and released me, both of us reluctant to part.

Harriett gasped and worked a silent sassing mouth. The two women stretched their necks our way and locked eyes with me, a mix of wonderment, surprise. Then Harriett whispered again to Eula, but the head librarian wagged her head and disappeared back inside.

Harriett stomped off toward the dry goods, her angry skirts scattering leaves.

Jackson led us inside the courthouse and down the hall to a small office. "It's the wedding couple," Mr. Dalton, the banker and Jackson's friend, called out a cheerful greeting. He looked dapper in his suit. Doc stepped forward and kissed my cheek, thumped Jackson lightly on the back. "What a pretty bride, Bluet. A blessed day for a wedding indeed."

The officiant slipped a finger under his bow tie, straightening the band. In a minute, his wife came into the room with a Bible. "Good morning. I hope I didn't keep you," she said, her eyes darting over the faces before landing on mine.

"Ah, good morn', Margie, meet our lovely couple, Jackson and Cussy," the justice said. Margie murmured a shy hello. She opened the Bible, found a page, then passed it to her husband and took the spot beside him.

The justice said, "We are gathered before God and man today to join this couple in holy matrimony."

Honey rested her head on Jackson's shoulder, and he reached for my hand.

A sharp rap on the door interrupted, and coal miner Howard Moore poked his head inside. "Pardon, sir, but I need you to stop the ceremony."

"What's the nature of this?" the justice scowled. "This is a legal and holy matrimony."

A chorus of fizzling gasps crawled around the warm room.

Jackson tensed, and I gripped his hand in a dampening clasp.

"Take your leave," Doc demanded and squeezed up front, glaring hotly at the miner.

Mr. Moore shook his head. "I need to have a word with the officiant. It's mighty important. Won't take long." He twisted his hat in a hand, anxious.

The justice quickly excused himself and left the room. Doc leaned in between us, wrapped his arms over our shoulders and whispered, "I'm sure Justice will be right back and will have you married within the hour." He nodded firmly and took his place close behind us.

We stared at the door, watching.

Honey fidgeted in the heat, wriggled in Jackson's arms. The air felt like it had wrapped the room in molasses.

When the justice returned a few minutes later, Mr. Moore and two other miners who had brought Pa home that August night pushed into the room with us.

"Cussy," the justice said, "the men have something important to ask of you."

The miners were pink-faced and scrubbed, with worn hats clasped to their bellies, dressed in clean but coal-stained work britches and pressed shirts.

Puzzled, I murmured my consent, and Mr. Moore stepped forward.

"Ma'am, uh, Miss Cussy, the last words of your dear pap was for you. He asked that I stand in his place should this marriage come to pass. And I promised I would... And iffin' it's alright with you, Miss Cussy, I'd sure like to keep my word and see you knotted an' done right. Be honored to give you away, ma'am."

"Yes," I barely breathed.

"Very good, Mr. Moore," the justice said. "We can now begin the ceremony with your passage."

Mr. Moore took the empty spot by my side, pulled out a tattered piece of paper, and said, "Elijah asked me to read this, Song of Songs 8:6."

And very carefully, Mr. Moore did. "'Place me like a seal over your heart, like a seal on your arm; for love is as strong as death, its jealousy unyielding as the grave. It burns like blazing fire, like a mighty flame,'" the coal miner read.

Slowly I turned to Mr. Moore and saw Pa there with his burning candle, speaking through him.

The ceremony didn't last more than five whirlwind minutes and came to a close when Jackson kissed me, and the justice of the peace pronounced us Mr. and Mrs. Lovett and kindly added *And Miss Honey Lovett*. A flurry of kisses, congratulations, and pats on backs passed around the stuffy room.

Outside, I was surprised to see Birdie with her boy waiting on the courthouse steps. R.C. and his young bride stood beside them, and Martha Hannah, Devil John, and the young'uns lingered nearby, along with a few other curious bystanders.

A secret flickered in Jackson's eyes.

"Did you invite these folks?" I asked.

"I may've mentioned the wedding to a few when I was clearing your paths, checking on your route."

I was thrilled that he wanted my patrons here for me, even more that he'd taken over what Pa'd done: clearing the briars and brush trails to keep me and Junia safer.

I spied Timmy Flynn and his mama standing back in the little crowd. Timmy ran up to me, handed me a scraggly daisy, and hugged my waist before disappearing behind his mama's skirts.

Small cheers and well wishes lifted into the air as my patrons gathered around to watch us depart.

Jackson helped us onto the wagon. A young man limped over and introduced himself as Alonzo, Loretta Adams's nephew. He reached up to hand me a bulky package. "Aunt 'Retta sent me to deliver a gift. God bless ya, Mr. an' Mrs. Lovett." His greeting was slowed with whiskey.

"Thank you for coming, Alonzo." I passed Honey to Jackson and opened the present. It was a neatly folded calico quilt with colors of many hues. Miss Loretta's note read:

October 20, 1936

Child,

May your union blossom and your lives be filled with all the precious colors of God's glorious fabrics.

Your library patron,
Miss Loretta Adams

I looked at Jackson and our beautiful child, then turned my gaze toward the colorful Kaintuck mountains and back to my precious patrons, feeling blessed by the glorious tapestry they had given me, by their lives that enriched mine. I didn't want to leave, needed to give my thanks, linger, and share this moment, this time, with each of them. I loved these folks, and for the very first time, I felt them loving me back.

From behind, I heard someone call for Jackson. Once, then more urgent. "Hold up, Lovett."

It was Sheriff and his deputy, and they looked agitated. Doc followed close on their heels, his face just as red.

Jackson handed Honey back up to me.

A door creaked open, and Harriett stepped out of the Library Center and folded a smugness into her crossing arms.

Confused, I searched the faces of the lawmen, stiffened atop the wagon seat.

"Davies Kimbo, you have no qualms with these good folks." Doc rushed up to Jackson's side. Most of my patrons milled about and stared, straining to hear.

Sheriff Kimbo ignored the doc.

Despite the cool fall day, Honey's face grew flushed, and a fussy whine rose from her. I patted, rubbed her back with my darkening hand, jiggling her on a knee.

"Jackson Lovett, you're under arrest," Sheriff said.

Jackson spun around, puzzlement crawling into his bright eyes.

"What? What's the meaning of this—" Jackson demanded.

"Miscegenation laws. Kentucky law says intermarriages between Negroes or persons of color in Kentucky are prohibited and punishable," Sheriff clipped.

"That's absurd," Doc said. "Your kin, Charlie, sure 'nough married her, Kimbo."

"Bluet can't marry again," Sheriff said flatly. "The law was revised this June, and it now states clearly and includes *any* color, *any* mix."

A bigger crowd gathered, pushed forward, closer now.

Someone yelled, "Lock them sinners up, immoral!"

Another cried "No!"

And one more shouted, "Heathens!"

I gasped. It had never happened here, but I'd read about the laws in the city newsprints and know'd they were being enforced in other places. Folks were charged and thrown in jail for courting someone not like themselves, for taking another color to their marriage beds. It was an ugly law that let mere folk lord over different-type folks, decide who a person could or couldn't love.

"You got no quarrel with me, Sheriff," Jackson said, dismissing him and lifting a foot to get into the wagon.

Sheriff shifted and squared his shoulders. "The law clearly states that marrying a colored destroys the very moral supremacy of our Godly people and is damning and destructive to our social peace."

"I'm taking my wife and daughter home," Jackson told the sheriff.

"You listen to me, Lovett. You think you can jus' waltz back in to Kaintuck with your highfalutin ways and soil the good people. No, sir, this ain't the west!" Sheriff's face heated with a fury.

The crowd's voices rose like a swarm of angry bees.

Honey startled with a whimper and rubbed her tearing eyes. Again, I patted her back and clutched her closer to me.

"Tha's right!" Someone in the crowd punched the holler.

"They ought to be horsewhipped," another bellowed. "Ain't natural, ain't right, Sheriff."

"Shut your mouth, Horace! *You* ain't right in the head," another lashed back.

"You best come peacefully, Lovett," the deputy warned.

Mr. Dalton pushed through the crowd and said, "I will have you answering to Mayor Gibson for this, Davies Kimbo." He turned and made his way back to the courthouse.

"Stop this foolishness, Sheriff," Doc said loudly. "No law has been broken. A simple pill can turn Bluet white."

A hush fell over Troublesome, and then another buzz climbed into the air and seemed to deafen me, making me light-headed.

Some looked up at me and pointed; others wagged tongues to their closest neighbor.

Honey buried a sob against my chest, and I tried to speak softly to her above my own loud heartbeats.

"It's the truth, Davies," Doc said.

Sheriff glanced at me, unsure, then shook his head and said, "That's hogwash, Thomas, and you can save it for the judge. He's being lawfully charged for fornication and the unlawful marriage and cohabitation with a colored and mixed citizen."

Fornication. Dumbfounded, I opened and closed my mouth, and the scratched denials trickled out. "No, no—"

Jackson's voice toppled mine. "Go to hell, Kimbo."

"Dammit," Doc's curse laddered atop of Jackson's. "It's lawful, and I'll attest Bluet has a medical condition and can be treated with pills."

"It's true, Sheriff." R.C. stepped forward and tucked his head. "Yessir, it is. Seen it for myself. Miss Bluet, uh, Book Woman, was a white 'fore my very eyes."

"She's a gawdamn colored!" Sheriff turned and told the stirring crowd. A man and woman jeered; another gasped.

Again, Honey fussed and squirmed in my arms, and I tried to rock her.

Jackson glanced up at us, his face rigid with grief, worry, and a hint of something troubling.

"I seen it, Sheriff, and so did my Ruth," R.C. said, quiet but insistent.

"You get on back to your fire tower, lad, or I'll see to you fighting a bigger fire with them whimp'd park ranger bosses of yours," Sheriff barked.

A few folks guffawed.

R.C. flinched, and his freckled face turned penny orange.

Doc cursed and then pleaded, "Davies, she's a decent woman, for God's sakes—"

Sheriff cut an eye to me. "I know Bluet's a good enough lass, but she's a colored one jus' the same." He shot out an accusing arm to me. "And I know damn well you already attested to her being of fit body and sound mind!"

Harriett stepped out of the crowd to glare, and I dropped my gaze, remembering Doc had told her just that.

Doc looked to Harriett and the sheriff, studying, then turned back to the assistant supervisor, a contempt rising in his wrinkled brow.

Harriett's cold eyes filled with defiance, and she tilted a triumphant chin skyward.

Jackson's eyes tightened, and he tossed his hat into the back of the wagon and loosened the collar on his freshly pressed shirt.

Doc shook his head. "She's not colored. I've told you: it's a medical ailment and—"

"She sure enough *is*," Sheriff thundered. "An ailment on these good folks. Step aside, man."

"We're lawfully married, Sheriff." Jackson fished into his pocket and pulled out the folded marriage license and flicked it open.

I tried to speak, but the words thickened in my throat, smothering. Honey squalled, and I lowered her onto the boards with shaky hands, trying to calm her so I could go to my husband. She quieted some, and I climbed down and went to Jackson's side.

A few of my patrons lifted their voices. "He's right. Let 'em go. Leave them in peace, Sheriff," one man called out from the back of the crowd, and I could tell it was Devil John.

"Best move along, Devil, lessen you be thirsting for something a little harder than what you can swallow—or are you wanting to spend more time with me again and let your paying customers go thirsty?" Sheriff shouted.

A few snickers floated in the air.

Devil John took a hard step forward, but Martha Hannah grabbed hold of his sleeve, whispered into his ear.

"This is a sham, and I'm taking my bride home. Let's go, Cussy Mary." Jackson reached for my arm.

"It's the law, and the law says she's just another nigger," Sheriff spit and grabbed Jackson's sleeve.

The words lay thick atop the crowd's energetic whispers. Then Harriett's hisses reached my ears. "A damnation. Sinners."

Jackson growled a low curse and leaned in toward the sheriff, then swung, and his fist landed square on the lawman's face. The marriage license floated to the ground.

Sheriff's head snapped, and he turned partway, wiped his cracked lips, and spit out blood. The deputy flew to Jackson's backside, latched hold of his arms, locking him in a hug. Sheriff drew back an arm and punched Jackson in the gut and thrust another to his head and one more to his middle.

I cried out for Jackson. Doc gripped hold of my arm and yanked me back.

Deputy shoved Jackson forward.

Jackson staggered, and I screamed and broke free of Doc just as my husband slumped to the ground. I bent down to Jackson, but the deputy stepped in front of me.

Doc cursed and rushed over. "Stop this, Davies! Stop, I say!"

"Take the wagon, Cussy," Jackson rasped as he tried to pull himself up to his knees. "I'll…" He pressed a hand on his side.

"I'll be along shortly." Doc laid a concerned hand on Jackson's shoulder, but he shrugged him off and took a breath, blood trickling from his brow. He got partway up, when Sheriff swung his boot, kicked him in the side and once again in the gut.

Jackson crumpled to the ground, struggled to rise to his knees. Sheriff got in one more hard kick.

"*Lie still!*" Sheriff ordered.

Jackson's jaw folded and smacked the earth, a flurry of dust rising. Then the deputy hefted a boot and brought it down on Jackson's leg. I heard the sickening sound of bone shatter fold into Jackson's scream, his cry echoing mine.

From the crowd, a single applause lifted and several protests rose, but no one dared step forward.

Jackson stretched out his arm and tried to pick up the dirt-stained marriage license near him, leaving a bloody print on the paper.

"I said lie still, boy, lessen you want to end up as jus' another dead nigger lover." Sheriff drew his gun from the holster. "Get on home, folks, before I lock you up for meddling with the law."

A few of the townsfolk slowly turned away, taking their leave, their grumbles falling into purring whispers.

Jackson moaned.

Sheriff pointed the gun at him.

"No, please don't hurt him." I dropped beside Jackson, huddled over him, begging. "Please, Sheriff, we don't mean any harm. Just let us go."

Jackson grunted one last time and passed out.

I cradled his face. "Jackson, wake up, *wake up*—"

Sheriff holstered his gun, then knocked my thigh with his boot, leaving a dirt stain on my wedding dress. "Get on."

A war cry erupted, and R.C. came charging at the lawman half-bent, his head aimed toward the sheriff's belly. But Sheriff had a bigger might, swiftness over the young boy, and grabbed R.C. by the shoulders and flung him to the ground.

The lawman planted a boot on the boy's chest. "You assault

me ever again, fire boy, and you'll be sitting in a prison cell if I don't stomp you down into the fires of hell first."

R.C. knocked his leg away, rolled over, and rose. "*You*—you keep your stinkin' hands off Book Woman!"

Ruth cried out for R.C., rushed up, and dragged him away.

"Bluet," Sheriff said, "you go on, girl. Take that colored babe of yours back to your holler 'fore I arrest you, or worse."

The sky seemed to tilt, and the earth moved as I squeezed my burning eyes and looked up at him. *Worse.* Pa's words struck like a cold steel blade. *Blues, many a colored have been hanged for less.*

"Someone fetch my bag," Doc hollered, as he folded his coat under Jackson's head and worried his healing hands over Jackson's busted bones.

A wail struck high, pierced and melded into old Kentucky winds, sweeping it into the pines, rattling me. I came to my senses and recognized Honey's cries.

"I've got him, Bluet. Give me room," Doc said.

I rose, my legs near folding, my arms reaching to the wagon for support.

I looked back at my battered husband and my heart ached, weighed heavy like stone.

Sheriff moved closer to Jackson and nodded to his deputy. "Let's get him up an' over to the jail. Doc can tend to him there."

The deputy motioned to two men. They lifted Jackson up and carried him across the street to jail, Doc fussing and following closely behind them.

Sheriff rubbed his hurting jaw, lightly touched his crooked nose. He winced, then spoke low, "I'm letting you go, Bluet, because of Elijah and the sacrifices he made for the good miners here. And I know how easily Lovett could've tricked a simple-minded Blue."

I stared at the sheriff, stunned. Honey's whimpers turned into a mournful wail, and I heard my family's burdens, their struggles, and the unspeakable horrors they had bore in the child's heartbreaking cries. A blinding fury balled into angry fists, and I drew a fire from it and raised a darkening hand.

"Pa was your miner's sacrifice, *your mule*," I said, locking eyes with the lawman, "and my *good* pa and many a *good* Blue made sacrifices so you and your kin wouldn't have to." I looked out into the crowd. "So you and your white families would be safe—have the protection, the life we never had, the life you take for granted." The disgust rose high in my voice, straining ugly and thin.

Murmurs rose from the hillfolk, and I saw the truth of my words reflected in solemn faces.

Sheriff cast his eyes downward, nudged the marriage license with his toe, then brought his heel down, ripping it in half. "The law says we're done. Now don't let me catch you loitering around here again unless you're on book business."

Our marriage had been halved as easily as an apple, and the split cast an unbearable grief across my heart.

"Get on, Bluet, 'fore I arrest you an' send that afflicted babe over to Frankfort to the Home of the Idiots," Sheriff said with a finality that hung in the air.

"*My baby*," I said in a voice so small it was lost to the wind. Shaken, I gripped the wagon rail and glanced inside at the teary-eyed child lying on the planks. Honey stretched out her arms for me, hiccupping between whimpers.

He would do it, send her to the old asylum for feeble-minded and idiot children—the horrid place for the demented or different young'uns nobody wanted.

I felt my knees sag. Fear punched at my insides, twisted, leaving me weak and sickened.

Devil John brushed angrily past the sheriff to my side. "The election's just three weeks away, Davies Kimbo, and I'll sure enough enjoy spending my time seeing you ousted. The town will have your badge for this. *Your livelihood.*"

Chants rumbled from the crowd and turned into a roar. "*Take his badge. TAKE HIS BADGE!*"

Hearing the protests, Harriett spun on her heels and fled over to the Center. Eula burst out the door and blocked Harriett. The head librarian's face writhed with rage, her words and talking hands flying hot and fast at her simpering assistant.

"*BADGE, BADGE*," the crowd thundered, their chants pounding down the dusty street, rising up into Troublesome's ageless tree-thick crags.

Sheriff stepped backward and placed a curling palm over his holstered gun. "Get on home, folks, 'fore I throw the lot of you in jail."

The deputy edged closer to him and gripped his gun, his eyes nervously darting around. "You heard him. Move along. Now!"

Folks quieted and slowly parted.

"I can tote you and the babe safely home, Book Woman," Devil John offered.

I shook my head and grabbed the wagon seat.

Sheriff turned his back to me, signaled for the deputy to unfetter our horse from its post. "Get on back to where you belong, girl." He raised his hand and flicked a dismissal. "Where the law and God sees it fit for your kind."

I glanced down at the tattered, bloodstained marriage license. Numb, I pulled myself atop the wagon. There was nothing more to be said. The sheriff, God, and Kentucky had said it for me.

It had been foolish to dream.

I snapped the reins.

Dreams were for books.

Forty-Seven

November 27, 1940

Dear Queenie,

Thank you for the books. My patrons were thrilled to receive them. I was pleased to learn of your grand news that the education in librarianship is nearing completion and your graduation is almost here. Librarian! It seems only yesterday when you left Troublesome. I am happy your family is well, and pleased to inform you we are fit too.

I'm much obliged for the new book you sent Honey for her fourth birthday. It's one of her favorites. She demands I read it to her at first light and every night, and insists I call her Mei Li.

Yesterday, my daughter declared she will be a librarian, and I dream it for her.

The new library building is coming along, and soon Troublesome will open its first borrowing branch. Last month, I received an invitation from the Kentucky Federation of Women's Clubs in Louisville, and was given an award for outstanding service and dedication to the Pack Horse project.

Much to my surprise and Harriett's loud protests, when I returned to the Center, Eula quietly took down the 'No Coloreds' sign and tossed it out into the trash.

Jackson is doing well, though I fear he still suffers from the beatings and hasn't fully healed since his release from prison. He has been looking for a place for us up north near Meigs Creek in Ohio. He learned the community is also in dire need of the Pack Horse librarian services.

Mr. Dalton has been most generous. Since one of the conditions of Jackson's release was that he cannot reenter Kentucky for 25 years, he has been helping us out and was finally able to privately sell the last tract on Lovett Mountain. Though Davies Kimbo was voted out and never reelected, I've been told he watches around town for Jackson's return and has made it his moral duty to keep him banned.

We pray that the laws of the land will change to favor all unions, all folks one day. I remain hopeful for our safety and our future.

I must close for now and pass this to Mr. Taft so that he can post it safely over in Warbranch for me tomorrow. Give my best to Willow and the boys. Write to me soon.

Your friend,
Cussy Mary

"Mama, I wanna read the book Miss 'Retta gave me," Honey called out.

I raised the tip of the pencil and paused at my signature and pulled my gaze up from the letter, the brown parchment buckling, rippling under my hand.

Honey held up the colorful storybook, *The ABC Bunny*. A crooked smile sat soft on her pale-blue face, brightening the shadow-darkened cove and warming our cabin that Pa'd built for me and Mama long ago.

"I read you happy story, Mama." Honey hoisted the book higher. "'Bout Bunny makin' different friends. 'Bout Kitten, Funny Frog, an'...*oh!* Porcupine!" She marched over to me. "Books'll learn you, Mama. I'm Book Woman, an' I read you this one."

"Come on, li'l Book Woman, let's read on the porch while your mama finishes her letter," Jackson said to Honey, and lightly squeezed my shoulder.

He'd be gone back to the Tennessee hills before sunrise but couldn't get enough of Honey—or me of him—on these precious secret visits.

I tilted my chin up to meet his eyes.

"I want to hear our happy story." Jackson's gaze lingered briefly on mine, and then he scooped up a squealing Honey and carried her outside. "Read to me, li'l Book Woman," he sang out. "Read your papa the happy story."

Junia whinnied, calling out to them.

My heart lifted, and I smoothed down the thick paper with my palm and penned *Lovett* to my signature with a hope-filled prayer.

Author's Note

Inspired by the true and gentle historical blue-skinned people of Kentucky and the brave and dedicated Kentucky Pack Horse librarians born of Roosevelt's New Deal Acts, *The Book Woman of Troublesome Creek* showcases a fascinating and important foot-note of history.

In writing the novel, my hope was to humanize and bring understanding to the gracious blue-skinned people of Kentucky, to pay tribute to the fearsome Pack Horse librarians—and to write a human story set in a unique landscape.

Methemoglobinemia is the extremely rare disease that causes skin to be blue. In the United States, it was first found in the Fugates of Troublesome Creek in eastern Kentucky.

In 1820, Martin Fugate, a French orphan, came to Kentucky to claim a land grant on the banks of Troublesome Creek in Kentucky's isolated wilderness. Martin married a full-blooded, red-headed, white-skinned Kentuckian named Elizabeth Smith. Martin and Elizabeth had no idea what awaited them. They had seven children, and out of those, four were blue.

It was against all odds that, oceans away, Martin would find a bride who carried the same blue-blood recessive gene.

Methemoglobinemia is most commonly acquired from heart disease, or airway obstruction, or taking too much of certain drugs. When acquired, it can be life-threatening.

The Fugates' methemoglobinemia, however, was congenital.

Most of the Fugates lived a very long life, into their eighties and nineties and without serious illnesses related to their blue skin.

Congenital methemoglobinemia is due to an enzyme deficiency, leading to higher-than-normal levels of methemoglobin in the blood—a form of hemoglobin—that overwhelms the normal hemoglobin, which reduces oxygen capacity. Less oxygen in the blood makes it a chocolate-brown color instead of red, causing the skin to appear blue instead of white. Doctors can diagnose congenital methemoglobinemia because the color of the blood provides the clue. The mutation is hereditary and carried in a recessive gene.

I've modified one historical date in the story so I could include relevant information about medical aspects and discoveries. Instead of the 1930s, as is the book's era, it was actually in the 1960s when Madison Cawein, MD, a Kentucky hematologist heard about the blue-skinned people and set out to find them. In the 1940s, a doctor in Ireland made similar discoveries among his people.

Dr. Cawein found the Fugates tucked in isolated hollers, in the thick-treed hills of Appalachia near Ball Creek and Troublesome Creek in Kentucky. The doctor convinced them to let him draw blood, then tested, analyzed, and drew more blood. The Fugates were gracious and kind people, according to Dr. Cawein's reports. After testing and research, he discovered the Fugates had congenital methemoglobinemia.

Cawein first treated the Fugates with methylene blue injections that instantly turned their skin white. But the drug was only a temporary fix. Methylene blue, first used to treat cyanide and carbon monoxide poisoning, generally is secreted in the urine within twenty-four hours and can cause unpleasant side effects in the interim. The doctor left the Fugates a generous supply of oral methylene blue tablets to be taken daily. Cawein also became a protector of the Fugates, and when news media and Hollywood came to Kentucky to see the rare people, he refused to disclose their whereabouts.

With the help of the elder Fugates, their Bible notations, and their recollections, Dr. Cawein charted the family and traced their ancestry back to Martin Fugate.

In 1943, Kentucky banned first-cousin marriages, and the ban continues there and in most other states today. This prohibition in Kentucky was not only to prevent birth defects; it was sought for other reasons, as well. The Ku Klux Klan lobbied for the ban early and fought vigorously for the bill's passage to keep white supremacy pure, while others wanted it to keep feuding mountain clans strong, which prevented young lovers from marrying enemy cousins and turning disloyal and increasing a clan's numbers. Anti-miscegenation laws in Kentucky were in effect from 1866 until 1967. For anyone convicted, the penalty was a fine or imprisonment, or both.

From what we know, the Fugates originated from France and were descendants of French Huguenots. Could the Fugates' medical anomaly mean they were true "blue bloods" descended from European royals? The Fugates were linked only to inbreeding instead of being embraced for their very uniqueness. Even when first-cousin marriages were legal across the United States, the Fugates were shunned and shamed, suffering in isolation because of their skin color and inherited genes.

In 1913, the Kentucky Federation of Women's Clubs convinced a local coal baron, John C. Mayo, to subsidize a mounted library service to reach people in poor and remote areas. But a year later, the program expired when Mayo died. It would be almost twenty years until the service was revived.

The Pack Horse Library Project was established in 1935 and ran until 1943. The service was part of President Franklin D. Roosevelt's Works Progress Administration (WPA) and an effort to create jobs for women and bring books and reading material into Appalachia, into the poorest and most isolated areas in eastern Kentucky that had few schools, no libraries, and inaccessible roads.

The librarians were known as "book women," though there were a very small number of men among their ranks. These fearsome Kentucky librarians traveled by horse, mule, and sometimes foot and even rowboat to reach the remotest areas, in creeks and up crags, into coves, disconnected pockets, and black forests, and to towns named Hell-fer-Sartin, Troublesome, and Cut Shin, sometimes traveling as much as one hundred or more miles a week in rain, sleet, or snow.

Pack Horse librarians were paid twenty-eight dollars a month and had to provide their own mounts. Books and reading materials and places for storing and sorting the material were all donated and not supplied by the WPA's payroll.

With few resources and little financial help, the Pack Horse librarians collected donated books and reading materials from the Boy Scouts, PTAs, women's clubs, churches, and the state health department. The librarians came up with ingenious ways to provide more reading resources, such as making scrapbooks with collected recipes and housecleaning tips that the mountain people passed on to them in gratitude for their service. The book women colored pictures to make children's picture books, journals, and more, all the while vigorously seeking donations.

Despite the financial obstacles, the harshness of the land, and the sometimes fierce mistrust of the people during the most violent era of eastern Kentucky's history, the Pack Horse service was accepted and became dearly embraced. These clever librarians turned their traveling library program into a tremendous success.

In the years of its service, more than one thousand women served in the Pack Horse Library Project, and it was reported that nearly 600,000 residents in thirty eastern Kentucky counties considered "pauper counties" were served by them. During those years, the beloved program left a powerful legacy and enriched countless lives.

Finally, courting candles. The spiral design of courting candles over a hundred years ago was likely created to keep the melting candle in place and from slipping—a mere practicality, more folklore than fact—though they certainly could have been used later by a patriarch to teach a daughter to respect his judgment and as a way to screen for potential suitors.

Still, I found it a commanding and curious induction of courtship. How powerful that the candle could be the source of someone's lifelong misery or joy, and passed on in different generations. How wonderful the conversations that must have taken place around and over it.

The Susan B. Anthony stamp was actually issued in August.

A Final Note. Dearest Reader, this is one of the most important books I've written to date. Dear in all ways, loved in a million more. I have tried to present the novel with precise historical backdrops, which involved in-depth research; interviews; meetings with hematologists, doctors, firewatchers, and others; studying Roosevelt's WPA programs; and living in Appalachia. If anything is omitted, or befuddles, it is strictly unintended and the fault of me, the author.

Images from the Pack Horse Library Project

A special thank-you to Lisa Thompson, Librarian II Archival Services Branch, Archives and Records Management Division, Kentucky Department for Libraries and Archives.

Book carriers ready to take the trail from Hindman, Kentucky. Known to the mountaineers as "book women," their arrival was always a welcome sight to the mountain-dwelling folk.

Sometimes the short way across was the hard way for a horse and rider, but schedules had to be maintained if readers were not to be disappointed. Then, too, after highways were left, there was little choice of roads.

The interior of a Pack Horse Library Center at Wooton, Kentucky. Main libraries were located in county seats, but attractive centers supplied outlying communities with reading materials.

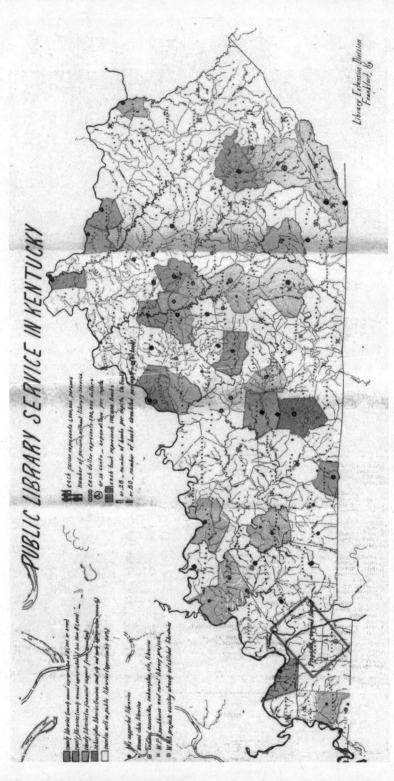

PUBLIC LIBRARY SERVICE IN KENTUCKY

Courtesy of Archival Services Branch, Archives and Records Management Division—Kentucky Department for Libraries and Archives

When newspapers passed circulating usefulness, they added comfort, cleanliness, and warmth to the bare walls of a mountain cabin.

The Pack Horse librarians delivered 3,548 books monthly.

RIGHT: The "book woman" did not always have a bridge to cross and had to find a shallow ford.

BELOW: Invalids, shut-ins, the old, and the blind would receive the benefits of books. If they were unable to read and there was no one to read to them, the "book woman" found time to read to them.

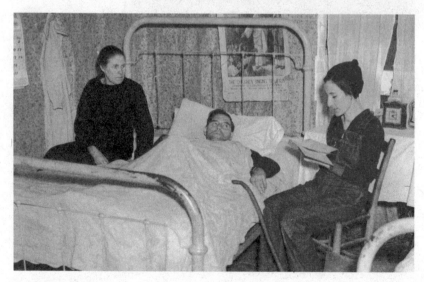

Schoolchildren were encouraged to take books home to read. The closing of school did not end this habit, for children continued to meet the carrier at the schoolhouse. Many children read aloud at home to their parents who could not read. Children's books were greatly in demand, and there was always a shortage of them.

Neither snow-covered hillside nor lack of roads daunts the "book woman."

Library service was not restricted. White families, black families, and teachers had the opportunity to benefit by library use. Library centers for blacks were established in black communities.

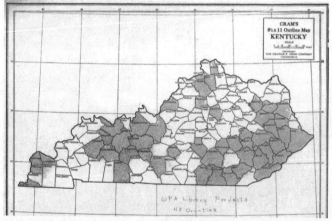

Winter and summer alike found the "book woman" reaching the mountain readers. Farm journals and agricultural bulletins of the state and national government gave mountain farmers knowledge for improvement of their crops; however, the demand was far greater than the supply.

Schoolhouses like this only had a few textbooks. Teachers selected books for reading and class work from Pack Horse libraries. During the four years of WPA service, there were frequent reports of better schoolwork due to the books furnished by WPA carriers.

A Pack Horse librarian delivers books to a patron.

Reading Group Guide

1. The Kentucky Pack Horse program was implemented in 1935 by the Works Progress Administration (WPA) to create women's work programs and to assist economic recovery and build literacy. Looking at the novel, how did the program affect the people in this remote area? Do you think library programs are still a vital part of our society today?

2. How has a librarian or booklover impacted your life? Have you ever connected with a book or author in a meaningful way? Explain.

3. Missionaries, government, social workers, and various religious groups have always visited eastern Kentucky to reform, modernize, and mold hillfolk to their acceptable standards. Do you think Cussy faced this kind of prejudice from the outside world? Is there any prejudice or stigma associated with the people of Appalachia today?

4. How do you think Cussy's father feels after he marries her off to an abusive man? Why do you think he agrees to Charlie Frazier's proposal in the first place? What do you imagine life was like for an unwed woman at that time?

5. Imagine you are making a community scrapbook like the ones Cussy distributes to the people of Troublesome. What would you include? Do you think these materials were helpful to Cussy's library patrons?

6. When Cussy receives the cure for her blueness from Doc, she realizes there's a price to pay for her white skin, and the side effects soon become too much to handle. If you were in Cussy's shoes, would you sacrifice your health for a chance at "normalcy"? If there weren't any side effects, do you think Cussy would have continued to take the medication? Would you?

7. How do you think Cussy feels when she is ostracized at the Independence Day celebration, despite her change of skin color? Can you relate to her feelings of isolation? Do you think these kinds of racial prejudices are still prevalent today?

8. Cussy has to deal with the loss of many loved ones in a very short amount of time. How do you think she handles her grief? Which loss was the most difficult for you to read?

9. What do you think life was like for the people of Troublesome? What are some of the highlights of living in such a remote place? What are some of the challenges the people on Cussy's library route face?

10. Back then, entering into a prohibited or interracial marriage in Kentucky was a misdemeanor that could result in incarceration, and we see these racial tensions attempt to sever Cussy and Jackson's relationship. Discuss anti-miscegenation laws and marriage laws. Do you think this kind of prejudice still exists toward interracial couples?

11. What do you think happens to Cussy, Jackson, Honey, and the other inhabitants of Troublesome after the story ends? Imagine you were Cussy. How would you feel leaving Troublesome for good?

A Conversation
with the Author

What drew you to the stories of the Pack Horse librarians and the blue-skinned people of Kentucky?

Years ago, I stumbled across these heroic librarians of the Great Depression and the rare blue-skinned Kentuckians, and I couldn't stop thinking about them. I wanted to embrace their strengths and uniqueness in story. There was such rich, magnificent history in the two, I was surprised I hadn't seen them in a novel, that neither had been given a footprint in literary history. I knew it was time for the wider world to experience them in a novel, to learn about, to see, the glorious Kentucky female Pack Horse librarians and the precious blue-skinned mountain folk.

Your novel is deeply rooted in the history of Appalachia. What research did you do to bring this time period to life?

Research is my favorite part of the writing process. I spent thousands of hours exploring everything from fauna to flora to folklore to food, as well as longtime traditions indigenous to Appalachia. I'm also able to live in that landscape and spend time with native Appalachians who have taught me the lyrics and language of their people and ancestors. Other research took me to coal-mining towns and their history, visiting doctors, speaking with a hematologist to learn about congenital methemoglobinemia, and exploring fire tower lookouts and their history. Years ago, I started collecting everything I could find on the Pack

Horse librarians, poring over archives, old newspapers, pictures, the history, etc. I spent many hours on Roosevelt's New Deal and WPA programs and conducted interviews. And last, there was the fun and interesting research on mules.

What does your writing process look like?

I've long been a kitchen table author, one who sets aside the recipe, forsakes the rules—the do's and don'ts, the shant's, shouldn'ts, and won'ts. This doesn't mean I don't respect the rules—it simply allows me the unleashed freedom to create the story intimately and lyrically, as if I'm sitting at my kitchen table across from you and telling it. There's the occasional detour, of course, and sometimes I take out the guardrails going one hundred miles per hour. And there's piles of research papers, the countless scraps and sticky notes littered everywhere in my office, on my desk and shelves. My dear husband usually creates cool, detailed drawings of my fictional towns to anchor and keep me straight. At all times, there's my beloved rescue pets wandering in and out of my office. Music is a must-have, and I try to create a playlist to reflect the moods and themes in my stories. My music influence is broad, passionate, and can dip into everything from opera to bluegrass to rock, and on to classical, big band, jazz, rap, country, and indie. During edits, all is quiet, and I'm slow, turtle slow, and also painfully meticulous, and can absolutely sit on a single paragraph for days, working and fretting over it. I generally devote anywhere from eight to fourteen hours a day to writing, research, and book-related stuff.

Did your own experiences living in Kentucky inspire or influence any of the descriptions in the book?

Yes, Kentucky is both a beautiful and brutal place full of fascinating history, varied landscapes, complex people and culture, and I'm fortunate to live in a region that I can draw on from the heart.

Do you see any similarities between yourself and Cussy? Differences?

I grew up under the grinding heels of poverty, spending my first decade in a rural Kentucky orphanage, moving on to foster care, and then finding myself homeless at age fourteen. I can relate to marginalized people and have much empathy for Cussy and her family, anyone who has faced or faces prejudices and hardships. It's easy to feel their pain deeply, particularly if you've gone through hardships in your own life.

If you had to choose, what is one of your favorite moments from the novel?

One of my dearest is when young Angeline takes Cussy Mary's hand, despite knowing the implication of being friendly with a blue, and rings a simple truth by saying "Hain't no harm. Our hands don't care they's different colors. Feels nice jus' the same, huh?"

Throughout the novel, we see the positive effects the Pack Horse library service has on this small, remote community. Do you think libraries still have that kind of impact today?

Absolutely, and now more than ever. As I mentioned earlier, I was raised in an orphanage. Later, as a foster child in 1970, I remember going to my first library one lonely summer and checking out a book. The librarian sized me up and then quietly said, "Only one? You look smarter than a one-book read, and I bet we can find you more than just *one*." She reached under her counter, snapped open a folded brown-paper sack, handed it to me, and then marched me over to shelves filled with glorious books. I was shocked that I could get more than one book, much less a bag full of precious books, and I was moved by her compassion, kindness, and wisdom. Librarians are lifelines for so many, giving us powerful resources to help us become empowered.

What are some of your favorite libraries to visit?

I love hitting the backroads to seek out small-town libraries. These places are treasured cornerstones filled with social mores—hidden gems that offer an opulence of customs, inspiration, and warm hospitality.

Who are some of your favorite authors to read?

There are so many talented writers out there to pick from, it makes the choice difficult. However, one influence and much-loved author of mine has always been E. B. White. *Charlotte's Web* is a jewel that tapped into my love for nature and animals. And every time I read it, I learned something new. It has that wonderful Hitchcockian first line—"Where's Papa going with that ax?"—and is infused with magical verses of dewy spiderwebs, "Some Pig" miracles, and unconditional friendship. *Some Book—Some Author!* Harriette Simpson Arnow, John Fox Jr., Gwyn Hyman Rubio, and Walter Tevis are some of my longtime favorite Kentucky novelists who wrote unforgettable masterpieces. Each one brings the pages to life with rich, evocative landscapes, beautifully told stories, and highly skilled prose.

What do you hope readers will ultimately take away from Cussy's story?

Poverty and marginalization are not so much economics or politics or societal issues as much as they are human issues. They are best grappled with by reaching deep into the lives of those suffering them. Knowing one small piece of this world—the earth, the sky, the plants, the people, and the very air of it—helps us to understand the sufferings and joys of others ourselves.

Acknowledgments

Thank you to the dear readers for allowing me into your home. To the darling and dear Kristy (Kristy Bee) Barrett, Judith D. Collins, Kathy Shattuck, Tonya Speelman, Carla Suto, Linda Zagon, and many other readers and reading groups and bloggers who generously and tirelessly cheer on my books and others'. You are a precious gift to writers everywhere.

And I'd like to add a little honey poem for Kristy:

> *A Bee-auty named Kristy "Bee" Barrett*
> *Collects each book like pollen to share it*
> *This novel-love bee,*
> *Is our sweetest sweet pea—*
> *Sweet as honey and buzzing with merit!*

My gratitude and love to Bry City mountain man and former lookout Ron Cole for sharing a Christmas dinner and your inspirational stories about you and your family's historic fire-tower home. And also to dear Honey Bee for your always gracious hospitality and kind support.

Much love and appreciation to Eon Alden and Chris Wilcox and the rest of the gang for unstintingly peddling my books. I am extremely grateful to cherished booksellers and librarians, for all your dedication and passion that goes into helping my books and others' find their way into the hands and hearts of readers.

Many thanks to the lovely playwright Amina McIntyre for sharing a meal and inspiring me with the antique courting candle at Black Acre Conservancy.

To my editors, the brilliant and hardworking book women, Shana Drehs and Margaret (MJ) Johnston. I am forever indebted to you for your sharp eyes, wisdom, and foresight, for rolling up your sleeves to make *Book Woman* achieve its very best—for making a good book great. My appreciation and many thanks to Diane Dannenfeldt for her exceptional copyedits, Carolyn Lesnick for her proofreading, and to the energetic and enthusiastic Sourcebooks team, for whom I am enormously grateful. Thank you, Sourcebooks, for letting me give these fierce librarians and precious, brave Blues a voice.

To my terrific Writers House agents, Stacy and Susan, who immediately championed this book and gave it their unwavering support—you are the very best a writer could ask for in agents. *And, Stacy, this one is for you.*

Writing is oftentimes a solitary journey, but this one was made easier by having the support of a kind and immensely talented book-woman tribe: mad love and appreciation to Joshilyn, Karen, and Sara.

Gratitude and love to G. J. Berger, my dear friend and critiquer.

Love to my beautiful and wise children, Jeremiah and Sierra, forever. To my husband and always-first reader, Joe, thank you for catching my misspellings and incorrect math and seeing me through. You are first and foremost the reader I love writing for and being with. I love you like salt loves meat, always.

About the Author

Photo credit: Leigh Photography

Kim Michele Richardson lives in Kentucky and resides part-time in western North Carolina. She is an advocate for the prevention of child abuse and domestic violence and has partnered with the U.S. Navy globally to bring awareness and education to the prevention of domestic violence. She is the author of the bestselling memoir *The Unbreakable Child* and is the founder of the tiny home Shy Rabbit, a writers/artists scholarship residency. Her novels include *Liar's Bench*, *GodPretty in the Tobacco Field*, and *The Sisters of Glass Ferry*.